MW01228473

THE PRINCESS OF AENYA

NICK ALIMONOS

Books in the Aenya Series
(in chronological order)

The Feral Girl

Ages of Aenya

— City by the Sea
— The Serpent's Eye
— Flesh & Steel

The Princess of Aenya

The Magiq of Aenya (forthcoming)

ACKNOWLEDGMENTS

I would first like to thank my parents, Arthur and Angie, for bringing me into this world and teaching me the value of perseverance. To my beta readers, David Pasco, Tobias Thölken, Hynde Belahsen, and my editor, Ava Justine Coibion, you helped make this story the best it could be, and for that, I am in your debt. To my children, Jasmine and Sophia, thank you for inspiring me daily, and to my nephew, Fonda Karapateas, I owe you for the character of Ecthros. Shout outs go to my talented illustrators: Noah Bradley (cover) and Becky Barnes (unicorn). Last but not least, I owe a special thanks to Michael-Israel Jarvis, who collaborated with me on "Noora's Song."

For Hynda,

My Radia

OCEAN

Crown of Aenya Mountains

Northendell

Tyrnael

Dark Hemisphere

Nimbos

Fei Country

Hills of
Gasemen Naar

Nr Wadsu River

Nasica River

Hedonia

Potamis River

Hills of Tororo

Yefira

Campania

The
One
Sea

AENYA

2000 km

I sing the Goddess that is in all,
who gilds the wheat and sun born rye,
who, in dreaming plains we seek her call

In the greenwood, in the elms that fall
from sundered root to shaken ply
Her eternal verse brings breath to all

In the hornèd moons that nightly rule
her silver sisters dance the sky
and from dreaming plains attend her hall

Even in the sore and weeping gall
there is the ballad which brings release
there is the Goddess of great and small

In streams deep and mountains tall
from lover's rage to felled knight's wreath
Zoë sings her song, who is in all

Do not dread and shrink from winter's pall
or of Luna's chill bite be dismayed
For Zoë, dying, sleeps in snowy shawl

And Springs born to sing the gilded corn
so broken hearts are once more allayed
when mourning moons break to Sun of M

*O*nce, not long ago, there lived a king in the land of Tyrnael, who had but one daughter. This daughter he loved with his whole heart, but upon her eleventh year, she fell ill, her cheeks paling like the petals of a dying ilm. Never leaving her bedside, the king called for every physician in his kingdom, but all were at a loss, for her ailment was unlike any they had seen. With enduring hope, the king sent emissaries to lands near and abroad, and learned men did arrive from as far south as the One Sea and from as far east as Shemselinihar, yet all were utterly mystified by her sickness. Beset by grief and desperation, the king offered all that he had, his very kingdom in recompense, to save his little girl from doom.

And it so happened, that upon this decree, a wizened sage appeared at the gates of the Compass Tower. Examining the girl with care, he declared with confidence that he could make the girl whole again, brewing an elixir so that she might drink of it and become well. And shortly thereafter, the rosy hue returned to the little girl's cheeks. Overjoyed, the king asked what the stranger wished from him in return, reminding him of his vow.

"So long as you know," the sage said to him, "I can stay the hand of the Taker, but only for a time. At the close of three days, before the moon eclipses on the third night, if she does not drink of my elixir, Death shall surely claim her."

Hearing this dreadful prophecy, the king turned ashen, but the sage comforted him, saying, "Be not dismayed, for it is not beyond my power to procure this remedy, enough to keep your daughter in bloom for her remaining days. Yet it is not without its price."

The king readily agreed, preparing to surrender his great wealth, his kingdom if need be, but the sage asked for one small thing, and one thing only, in return for his ministrations, that the king take as his own a young boy to be adopted. The sage's own son.

1

Radia

Radia loved to watch the morning creep in from beneath the moon, the sunlight washing the dark gray shadows from the mountains to reveal their emerald glow. Foothills glittered with the various places she longed to visit, and as the light of day continued to spread, the familiar sights of her city emerged, one by one, from the gloom of night. Atop the Compass Tower, a thousand feet above her slumbering subjects, she watched the world unfurl like few ever could. Tyrnael radiated like spokes of gold, its spires rising like lotus flowers, its terraced hills green with moss and hanging vines and tall grasses. Arches moved between each structure and beyond the city, reaching impossibly outward. Once, the bridges served to unite the surrounding kingdoms, with the Compass Tower at its hub, but those days were long forgotten and the framework of steel and marble fallen into disrepair. Tyrnael was a city of unearthly beauty and wonder, if only one did not look at the cracks.

And all of it is mine, she reminded herself again. But the enormity of that truth failed her imagination. How could she truly rule anything when, throughout all her life, every last thing was done *for* her? She did not know to prepare meals or sew and, without Larissa's aid, she was helpless to lace her own bodice. Not that she wanted to. Her queenly raiment was heavy and stiff and stymied the flow of blood to her limbs. Most mornings, she could scarcely touch her toes, but dressing maintained the hierarchy, helped her subjects to know their place. Or so her advisers impressed upon her time and again. *A lady of royal birth cannot be seen half-naked like some commoner!*

Everything was different now. She stood upon the balustrade dressed in a gown of translucent white samite, the color of foam left behind by a crashing wave, and inlaid with gold thread and beads of pearl and lapis lazuli. Larissa had the good sense to match the gown with the late queen's tiara, which shone from Radia's forehead in pure platinum. *What would I do without her?* Today of all days, Radia needed to look the part, fifty-fourth descendant of the Zo, ruler of Tyrnael, princess of Aenya. Her youth, spent frolicking in the gardens and diving into fountains and being chased by tutors, was over. She was fifteen and a woman, and her father was dead.

Radia gathered her hem in her fists and moved away from the bailey, the silhouette of her bare feet showing through the fabric. She followed the arrow etched into the granite floor like a child on a balance beam. Every arm ended in the same rune, indicating *south*. As sovereign of the world, Radia stood atop the planet, at its pole. She was *True North*.

There was no roof above her, only the sun and turquoise moon and fading galaxies. A curved wall with its crescent of steps protected her from the chilling altitude. Her throne rose like a spire, the highest point for more than a hundred miles, but she could never imagine herself, or any other person, upon that chair. It was her father's place. With each breath, she could feel his absence, a gnawing emptiness in the heart of her being she could not shake. Now, more than ever, she needed his courage and counsel—he had always been around to provide her with just the right words. Though she found herself shielded from the ways of the world, Radia was certain of right action from wrong, good from evil. She knew it from the many stories her father told and the books he bequeathed her. Heroes of old, *batals of legend*, lived in her imagination, offering her their guidance. No hero would allow the kingdom to continue down its current path and neither would she.

Radia climbed to the top of her dais, the accouterments of her station heavier than ever, the train of her gown, thrice the length of her body, spilling down the steps and across the floor like a carpet. To sit where her distant forefathers' buttocks had rested for untold aeons felt wrong somehow, forbidden. *Royal butts*. She grinned at the thought of it. Beneath all that fancy clothing, they were all the same. Human. Her throne of amethyst crystal was quarried from the core of the planet, and pressed hard against her shoulders. She resisted the urge to tuck her legs in and sit sideways, but the arms were too far apart and she felt herself sliding forward. *Whoever sat here comfortably? Were the Zo made up of giants?* Everything was built to exude authority, she knew, but could she project power from the throne, as her father did? After fidgeting some more, she managed a stately position, with elbows tucked in and backbone arched and chin up.

"Father, help me." She said it for his ghost to hear, and with her heart throbbing in her throat, reached for the topaz switch in the armrest.

Archers gathered like silver birds along the periphery wall, up and around the spiraling stairwell. Their composite longbows reminded her of goose wings. Facing the throne, rising from a wide berth of steps, a contingent of knights flanked her in two columns, their sarissas swaying high above the ib feather plumes in their helms, the unicorn sigil of Tyrnael gleaming from their cuirasses. It was her *praetorian guard*. The sixteen knights swore fealty at her coronation only cycles before, the last and only time she sat the throne, up until now. It made her ill at ease that men she hardly knew should offer their lives in such a way. At the very least, she could learn something about them, if they had wives or children, but she was never good at matching names to faces. The praetorians were an elite few, carefully selected from among the tallest and strongest, and indistinctly handsome. Only one was difficult to look upon, perhaps the most hideous man Radia had ever seen. His face was creased, like a sheet of papyrus crumpled and straightened again, and when he carried his helmet under his arm, there was not a single follicle to be seen on his scalp. When she first met him at her coronation, all she could do was stare at the scar dividing his eye and lip. She could not fathom why he had yet to fix his face, but he seemed oblivious to it. *Why ever would he choose to become my protector, looking like that, and whoever was so negligent to appoint him?*

Her brother was last to enter. His presence made her grip the edges of the throne. When they were children, they played at pretend, and she may even have loved him then. But even as a boy, he loved to pull the wings from the butterflies, slowly and methodically, watching and delighting in the agony he was causing. She used to cry and threaten him with father, but the king only listened sympathetically, taking no action. When his cruelty evolved from torturing insects to hammering frogs, she had had enough of him, and what love she might have felt waned to nothing. *When I am queen, I will see you pay,* she remembered herself thinking. Now father was dead and she had the power. So why did she not feel powerful?

To anyone looking upon him, Radia's brother was a monster. From horn to heel, he was iron the color of rust and blood, and he bristled with spikes like some demonic urchin, with pike-like horns that protruded from the sides of his helm. His mask gave the impression of a face, with absences for eyes through which to look out. Radia understood the need for a soldier to coat himself in armor, but war had never been known in Tyrnael, not for a thousand-thousand years. His readiness for battle was unnerving, and yet it would not have surprised her if she caught him sleeping in his suit. The cacophony it made, as each metal plate grated against another, was an assault to the ears, and a further insult to her rule as he marched before the throne. Zaibos exuded the power she failed to gather, even as he fell to one knee before her.

I must not be intimidated. "You may remove your helmet," she managed, without a tremor in her voice.

He tugged at his horns, but what emerged from underneath the mask was no less fierce. A perpetual scowl was etched across his jaw, as if his face were made of stone, and his eyebrows were dark and bristly, like dead caterpillars above deep-set, iron-hard pupils. The hair that spilled over his shoulders was black as pitch and, about his chin and cheeks, a beard grew like a thorn bush.

Radia immediately became conscious of her small, girlish features. Her mismatched eyes, one turquoise, the other violet, stared back at her sixteen-fold from the praetorians' rounded helms. Her cheekbones were framed by golden braids—not blonde, but gold. Brother and sister looked nothing alike, but they were not of the same blood.

"Why did you call me here, sister? I am very busy."

"You will address me properly, Zaibos. *Your Grace* will do, but not *sister.* Not here, when I am on my throne." Her voice felt small, swallowed by the space. She sounded more like a songbird than a monarch.

"Very well," he groaned, adding, with a measure of contempt, "Your Grace."

"Seeing as you are busy, I . . ." she started, *No, stupid, use more forceful language!* "Tell me all what you have been doing with your time."

"*Doing*, Your Grace?" His eyes were steel—two archers taking aim.

"I know you have been doing things . . . taking distant forays into the dark hemisphere. I hear rumors of battle, that you return with blood on your armor."

"I act upon my duties, Your Grace, those bestowed to me by your father."

"And what duties might those be?"

"Protecting the kingdom. *Your* kingdom, of course."

"From whom? We have no enemies. Tyrnael has not known war since before the Cataclysm!"

"That is precisely the matter. We have become a stagnant civilization. Tyrnael was once known throughout the entire world. Now we exist as myth, in songs. The greatness our people once knew has been denied too long. Empires grow out of conquest. If we go on as we have, hiding behind our mountains, without the conquered to fill our bloodlines, we will continue to decay and in time be forgotten. And so, as I told you before, I am doing my duty, and protecting the realm."

"Do not speak to me as if I am a child, brother. I've read the histories, but we need not go to war to be great again. There are other ways. We can send emissaries to the Outside, make ourselves known. Build friendships and alliances."

His armor rattled with laughter. "Friendship? I fear you are much too young, sweet sister. If we open our gates to the world, the world will come in like a flood, rob us of our secrets. They have always sought what we possess. Why else have our people hidden for so long? If we had only the numbers to fill our ranks, to build true armies, I'd welcome the chance to defend our borders. But alas, Your Grace, a child is born only once in a cycle if we are fortunate, and the rate is decelerating."

At fifteen, Radia could count on her hands the number of girls she knew her age. Larissa used to tell awful stories of mothers losing their newborns to theft, and it always upset her, as if her handmaiden was telling lies. Childbirth was a miracle in Tyrnael. But its perpetuation could not justify the cruelties of war.

"How do you do this, then? Make conquests without armies?"

Zaibos was standing, his helmet clanking under his arm. "Alliances have been made. In the dark hemisphere," he explained, "there are denizens of the sunless lands, bogren and horg of countless number, who seek to sate their bloodlust."

Horg and bogren? Those were the names of inhuman things, a product of nightmares, fitting company for someone like her brother. "You can't—it is forbidden!"

"It was your father, the king—"

"My father would never!" she cried. "He loved peace, something you've never understood! These actions have nothing to do with the good of the kingdom. You satisfy *yourself*, and your hunger for cruelty!"

Radia was standing without realizing it, shaking with rage. Father would never have done that. A princess should be composed, speak firmly but never rashly or in anger. She was still only a child. Everyone could see it, her brother most of all. If only there was a kind face amid the masses, someone who loved her, she might find a measure of courage in it. Larissa had pleaded to stand beside her, but Radia was too stubborn to listen, fearing that keeping her handmaiden close would make her appear weak. She had rejected her father's most trusted adviser as well. Anabis was kindly and wise, but he stressed patience and moderation, when what was needed here was boldness. Now, Radia wanted nothing but to end this ordeal, return to her dolls and books. She could not even find the strength to match eyes with her brother, focusing on her feet instead, dismissing him with a tremble.

She waited, battening down the heart in her chest like a sail in a windstorm, but to her dismay, there was no sound of retreat, no reaction to her command. The court was frozen in place. Zaibos did not move and his archers stood like stony sentinels. Had they not seen her gesture? Would she lose face in repeating it?

"No. I am not one of your handmaidens, sister, to be sent away so easily." His tone was like the hiss of a snake when it threatens to bite.

"I am in charge here, Zaibos, not you. Am I not the blood of the Zo? Am I not True North?" She was pleading now, not with him, but with the others in the room.

"Titles do not confer loyalty, Your Grace. There is a high price to pay for that. My men die for me on the battlefield. But what do you know of such things? The power of Tyrnael lies with me. I command the army. What do you command? Cooks and seamstresses?"

Radia had prepared endlessly for this day, rehearsed every word, and yet she stood paralyzed, robbed of speech. Her pretty gown and seat of amethyst meant nothing. She could see the doubt in the eyes of her protectors, and dread crawled into her mind. "This is high treason, Zaibos! Be dismissed or I'll—"

"You'll what? Have me hanged? Beheaded? Drawn and quartered? Does your compassionate heart have the strength to enforce your dictates? I think not. And yet you cannot accuse a man of treason without carrying out the sentencing. You are weak, my sister, and innocent."

Spurred by the insult, Radia found her courage. "Guards! Take him to the dungeons!" But even as the words escaped her lips, she knew she had made a mistake. Zaibos donned his helmet, becoming the monster again, and none dared move against him.

With his back to the throne, he addressed his archers, the voice from his faceplate sounding eerily. "I had hoped for a peaceful transition of power—no angry mobs to contend with, no rebellions to quell—but now you've forced my hand."

By the Ancients! He is going to kill me.

She had always known him to be cruel, and this frightened her, but she never imagined dying by his hand. Did their childhood memories mean nothing? *No, he is a monster, nothing like my father, or me.* Sensing the threat at last, her praetorians moved into action, joining together with their sarissas thrust outward like an immense morningstar.

Zaibos was undeterred, walking against them, armed only with the poison of his tongue. "Who among you is prepared to die for this girl? She slumbers here in this tower on silken sheets and sups from silver goblets every night. And what have her people become? We are like lichen under a rock, living in the shadows of past glories, and she would see to it that it ever be so, that we continue to bend the knee and serve, until her children come of age and the cycle continues! I say no more! The progeny of the Zo ends here. Do your duty and spill your blood here and now for this undeserving brat, or follow me into a new age of Aenya."

Radia's guards did not flinch, not until Zaibos raised his gauntlet, and the chamber echoed with the sound of drawn bows. Knights broke rank in turn, until the phalanx fell apart, and a mere six stood before the dais, torn between duty and self-preservation.

Only one spoke out. "I am."

"You are what?" the monster barked, towering a head above him and every other knight, but the guard with the scarred face did not step away.

"I answered your question. I am prepared to die for this girl. There is more to life than death."

"Then you are a fool!" Zaibos's blood-red gauntlet came down and hundreds of arrows reached into the sky, perched in mid-air, and dropped with sudden terrible force.

Men were dying at her feet, clutching at the seams of their armor, their eyes wild with terror. Feathered shafts grew from their knees and throats and the open grills of their helms. Her guards were young and naïve to battle. The *praetorian* was an honored position, but their training was ceremonial, more dance than combat. The unicorn sigils were lined in red and blood was pooling across the floor, staining the hem of her gown. A second volley of arrows arched into the sky, silhouetted against the sun, and not a man remained to shield her from them. After only fifteen years, less than a tenth of her father's age, her life was to be cut short. She closed her eyes to welcome the end.

I hope it doesn't hurt much. Don't scream. Don't weep. Give him nothing.

Arrowheads were chiming like rain on a plated roof, and she waited, with no place to run or hide. *My dress will be all bloody, and Larissa worked so hard to ready it.*

But death did not come. Nor pain. When she dared to look again, the view was saturated with the scarred visage of her last remaining guardian, the only man she had ever seen stand up to her brother, and he was groping at her thighs—no, that wasn't right—he was shielding her with his armored body.

"I should be dead," she murmured, checking herself for holes to make certain she wasn't.

"You're not out of this yet, Your Highness." He played with the switches on the armrest until finding the one he needed. The throne started to turn into the floor with the both of them on it. Everything was spinning. Stone masonry was passing over her eyes. They were in a long vertical shaft and dropping quickly. When the throne settled into place, dim orbs of light played with their shadows. They were in a blue room large enough for two to stand abreast.

"Are you hurt?"

Radia could hardly think or hear. What she witnessed only moments before dominated her vision. "No, but what of you? You should be—"

"The throne was built by the Zo," he remarked, "for just such an occasion, no doubt. There must be a field within range of it, or we're both just terribly lucky."

Tears ran hot across her cheeks. "Those men . . . they're dead because of me."

"They did what was expected of them, Your Highness," he replied. "Now you must do the same. Run."

But Radia did not leave her chair. "I can't—"

"They won't be long," he said, pulling the longsword from his belt and moving forward, as if to gut her. "We'll have to be quick about it." He worked the blade through the fine muslin fabric. "You'll forgive me, Your Majesty."

Radia could not watch. It was her great-grandmother's dress, but when he had sliced through it, she could feel the air on her knees, the freedom of motion. "That's good."

He nabbed her by the wrist, harder than she would have liked, and dragged her through an open archway. A flight of steps led up and another set spiraled downward. She could hear the stomping of boots above, the clank of armor, the rattle of arrows in quivers.

Walls pushed on them from both sides as they took to the stairs. The descent was steep and narrow, with just enough space to set her foot.

"I think they hear us!" she murmured.

"Be quiet, will you?"

Radia stole back her arm, which was already sore. This guard of hers acted nothing like the heroes in her fairytales. "Are you rescuing or kidnapping me?"

Again, he brandished his longsword, as if to attack her. She followed the length of steel to the line of marching boots crossing the stairwell like some monstrous centipede. In that same moment, an archer poked his head under to spot them, and a volley of arrows ricocheted overhead, clacking and clattering like hailstones.

He grabbed her again, moving faster than she thought he could in mailed knees and greaves, traversing the steps in twos and threes. Even in her bare feet, she had difficulty keeping pace. "We need to reach the bottom before they do. If we give them a clear shot, we're done for."

"Who are you," her voice echoed, "and why are you helping me?"

His silence was infuriating, and if not for the threat of death, she would have refused to move unless he answered.

They continued on, her right hand following the inner wall to maintain balance, moving down and down until the whole of the tower opened into a vast hollow. The stairwell curved for hundreds of feet to the bottom and went up just as far. Seized by vertigo, she reached for a support that was not there, finding only a sudden empty drop. Even her praetorian slowed pace, moving with deliberation.

They circled the tower as they descended, watching the archers chase precariously from across the other side, looking miniscule where Radia had been only seconds before. A few took aim, but their footing was too narrow and the updraft carried their arrows every which way.

The base of the tower led to an inner courtyard. Sunlight from a domed ceiling streamed across the walls, gilding the granite frieze-work, the sculpted planets and the replicas of cities, the great orators and scientists and heroes immortalized in stone. It was a marvel of antiquity from the Age of the Zo, but there was no time to wonder at it.

Beyond the courtyard, they passed through the pleasure gardens, through citrus groves and stone ponds, under the cover of grapes growing from a trellised ceiling. Faerie butterflies with luminous azure wings, some the size of her palms, fluttered about their ears, as pods with purple and pink buds threatened to knock them over. Radia could spend days in the gardens reading, or chasing the phosphorescent fauna, without stuffy tutors or stuffy clothes, but such frolic would never come again, she realized, nor would she sleep again in her soft bed, or know the company of . . .

"Wait! Larissa."

"Your Highness, we must hurry—"

"I go nowhere without my handmaiden!"

"I did not swear an oath to protect Your Highness's handmaiden!" he growled. "Follow me!"

"I won't and you cannot make me." She crossed her arms over her chest. "Am I not *True North*, am I not—"

"Alright, then. Where is this girl of yours?"

"In my chambers, of course, where else—?"

"Are you insane? A hundred men are coming for us both, and you want to go to the one place they'll most expect us?"

"If you wish to protect me, you'll simply have to do it there."

"Where?" he barked.

Holding the threads of her gown, she skipped to the edge of the enclosed garden, through an arcade of jasper, tourmaline and chalcedony, and out to a postern door. Another rumble echoed through the walls, succeeded by the pitter-patter of water droplets. "That isn't the army—it's a storm," he remarked, pushing through to the outside.

The sky was somber gray and the stones below were slick and glistening. The rain was falling hard and harder and sideways with the wind. "The sun was ablaze only moments ago," he said with a bit of confusion. "The gods must be smiling on us. This will give us cover, skew their arrows at least, should they find us."

Radia followed him and secured the door. It would be some time, she figured, before her brother's men could determine where she'd gone.

The ledge led directly to a one-man bridge. It seemed to be suspended in air, with nothing but sky on either side, crossing high above hills and waterfalls and tiled rooftops. A lone minaret stood a great distance off, like a lance passing through the turquoise moon.

"What are you waiting for?" she asked.

He stared over the brink, as if measuring the distance to the bottom, which shifted with the motion of the clouds. "There has to be another way."

"To my bedchamber? It's right there," she said, pointing, "in *that* tower."

He took a wary step onto the bridge, clutching the railing firmly. Radia paced behind him, lifting her cheeks to the rain to take the brunt of it, letting it rush down her neck and clothes and drip from her braids. It was invigorating, empowering. "Go!" she cried, shoving him.

"Are you sure this is safe?"

"Wait. You're not afraid of . . . Are you afraid of heights?"

"I do not prefer them."

"You faced off against my brother and his army and now you shrink before a bridge?"

"Men I can handle. The ground far below us is another matter."

"I walk this way every morning, noon and evening, as does Larissa. Now make haste before they find us!"

The royal bedchamber was in order. Frilly, her swan, drifted lazily in its fountain pool, and behind the silk partitions of the room, her bed was straightened with linens newly washed and pressed, and her collection of dolls and perfumes was neatly arrayed, and her books were all on their proper shelves, except for the one she was reading, the fairytale collection with the unicorn seal on the cover. Yet her handmaiden was nowhere to be found. *Larissa, you have been so good to me. How can I leave you behind?*

Radia twirled about the room, anxious to know what had become of her companion, the larger predicament dissolving from her mind as her protector paced to and fro.

"So, where is she?"

"I don't know," she said, running a finger over a jeweled comb. "Maybe the stables."

"*Maybe the stables!*" he roared. "You said she would be here!"

Radia recoiled, frightened by his sudden temper. "I said no such thing. I sometimes find her here, is all. But she does love the stable ponies. We might find her there."

"Princess, for the sake of your life and mine, we must depart this castle immediately. Do you understand what that means? *Immediately!* No more detours!"

"If I'm never coming back, let me at least pack a few things, change out of this outfit, which you managed to ruin, by the way." She tucked her book under one arm and reached for a small box encrusted with gemstones. The lock was a gold heart fastened by a dagger. Book and box went into a satchel, and she then proceeded to fight with her great-grandmother's gown, but the lace was too tight about the waist and held her like a giant's fist. "Praetorian, if you would come here a moment—"

"Princess, please, we haven't time for this," he argued. "We must—"

A loud bang interrupted him and they both stood at attention. Nothing could ever threaten her here, she had thought, not where she was born, not where father had sat when she was ill, reading her fairytales. She had not been able to imagine life ending where it began, and yet she could hear them beyond the walls, men clamoring to run their swords into her heart, and the illusion of her sanctuary shattered with the sound.

The praetorian pushed furniture against the door, but already it was splintering, throwing intricately patterned wood chips into the pool, ruffling Frilly's feathers.

"Is there another way out?" he cried. "A trap door?"

"The mirrors!"

Radia showed him to an octagonal dressing room. Tall, oval mirrors stood on each side. Reflecting at them was his scowling, hairless head, a long scar cutting through his eye and lip. Her image stood at his side, with her spun-gold hair and eyes of different colors, turquoise and violet, so much like the moons.

He shook his head. "What is this? This is a . . . a waste of time!"

"Have you lost all your faith? Look closer."

"I see nothing."

"Only our reflections," she answered. "See?" It was true. There was no wall or curtain behind them, nothing to indicate their surroundings but a blurred, glassy surface.

In the other room, a door was coming to pieces, chairs were clacking, tables were squeaking and groaning, and pottery and crystal were being shattered. Someone fell into the fountain with an obscenity, and Radia's bird gave an awkward squawk that she sensed was its last.

"Princess, I've failed you. There is nowhere to run—there *was* never anywhere to go." He drew his sword from its sheath and moved toward her, his eyes pained.

"No," she whispered, "you haven't, not yet. And you may call me Radia." She offered her hand, not as a superior, but a friend. "Tell me your name, praetorian?"

"I am called Demacharon."

The soldiers were in view now, their plumed helms bristling like the combs of angry roosters, their arrows nocked. Radia gave them a final smile and pulled on his arm, and together they fell through the mirror.

It was like falling suddenly and unexpectedly through a trap door, like having your mind and stomach exchange places, but the moment passed quickly. Radia was on the ground beside her protector, bent double, gasping, retching. As much as she wanted to empty her bowels, only lines of spittle dangled from her lips, as she had been too nervous that morning to take breakfast. Anabis once explained how the Zo traveled throughout Aenya, and even between stars, in such a manner. Hand-in-hand with her tutor, she had once jumped inside a mirror, but the disorientation and sickening feeling that ensued dissuaded her from ever trying it again.

Demacharon found his footing like a drunkard. "You should have warned me about that."

"I'm sorry. I didn't think there was time."

"Where are we?"

The floor was a rough-hewn flagstone covered in hay, with crabgrass and other weeds growing from between the cracks. Fires burned from sconces, throwing long shadows about the room, glittering in the oval mirror at their backs. In the adjacent hall, they met with rows of halberds, swords and spears, shields in piles and men made of straw.

"Why does it smell so foul?"

"This is the armory," he answered. "You couldn't have picked better unless you wanted to visit Zaibos's personal chambers."

"Hey—I didn't choose this place—every mirror has its twin! We end up where the other is. I had no idea it would be here."

"You should have said so before," he said, smashing the silvered glass with the pommel of his sword. "Now they cannot follow."

"Is there any way out of here?"

He examined the rack of weapons before him, weighing a gladius in his hand. "Of course, but without anyone seeing us . . . there's the rub. This might not be entirely fruitless, however."

Radia watched him mull over their options. It was a strange thing to put her faith—her very life—in the hands of a stranger. And yet, what choice did she have? There was no one to trust but Larissa, and what good was a handmaiden at such a time? *Poor Larissa.* She could only hope that no harm had come to her, but knowing Zaibos, that hope was faint.

Demacharon pulled off his cuirass. His upper body was discolored in places, and it took some time for Radia to recognize the bruises for what they were. Lines cut through his chest and side, marks drawn by weapons. She could only imagine how such wounds must have hurt him. Her spine began to tingle at the sight, and her body grew numb.

As he searched among greaves and gorgets and sallets, she reached out, gently touching him. The skin on his shoulder was raised in the shape of a trident. "What is that? Did they—did someone brand you? Like a horse?"

"It's nothing," he said, donning a breastplate of boiled leather. "A memento from another life." He strapped the gladius to his hip beside the longsword, and turned to her, pressing a dirk into her palm. "If something should happen to me, do not hesitate to use this."

"A knife? I don't think I could ever—"

Voices filled the room and Radia knew they were no longer alone. There was no place to hide or to run. Demacharon tightened his belt and walked into the common room, where a contingent of soldiers awaited them.

Eight surrounded them, weapons in hand, and a young man stepped forward. He was uncommonly handsome, even for a soldier, and the unicorn emblazoned across his torso galloped in the torchlight.

"Did you think you could escape us, traitor? We have men posted at every exit and mirror. Hand over the princess and the king will make your death a painless one."

"What a generous offer, Captain Sligh." Demacharon slid his longsword from its sheath. "How could I pass it up?"

"Wait!" Radia cried. "Traitor? How can this man be a traitor? He saved my life! He is the only one loyal to me."

"You have been misled, Your Highness," the captain replied. "Alas, you are a child, and could not have known better. You are not to be blamed."

She stood between the two men, trying to look tall, but she was short for her age, and barefoot. "What are you going on about?"

"Did you truly believe you were being rescued? That this man—*this man*—an admitted outsider, would risk his life for yours? The world does not work this way, princess. This is not one of your fairytales. No one gives his all unless there is something to gain, and a princess of Tyrnael is no chimney sweep's daughter—no, you are a jewel among women. The crown on your head alone is worth his weight in gold!"

She snatched the tiara from her head, tossing it to the floor where it rolled out of sight. "Is it true?" she said, turning to Demacharon. "Are you a foreigner?" But she knew the answer before asking. Why did he look older than her father did on his deathbed, yet move like someone half his age? And why did he have trouble pronouncing his words—a detail she had not noticed while fleeing for her life—if the language was not new to him? It all made sense now.

Demacharon lowered his sword. "It is true I was not born in Tyrnael, but I am sworn to you, the true heir, not the half-breed monster who would call himself king."

"The throne is his birthright," the captain rejoined. "After all, he is eldest born."

Radia could feel her cheeks boiling with rage, a rage that came in the face of blatant lies. "Zaibos is not of my blood!" she cried. "His father was not my father! He is the usurper, the traitor!"

"Politics aside, our liege has taken the throne for the betterment of the empire, but does not wish harm upon his kin. He told me so himself."

"I may be young, but I'm no fool," she answered. "I heard my brother's words. He intends to kill me! Shot arrows at me!"

"Not at you, Your Highness. If we had wished you dead, you would be. Consider that a hundred arrows came your way, and miraculously you were left unharmed. It was the conspirators who were executed—your praetorian guard—led by this man whom you fancy a hero. We suspected the plot from the day *he* requested the position. Otherwise, we never would have allowed him near you."

"So . . ." she murmured, "all this was some sort of charade?"

"Forgive us, but it was necessary to uncover the truth. When this man came forward to speak, we knew our people were involved, that they meant to steal you away to the South, to lands beyond the Crown. Come with us now, and King Zaibos promises you will sleep safely tonight in your own bed."

"No," said Radia. "He is an honorable man. I can . . . sense it."

The captain raised his blade. "If you will not surrender peacefully, you will be forced to watch him die!"

The two men came together faster than Radia could have imagined. Swords flashed, painting the air silver, ringing with deadly music. Sligh seemed sure of himself, dancing around her praetorian, lunging and parrying more swiftly. Demacharon retreated against the wall, defending blow after blow.

"I've always admired your way with a blade, but I never trusted you."

Demacharon pedaled backward into the narrow recess of the hall as the captain pressed and taunted and mocked, his longsword flying wide, chipping at the masonry, raining dust on them both. Her champion seemed to be weakening, and Radia feared for his life.

"Tired, old man?"

There was a sudden, somber look in Demacharon's face that startled her, a darkness she had not yet seen. "You've never killed a man, have you? Never watched a man's eyes as the life ebbs out of him?"

"W-What does that—?"

"It means you're green, boy. You can't cut me down because you don't want to. Me? I've killed my share, men much younger than you—watched soldiers die before you were born. And I have nothing to lose."

There was an edge in his voice, enough to make the captain hesitate, and in that instant Demacharon lunged forward, embracing him. Radia was suddenly afraid for them both. She had witnessed the horror of men felled at her feet and did not wish to relive it again. In her most authoritative voice, she demanded, pleaded for peace, stopping short of throwing herself on Demacharon's arm, but when he released the captain, she could see the blood flowing and the red-stained gladius in his other hand. The boy's brow beaded with sweat and the color rushed out of him. She could see the disbelief and confusion written across his face. Radia watched him shudder and grow cold and his pain became her own. She moved a hand to her nostrils to staunch the flow, her blood spilling over her fingers, across her lip and chin.

"Not again," she heard herself saying. "Not now."

Demacharon was calling her name, but his voice was a distant echo. The boy was dead and she was falling beside him, down and down into the dark spaces between worlds.

2

Demacharon

When there is only silence and darkness, I find myself comforted. There is peace in not remembering. But sometimes, when exhaustion forces my eyes, I go deep into the maelstrom, down into the abyss between realms.

It is not a dream. An awful clarity pervades every little detail. I could describe, if you were to ask me, the shape of each rock on that damnable plain. But at first I am only aware of dread, not merely the feeling of it, but a pervasive, palpable reality, like a knife entering my very being, causing me to sweat and tremble.

No sun casts its light over this land. No stars. No moons. What dim glow permits my sight to function, I cannot say. The sky is the wrong color—perhaps you could call it violet, the deepest shade one could fathom—but is in truth like nothing the eye can perceive. Only rock and gravel populate the surface, and the bottomless trenches and distant mountains create an austere panorama. Even in the most arid of deserts, there are cacti and lichen, and lizards and serpents crawl over the earth. In this place, not a soul abounds. I look for direction, some sign to lift my spirits, but I am utterly lost. The terrain is without feature but for the hilly silhouettes on the horizon.

Might those peaks promise better pastures, a city perhaps, a place where vagabonds gather? I wonder, holding fast to hope, and yet the way the mountains are arrayed—how they loop and twist at impossible angles—disturbs and disheartens me.

Who am I? What is my purpose? How did I come to this unfinished creation, this place abandoned by gods? And how can I still breathe where there is no vestige of life? At the fringes of my mind, my name teases me, but it is a long-lost memory. I cannot even be certain as to the nature of my existence, of whether I am a man, woman, or other, or if, before this very moment, I ever lived at all. The only clue to my identity is a tiny wooden carving in my palm, a trireme the length of my forefinger, meticulously engraved with a battering ram and a double tier of oars flat against the hull. The standard etched into the lateen sails, the trident, is familiar to me also. Was I a sailor once? A captain? I only know that the ship is dear to me.

The carving is the one constant, for I sometimes find myself in rags or in the full regalia of a centurion, or else entirely naked. It matters little, for clothing is unsubstantial here, as is the flesh. My body is numb to cold, and thirst and hunger are but wistful memories. Rocks tear across my soles, but no blood appears, and I feel no pain. I am a hollow vessel adrift in the waters of beyond.

Solitude consumes me, and I long for nothing but to expire, to cease this tired existence. I have fallen through all the layers of being, and there is no greater depth for despondency to take me to, and still, even in this remotest of hells, there exists a glimmer of light. I cannot tell its nature, whether it be a sun or star or some great lighthouse-fire calling lost souls to hopeful shores, but dread and despair recede from it like the night shrinks from the day. The light is life. Hope. I cannot but follow it.

For how long do I trek across that plain? A day, a year, a hundred thousand years? There is no answer, for in this *otherwhere*, time does not exist. And yet, however great my travail, the light remains eternally beyond my reach.

At last, I come to a pen for goats and hens and other livestock. The fence is unremarkable as fences go, with rivets showing between the seams, but to me, it is a work of exceeding beauty. Anything besides rock and gravel is a sight for weary eyes. Even the earthly feel of it—its grainy cedar planking against my fingertips—gives waves of pleasure. I wonder where the farmer must be, and his animals. I stand awhile, delighting in my discovery, as the ethereal light continues to beckon. But I fear to leave that place, *because it is a place*, a memory, a tether to my childhood.

Beyond the pen, shapes flit to and fro, inking the ground with elongated shadows. Only living things move about so, and whatever their manner, I think it of no consequence. To escape my loneliness, I would befriend a bogren, but the fence prevents my crossing. It stands to my thigh and yet I cannot climb or leap over it. Some force keeps me and does not let go. With every part of my being, I struggle against that barrier, until I surrender upon the railing, resting my palm against it, and the fence is suddenly behind me. It was the little wooden ship—my key—permitting me passage.

The space beyond is choked with people, though I did not see any when I was still on the other side. They press me, shoulder to shoulder, knocking me about as they bustle past. Some are dressed in rags, others in fine embroidered silks or gleaming mail, and more than a few are utterly naked. Paupers and merchants and soldiers, highborn aristocrats and priests and kings—they are all mixed like fish in a fishmonger's net. I recognize the garb of the Hedonian, a man from my own city, and a great many from Thetis, Thalassar, Northendell, and Shemselinihar. But an even greater number are foreign to me, perhaps races from beyond the map, or extinct peoples from the pages of history.

They do not seem to notice me, nor do they speak to or acknowledge their own in any way. Here is a continent-sized population—a host too vast to measure—and yet they are blind to themselves, each man and woman and child a stranger. Their eyes are soulless, lost and bewildered, but some power drives them, causing them to swarm about like gnats, eternally searching. It is a placid mob, a procession of the mad, and a thought seizes me with terror, that I must count myself among them, that I am surely no different.

Again, with the talisman in my hand, I find my way. The ship is my identity, my purpose. Holding fast to it, I push through the mob, shouting and beating them with my fists, but my blows do not sway their desperate course. No matter, I am determined to persist, to not become one of them. The light is my salvation and the ship my passage.

Ages ago, I leapt from a high place, and the ground raced up to meet me, and I found myself in this dreadful place. But now, guided through this sea of faces, I find them at last, and know myself at once. They are within my reach, the two I came in search of, the people for whom I surrendered everything. She wears the same black tunic and shawl. Our son clutches her hand, and she is leading him through that awful gathering, her face despondent and broken, her hair ashen, her face resembling a drowned woman's. The boy at her side, despite his age, shares her deathly aspect.

I push bodies from my path, reaching, screaming their names lest she move away and is lost to me again, but she cannot hear. Fighting for every step, I finally reach her and grip her by the shoulder, forcing her around to see my face.

"Niobe!"

She stares and stares, as if through a window, offering no reply.

"Don't you recognize your husband, Niobe? It is me!"

I tilt her chin, so that she might gaze fully into my eyes, but she is dead to the world. The boy holds to his mother out of some habit, I realize, like the fingers of a corpse stiffened about some precious remnant from life. No tenderness resides in their clasped-together hands, for he does not know his mother, nor she him. The thought occurs to me how the two came to be joined for all eternity, yet strangers to one another. Before my fall, Niobe came seeking our son, and after finding him forgot herself and was lost, just like the others. Surely, I am to follow, but I refuse to accept the truth of it.

I shake her, lovingly, angrily. "Say something, Niobe! Speak to me, I beg you."

I plead with her, embrace her as if she might become immaterial and slip away, and still she does not know me. On my knees, sobbing and quaking, a terrible certainty takes root in my mind. It is imperative that they know me. If they do not speak my name, I will soon forget it and, by not knowing it, will cease to exist.

Surrendering hope for my wife, I turn to my son. How often has he run into my arms? For how many countless nights have I cradled his head and heard him whisper that he loves me? Surely, he will remember—gods be good, let him remember!

"Astor, please look upon me. Look kindly upon your dear father, so that I know that you know me." But he only stares, his face contorted as if searching for a memory.

I can feel his wrist, slender as a sapling, and yet there are no veins, no pulse—he is just as I found him all those many years ago, the day my Niobe came down to this place in spirit. I touch his side and recoil. The gash is still there, from when the creature spilled his entrails on the sand. I reach for my face, finding my own scars, each one a reminder the monster left me of the life I failed to save. He had been playing by the shore that morning, playing with his . . .

"Wait!" I cry. "The token!" Pressing the wooden ship into his palm, I watch as he ponders it. It was my gift to him on the day I shipped out for war. He was never without it. He will remember the ship and remember me. I do not doubt it.

My son does not speak, but I can see the change in his eyes, a spark of recognition. Niobe is also beginning to see me, and I come to her aid, recounting memories, from when our lips first touched on the shores of Sarnath, to our wedding day when we danced on gold-painted litters, to the evening when our newborn son first wailed and trembled in my hands. Slowly but surely, they are coming to know me. We will exist together, be it in this horrid place, yet no longer in solitude.

But, in piecing together my identity, I become recognizable to others I knew in life. Like vultures to carrion, they swarm about me, whispering awful things in my ears. Shame falls on my heart like an anchor, and everywhere I look, there are faces—faces without bodies—growling and hissing and murmuring. This one I slew in battle when he was very young. Another was unable to pay his taxes and so I had his home burned to ash. Still another lost his sons at my command. They are pulling at me now, tearing my clothing and hair. I try to fight them but am outnumbered and overwhelmed. Hands pin my arms and legs. Niobe is calling out to me and to the crowd, weeping for mercy, as is my son, Astor. The two of them know my name, but have no knowledge of my misdeeds, and those I have wronged will not release me. I am dragged away from my family, watching my wife and son shrink from my eyes, framed by those horrid faces. Fingers fill my nostrils like worms, bury my mouth, and dig out my eyes. Having given my token to my son, I am dragged back to the fence, thrown over it into the blasted plain. My eyes are gone now, yet still, I can see it—somehow I can see the light. In that last moment, I recognize the source. A city. By the gods, the light is a city!

I do not fear to die as other men do. The great mystery does not cause me to dread my eternal sleep. It is the certainty of that undiscovered country, and in knowing what awaits me.

3

Hugo

Hugo found he was unable to concentrate, his head full of the rumors that were spreading exponentially, like a wildfire, from one terraced neighborhood to another. If even half of what he had heard was true—no, he could not allow his mind to follow such a dark path. Besides, nothing of the sort had ever happened in Tyrnael. History was rife with calamitous moments, but they were not living in such a time. The present was dull, ordinary, and secure. *The Lawgivers*, in their vast wisdom, had made certain of it.

He continued eastward along the stony promenade, following a pillared arcade heavy with vines, scarcely noticing anything but his feet, and the way in which the gold-limned pavers gave way to featureless gravel. Few people traveled this route, and fewer highborn. The eastern edge of the city was a place for manual laborers, for crop-workers and trash collectors. For eloai.

The pathway narrowed to an open plateau, which stood apart from the monoliths and white-gold spires dominating the city. The landing extended out to a natural outcropping, overlooking the Great Chasm in the East. The morning air was crisp and cool against his face, and the turquoise moon hung low in the sky, having almost vanished against the blue horizon. Larks called for lovers, dandelions swayed in the hills, and leaves quivered from their branches, and in his reverie, he walked suddenly into a wicker basket brimming with hockenberries. The tiny round fruit sprawled every which way, rolling off the path to fit neatly into the spaces between the paving stones, and he found himself simultaneously apologizing and stooping to gather up the result of his carelessness, staining the ground with dark purple splotches with each of his steps.

"I am so terribly sorry," he repeated.

The young girl was barefoot, wearing the white, knee-length peplos common to the eloai. She was too busy squatting over berries to look at him, answering, "No, no . . . it's entirely my fault."

"How could it be?" he urged. "I wasn't watching where I was going."

"No," she insisted, never lifting her gaze. "I should learn to be more careful."

By now he had gathered a good handful and was beginning to refill the basket. "You may need to rewash these. Goats tread through here sometimes."

She glanced his way, saw what he was doing, and gave a short gasp of alarm. "Please, kind sir, you needn't help me."

He dumped another handful into the wicker receptacle and bent down again. The work was tedious, but he was delighted all the same. "I don't mind. Really."

"You shouldn't," she remarked matter-of-factly.

"But why?"

"Well, because . . ." She stood to face him for the first time, her cheeks reddening, depositing the last of what could be salvaged into the basket, and in her pale gray eyes, he could see the wheels of her thoughts turning. "Because, I'm an eloai, and you're a . . ."

"A soldier?"

A streak of fear shot across her brow. "You're a soldier!"

"Is there anything wrong with that?"

"No!" she exclaimed, a little too loudly. "Of course not. It's just that—I'm not even supposed to be here. I switched jobs, you see, because I wanted to pick berries. I thought it might be fun. You won't tell anyone, will you?"

"Why would I? What's wrong with—?"

She ran off before he could finish speaking, hockenberries jostling in her arms, more than a couple dropping and rolling off into the dirt. Hugo could not help but snicker as he watched her go. Eloai did not wear makeup, fancy clothing or jewelry, and their hair was trimmed to the shoulder, falling whichever way nature allowed. Male and female alike, they were born to be simple, and yet for Hugo, they were like certain ordinary trees or flowers, often going unnoticed, yet possessing an unassuming beauty, if one was to simply stop and take notice.

He continued down to the foot of the Great Eastern Gate, and the bridge spanning the divide between the two hemispheres. The colossal arches were worn by wind and sun and the ravages of time, overgrown with blazing stars and chicories and perennials. On the north flank, the stone creature rising from the base had collapsed into a mound of rubble, leaving only its hindquarters, but on the southern end, Hugo could make out the semblance of a bucking horse, dressed from hoof to snout in green creepers, with a single horn spiraling up from the head like a conical lance broken at the tip. He stood fretfully upon the landing, overlooking the sheer drop of the Tectonic Chasm. It was like peering beyond the end of the world, the bridge crossing the divide vanishing into the gray ether. Whether he could continue along the expanse until reaching the eastern half of the world, he could only guess, but the distance, he knew, was many leagues. Turning north to the Celestial Hill, he observed the Compass Tower, which loomed like a gilded spear rising from a white fist. His impatience growing, he tried to gauge how far the violet moon had traversed across the broad face of the greater turquoise disc, and his eyes drifted again to the statue of the unicorn, to the standard of his people. He had only chanced to see the animal once in his youth, on guard duty at the royal stable, and did not know whether other such creatures existed, only that the one he was fortunate enough to have witnessed was hundreds of years old. Legend had it that the thirty-third descendant of the first king, Queen Lumina, was so pure of heart, that after she had fallen asleep in a neighboring glade, a unicorn came to rest its head on her lap. The divine creature became enamored by the princess's charm, and in time came to dwell with the royal family. And so the embodiment of the sigil Hugo wore on his breast remained, upon centuries, among the king's equine stock.

His appointment arrived at last. Hugo watched him emerge from the direction of the tower, his black charger sidling up to the gate. The man was meticulous in the handling of his beast, wasting no time dismounting, the unicorn crest emblazoned across his cuirass gleaming in the morning sun. Hugo recognized his pale face and gaunt cheeks, and embraced him from wrist to elbow.

"Mandos! What's this all about? What's happened?"

"It is . . . a great day," Mandos answered hesitantly. "Not only for us, but for every citizen of Tyrnael."

"Oh?" Hugo could sense some measure of insincerity in his voice, even as the other looked upon him in earnest. "I'd heard differently. That there's been some kind of violence. That several people have been killed."

"I won't deny it. Good men were taken from us today. Brave souls. Praetorians mostly. But the lot of them were traitors."

"Traitors?" Hugo mouthed the words incredulously. "How can that be?"

A look of resignation crossed Mandos's face. He was middle-aged, but appeared much older. "You'd best believe it, my friend." He fastened his charger to a spiral of rock, and the animal remained motionless, as if turned to stone. "These are troubling times, which is why I so urgently sought you out, to prevent the lies from clouding your judgment. I also needed to know, for my own sake, that you could be trusted. That you could be loyal."

"I would never betray the princess, Mandos," he said softly. "You know this."

He stood quietly before speaking again, choosing his words carefully. "Aye, but that's the rub. The princess is missing. She might even be dead. Which is why we must turn our attentions to the greater good. Think upon what is best for Tyrnael and its people. Our allegiance is to them."

"Of course. And I agree. But you say the princess may be . . . dead?" His heart ached even to say the words. "That can't be, Mandos."

"We are still uncertain as to what has happened to her, precisely." He turned to his horse, casually brushing its shimmering dark mane with his gloved fingers. "After the guards were massacred, Sligh attempted to rescue her, but was killed in the process."

"Sligh was a good man! I knew his family. Generous people. I supped at his house many a time, attended his brother's joining."

"He will be avenged. All of them will."

Hugo sat against the base of the arch, his legs weary. Such things never happened in Tyrnael. Their kingdom was a bastion of liberty, the envy of all Aenya for untold ages. And although he had been trained for battle from a young age, he felt unprepared for it now—for just such a trial. Instinctively, he groped at the brass pommel at his hip. "What do we know about these traitors? Where do they come from?"

"Foreign insurgents, who else?" Mandos answered matter-of-factly. "It's just as Zaibos warned us about. Though some of us refused to listen," he added with disdain. "We allow these strangers into our borders and you see what happens."

Hugo did not speak. Something had changed in the timber of Mandos's voice. There was a sudden edge to it that gave him pause. He glanced away, toward the bucking unicorn made of stone. Its foundations, he could now see, were crumbling. "That can't be. What would outsiders want with Radia?"

"They want what we have, Hugo—our prosperity, our long life—and they'll kill to get it. How many times has the commander spoken of this? Tyrnael cannot remain hidden forever. And now that they know we're here, we must become strong, to protect the people we love. The old ways can no longer sustain us."

Hugo crossed his arms and took a step back. "Seems awfully convenient, these foreign-born kidnappers. I mean, it's just what Zaibos would have wanted."

"What *he* would have wanted? Just what you are suggesting, Hugo?" He scratched at the finely trimmed hairs of his chin. "Zaibos wants what we all do, security in Tyrnael, for everyone, for children and the elderly to live free from harm." Mandos was never one to raise his voice, but now, he had become uncharacteristically passionate. "Our ancestors were masters of the universe! All of Aenya worshiped the Zo. Now look at what we have become. Look at these ruined colonnades, these broken bridges—we are wasting away here, wallowing in the shadows of past glories. But we could rise again!"

"We needn't master others to be great. The Zo led through wisdom."

"And that wisdom came at the point of a sword." An angry glint danced in his eyes that Hugo had never seen before. "You cannot teach without authority, and authority necessitates power. That is the hard truth Zaibos has helped us to learn."

"Men who desire power never make for good rulers," Hugo stated flatly.

"Empty rhetoric," Mandos shot back. "Platitudes for a schoolboy."

"We have had peace and prosperity for ages, under the reign of Solon and his forebears. But what you are proposing . . . it can only lead to tyranny."

"If we sit and do nothing, they *will* infest our city. More are crossing every day. First they ask to barter, then they set up shops—next they will be living alongside us, cavorting with our women and our children. Is that what you want? Hedonians, Delians, Shemites—the whole stinking lot of them—diluting our culture, dirtying our bloodlines?"

"Newcomers enrich us," Hugo replied. "They bring fresh ideas, new kinds of music, art, food. That is what Tyrnael needs to thrive. Isolation is what's been killing us."

Mandos's face changed again. He looked almost apologetic. His voice came softer now, his words sounding with greater diplomacy. "Sure, we can adopt what we find useful, but we must control the flow of who comes in and who doesn't. Without borders, we surrender our sovereignty. And now that the old dynasty is gone, we have the opportunity to strengthen ourselves."

"Gone? Wait—I thought you said the princess may still be alive?"

"Alive, dead . . . what matters is the imminent threat to our homeland."

Hugo was beginning to see with whom he was speaking, and it frightened him to realize that the man he thought he knew was no more. "Are those your words, Mandos, or the commander's?"

"*King* Zaibos," he answered icily. "And yes, he has taught me much, for he is a great man! A man of vision, and strength."

"But, is he a good man?" Hugo challenged.

"At times like these, we cannot afford to be fastidious. We must sometimes take a step back before moving forward. Zaibos is doing what none have had the will to do. He is making the hard decisions."

"I don't trust him. Zaibos will say and do anything to get what he wants. Don't forget—hubris caused the downfall of the Zo, and the cataclysm that followed."

"Well, you know me. I was never very good at history. I chose to focus on my sword."

"Then you should listen to someone who paid attention to the lecturers!" Hugo's fists were clenched at his sides. He felt betrayed, by everything he knew of the man, a fellow defender of the dynasty.

"No, you listen. I've always thought very highly of you, and that is why I am going to pretend this exchange never took place." Slowly, Mandos turned away, clutching the reins of his charger. "Things are going to be different from now on, and if you are wise, you will know where best to stand. Please don't take this as a threat. This is me . . . at my most charitable."

4

Eros

Eros sat across the table from a man long rumored to be a monster—not merely a savage, but a literal demon. He could now see what he long suspected to be true. Rumors could be used for deception and intimidation, and as Eros made his living by such methods, he had to admire the implementation. Even without the blood-red helm of spikes, Zaibos was a monstrous figure to behold, taller by a head than himself, with shoulders like a horg. The king of Tyrnael sat, even now, in full plate, as if the armor was a part of him. An elaborately wrought-iron chair, riddled with gaps, accommodated the spikes protruding from it.

"The world is full of black hearts, but mine is the blackest of all," the king roared. "I like the sound of that, don't you? It's like poetry."

"I care only for the poetry of stealth," Eros answered, "the dagger in the night, silent as a gliding owl."

Zaibos's lips curled into a wicked grin, his beard swaying like hanging moss. "I like you, assassin. You do not fear to look into my eyes and speak your mind. That is just the kind of man I need." His fingers greased with fat, he tore into his meat like a sabretooth, and downed the mouthful with mead.

Eros did not feel hungry and only sipped at his chalice, which was heavy enough to use as a weapon, should the need arise. He leaned into his chair, trying to look at ease. It was not as though he had never met with evil men before, but he was accustomed to making deals under cover of the moon, in lonely alleyways and forgotten alcoves. Here, the sun was full on his face, and colorful tents surrounded them. Soldiers bustled to and fro, grinding swords on whetstones, picking straw men with arrows, testing weapons against armor and muscle with muscle.

"You've not yet told me the job."

Zaibos picked his bone clean and spat greasy slivers with his answer. "I want the princess's heart—in a jewelry box I will provide you."

Despite his murderous inclinations, Eros could not rein in the surprise in his voice. "Isn't Radia your sister?"

The king's eyes were like dull steel. "Should that matter?"

Eros took a swig from his cup. The mead tasted bitter. There were times when he had refused to take money, usually from a husband who still loved his wife, when he could still see the hurt in their eyes, the sort of desperation that would result only in a regrettable and impulsive act, and in those instances he would talk his would-be clients into less bloody resolutions.

"The life of the heir to the throne will cost you a mighty sum." In truth, Eros had never killed anyone of royal birth, but he assumed that the fee must be higher.

"The cost is irrelevant." He slammed the chalice down and wiped his chin. "Here in Tyrnael, we have never wanted for precious metals, or for anything our ancestors could readily produce. I could make your likeness out of solid gold, if you wished it."

"That won't be necessary."

In a clearing not three steps from their table, two men were making a raucous noise with maul on shield, sword on helm. Eros wondered, were they preparing for war? Did this have some connection to the princess? He could only guess, but sigils and banners meant nothing to a man of his profession. There would always be the need, in any society, for dirty deeds, for men in the shadows to maintain the illusion of stability. No matter who ruled in Tyrnael, whether Radia or Zaibos or Skullgrin himself, Eros would blend in like a chameleon, because he had come into the world as few others did, a man born without identity.

A possibility occurred to him in that moment, one he could only dream of since the time he was old enough to understand injustice. He quivered with the thought, wondering if it was even possible. And why not? Zaibos was the master of Tyrnael and the secrets of the Zo were at his disposal.

"Gold does not interest me. Nor jewels either."

Zaibos smiled, as if let in on a perverse joke. "Lands, then? Titles? A lordship, perhaps?"

"What need does a man with my talents have of lands? No, what I desire is . . ." and he pulled his hood away to reveal the brand on his forehead, a serpent with an extra head for a tail— the shame mark. His *aleph*. He offered nothing more, waiting for his employer to catch on, fearing the derision known to him since birth.

Zaibos twisted his beard, slicking it with the grease from his fingers. "All this time, you've kept it hidden from me that I should not be speaking to you."

"Does it matter what I am?" Eros said angrily. "The manner of my birth? Or what I can do?"

Laughter echoed from the monster's metallic frame. "Relax! What do I care of the taboos of Dis? I could raze that city to the ground and kill everyone who ever shunned you. Or I could fix that here and now, with my knife."

"The mark is a part of me. A man who is not seen or spoken to cannot be questioned or sought after. It is the most useful tool in my profession. What I request is not for me, but my mother, who carries the same mark. No one has spoken to her since the day I was born. In Dis, shit-covered pigs are treated with greater respect. If there is any way to undo the mark, to make her visible again . . . That is the fee I request—a life for a life."

In the arena beside them, a giant of a man with a gleaming maul struck a powerful blow, and his opponent fell to pieces, armor scattering like fragments from a porcelain doll hitting the ground. Zaibos watched with delight, seeming to forget their conversation, but as the fallen warrior's broken body was carried off, he turned to face Eros. "Our scientists can give your mother a new face. She will be young again, unblemished and beautiful. But first, you must prove yourself capable."

"The child should pose no trouble. If you call away the guards, I will be able to—"

"Not so simple! Radia is not as foolish as she seems. She has fled the castle, possibly the kingdom, and is not alone. Her lapdog protector, a Hedonian by the name of Demacharon—a dangerous man—killed eight of my best in single combat. Do you think that will be a problem for you?"

"No man is a problem for me, Zaibos."

"Oh? You're that good a fighter?"

"I do not fight men. I kill them. There is a difference."

"But if you come face to face with this Hedonian? What then would you do?" As if to illustrate the point, another man fell beneath the giant hammer. The way the helm was smashed into the skull, Eros doubted the man would live through the night. "A golden age is dawning upon Aenya, and as in days of yore, Tyrnael will serve as its capital. No weakling can rule over this new utopia—the princess's weakness, like that of her ancestors, has been a blight on our people for generations. She represents all that I aim to cure. Now, if you would join my cause, and show me your strength!" With a broad sweep of his gargantuan arm, Zaibos gestured towards the sparring champion.

Eros bristled. Any other time, he would have balked, no matter the offer. But Zaibos frightened him like no man ever had. And the possibility of saving his mother from the mark of invisibility, of removing her aleph, was too tempting to walk away from. Still, lines of respect had to be drawn. "Understand this—I am not one of your soldiers to command. But if you need me to demonstrate my services, I can oblige you."

The sparring champion, Horgin, much like the king himself, was heads taller than the assassin and covered in iron from head to toe. Horgin opened his helm to wipe the sweat from his brow. The sun was cooking men in their armor, and by now the brute was sure to be stewing. Good, Eros thought—heat makes a man slow to action.

"This is what you bring me to fight?" he barked, shaking blood and entrails from his weapon. "A peasant-insect?"

It was all a song and dance to Eros, the roaring and chest pounding of a halfman, an attempt at intimidation that did not faze him. "Is that a fresh term you've invented? Peasant-insect? How unexpectedly clever."

Horgin lobbed a ball of phlegm at him, but Eros dodged quickly enough to avoid the sticky mess. "Was that your first attack?"

Feigning outrage, the giant slammed his faceplate down and moved into an offensive posture. Squires rushed to the assassin's side, offering a variety of swords, axes, and maces, but Eros brushed them off. The only items he needed were already in the pockets of his cloak and hidden around his waist—they consisted of one dagger, a particularly nasty species of spider in jars attached to his belt, spools of a special silk thread from a worm found only in one part of the Dead Zones, and a sling.

Eros stood, motionless, imagining that the gathering onlookers must think him paralyzed with fear. Horgin hesitated in moving to kill him, perhaps out of pity, or the shame of striking down an unarmed opponent. At last, Zaibos raised a thick finger, giving the order to proceed. The distance between the two men was not more than two strides. Horgin had to but bring up his maul and Eros, sans helmet, would have his brains turned to porridge. But just as soon as Horgin took his first step, the spiky head of his weapon catching the light, he was lying on his back, inexplicably screaming, tears of blood trickling from his left eye. The crowd gaped at Eros with a mix of horror and admiration, and from more than a few mouths came the word *sorcery!* But he could see the recognition in the faces of a few keen-eyed observers, those who saw things as they happened, those who had been focused not on Horgin, but the assassin. They saw the cloth sling, now crumpled in his palm, and the flash of something quick and round and heavy.

Eros strolled over to the giant's fallen body and plucked the metal object from the metal crater in Horgin's helm, the space where his left eye had been.

Zaibos looked impressed, and Eros couldn't help but feel a measure of pride. "It seems my faith in you was well-placed. How did you do that?"

Eros kept his tools of the trade a closely-guarded secret, as to show anyone would compromise his ability to work, but for the self-appointed king of Tyrnael, he made an exception. From a hidden pocket, he produced a silvery-grey sphere etched with runes. It was smaller than his fist, but so heavy that it was tiring to hold. Each time he used the sling, he risked dislocating the joint of his shoulder.

"Iridium," he explained. "The heaviest metal known to man and more highly prized than gold. Cuts through armor as if it were papyrus. Horgin never thought to shield his face, not while wearing his helm, which is why he is lying on the ground and I am not, although I made certain, in case you needed him, that he live—he'll only need to be more careful watching his left side.

"If this Hedonian is anything like the soldiers I've known, he should fall just as easily. If he fights to protect the princess, then he is a man with ideals, with honor, which is all the better for me, because I am not hindered by such considerations."

"You're a man of my own heart, so you shall have all you desire!"

As he slipped the iridium back into his pocket, Eros could not shake his discomfort. Zaibos looked as if he could not be more pleased, and to the assassin, that was the most unnerving thing of all.

"So you want her heart in a box. Why not her head?"

"I see your meaning. You suspect I cannot trust you? Yes, you might offer me a pig's heart instead, but my people have ways of knowing. For each life, there is a signature—in the blood, teeth, and hair. What I desire is her essence, her soul if you will—that which makes her what she is—and so you must bring me the container in which the soul resides."

Eros considered the king's words. Did the soul truly reside in the heart? He had never seen evidence of it, even when cutting the organ from a man's body. "One last thing, then. How old is she now?"

Zaibos eyed him accusingly.

"If she has gone into hiding, she is likely in disguise. If I am to go looking, should I ask for a twelve-year-old girl? Thirteen? Fourteen?"

"How should I know? I am not her nanny. Although I believe she has just flowered, so she must be fifteen, sixteen. To a barkeep's eyes, it will make no difference."

Fifteen. Almost a child.

"Besides," Zaibos continued, "the greatest fool in the land could not mistake her for a peasant. No one who sees those eyes can fail to notice—"

"The Moon-Eyed Princess," Eros murmured. "So what they sing of her is true? One eye is turquoise, like the greater moon, and the other violet, like the lesser. I thought it just a fanciful rumor."

"Fanciful, yes, and accurate, much to her detriment."

From the time he was old enough to hold a blade, Eros had been running "errands," or so he would tell his mother. It began with a pesky dog who liked to steal the butcher's scraps and evolved from there, to debtors and creditors, and witnesses of crimes. Most men were wretched things, undeserving of life, and most women fared little better. Relying on this principle made his job all the easier, which is why, for an innocent life, he charged a higher fee. But this princess was like no other quarry. If what he had heard was true, she was a paragon of virtue—her clemency legendary. There was also the story of her illness. Not a heart in Tyrnael was unmoved by it. The young princess, a child of six, had stood at Death's door, as the king turned mad with grief—if the bards are to be believed, his hair had become white overnight.

Whatever the truth, no man or woman was greater loved than the daughter of Solon. But if Eros could bury his pity enough to bash a hungry mongrel's brain in with a rock, he could run this errand. The dog's death put five silver coins in his pockets, enough to feed himself and his mother for a cycle. It was his way, and his mother was the only thing that mattered to him, all that he loved in the world. For her, Eros would strangle an infant in the cradle.

5

Ser Marek

HERE LIES SOLON VII
KING OF TYRNAEL
53rd Descendant

The letters etched into the granite stared back at her, powerful and eternal. Her father's death was fresh in her memory, but the writing was in the archaic tradition, a spelling and dialect reserved for the aristocracy. Each line she traced with her fingertip, as if to embrace her father.

"You're well?"

By the dim torch in his hand, she could make out his unpleasant features, the scar running the length of his face deepening in the shadows, the pate of his head catching the light like the moon.

"You brought me down to the crypts?"

He fitted the torch into a sconce on the wall. "What better place to hide? Men fear death and dark places. And I was not sure you were coming back to me. Your father's tomb seemed a good resting place."

The hem of her dress was wet and stuck to her thighs, and her bones ached after kneeling before the king's epigraph. Water trickled and pooled underfoot, numbing her bare soles. She was grateful, at least, to have slept high and dry above her father's body, touched only by the damp chill of the catacombs. She found her father's likeness upon the sarcophagus—the silhouette of his kindly face—to be a comfort in the darkness.

"Didn't you think to check my heart? My breathing? You thought I was dead?"

"Not dead, but dying, perhaps. You lost all color and grew cold. Soldiers fallen by the sword have looked more lively. I thought I'd failed you, that one of those bastards had got to you, but I could find no wound. What was it that ailed you, princess? Are you ill?"

Her lips and nostrils were encrusted with blood. She put a hand to her face and remembered the captain, little more than a boy, the way his eyes looked when Demacharon thrust his sword into him.

"Is there something you haven't told me? I cannot protect you if you keep secrets from me."

"I don't want your protection." The ground was rough and uneven, scraping her heels as she moved away from him. "You're no more than a murderer."

He pursued her, his footfalls echoing down the sarcophagi-lined passage. "Radia, I am a soldier. I did my duty."

"You killed Sligh. And the rest, did you not? Otherwise, they'd have followed us here. I am not an ignorant child, you know."

"I never thought you were. But you must understand—it was them or us. There was no choice."

"Did you enjoy it, killer? Did you relish watching them die?"

He raised his hand suddenly. She could feel his rage, his desire to lash out, but there was something else about him, a deep well of sorrow.

"Maybe Sligh was right about you. You're my kidnapper and you intend to ransom me. Well? Have out with it. I prefer to travel as your captive than as your fool."

Demacharon dropped to one knee. "Forgive me, princess, I would never—"

"Why then? Why risk yourself for a princess who has lost her crown? You cannot hope to challenge Zaibos, not without an army, and I have nothing with which to aid you. My power was the throne, and my wealth within the tower. Without them, I am nothing. You fight in defense of a well-dressed beggar."

"I did not swear an oath to a beggar, but a princess of Aenya, and I aim to honor my oath. It does not matter what you believe you have become. You are and shall always be the rightful heir to Tyrnael. The people of this kingdom know it. And this is where you err, because power comes not from the throne, but the people who look to it."

"If you still believe in me," she said softly, after a time, "will you swear to me again? Do whatever I bid you?"

"Ask that I turn my sword against myself, and I shall."

"No!" she exclaimed. "Why must everything be about killing with you? No more deaths! Swear this to me."

"Radia, don't be unreasonable. If we are attacked, how can I—"

"Swear it," she cried, "or else, I am a beggar and, worse, follow in the footsteps of a murderer. That I will not accept."

He lifted his hand and she took it. The skin beneath his knuckles felt calloused and aged in her silken hand. "Lest my lady bid that I break this oath, no more shall die by my hand."

Her senses portrayed him as a man of his word, but she also wanted to trust him. Alone and on the run, what could she hope to accomplish? Where could she hope to go? Yet she recognized that desperation could blind her to the truth. In the past, Zaibos, and those in his thrall, had found it easy to deceive her, because she could not fathom the darkness that resided in the hearts of others. Deception was as foreign a concept to her as the bogren. Radia could never bring herself to say anything but what came into her mind. She used to argue with her father, that if only the world spoke as she did, without filter or subtext, evil could not exist.

"I am an empath." Her voice traveled the corridor, rebounding from the stone berths of the dead.

"What does that mean?"

"It's a family trait. My mother had it, as did my father to a lesser degree. Each generation loses a bit. The Zo could read thoughts. I can sense people's feelings, their joys and their sorrows."

"So, you're telling me that with Sligh, and my sword—"

"No. I do not experience their physical pain, but I felt his anger at losing the duel, and regret for all the days he'll never see. I could feel his fear most of all, of the end, of the netherworld that awaits us all."

"Alas, if I had but known . . . Is that why you swooned?"

"That was part of it." Even now she did not know to lie, but found it easy enough to skew the truth. And why should he know? He was still a stranger and the reasons for his loyalty did not sit right with her, despite his declarations.

"Why did you not pass out in the throne room? Many more deaths there."

"I was afraid for my life," she answered. "I cannot sense other's emotions if I am focused on my own."

"And now? Can you tell me what I'm feeling?"

She shut her eyes and other material senses, closing all but the center of her being, which opened to receive him. Emotions passed freely between them, like air from his lungs to hers, but only she had the power to perceive it.

"Hope," she murmured. "You feel hopeful." But there was much more she did not, could not, say. Buried beneath the surface of his consciousness, there was loss and yearning, and something she only vaguely recognized. It frightened and nearly consumed her, and so she fled from it, shutting herself from him.

"Anyone could have guessed that," he said. "We're both hoping to get far from here, unless you plan on setting up house."

The light from his torch glazed the walls of the catacomb, but could not penetrate the darkness. She could see nothing but her father's tomb and two more beyond it—her mother's and grandfather's.

"If you're ready, we follow the water. Where it flows, there must be a way out."

Radia stood near enough to touch him, for the light and warmth of his torch, shivering as the crypt grew colder and wetter. They visited each of her forefathers in turn, and she spied each name as they passed: KYLIS III the 52nd, MIRO the 51st, NOBORON XIX the 50th, SOLON VI the 49th, and so on, further back in time, where the shadows deepened and the tombs turned more rounded and decrepit with age. After the tenth inscription, the writing became illegible—a barely perceptible scrawl in stone—or vanished altogether.

Whoever cared to honor the dead were long gone themselves, she considered, and she was ashamed to not know them. An elaborate tapestry in the castle library displayed a tree with over ten millennia of branching generations, where the first of her ancestors, K-Lon the 1st, was set in its roots. She was made to study history beside that tapestry, but Radia preferred real trees to stitched ones, for she had always loved the living more than the dead. She supposed that, many years from now, no one would remember her either.

They continued without a word, comforted only by the sounds of their shuffling feet and the crackle of a dying flame. The air smelled of decay. Certainly, no sun, no living breath, had touched the place for untold ages. It was unnerving to think what eyes last looked upon these stone berths, so wrought with time they scarcely seemed manmade, but like aberrations of geology. Webs sometimes broke against her face and caught in her hair, the threads sticky and thick as a fishing line, but she feared more to step on a spider than be bitten by one.

In the waning glow, the walls were vanishing, and the tombs turning to mere silhouettes, but the course of the water continued, never higher than her toes, leading them around corners, diverging from distant cousins to lesser-known uncles. Demacharon lowered his torch and the water glittered like flecks of gold. "We're losing the light and there's nothing left to burn."

"What about our clothes?"

"I've only got leather and bronze," he replied gruffly. If he was grinning or scowling, she could not see it.

"My great-grandmother's dress. You've already ruined it, and it is doubtful I'll be attending court soon."

"I'd sooner dig up a king and make kindling from his bones."

"No, it's really of no use to me. It's wet and frilly. I'd be warmer with a fire."

"That isn't the point. You're a princess, and you cannot be seen like some wild human."

"Do wild humans truly exist?"

"They most certainly do."

"Have you met any yourself? What are they like?"

"They are barbarians. Savages. People that behave like animals, like the Boro and Xerente, and the Ilmar. Even when we showed them how, they refused to capitulate, to wear any clothing or—"

"Really? Some people don't wear clothing?" She thought back on every rib-pinching corset she was ever forced into and considered how wonderful it would be to go without. But before she could speak her mind, his hand flew to her mouth. She started to grow angry when the clamor came again. It sounded like something scurrying—something frantic and fearful and very large.

She listened intently, to their breathing, and to steel sliding on steel. "Hush." The torch was down to embers, but she could make out the longsword in his hand. "We're not alone."

"Rats?"

"Not likely."

His hand fell on her wrist and they moved together cautiously, but the flicker of his torch could scarcely give shape to their surroundings. Webbing crossed the passage more frequently, until Radia was spitting it out, pulling it from her ears. Much of it was like rope and more than once she had to push her way through. At some point, when the webbing grew too dense, Demacharon made use of his sword. Their torch, by this time, was like a single firefly in pitch-black space, but before it went out completely, Demacharon touched it to the webs, and the flame began to grow, crawling along the ropey threads to form a blaze. When the hall was sufficiently lit, Radia could tell that what she thought to be webbing was not—the fiber differed in texture—and she could also see, hanging from the ceiling, fleshy green sacks containing dozens of pods. Something was squirming within each one, pushing against the translucent membrane housing it. They were alive. And they were everywhere.

Demacharon wrapped the finer threads about his torch until the room glowed with the reds and yellows from his fire. The sacks oozed and dripped in the light, and she decided against touching them, but there were other curiosities to behold. Long, tapered, ivory stems seemed to be growing out of the masonry. Before he could stop her, she pried one from the wall. It was larger than her palm and curved to a point.

"Don't touch the tip!" he warned, more loudly than he intended. "There may still be acid."

"What is it?"

"It's a nail, from a very large creature." He sounded agitated and fearful. "They live in caves and manmade dungeons like these, and propel themselves along the walls. Quite rapidly, I might add."

When she looked again, she noticed the grooves in the stone, long lines running every which way. "Perhaps we could make peace with it? Communicate with it, somehow, and soothe it?"

"Princess, this monster has no eyes nor ears. It can't even smell. But it more than makes up for that with five arms ending in acid-tipped claws, and rows of acid-tipped teeth, and a very sensitive hide that senses whenever prey is nearby. It lives for two things and two things only—eating anything stupid enough to enter its lair, and hatching little versions of itself."

"So you're saying it's not all bad? That it's a mother at . least?"

"I am saying we should remain as quiet as possible, and avoid touching anything, especially these 'webs'. It's a kind of mucus that is shed from its body. When it hardens, the vibrations help the creature locate prey. We're lucky to have stumbled through so many without drawing attention."

Radia turned back the way they came. The monster's hardened mucus trails were everywhere. Moving through them would pose a challenge, she thought, but as she searched for a safer passage, the thicker strands started to oscillate like the cords of a lute, and the walls came alive, reaching with ghostly fingers down the corridor toward them, surrounding them. The sound of acid claws raking against the stone was unmistakable and Radia realized that Demacharon had spoken too soon, that their traipsing through webs had been a call to dinner. His hand clamped down on hers and they were off again. His pulse was in her veins, his fear in her heart.

Darkness swallowed them as they turned the corner. She groped at the air, feeling her way around, avoiding the tombs as best she could. Whether they followed the water's course or moved against it, she did not know, but the water deepened to her ankles, and there was the distinct impression that the ground was sloping, that they were zigzagging down a series of ramps. But the clawing only intensified. She glanced over her shoulder and immediately wished she hadn't. An iridescent green glob was tearing through the corridor, its many limbs flailing in their direction. They broke through one tangled mass after another, each one denser than the last, making them stumble and slow.

We are doing what it wants. It's chasing us into its trap, into the heart of its lair.

All she could hear was the awful click-clack of nails on the wall, drowning out the frantic noise of their feet and lungs. At any moment, she would be joining her ancestors where they lay. She would die with someone whom she could scarcely call a friend, never to see Larissa again, never having the chance to make a case before her people.

Like a fly in a spider's silk, Radia was trapped. Milky threads, broad as her wrists, clung to her arms and ankles. Demacharon moved to defend her. She appreciated the gesture, but unless the monster was to eat him first and become full, she doubted a single human would satisfy its appetite. Radia could now see the concentric rows of crystalline teeth formed in its mouth. To appear threatening— as much as a man with a longsword and a torch could be— Demacharon bellowed at the monster, and it did give pause, creeping away from the flame and back along the corridor. She had to admire the elegant way it moved, its spindly arms pushing off the floor, with a claw at each wall and a fifth hooked to the ceiling.

"It's sizing me up," Demacharon cried, "but it won't be fooled long! Run, princess!"

"No! I won't stand to feel your death." Even as she spoke, she was snapping off threads, to create a tunnel she and her companion could escape through.

"I die every night," he called back, cutting a wedge between the monster's teeth and gums. "What's one more?"

The threads were crumbling in her fingers now. It occurred to her that over time, they must become brittle. When enough were pulled to clear a path, a second opening appeared to her left, and without another thought, she tugged Demacharon through it just as his longsword disappeared in the monster's gaping maw.

Together they tumbled into darkness, and at once she knew it was no corridor, but a wide space, sizable for a crypt. If the monster could only move by propelling itself through narrow spaces, they might be safe here. Either way, exhaustion had set in, and running was no longer an option.

Demacharon slid to the floor. "Damn thing has no vitals, no weak spots . . ."

"Are you hurt? Did it bite you?" she said, reaching down to touch his shoulder.

"Am I missing a limb?" he half-grumbled, half-laughed.

"How can you joke at a time like this?"

"It cuts tension before battle, or when there's a monster lurking around the corner, waiting to devour you." He was wincing. "Although my shoulder feels chewed up just the same." She gave him a puzzled look. "Try swinging a weapon around for forty years. I will say this—I'm past the retiring age for killing monsters."

"Where's the torch?"

"I dropped it."

"Dropped it? Why? We needed it."

"Oh? Is there anything else you need? A cup of warm milk?"

"You're the most uncouth servant I've ever had!"

"*Uncouth*? I don't even know that means."

"Never mind. I'll get the torch."

He reached for her ankle but the ache in his arm made him sluggish. She appeared a few moments later, grinning and with a torch in hand. Much of the webbing he had wrapped around it had burned away, but fortunately, the floor was littered with potential kindling.

"I could not find your sword."

"It's gone. Eaten away." He rose to his feet with a groan. "We can't stay here, but as soon as we take a stroll down that hall, we're supper."

"Perhaps there is another way." She carried the torch from corner to corner but found no exit. Her father's crypt was of stone and mortar, but the surfaces here felt smooth as glass, unlike any building material she had ever known. She moved away, bringing the torch to a raised platform in the center of the room. It resembled a mound overgrown with fungi and vegetation. With Demacharon's help, the sarcophagus took shape.

He stepped back to examine it. "Who rests here, I wonder?"

"No one. He's dead."

"A bit crude, princess, but I think you're catching on."

She gave him a quizzical look but did not bother to ask.

Digging into the edges with his fingers, centuries of lichen came off in clumps. Radia folded back her grandmother's sleeves and started to scrub, discoloring the finely woven fabric with yellow and pink and green. A knight's crest soon emerged—an exploding star—and beneath it, the arcane alphabet of the Zo.

"Can you read it?"

"I used to hate Anabis's old language lessons, but I suppose I should be grateful." Shining her light on the raised symbols, she read, "'Here lies Ser Marek the Brave, the Nova Knight, who slew a thousand by his sword, and became lord by his own handle.' No, sorry—that should be 'his own hand'."

"Very precise, wasn't he? I mean, he quit right after a thousand. Not one more or less. Nice round number."

"Oh, you're trying to be witty again, right?"

"More like sarcastic," he said, and after an awkward silence, added, "It's when someone says one thing but means another."

Radia felt her brow crease. "Why would anyone want to do that? Isn't that just like lying?" If the world beyond the castle was this confusing, she would certainly struggle to understand it.

Demacharon smacked his face and ran his hand down across it—what she assumed a common gesture among the southern city-states, though it meant nothing in Tyrnael.

"The real question is, who were these thousand?"

"Enemies of the Zo," she answered somberly. "This is just what my brother wants—a return to the glory days, when war spread like a flame across the whole of the planet. He wants to revive the Nova Knights, or something akin to it."

"Wait, there was a war? Over the entire world? Forgive my ignorance, I was never a student of military history, only tactics."

"I would not expect an outsider to know this. Nobody does. Aside from the few books in the castle library, our history has been lost. The Nova Knights were the elite. They united Aenya during the first civil war and kept peace afterward. It is said that they went into battle on birds of steel and fire."

"What does that even mean?"

"I can only imagine."

"Shouldn't you know? Is he not a distant cousin of yours?"

"Perhaps not. They lived prior to our dynasty, before the greater moon came into the sky, during the heyday of the Zo."

Demacharon looked dumbfounded. "And we, in Hedonia, thought ourselves ancient! How old are these catacombs, then? I thought they were built by your family?"

"Tyrnael was built upon the ruins of an older city, just as that city before it. As far as anyone knows, these tombs extend down into prehistory, from the age of the First Men, before writing and—" she turned suddenly to the dark passageway, forgetting her lesson. The walls were coming alive with echoes, the small hairs on her arms prickling with every scratch of nail on stone. It was doubling back in search of them. "You don't think it can come in here, do you?"

"If it does, I have only this." He slid the gladius from his hip—the blade was no longer than his forearm. "And I'd prefer not to get that close."

"Wait! Who 'killed a thousand by his sword'? We have an armory right here!"

"You intend to disturb this poor man's resting place?"

"There are only bones here," she answered, "and I think this Ser Marek will forgive us given our predicament."

"Are you certain? I have no desire to be cursed, or meet his angry spirit in the . . . in the afterworld."

She was pushing against the lip of stone, letting out the occasional grunt. "You fear the dead and not the living?"

He lent his strength to the task, though the top was enormously heavy and interlocked with the base like a set of neatly-fitted teeth. "We need to lift it," he said, wiping a trickle of sweat from his face. "It's hopeless."

The clawing sounds amplified, alerting them to the darkened breach in the wall. She stood beside him and watched, her heart frozen with dread, and in a flash of green the monster passed.

"It doesn't know we're here," she murmured. "We can hide."

"But for how long? Without water, we'll be dead in days."

"And if we step out there, we'll have only seconds."

"We could make another run for it," he argued. "Wait for it to pass and make for the opposite direction."

"We don't even know where we are! We may come to nothing but a dead end. We need what is in that tomb!"

"I told you, I cannot lift it. If we had six strong-armed men . . . but alas, with only the two of us," he shook his head, "the task is impossible."

Radia approached the tomb again, her eyes closed, her fingers moving gently across the smooth surface. She tried to remember the lessons, what Anabis had taught her about the Zo, their history, their customs, their burial rites. "We do not need men," she answered, as if in a trance, "only the right . . . *words.*"

Even she could not be certain of her actions or the language forming in her brain. Maybe it was nonsense, made-up gibberish. Or, she hoped, some recollection remained in her, from before birth, from the time of her ancestors. When nothing happened, she started to feel the fool, but she continued to chant and wave her arms, just as the priests of old in the library murals.

She felt a vibration at her feet and looked over to see Demacharon's jaw drop. The sarcophagus righted itself like a man rising from sleep, and before either of them could speak, the sides flew apart, revealing a body of gleaming silver.

"I've never seen armor like this." Wonder gripped Demacharon's voice. The Nova Knight was fashioned out of metal, with every muscle and sinew shaped into the suit. Only the helm was of simple geometry, with a single slot for the eyes, and a red crest blooming from the cranium. "I can't see any seams or weak points. And this alloy . . . untarnished all these years, without a blemish of any kind—you'd think he was entombed yesterday. I've seen such a substance once before."

Radia could see her mismatched eyes mirrored in the helm, her lips stretched across the breast, her bosom warped in the clefts of the abdominal muscles. "Could you wear it?"

"If going to war, yes. This must be iron or something heavier. I can hardly imagine how he moved about in it, if not for some sorcery. Besides, every eye in the city would be upon us, which is the one thing we don't want. What we need is a weapon, something that can be hidden, so nobody knows we were here."

A simple scabbard of black leather hung from a gilded belt. With some hesitation, Demacharon removed it. Radia felt a twinge of guilt for purloining that which was unmoved for well-nigh eleven thousand years. When he pulled at the pommel, however, Radia had to laugh. The blade seemed to be missing. So much effort, and for naught. But Demacharon did not share in her mirth. He simply stared at her with the broken haft in his hand, which only made her break into laughter again.

"What is it?"

"You were right—it does cut tension. It may not sever anything else, but distress is no match for such a blade! Ha! I should have appointed you court jester."

"I still don't see—" he began, when suddenly, the blade made its appearance and humor gave way to wonder. She reached for it, marveling, but when he moved away the blade vanished again. "Don't touch it. You'll cut yourself."

"On what?"

"This," he replied. He turned the sword about and the blade winked away, reappeared, and was lost again.

"It's a two-dimensional sword," she exclaimed. "You can see the flat side, but it disappears on edge."

"Remarkable." He twirled the weapon in his palm over and over. When visible, the blade was flat and straight, like a

56

yardstick, with rectangular patterns cut into the steel. "It's too narrow for the eye to see. This is Zo-tech, without question, greatly beyond the ablest blacksmiths of Hedonia. Forged with magic."

"Magic is what people do not understand," she said matter-of-factly. He gave no response, and Radia feared she had insulted him.

"There is writing on the hilt."

"*Severetrix*," she read. "It is the weapon's name, I believe, roughly translating to, 'hair-splitter'."

"That is appropriate." He paused, listening for the faint sounds of the beast clawing its way through the catacombs. "I do not know how to use this weapon, princess. My instincts tell me a thing so slight must also be frail, but so sharp as to sever the arm of Sargonus himself."

As he spoke, the room seemed to grow colder and her senses dulled. The fire was dimming, as was Radia's strength. A princess was unused to adventure, to going without food and water while traveling abandoned places. More than anything, she longed for the softness of her bed, the warmth of her tower with braziers blazing at every corner.

"I won't last the night," she said. "Make do as best as you can with the two-sword and let's be far from here."

"I cannot meet that thing in the corridor. We were lucky to escape unscathed before. Only a scratch and the wound will fester, and without proper attention, result in terrible, agonizing death. And since we must go into hiding, we cannot chance a visit to a healer."

"You are right, of course," she replied. "I cannot ask so much of you."

"Princess, you misunderstand. For you, I'd suffer a hundred deaths from this monster. But no, there is another way. We must lure it here, where it cannot take full advantage of its arms. But I am unsure of how to do it. Without those webs strung across this room, it may not even know we're here."

Before he could seize her, Radia ducked through the opening that led into the corridor, peering through the white interlace of thread into the darkness beyond. Now that she was not running from it, she could open herself to the creature, sense the gnawing hunger defining its existence, a craving no human could fathom. But she could also feel its trepidation, a desperate need to protect its offspring. The greenish, translucent pouches were hanging overhead, and she understood what she had to do.

"There's no other way," she explained. "The sacks emit a wave, a frequency, like the webs—"

Demacharon moved beside her. "I don't know what that means."

"Sounds we cannot hear. And if they are being threatened, they'll cry out." She tore the fleshy membrane from the wall and hurled it to the ground, watching the small greenish balls clash and clump and squirm inside. "Stomp on them," she insisted, as her tears began to form. "I can't bring myself to do it, so you'll have to. Kill its children and it'll come."

"Radia, it isn't . . . I mean, it's just a—"

"I know!" she cried, weeping uncontrollably. "Do it!"

Almost as soon as Demacharon had crushed the contents of the sack with his boot, the tetra claw beast came barreling from around the corner, propelling itself with tremendous speed. Demacharon and Radia dashed back inside the crypt, scrambling to the far sides of the room to where its claws could not reach. Without the narrow sidewalls and ceiling to support its weight, its spindly legs collapsed, and the monster lost its spherical shape, transforming into an even more hideously deformed lump of teeth and flesh. Radia balled into the corner, overcome by anger and despair, as Demacharon taunted the monster, popping one embryo after another under his boot. The horrid mass let out a squeal, far from a human sound, but piteous all the same. It flailed forward, lunged at him with circles of teeth. But he moved more quickly, flanking and gutting it, Severetrix slicing effortlessly through the monster's skin. Twitching and groaning, a yellowish fluid pooled from its stomach—most of its body was stomach—and the long-digested remains of Radia's ancestors spilled forth. Unable to bear the sight and the stench, they escaped into the hall, gasping and fighting the urge to retch.

Parts of his greaves, boots and some of his cuirass were eaten away, burned by the acid, but if he was hurt, he did not show it. The two-sword, yellow with bile, became flawless again as he shook it.

"Are you hurt?" he murmured.

Her heart felt empty. Where life had once been, there was only cold emptiness. She wiped her eyes and he came into focus. He was afraid, but not for himself. She could feel that now like never before. *He cares for me.* She did not understand how or why, yet knew that he did.

Slowly, she shook her head, indicating that she was unhurt, wanting to say more.

"We should go," he said softly.

It was enough. Words were wasted when breathing came so heavily, and together they faced the darkness, and went.

6

Larissa

More than two dozen horses slept in the royal stables and Larissa loved every one of them. She knew their names, which creatures had fathered which, and could count their days since birth. If a mare cantered with a limp, Larissa fretted over it as though it were a sick child. Tending to each animal's need was no easy task. Leading a mare around a millstone could be exhausting. She sweated, and a putrid mix of mud and dung sometimes caked her feet and legs, which made her less than popular with the maids responsible for scrubbing her footprints from the castle floor. Most other servants, from the laundress to the scullions, avoided speaking to her or did so with contempt. The work of a stable hand is beneath an attendee of the royal court, they would remark, when they thought her out of earshot. But Larissa never took their comments to heart, for like her mother and mother's mother, she was eloai, and bred to be content with life.

Among the hierarchy of servants, Larissa held the highest position, though she had never desired status, for eloai were incapable of ambition. A whim of fate, rather, and a shared love for animals—and one in particular—had elevated her to the right hand of the princess. When Radia fell ill, King Solon had sought out every treatment available. When the alchemists of Tyrnael failed to cure his daughter, he turned to mystics from Hedonia, and when their methods proved fruitless, he sought seers from Shemselinihar. With his four-year-old daughter at the gates of death, unable even to lift her head from her pillow, Solon acted in desperation, seeking to study the unicorn, which was said to be immortal.

The solitary creature in the royal stables cast no restorative magic, though the daughter of the king grew to love the animal nonetheless and, after a time, when Radia became whole again, she returned often to the stables, and the girl who helped her mother tend to the animals became her playmate. Raised side by side, close as sisters, the lowest and the highest born grew into maidenhood. And after ten years, Larissa could offer Radia something no other servant could. At the princess's insistence, the lowly eloai, who shoveled manure in the morning, stood at the foot of the throne as Radia's caretaker, but also, her closest friend.

Throughout their childhood, the unicorn remained in the stables, serving as a bond between them, never aging, never less beautiful than the day Larissa first looked upon her. Her white sheen resembled the spume of a crashing river, but a ghostly luminous blue enveloped her in the starlit hours, like the smaller moon when it sails behind the clouds. In shape, the unicorn stood between a colt and a deer, but moved far more gracefully than either. Vain and proud, she never passed still waters without stopping to gaze at herself, and whenever she approached the animals, they twirled their tails and backed into their stalls, not in fear or with disdain, but out of reverence. For the unicorn, Larissa knew, was not one of them, but a goddess of the wood and all woodland creatures, and the human name given her was Amalthea.

And yet, despite her grace and beauty, Amalthea was a prisoner. How long ago had she been captured, none could say. Larissa's mother had known her since childhood as did her mother's mother. Larissa knew that the unicorn was immortal, so it could very well be that the Zo ensnared her millennia ago, with the golden ring and talisman that was fitted to her horn. But more than that, when Larissa gazed into Amalthea's immense fawn-shaped eyes, she did not see a low-born stable hand, but a young woman of noble stature, someone of importance. Though it occurred to her to liberate the creature, the stable girl loved the unicorn and was convinced that the unicorn loved her in return, and would miss her if released into the wild.

Having cleaned and watered and fed the animals, Larissa strolled into the hayloft to douse herself, using the same bucket she did to scrub the horses. Water soaked into her clothing and trickled down her body to dissipate under the straw. If ever the unicorn defecated, Larissa did not know it. She appreciated the creature's fastidiousness, herself not wanting to come close to others if she were smelling of sweat or feces, though sometimes she could not avoid such situations, and they greatly embarrassed her. The unicorn loathed the touch of linen or hemp or any material of the loom. Larissa could sympathize, but felt indecent going without clothes, and though no one bothered to visit the stables so late in the day, she never risked undressing where someone might see her, even to bathe. But having her peplos cling to her body made her shiver. As with most garments worn by the eloai, the single-piece tunic was cut a hand below the waist, leaving the thighs bare.

When she finished bathing, it was time to release Amalthea into the hayloft—this was a simple matter of lifting a latch inscribed with runes. Upon doing so, Larissa had to stand some distance away, for the unicorn always came rushing forward in a flash of blue-white, sudden as a bolt of lightning.

"How are you today, my lady?"

Amalthea's eyes stared knowingly into hers, black and blazing, and she tossed her head as if to say, *fine* and *thank you*.

"Your mane is looking so very lovely today," she replied. "But, oh! Is that a tangle I see? Please, don't be offended—it's only a little tangle, the smallest I've ever seen. Will you be so kind as to let me comb it?"

Larissa repeated the words day after day, and each time she pretended they were new. The unicorn's mane rarely needed tending, but she loved to comb through it, and Amalthea enjoyed the attention. But one could not groom a divine creature with just any common comb—the unicorn's had been a gift from Lost Aea, fashioned from the jaw of a wakefin, and inlaid with pearls from the depths of the One Sea. Realizing she had forgotten it, Larissa went to her vanity, when she froze in midstep. Someone was in the hayloft with her. She could feel the hairs of her neck prickling, and the unicorn stood entirely still, never lowering her gaze.

"Beautiful, isn't she?"

He was thickly dressed in earth tones, like a merchant, but with a hood concealing his forehead and partly his eyes. "I've never seen such a horse."

Larissa found herself walking backward until the unicorn's muzzle slipped under her arm. "She's not a horse."

"Well, it's a magnificent creature, nonetheless. Have you ever ridden it?"

At that, Amalthea took to protesting, whickering and stomping her hooves. "Please don't call her 'it'. She hates that."

"Very temperamental, isn't she?" He moved closer, under the torchlight, and she could see his dark, sharp features. Despite her unease, she could not help but find him handsome.

"A young knight tried to mount her once. He went into the infirmary with his armor punctured and his ribs broken. The horn missed the heart by a thumb. I don't think she missed it by accident."

"I find that admirable. To be powerful yet merciful."

"Have I seen you before? Are you a knight? Or a servant of the castle?"

"Oh, I doubt we've met." He reached out his hand and she spotted the sheath at his hip. "They call me Eros. And you?"

She did not like the casual way he went about introducing himself. What did he want from her, and how did he know to find her, anyway? She had no desire to divulge her name, or any other information, but custom demanded an answer. "My name is Larissa."

"A beautiful name," he said, "for a beautiful girl."

The distance between them was growing shorter and she could feel his eyes, intense and focused as dagger points. Suddenly, she felt very exposed, and quickly covered her bosom lest the wetness of her peplos reveal the nipples jutting beneath it. "My mother was beautiful once," he intoned. "If only you could have seen her! But alas, you're much too young to have had the opportunity. She was a performer, the finest in all of Dis. They worshipped her on stage—how she sang the epics, how she tilted her head so that her hair turned to pure gold in the sun." He laughed, though she could not see the humor in what he was saying. "Beauty is quite the trap, is it not? Ah, but I am remiss. You stand before me, in this ripe moment of life, and I prattle on of days that shan't come again. Forgive."

Larissa's discomfort only continued to grow. Who was this man and why was he talking about his mother? All she could think to do was be polite. When someone is kind, there is nothing to fear, or so her mother taught her. "Please, I am to be forgiven, not you," she said with an abrupt curtsy. "You startled me and I quite forgot my manners. Permit me to start again. I am Larissa—how may I serve you?"

"Oh, I can think of many ways, but what I need first and foremost is a bit of information. I hear tell you are well-acquainted with the princess, that none in the kingdom know her more intimately."

She sensed what he was after, but chose to play the fool in an effort to stall him. "What would you have me tell you?"

"She has fled from the tower. Where did she go?"

"I am at a loss, I fear." She tried to keep emotion from entering her voice.

The gradual way he closed the space between them was beginning to feel like a noose about her neck. She wanted to run the other way, to scream, but his will and the way he stood over her now overpowered her. "Shall I ask again?" An edge to his voice frightened her. "I know a great many ways to learn whatever it is I want to know."

"I swear that I know nothing! They told me she went away."

"You are either very stupid or very foolish, Larissa." He placed his hand over hers, and she found it to be uncommonly soft, the skin of a prince. "Your dearest friend and confidant abandons her tower for the first time since she was born and tells you nothing? Did you not consider that the least bit odd? Were you not disappointed?" He tightened his grip, crushing the small bones in her palm.

"Please, I know nothing, good sir. I swear it! I am simple and do not think on such matters, and . . . you're hurting me!"

"Indeed," he said, pulling away, "and so you may be speaking truthfully. It may not be in your nature to deceive. But you can still be of use to me. You know how she thinks, her weaknesses, where she might go to hide."

It was true that Larissa did not know where the princess had gone. Part of her believed the story, that an urgent mission had called the princess away, but some doubt churned in her head, and she couldn't help but reject what the knights had told her. Eloia were born to do what they were told, to never question those superior to them, but she could not remove from her mind Radia's sleeping chambers in disarray, the curtains torn, the feathers strewn from the pillows, and the swan, floating lifeless in the fountain. At the time, she kept her mind busy with tidying the place. If only she was permitted to do her duty until the princess returned, it might ease the darkness creeping into her head, but the guards forced her away, and so she went down to the stables to find her comfort, her unicorn. Now, with the words of this stranger, her greatest fears erupted to the fore—the one she loved most in all the world was in danger.

"What has happened?" she said at last. "Why do you seek the princess?"

"Do you want the truth? Or another lie? You deserve a choice, at least."

"What else but the truth?"

"Very well then. I doubt I could have deceived you long. You're a stupid girl, but with good instincts." He slid the dagger from the sheath at his hip. It was black as obsidian, and runes were engraved into the blade, but she could not read them. "Do you see this? When I find your princess, I am going to stick this into her sternum, a bit beneath the ribcage, and cut out her heart. And you are going to help me do it."

Larissa was wiping her eyes before she even knew that tears were forming. The mere thought of Radia being hurt felt incomprehensible to her, unbearable. "Why? Why would you want to do that? What has she ever done to you?"

"Nothing!" he exclaimed, "and I am certain she is a guiltless creature. I pity your mistress, loathe the terrible thing I must do to her. But the world is a cruel and dark place, Larissa, full of cruel and dark people. Believe you me, I would have preferred the role of the hero. Who does not wish to be showered with adoration? Have his deeds sung for generations? But alas, that was not my lot." He slipped his hood away for her to see it, the twisting 'I' branded into his forehead, but she did not know what it meant. "My fate was chosen for me. An abomination gave me life, you see, and so I was marked at birth . . . an *abomination*."

"I won't help you, no matter what you say."

He twirled his dagger like a painter would a brush. "You will, I think."

The stable felt cold, more so than before, and she still dripped from her crude bath. Every sound thundered in her ears as he moved—the crunch of straw beneath his boots, the hooves of the animals whickering in dismay.

"Are you going to kill me?"

"Perhaps. But I'd greatly prefer that you live. You are lovely and kind, and faithful to your mistress."

"In that case," she managed, eyeing her reflection in the blade, "what are you doing, with that?"

"I am going to ask you a simple question. Can you read what is written here? No. I suppose you can't. It says, 'There is no god but the Taker.' Truer words have never been written. Take the most pious of men, priests who devote their entire lives to their deity, having sworn every oath under heaven, and before me and this blade, all their swearing comes to nothing, for there is only one god they truly fear. Knowing this gives me one advantage over other men, and this trick keeps my pockets heavy. Therefore, I ask you, whom do you love more, the horned horse or your mistress?"

She stood shivering and covering her head, but could surrender no reply.

"What's the matter? Speechless? Allow me to answer for you, then. Naturally, a human such as yourself must love her kind above all, and yet, I'd wager that your base instincts work against you, that to save this beast today, you forfeit the one you love most come the morrow."

Larissa was numb with despair, even with Amalthea nuzzling her back, offering comfort.

"Make your choice!" he cried, "do you help me find Radia and allow this beast to live or do you watch it die, right here, right now?"

"I . . ." Larissa collapsed to her knees. "I cannot . . ."

"So be it." He raised his dagger to strike, but the unicorn did not stand to be slaughtered. Horn and dagger clashed and the latter went spinning from Eros's grasp. As he fumbled for the weapon in the hay, something occurred in Larissa's mind, a completely alien, wondrous realization. No one was telling her what to do and yet she knew, and if she had to give it a name, it could only be *inspiration*. Rising to her feet, she clutched Amalthea's horn, and pulled at the ring.

"Go! Be free, and find Radia! Carry her far and away!"

Amalthea fixed her gaze on the stable girl with eyes like stars against the dark of night. As the ring dropped from the tip of her horn, the space around them warped and twisted, as if the world was made of liquid, and the unicorn vanished in a blaze of blue and white.

7

Theádra

My son wears my helmet, much of his head and neck having disappeared under it. With each movement he makes—each miniature jab and thrust—he must steady the bronze dome with its crest of red streaming horsehair. He brandishes his wooden sword, threatening the hanging braziers, surrounded by the enemies in his imagination.

"Careful, Astor," I say, "lest you slay your mother."

Niobe stands at the entrance to our bedchambers, looking unamused. "Inform our heroic little son that the moon has passed and that he should be asleep!"

"Alas!" I cry. "The greatest of children's foes! Bedtime and a mother's wrath!"

She is tapping her foot, glowering, but I cannot help sharing in the boy's mirth. I have been too long from home, and too soon shall return to the campaign, where my footmen will fear me and strange faces in unnamed lands await to slaughter me.

"Now!" she insists.

I pull her to me, but she resists my lips. "Have I told you how beautiful you look?"

"Several times this evening, but it will not avail you. I am your wife, not some hussy who swoons at a young commander making eyes at her."

"Oh, but you did once! Alas, I've conquered many lands, but fight my greatest battle at home! There are no siege towers to breach my lady's heart, no arrow—"

Before he can finish, the amphora on the mantel meets the wooden sword and tumbles to the floor. In an instant, the story told along its outer rim is no more, its heroes, gods, and monsters broken to pieces.

"Now look! Who will sweep this mess? The maid is abed, where my son should have been a passing ago, and I hate to rouse her."

I remove my helmet from the boy's head and place it by the foot chest, where I know he loves to stare at it. But in seeing the ceramic pieces, his eyes, wide and blue as the Sea, begin to water.

"No need to weep. It was just some old pottery—I can buy your mother another."

"My mother gave me that!" she cries from the adjacent room, where she searches for the besom.

"Come, Astor—a good soldier obeys orders, and the master of the household commands you to your barracks."

"But Baba, I thought *you* were the master."

I run my hand through his gold, short-cropped hair. "I command the legions of Hedonia, but no one outranks your mother. Understood?"

"Certainly, Baba. But what is a *barracks*?"

"It is where a soldier sleeps."

He nods, but his eyes are already wandering to the shelf facing the bed. "Won't you read me a story, Baba?"

The night is no longer in its infancy and Niobe grows impatient, but I know that I might be called away in the morning, to be absent for cycles, possibly years. "You are the master of my heart, Astor."

With sudden eagerness, he leaps onto the mattress, tucking his legs beneath him, the memory of broken pottery gone from his face. He realizes he has forgotten something and leaps down to fish through his toy bin, which holds a wooden aurochs pulling a wooden cart, a scaly ceramic saurian and a tiger painted green, and tiny hoplites in bronze with spear and shield, but only the ship matters. It resembles the *Mare Nostrum*, the double-oared trireme his father boards for war. Astor is hopeless to sleep without it.

I turn to the books as he assumes his place on the bed. "What will it be tonight? The Batal who slew the two-headed giant of Abu-Zabu? Or the Batal who fought the prince of the snake men?"

"Um, Baba . . . no killings tonight. I want the one with the princess in it."

"Are you sure? It's not like a man to want to hear of princesses. I thought you wanted to become a great warrior?"

He leans his head on my arm. "I want to grow up to be you, Baba."

Though part of me takes pride in thinking of Astor all plated in bronze, leading men to victory on some distant foreign shore, a greater part fears such prospects, preferring he remain safe behind the walls of the city as a magistrate or a mason, or even a scribe.

A bucking unicorn traced in gold adorns the front of the dark leather book. I try and recall whether such beasts exist. Much of the world is unknown and I've encountered stranger creatures in my campaigns.

I begin on the first page, reading slowly.

Long ago in a faraway city, lived a king in a shining tower of alabaster. The surrounding countryside was prosperous beyond measure, so that even the streets glittered with gold, and the people never wanted for food or shelter and knew nothing of sickness and war. Lovely to behold was their queen, and the king loved her dearly, yet no children were born to them. Longing for an heir, the royal couple entreated the gods, offering alms of milk and honey, and after seven years and seven cycles, the gods gave answer with an infant daughter, while taking from the king his queen.

As the years passed, the princess of Aenya became ever more beautiful, with a face like alabaster and hair like spun gold. In the courtyard, when she lifted her voice in song, the bards wept, and when she went to lessons, the elders marveled at her wisdom. Everyone who knew her, loved her.

All was well until her eleventh year, when the princess fell deathly ill. A black cloud descended over the land that day, and not a man could be found who did not wear a somber face, and not a mother there was who did not weep for the dying princess. Never leaving her bedside, the king called for every physician in the kingdom. Seven physicians arrived, and seven were dumbfounded, and the princess fell ever deeper into the grip of the Taker. The king's hair was white with grief when he again assumed the throne. Calling for his emissaries, he decreed that any man finding a cure for his daughter be offered his very kingdom.

And so, one fateful day, an old wizard came knocking . . .

Turning to the next page, I hear soft snoring beside me. He never stays awake beyond that part, and I never bother to read further. Closing the book in my lap, I see my wife with a besom in hand. Her chestnut hair shows the first streaks of silver, and her eyes look soft and tired. The years have weathered her, but by the warm light of the fire, she remains beautiful. As I watch her sweep, a dark mood falls over me, and I cannot be certain when it is that I begin to doze off, but daylight is pouring in through the windows and my wife approaches me, her brow lined with worry.

"Have you seen Astor about?"

The book falls with a thud to the floor as I shift under the covers. "Is he not sleeping?" I reach for some sign of his presence, his small body, a crop of hair, the limb that pokes me in the ribs in the deep of night, but my hand meets nothing but tangled bedding.

"He went out early," she says. "He was going on about sea-monsters, and he had his boat with him."

"He went beyond the wall, then, to the shore."

"Do look for him, will you? A mother worries."

I am overcome by some dreadful premonition, though I know not why. Astor has explored the city countless times, and yet my heart is falling into the pit of my stomach. I don my cloak casually, so that I not alarm my wife, and head through the postern door.

The air breaks against my cheeks as I lean over the balustrade. Bits of sand collect in my eyes and beard. Across the wall, the banners twist in the wind, fighting to hold to their towers. I take the zigzagging steps two-by-two down to the shore. Waves crash into the breakers violently, white-capped, spraying mist over the city, and the cold air and gray sky betray the Sea God's foul mood.

I feel an urge for haste, but also hopelessness, the sense that I cannot move swiftly enough. The Sea calls and yet I dread what awaits me—a gate to a terrible place, a place without memories.

At last, I see him. He is huddled alone by a reef, the toy ship in his hand, talking fervently to himself, acting out some scenario in his head. A slim green form slips from the water and moves toward him.

"Astor!" I call to him again, but the waves drown my voice. He does not see me or hear my warning.

"Astor!" I scream.

And scream, and scream.

The name was ringing in Demacharon's ears when he came to on the floor of the cavern. The pang of losing his son never dulled with time, and waking brought every memory to the fore, shattering whatever small peace he found in slumber. Astor was with him when he laid his head down to rest and remained when he arose. The scar dividing his face burned with the memory still, and he was only thankful that the dream did not lead him beyond, to that *other* place.

His joints cried in protest as he pulled himself to a seated position. Every sword that nearly cut his life, every mace that ever rattled his brains within his helmet, and countless other injuries, they greeted him each morning, and the rocky floor did nothing to ease his soreness. It was a hard place for any man to spend a night, but he had known worse, and pain was the mark of a life well spent. Only his duty mattered, kept him sane and alert. Without it, he was lost, he was . . .

"Radia?"

Beside him was nothing but gravel and bare stone. Startled, he called her name again. Knowing she would not have returned to the crypts, he followed the sound of trickling water down to the broad expanse of steps cut into the rock. What had been a void the night before now blazed with light. Veils of mist obscured the immense cavern's far reaches, out of which came a distinct roar like a torrent of water. Above him, amorphous formations spiraled from the ceiling like melting candles, where moisture collected and wept into pools below. Here and there stalagmites twisted up to meet stalactites, like the teeth of some malformed creature.

He continued down the steps, climbing over layers of cream-colored stone, the floor of the cavern angling inward to form a striated bowl. Sounds of water echoed about, guiding him, until he heard a melody. She was humming. It might have been the mist, refracting the sunlight percolating through rifts in the rock, or that he was still in that twilight stage between wakefulness and dreams, but when he saw her she was like some ethereal creature, magical and otherworldly. Radia leapt and twirled, a dancer whose face shows no concern for the world, and she was naked but for her tresses, which were gold as morning sunlight and streamed like a river down from her neck and shoulders. It was oft-said that the princess of Tyrnael was the loveliest creature in all Aenya, and when he had taken his oath and first saw her upon the throne, his breath had stopped short. But seeing her as she truly was, without any of the trappings of custom and ceremony, there could be no doubt. If he were a younger man, less blunted by brothels and the human spoils of war, he supposed his heart would have burst. But a younger Demacharon would have seized her, raped her, and the man he now was would despise him for it. She was the daughter he could have had, had Niobe not become barren with grief.

"What are you doing? Where are your clothes?"

"Now you've gone and ruined my focus!" A butterfly, azure in color, fluttered playfully at her fingertips. She was either attempting to catch it or following its movements. "Couldn't you see the butterfly?"

"Where are your clothes?" he asked again, more firmly.

"Oh, those raggedy things? I tossed them."

"You did what?" He sounded angry, and tired, and paternal without meaning to be.

"After your brutal tailoring job, there wasn't much to be salvaged of my great grandmother's dress, was there?"

"Did you not have undergarments, at least?"

"After slogging through crypts and monster's entrails? Those things were rancid. Princesses needn't stink, you'd be wise to know. You could use a good washing up yourself, I'd imagine."

"My lady, please tell me you won't be making a habit of this. The people of this kingdom look to you. Or will. As their ruler, you cannot be seen prancing about—"

"Prancing? Now really, what's so awful about prancing?"

"Don't play coy with me. You know what I'm getting at."

"There's no one about—I checked. Nobody who matters, anyway. Well, *you* matter, of course, but not in that way. You know what I mean!"

"No, I do not. And a princess should never be seen by her subjects, not even her protectors—"

"Goodness, now you sound like stuffy old Anabis! Well, I've got nothing else to wear, so look away if I offend. Blink, if you're able."

"You shouldn't wander off alone, either," he added, too weary for words. "How can I protect you if—"

"You talk in your sleep. Did you know that? Just ramble on and on about the strangest things."

"Why didn't you wake me?"

"Quite honestly, I was afraid to. You might have woken from some nightmare and taken me for a bogren. But it wasn't you that disturbed my slumber—I was cold and hungry and needed a drink. You may be used to this sort of thing, but not I. So, I came down here, and then I discovered the most amazing thing!"

Her enthusiasm made her all the lovelier, but did not inspire his curiosity.

"The butterfly told me how to find it."

"My lady, princess or not, if they find you stark naked and conversing with insects, they'll lock you away for sure!"

"She's quite clever for an insect, and she does speak, if you have only the ears to listen. Come away and see for yourself." She offered her hand and he embraced it. "It's down below just a little way."

He had forgotten she was a mere fifteen, only a few years older than Astor. Whether naked or fully clothed, he must consider her reverently. His only concern was for other people, men who could only mistake her innocence for indecency and wantonness. Evil was so far from her heart, she was blind to it, which made protecting her all the more difficult.

As they descended, waterfalls emerged from behind curtains of mist. The uneven ground slowed their progress, but centuries of flowing water had smoothed and flattened the stalagmites, which stood no taller than their knees, allowing her to hop with bare soles from one to another.

In a depression at the center of the cavern, a solitary tree stood aside a small pond. With no other vegetation to be seen, it was a peculiar sight. Leafless limbs sprouted from its ash-gray trunk, reminding him of an elk's horns. The princess knelt for a drink, letting her braids touch the water, and the ripples expanded to the edges of the pool like rings of gold.

"Are you sure it's safe? I've lost whole regiments to dysentery."

"It will rejuvenate you, as it did me."

In every way, the princess did indeed appear strong and vigorous, more than she should have been considering their lack of rest and nutrition. And the water was not stagnant. Trickling streams fed into it, yet the surface was still and shone like pure silver, and unlike the many other pools surrounding them, he could not see to the bottom, which suggested an underground aquifer.

Gazing upon himself, he was reminded of an old leather boot, scuffed and riddled beyond repair, the scar dividing his face like laces come undone. It pained him to see her reflection beside his, though he had never been one for appearances. He had known soldiers in the morning of their lives, deformed in battle, too ashamed to return to their lovers. With little pity, he would say to them, 'You need not concern yourself—nothing matters but the strength and will to do your duty'. Weighed by more than fifty suns, Demacharon wondered whether he still possessed the strength to do his duty and protect the princess. But to dwell on it would avail him nothing, he told himself, cupping his hands into the pool and allowing his image to fragment. The water tasted clear and surprisingly warm.

"This place is sacred," she remarked. "Life began here, with the earliest living forms to emerge on Aenya, the first children of Zoë."

"How do you know that?"

"I know lots of things. This tree here," she added, "is Theádra! Can you believe it? We've found Theádra!"

"It looks dead to me."

"But it isn't. Watch!" She reached under a branch and waited with her palm upturned. "May I have a pomegranate, please?"

To his amazement, something began to grow, no bigger than a seedling at first, but as the natural processes were greatly hurried, it morphed through every stage and color before his eyes, from a small, bright green sphere to a ripe and purplish oval. She offered him the fruit with a smirk. "Hungry?"

"That is . . . that is impossible." He held the pomegranate in his hand, dumbfounded. "If we could plant these elsewhere, we could use them to feed—"

"Oh no, we can never! Theádra is unique, you see. When I came upon her, I suspected she was the one, and then when the butterfly told me, well I simply knew it to be true. Have you never heard the tale?"

"It is not known in Hedonia."

Leaping across the pool, Radia sat cross-legged under the canopy of branches, and as if he were seeing it in some new light, the tree seemed to come alive in her presence.

"Theádra was a mortal woman, a queen of Tyrnael, who lived long ago, in a castle by the edge of a great forest by the dark hemisphere. She had six sons and six daughters, and was proud, never missing a chance to boast of their strength and beauty. Women who were barren, or had lost children in birthing or to illness, listened to her and lamented their fortunes, and after a time grew to resent the queen.

"At the altar of Fate, these women lifted their voices to beseech the goddess, asking why they could not have had but one healthy child, while the queen was given twelve. Fate did not listen, for her decisions can never be undone, but the god of death, Skullgrin, was moved by their pleas, and he sent forth a terrible host from the dark hemisphere, armies of bogrens and horg and creatures too terrible to name. By this time, Theádra's sons were fully grown, and as young men tend to be, they were blind to their mortality. Off they want to war, and while many proved valiant, all returned to their mother on the bier. Theádra mourned the loss of her sons, and her only solace was that her six daughters remained. But they would not remain long.

"The bogren host fought their way through the woods to the bright hemisphere, until they stood at the very walls of the city, greatly outnumbering the forces of Tyrnael. Their chief, who went by the name Bushwhack, asked to parley with the queen. His demand? That she forfeit six maidens, to be delivered in marriage, or the city was to be razed to the ground and its every inhabitant killed. Horrified at the prospect of giving any one of her daughters up, Theádra refused and readied for battle, but the mothers who now despised her made other plans. Unwilling to sacrifice more of their sons to a deadly siege, they stole into the castle in the eclipse of night, kidnapping the princesses and delivering them to Bushwhack. By morning, the bogren horde had retreated to the dark hemisphere, but Queen Theádra was overcome with grief. She went completely mad, running and screaming through the courtyard, pulling every hair on her head one-by-one until she went entirely bald. At last, she fled the castle to seek her daughters.

"Upon entering the woods, the queen became lost. Being so near the dark hemisphere, the night grew so cold that she lost all ten of her fingers, and would surely have died had she not taken refuge in a cave. There she remained many a night, weeping and calling the names of her lost children, until Zoë, Goddess of Life, came to pity her. Though the goddess could not bring her loved ones back from Skullgrin's domain, she could ease the queen's suffering by transforming her body into a tree, and her spirit into a nymph of the wood."

Radia was smiling as if no story could have ended more happily, and since there was nothing more to tell, the two sat quietly, listening to the falling of the water.

"What nonsense," Demacharon said.

Radia looked perplexed and disappointed. "You didn't enjoy the story?"

"Am I to believe this tree was once your queen? Besides, there is no such forest about, and the dark hemisphere is far away."

"It was ages ago, when the land was different," she explained, "and either way, a story need not be true for it to be good."

Demacharon spent the remainder of the morning asking the tree for fruits—pomegranates and melon grapes and banappes—which did little to sate his gnawing hunger. What they could not eat, they stuffed into Radia's satchel.

They climbed out of the depression, leaving the pool and tree behind to follow the thundering sound of water. The air became wetter as they approached the far edge of the cave, and the ground became increasingly slippery, so that Radia could no longer move briskly from pinnacle to pinnacle. Soon, beads of moisture gathered on their faces and soaked under Demacharon's leather cuirass.

Daylight flooded the mouth of the cave, which was broad enough for twenty men to stand abreast, and he welcomed the warmth on his cheeks. Shafts of sun combined with vapor in the air to form a rainbow, and Radia, mad with joy, ran off to catch it. But he was dismayed. The spray broke from a curtain of water spanning the length of the opening, and he felt certain that, beyond the waterfall, a sheer drop would present itself to them. He could see already that the lip of the mouth was sharp and wet, far too risky for climbing or any sort of exploration. Sensing his unease, Radia approached him, saying, "Don't worry. We'll jump."

He tried to peer over the edge, but his insides mutinied, and the spray left spots on his eyes. Even Radia could not hope to see what awaited them at the bottom. The water obscured everything but the blue of the open sky and a yellowish glare where a sun should be.

"You don't know what's down there or even how high this is. More than likely, there are rocks below that will break our spines like kindling."

"But there aren't any," she insisted. "I have already asked."

"I suppose the butterfly told you so."

"As a matter of fact—"

"I am not trusting my life to the imaginings of a child!"

"You forget your place, praetorian." She was suddenly a woman, commanding and confident. "I am still your master, and if I am to jump, you've no choice but to jump with me."

Holding fast to the satchel around her shoulder, she took a step forward, her foot landing precariously on a small sharp stone jutting from the face of the cliff.

"Wait!" He was clutching her arm, pulling her away. "If I must lay down my life for my lady, so be it, but you do not know, cannot—"

"There's a lake. It's quite deep. If you can swim, we'll be fine. Have faith in me. You *do* know to swim, don't you?"

There was a time when he would have followed any order without hesitation. He had, in fact, leapt from a mountain by his own will. But what she did not know, and he dare not speak of, was the place that awaited him and haunted his dreams. Still, to die here and now would bring an end to his nightly torments. He could think of no better way to leave this plane than by doing his duty. The greater thing to dread was the loss of the life he was sworn to protect.

With some reluctance, he tugged off his boots and shed his armor, and taking her hand in his, joined the fall of water. His stomach lurched up into his sternum and remained there, and for a long while he was deaf and blind within the torrent. Their hands having broken apart, he could not be certain whether she had fallen with him. His feet broke the surface first, and a stinging sensation ran up through his thighs to rattle his upper body, but he regained his bearings quickly enough. Kicking upwards, he came to the surface shivering. No large rocks were visible at the perimeter, but the lake was small in circumference. A short distance from where they dropped and they would certainly have been killed.

"Radia?"

He shouted her name, not seeing her on or under the surface. He circled the small copse twice before finding her in a crop of tall woundwort reeds, straining the water from her hair.

"Are you all right?"

"I only wish Larissa was here to do my braids, but otherwise, fine. A bit shook, to be honest. That butterfly did not do justice to the height of the drop."

"I told you that butterfly was a fool!"

She stared at him, digesting his words, until she burst. Her mood was infectious, and he was laughing despite himself, at the absurdity of it all. He was alive, after all. He had not known the feeling since the time before he could look into Niobe's eyes without pain and remorse, before Astor . . .

"By the gods!" he cried, as if stricken by an arrow. "Where is it?" He hurled down his scabbards, turning his belt inside out, and jumped into the water to search among his boots and leather cuirass. "It's not here! I've lost it!"

"What have you lost?"

Knowing it must float, Demacharon bloodied his fingers by the edge of the lake, digging through mud and stones. *If only the gods had taken pity on me—if only they had made me into a tree.*

"I have your boat," she said softly. She had crept up on him, and he turned to see her standing directly behind him. "That *is* what you're looking for, is it not?"

He went to snatch it from her palm, but she was swift, moving away to the far side of the lake.

"Don't play games with that! Give it to me."

"A child's toy? What is it to you?"

"If you can see into men's hearts, you must know what it means to me. Return it, I beg you."

"Your pain is wrapped up in this boat. I can feel it, but cannot imagine the reason."

"What do the concerns of a praetorian matter to you?" He was being brash, he knew, and knowing of her empathic power, dishonest.

"We are fast becoming friends, are we not? If you are to be my protector, we must at least be that to each other. Otherwise, how am I to fully trust you? It is true that I was too hastily abandoned by those sworn to me, and that you stood by my side, but what am I to you? Why do you keep faith? You are a puzzle box I cannot open, and yet this boat . . . I cannot help but wonder, is it the key to who you are?"

Friendship was not possible with so much hidden, yet how could he tell her of his past? One so innocent would only fear and despise him. "I was born and bred to be a soldier and a soldier does his duty. There is nothing more to me, my lady."

"Answer me one thing, then, does it remind you of someone? Someone dear to you?"

He turned away. Her probing, mismatched eyes were disarming. "It belonged to my son."

"Where is he now?"

"He is gone. Gone where I cannot follow."

All the mirth drained from her cheeks, and for a moment she looked aged. Without a word, she placed the ship into his palm and he slipped it back into the hidden pocket of his belt.

8

Ugh

U gh lived in a burrow deep in the bowels of Aenya. Immense roots twisted down from above, giving his home shape and dimension, framing the doors and passageways, but more importantly supporting the earthen roof. The floor was bare, without an animal skin to cover the dirt, but the walls consisted of colorful multilayered strata. An alcove dug from the granite base served as a bed and worktable, with a layer of chalky gray slate above it, followed by glassy igneous and a band of pale white flood silt. Though his home offered few amenities, a plethora of interesting things could be found embedded in the strata, like skeletons of animals he did not know existed and crab-like creatures that had turned to stone, and glittering metal deposits also, from iron ore, copper and tin. Once, while digging an alcove to place his tools, something gold caught his eye, no bigger than the crust from his tear ducts, and he did not hesitate to hide the treasure.

Ugh never concerned himself with boredom, however, as he was too busy thinking how to remedy the aching in his belly. If lucky, a worm or two might plop down from the ceiling, or a grub or beetle. Ugh spent much of his off time fishing the top for morsels. Most days he went home empty-stomached. Anything greater than a mole rat was difficult to come by, as larger prey tended to live nearer the surface. He could only imagine the taste of rabbit or swine, or human kid, but given his diminutive stature, he could never know such delights. As a lowly digger, Ugh fed from the scrap pile, from whatever the *bigger* discarded. When the pangs in his stomach were beyond suffering, he might settle for detritus—the leavings of saurians and other beasts—which tasted foul even to him and did little to sate his hunger.

But there was no need for detritus today. Noticing the faint luminescence beyond his door, Ugh had found the run leading to his home aglow. Blue algae caked the walls and brighter still were the clusters of truffles growing in the warm wet niches between the roots in the roof. Quivering with excitement, he gathered the mushrooms greedily, as many as his stick-like arms could carry, and retreated to his burrow, smothering the light to escape the notice of thieving neighbors.

With a flint, he started a fire, in a hole with dry roots and leaves, and set a kettle to boil. Most of his kind would not have bothered with the cooking, devouring the mushrooms immediately and licking the algae from the walls, but Ugh considered himself more refined than most. He did not wish merely to end his hunger, but savor the sensation of food filling his belly.

As the water popped and hissed, he brushed the algae from his fingers into the kettle, and worked the truffles with great care, peeling each cap from its stem and tossing it into the broth. A pungent aroma filled his home, making his mouth run with drool and his stomach pains more acute. Dizzy with hunger, he shoveled the remainder of the truffles in to boil. There was nothing left to do but grab his spoon and wait. But with waiting came a sense of dread. What if the smell of cooking made its way down the run to the other burrows? If his find was discovered, nothing would be left for him, being that he was much too small to fight. It occurred to him that his only chance was to hide what he did not eat that day, and with a spoon in hand, bolted from his door in search of fungi he might have missed.

He made several trips, hiding the truffles in the shadowy niches of his home, until he bumped his head against something hard and unyielding. Seeing two bogren standing in his doorway, Ugh made a noise that fell somewhere between a gasp and a shriek. Before they could give insult, he treaded backward, feebly hiding the panic on his face. The smaller of the two was Ack, a fellow digger with a lumpy face, toadstool ears, and a carbuncle nose, and whisker-like hairs sprouting from each lobe and nostril. Slightly bigger than Ugh, Ack could not wrestle much food away. But the bigger one frightened him. His wide, flat face resembled a misshapen potato, and despite having no neck—not one Ugh could see anyway—his head seemed firmly attached to his rocky yellow body.

It was a well-known fact that females of the digger caste died in childbirth. Should they manage to survive, mothers were summarily killed and eaten, umbilical cord and all. The last sound a mother made before dying became the newborn digger's name. Those fortunate enough to birth warriors, however, were permitted to live. Warrior names were unique, a mark of status.

"I am Grumblestump. Follow me."

Dialogue between bogren was limited if not nonexistent, which resulted in confusion and disorganization, arguments and insults, often bloodshed. Ugh tried repeatedly to fix this poorly coordinated system, but no one ever listened to a digger.

"Wait. What? Why?"

"Work," said Grumblestump. "Dig."

"But this is my day off," Ugh complained, "and you can't expect me to work on an empty stomach."

As always, Ack was looking about nervously, as if some creature were about to pounce on him. "The Master's here! He's come to inspect the Forge and we need to be seen working! Shirkers will be tossed in the magma!"

'Shirkers will be tossed in the magma,' was a common refrain among foremen, those insufferable creatures of the warren who were mostly comprised of former bogren warriors injured beyond usefulness, and typically missing limbs. For most workers, the foreman's lash was motivation enough, as Ugh's shredded backside proved beyond count, but when foremen exhibited an especially foul mood, or worse, a very jolly one, bogrens ended up in the magma. Watching a worker thrash and scream, his muscles and bones dissolving into a red paste, provided a source of great humor to all but one. Fearing to be that one, Ugh voiced no further complaint. He simply excused himself to retrieve his pick and spade, and while at it, stamped out the fire and stuffed his throat with uncooked truffles.

"Hold on a bit," said Ack as Ugh reappeared. "Is that cooking I smells?"

"Cooking?" Ugh echoed. "No, you must be mistaken."

"I smells it too," Grumblestump remarked, his wet, pig-like snout contracting.

Ugh pushed through them into the run and slammed his door. "Don't forget, shirkers will be thrown in the magma!"

For a moment, Grumblestump looked about him, confused and uncertain, divided between duty and his instinct for food. But at the urging of the two diggers, he continued down the run, summoning workers from every crack and mud hole they came to.

Bogrens were a noisy, stinking bunch, and the diminutive digger could barely endure it. Chins nodded against his skull, elbows poked his ribs, and knees jostled the tender bits between his thighs. If only they could move in an orderly manner, he might not need to suffer injury on his way to work. But to voice any opinion was a waste of time. As they continued to shove and trample one another along the dirt corridor, Ugh considered how much he hated his life—he was meant for better things, for some meaningful existence, but was doomed to be surrounded by gibbering idiots.

The heat could be seen a good way before the end of the run. Ashy embers and smoke wafted across their faces, smothering their sense of smell and stinging their eyes. The air quivered more noticeably the nearer they came to the Forge. Where the run ended, a drop presented itself, with a series of ladders leading downwards. In their eagerness to exit, bogrens sometimes pushed one another from the edge, never to be seen again. More than once, Ugh had watched steps collapse under the weight of too many bodies, hurling dozens into the depths. How far did they fall? None could say, for they were but one clan among thousands, many of whom lived in tiers far below, and the abyss was rumored to reach into the heart of the world, a heart of magma that pumped with the lifeblood of the bogren race. Perhaps the fallen ended there, to be devoured by the eternal flame, but Ugh had no desire to make this discovery first hand. So he waited, hiding in the shadows as workers passed him by. When only a few remained in the run, he carefully made his way down the ladder to the nearest platform, where bogrens gathered from the hundreds of exits dotting the shaft.

Shoddily constructed scaffolding and rope bridges crisscrossed the abyss, and when Ugh moved from one to another, he could hear the planks groaning and the threads twisting and snapping. Despite the obvious state of disrepair, no one ever bothered with maintenance. When a bridge or platform fell apart—resulting in the deaths of hundreds—it was simply rebuilt and replaced. Ugh supposed there was no point complaining, for catastrophic failure was entertaining. Just as with shirkers in lava, comedy and tragedy were one and the same in the minds of the overseers.

The whole of the Forge balanced precariously over the void on protrusions of rock. A nexus of chains and pulleys brought immense cauldrons from the hot glowing rivers below. Blue saurians, of the *bandersnout* variety, were tethered to winches to help with the load. The cauldrons were poured into molds, and as the molten shapes cooled, workers hammered them into weapons and armor. Ugh pictured himself in the smith caste, with chisel and nail, meticulously carving the Fist-and-Morningstar—the Master's standard—into every breastplate. He found the level of artistry in the job appealing, a thing that other castes lacked, especially his. Alas, he was born a digger, and a digger he would always be.

Grumblestump was nowhere to be seen, and without a foreman to give direction, Ugh stood perplexed, pick in hand. After a time, he surmised that they had been gathered not for labor, but to honor the Master. Just as the thought came to him, a great commotion swelled below, and every bogren clambered toward the center, over bridges and scaffolding nearing collapse. Obscured by a crop of skulls taller than himself, Ugh climbed the nearest ladder to look out from the mouth of the run.

A huge six-legged salamander, with burnished scales like roiling lava, was making its way through the gathering, snapping its jaws and threatening to tear the limbs from anyone who strayed too closely. The Master was saddled atop it, in a shell of blood-red steel, the spikes from his helm radiating like the flames from the furnace of the Dark God. At the sight of him, a tickle of fear ran the length of Ugh's spine, but he was powerless to look elsewhere. He watched as his chieftain, Bloodsnot, the biggest in their clan, approached him. The Master did not dismount, and only by his tugging at the reins did their chief escape from losing his head. A pair of smiths followed, an immense mace carried between them, a weapon too big for even Bloodsnot to wield.

"Bonecrusher," the chief declared. "A gift for the Master."

Taking the weapon in one swift motion, the holes drilled into the mace-head whistled, and as he brought it down again, the sound came sharp and deadly, ending with the cracking of the smith's skull. Admiring the show of strength and savagery, the onlookers cheered and hooted.

"A simple name, from simple minds," he said. "It will suffice, but I did not come for this."

"We have ten-thousand armor ready."

"I will take them. After we march on Northendell, I will need more. Many more."

"As you desire, Master. But we are prepared to do the fighting ourselves. My warriors stand ready."

"If Tyrnael is to relive its glory days, it will need men of vision and strength. Empires are not built by the scum of the world."

"And yet, you promise food, yes . . . food for all?"

"When I sit on the throne of Aenya, bogrens will feast like men."

9

Noora

A crude reflection of his face warped about the blade, his chin stubble flashing in and out of view as he attempted to trim it. Demacharon squatted in the tussock, trying to steady himself as he drew his dagger slowly across his cheek. Beads of blood were sprouting from his leathery skin—it was not unlike his campaigning days, when he and his men were out in rough country and supplies were sparse. Given the circumstances, it might have been wiser to let his hair grow. Zaibos's men would be looking for someone clean-shaven. But Demacharon had decided against this long ago—a beard would cover much of his scar, make the flayed skin less pronounced, and that he could never allow. The memory of that day, when he had failed to save his son, could never dull in his mind. In his makeshift mirror, Demacharon was forced to reflect on his sins.

"I'm back!"

How she managed to sneak up on him, a lifelong soldier hearkening for assassins, he did not know. Despite the heavily-wooded surroundings, her feet did not so much as snap a twig or turn a leaf. The greatest Hedonian ranger could not hope to match her stealth, and it made no sense, considering her sheltered, indoor upbringing. This was but one enigma among many. The night prior, the princess slept soundly—without a stitch to shield her from the chill air—on what he could have sworn was bare earth. By morning, she awoke in a bed of budding baby's-breath and dandelion. At least she'd had the good sense to dress herself, if the single sheet in which she was now garbed could be called clothing.

"What do you think? It's a bit less formal than what I am used to, but that is kind of the point, isn't it?" It was like a tunic or apron that slipped over the head. She tugged at the hem, which left most of her thighs bare, as if to show what was not there. As she turned, he could see that the garment was open on either side, revealing the edge of her breast and rear. "There was little choice in the matter, from what was hanging out there—"

"You stole from a clothesline?"

"It's not stealing! Borrowing. I'll return it later."

"Where is the rest? You're practically naked."

"How can you be *practically* naked?" she said. "You're either naked or you aren't. And if you didn't know, *this* is a peplos, the traditional raiment of the eloai."

"The who?"

"You don't know anything, do you? The eloai are submissives, bred for common purposes like cooking and cleaning, and mending."

"We had those too, in Hedonia. They were called slaves."

"Not slaves!" An angry blush came over her cheeks. "Eloai can refuse a request if they wish. But work makes them content."

"Are they compensated?"

"They are fed and housed."

"Sounds like indentured servitude to me. I had heard differently, that the people of Tyrnael were free—"

"They're not unhappy," she stammered. "They—"

"How would you know? No. Wait. I forget, you're empathic."

"Larissa and I are like sisters and I treat her as well. Though I admit that eloai tend to go unnoticed. The highborn do not speak to them but to request some labor. Which is why this is the perfect disguise."

"I still advise we cut your hair. Zaibos's men will be seeking a young girl, and it's hard enough hiding you with those eyes." The problem had been nagging him from the time they fled to the crypts. How do you smuggle a fugitive princess with such distinctive features? Even if the people failed to recognize her face, beautiful as she was, her mismatched eyes were unmistakable, her left the turquoise of the greater moon, her right a bright violet, like the smaller moon.

"Don't you think they'll be expecting that? Pretending to be a boy is as old as the first Batal. In the third century of the Suppression Wars, when Radamanthes the First was killed in battle after his saurian mount fell atop him, his sister, Phaedona the Third, donned a man's armor and routed the enemy, much to the displeasure of her father, King Elezares, who just happens to be my great-great-great-great—"

"Enough," he cried. "I get it."

"But whoever heard of a princess disguised as a servant? I never have. Have you? Besides, it is customary for eloai to avert their eyes. As your humble attendant, I can keep to myself without suspicion."

Demacharon hesitated to agree, but he trusted her knowledge of the city and its customs. Wiping the blood from his chin, he murmured, "It's a wonder the men don't press their advantage."

She stared at him, a puzzled look on her face. "I don't get your meaning."

"Forgive me." His words were not intended for her ears, and already he regretted them. "I should have learned by now to hold my tongue."

"No, I want to know. How can I govern justly if I do not hear from all of my subjects?"

"I simply meant that, with what you are wearing, there may be those men without honor, who would attempt to force themselves upon you."

"Force me? To what end?"

She was only fifteen, hardly a woman, raised her entire life away from peasants. And yet, could she truly be so naïve? "Radia, it is . . . a basic human function—"

"Oh, you mean sexual intercourse! I've read of that in the histories. It is forbidden."

"Well, I should hope so! Only savages go about raping—" He stopped short, recognizing the deceit in himself, and dreading her power to look into his heart, to discover the monster that dwelt there. How many beauties were brought into his tent in the dark of night, virgin daughters whose fathers had fallen the same day, wives of husbands murdered by his legion? The supreme commander of Hedonia had nothing to hide and none to hide from. Though it went unspoken, even his wife had understood that his actions on the battlefield were beyond reproach, the spoils of war a sacred right sanctioned by the priesthood. And yet, before this mere girl, Demacharon felt the stirrings of shame.

"You misunderstand me, I think," she went on. "Sexual intercourse is no longer practiced in Tyrnael. Has not been for centuries."

He pondered her words, thinking he misheard. "How can that be? How are the children—"

"There is a Committee. They decide what offspring are to be born, when, and to whom. A couple may appeal for a child and, if they are approved, an infant is grown in the Nursery— it's a building here in the city. I can show you."

It seemed beyond comprehension, but would explain her utter disregard for modesty. In Tyrnael, clothing was a matter of social standing—the more layered and richly woven the fabric, the higher the status. He recognized the aristocrats roaming the halls by their indulgent lace and ruffle. His own praetorian armor, which had covered him from head to heel in gleaming steel, maintained his status. It was no wonder the eloai, who kept out of sight, were accustomed to donning so little.

"Do you think us odd?"

"Cruel, more like."

"No, it is not. You see, after the Cataclysm, hunger, sickness, and war plagued our people. Aenya was a dying world and Zoë could not provide for her progeny. Children born into that time suffered the worst of it. Mothers left infants they could not feed to die in the woods. And so, my ancestors decreed intercourse forbidden, to curb the population, and thereby the suffering. Now every child is born to caring parents. No sicknesses or deformities exist among us. Nor does famine. Our keepers see to that."

"Better to let men die like men than be bred like cattle!"

"There are many ways to love, Demacharon, if that is your concern," she said. "Do not the bees love the flowers? And trees the sun?"

"You are a very strange girl, I think."

"Things can be both strange and true, wouldn't you agree?"

Her insight caught him off guard. How could she seem so innocent one moment and wise the next? "Your people cannot hope to enforce such a law."

"It was passed down centuries ago. My people have since lost the craving for it."

Demacharon shook his head. "Do you think Zoë meant for you to live this way?"

A troubled look came over her face as she contemplated this. He then remembered that he was a stranger and in no position to judge. Throughout his journeys, as legionnaire and commander, he had met with many inexplicable customs, more than a few of which he found repugnant. But there had always been a place he could return to where the conventions made sense. Now there was no such place. Like the peoples he himself displaced, he was a man without a country, looking to belong, if not in Tyrnael, somewhere.

Strapping his gladius to one side and the scabbard of the two-sword to the other, Demacharon watched the swaying dandelions kiss the tops of her feet, the wind rustling the leaves in the trees and the peplos round her body, the sunlight percolating through her hair in a golden halo. She was wondrous beyond compare, in ways his simple mind could not fathom, and it saddened him and made him deeply fearful. To keep such a girl secret, hidden from those who wished her harm, was a task beyond him, a task bound to failure and tragedy.

They walked a short while through a wooded area until coming upon a cobblestone path. As they set upon it, Demacharon could not help marveling at the glittering yellow substance underfoot. When he first arrived in the city, he stooped many a time to break pieces from the road, despite disconcerting stares from pedestrians. Its weight and texture, and the way it yielded between his molars, could only signify one thing. But his mind could not accept it.

"Radia. I've been meaning to ask someone about this, but felt a bit silly, should I be mistaken."

"You should never feel silly for anything, lest you want to."

He shook his head, confused. "This path we're walking, its construction, is it . . . gold?"

She thought for a moment, and replied, "Geology was never my best subject, but I believe so, yes. Why do you ask?"

"Have you any idea what gold is worth outside the Crown?"

"What do you mean by worth?"

"I mean wealth. Currency. Coin exchanged for goods and services."

"I don't know what you mean by that. But I do know that gold is a good building material, as it doesn't oxidize."

They continued in awkward silence, Demacharon too perplexed for words, until coming clear of the trees. What he had assumed was a forest was a segmented part of the city, what Radia called a *park*. Ahead of them, the golden road sloped downward, coursing like a river. At their backs, the sky was clear of foliage, and they could see the path winding up to the base of the hills, where dozens of waterfalls could be seen breaking against the sharp gray rocks below. Mountain and castle seemed to be floating in the air, rising from the torrential vapors, and from its peak, the Compass Tower climbed impossibly into the upper atmosphere in gold and white, like a spear in the hand of a stone titan. A nexus of walls, minarets, and bridges spread across and away from the whole, vanishing in all directions, to the limits of the city.

Radia stood beside him, watching, dumbfounded. "I've never seen it from afar, the place I've lived my entire life."

What could he say to her? That she would sit again upon her throne? Did she have the power to sense false hope?

Just then, a cloud passed over the sun, and the contours of her face deepened in the shadows. "I am afraid, Demacharon."

"No harm will come to you. I will see to that, my lady."

"No," she answered. "I am afraid of my people. I must seem so remote to them, so beyond reach. Would they accept me, do you think?"

"What are you saying? The people adore you."

"Do they?"

"In all my travels, I've never known so beloved a ruler."

"But is it *me* that they love, or the idea of me, my story?"

"If they come to know you as I have, they will worship you. I do not doubt it."

"You are too kind, praetorian. But, honestly, how can they ever know me, if I am to forever remain in hiding? Running from my brother?"

"Such concerns are for another time. We must go down to the city now."

They continued southward, the only direction one could move from the tower. The sun was clear and bright again, and a gust of warm air was blowing from the west, but a mountain chill was in the air.

"Another thing I have never understood . . ." he said, ". . . the further north one travels from the Sea, the colder it becomes. South of these mountains, the rivers are frozen— there is not but hills of ice and snow. Yet in this very spot, at the peak of the world, all is green."

"I know only what the myths tell us. The goddess set this place aside, for the people given her name, to shield us from the Cataclysm."

"And do you believe such things?"

"Everything is possible. There is also the westerly wind, that blows from the Dead Zones, where the land, they say, is hot as the inside of a kiln, where sand is turned to glass and clay into ceramic."

"Whatever the truth of it, the climate is unexpected and, I believe, what has protected you from invaders for millennia."

Demacharon and Radia reached the end of the path, which came to a sudden drop, offering a scenic vista. Disorientated by the altitude, he backed away from the edge.

Tyrnael spread to the horizon in a multitude of golden terraced hills, their rooftops lined with greenery, bridges above and below them connecting to each tier. He led the way down the zigzagging stairway set into the structure, taking care to cling to the inner wall, but Radia surpassed him, hopping two-by-two down the steps until reaching the street below.

Demacharon maintained a wary eye for soldiers, but the only person to cross their gaze was a barefooted girl, younger than Radia, wearing only a tunic and carrying a wicker basket filled with fish. A moment later, they passed another pedestrian, also barefoot, and just as plainly dressed. In any other city, the boy could have been mistaken for the girl's brother. But things were different in Tyrnael, he now knew. The common folk were all too common. Every man and woman shared the same face, or near enough to seem of the same family. No one was terribly aged, sickly, or deformed, nor could anyone be described as obese or scrawny. But what he found most unnerving was the silence, or the lack of one sound in particular—the merriment of children. Hedonia bustled with boys and girls playing at war or seek or kites. Here, not a single laugh or squeal of delight could be heard. Occasionally, a toddler might stumble into view, closely guarded by its mother, and that was all.

"This may be easier than I thought," Demacharon said. "Where is everyone?"

"Are you forgetting I am an eloai?" she whispered. "Servants don't know to answer such questions."

"What does it matter? We are alone!"

"The people are inside their homes," she explained. "Where else?"

"This won't do. We need to find a busy place, a market or something, where people congregate."

"Are we not trying to avoid being seen?"

"A servant should not ask questions," he said with a smirk.

She took him by the hand. "The Court of Festivals. I know where it is!"

In the narrow alleyways, away from windows and balconies, she skipped playfully along, leading him on. Moving onto the broader streets, where the occasional crowd was gathered, she became more reserved, lowering her eyes and hiding behind him, occasionally whispering directions. All the while, he wondered whether she was only guessing at the way, for the city looked differently from below, and she had never been permitted to roam freely from her tower up on high.

By midday, after a dozen wrong turns and dead-ends, they found the entrance to the market district.

An iron statue, vaguely resembling a man, stood in a fountain in the center of the square. Banners surrounded them, each marking a door and a profession: a baker's rolling pin, a butcher's cleaver, an accountant's quill, a smith's anvil. Radia's sigil was the bucking unicorn, gold on white, but it was nowhere to be seen. They turned into a wide lane flanked by wrought iron planters of yellow tulip and gardenia bushes, where the people were flocking. Their garments were of peacock feathers, or silks resembling crashing waves, or arranged of oddly cut shapes. One woman hid her face behind a beaked mask. Another sported a tall, conical hat, trailing a long golden tassel. Most were accompanied by their own barefoot eloai, both male and female, who stood behind with eyes lowered.

"Who are these people?" Demacharon asked.

"They are highborn. They dress like other races during festivities. See that woman there? She's an avian. And the one with the pointy hat is from Shemselinihar."

"It's a mockery! They've never been outside the Crown! If I see a 'Hedonian,' I'll punch him."

"Don't make trouble. You asked for a gathering. Here it is."

"All right," he grumbled. "Now hush."

Demacharon watched the decorated host mill about. It was like some twisted version of the bazaar in Hedonia. He avoided eye contact, keeping his ears open for news of the princess's disappearance, or of anything to do with Zaibos's movements, but there was only talk of plays and music. Giving his eloai a stern look, he merged into the crowd. They amassed under a domed structure emblazoned with a six-stringed bouzouki. A man stood before a set of massive double-doors, waving at the attendants queuing up to enter. With his ruddy cheeks and double chin, he appeared out of place, a refreshingly alien face.

"That is just what we're looking for," he told her, taking a place for them in the line. "Keep your head down and say *nothing*."

"Welcome to the Cosmos!" the pudgy man exclaimed, sounding like a high-pitched bird. "My name is Orson. And what might you be?"

Demacharon grinned.

"Well, I'll give you high marks for makeup, but that armor needs work!"

Radia squeezed his hand as if to say, 'don't hit him.' "What is this place?" he asked.

"You've never heard of the Cosmos Theater?"

"Not really, no."

"Why, it's only the most spectacular show in all the world! Singing, dancing, drama, acrobatics—whatever your fancy. Our acting troupe is guaranteed to rekindle your love of life, have you in tears by the end of this evening, or you can take back your barter."

"Barter?"

"You've nothing to barter?" He looked disappointed, like a giant, pouting baby.

"You don't take coin?"

"Coins are worthless in Tyrnael, so we don't ask. But we are a traveling show, and coins work most places, so if you've any to offer, I'll gladly take them off your hands."

"Travel? From how far?"

Demacharon could sense the irritation of a great many people at his back. They were eager to pass through the gate and he was holding them up.

"Terribly sorry, sir, but you'll have to offer something in trade or be off."

Radia pressed something into his palm, a sapphire the size of his thumb. Knowing how something of such value might come of use, it pained him to part with it. "Will this do?"

Orson's eyes drank in the violet shimmer, and glancing around for who might be watching, discreetly tucked the jewel into a ruffled breast pocket. "Yes! Indeed! Come in. As my honored guest, you will be seated at the foot of the stage!"

The theater was arrayed in tiers, with terraces at the top level and concentric rows for seating beneath. Braziers glowed orange in columns on every level, casting monstrous shadows against the walls. Chipped murals painted across the vaulted ceiling harkened to a far earlier age—knights with missing limbs, a floating sword battling enemies faded beyond recognition, a no longer frightening horg largely erased by entropy. Most structures in Tyrnael, he knew, were relics from a time forgotten, and therefore abandoned, or in this case, repurposed.

The usher led them down to the center floor, where a great number of circular tables were set, dismally festooned with brittle, dehydrated flowers. On a wooden stage, not two paces from them, an elderly man plucked his bouzouki.

"I like this place," she said. "It's fun being out."

"We're not here for fun, so keep your eyes hidden. I've yet to hear so much as a rumor. For all we know, Zaibos may have kept your flight a secret, which can only work to our advantage. But if the public is aware of it, and you are spotted, I'll be powerless to protect you."

Radia brushed her hair to the side and fixed her gaze upon the lifeless gardenia petals strewn across the table. "I still don't understand what's happened. My people would never stand for a bloody coup. They'd be outraged . . . revolt. Zaibos must know this. Why take the risk? Why not kill me in my sleep and claim some misfortune of fate?"

"Kaius the Tyrant," Demacharon replied. "He was commander of the legion in the twelfth century. Believing the clergy was unfit to rule, Kaius murdered the High Priest before hundreds, proclaiming himself god-emperor of Hedonia, Sargonus incarnate. He had the army for support and the city cowered before him. His rule was one of fear and intimidation. Zaibos wishes to do the same. He does not simply want to get rid of you—

he wants to change the people, make them afraid so that he can control them. What better way to intimidate the kingdom than by murdering you in open court for all to see? After this, none will dare challenge his legitimacy."

"It saddens me to think of him," she murmured. "I thought him good once. We used to pretend together, until he got older."

"There is very little *good* in this world."

"You cannot believe that. You're a good man, aren't you?" She lifted her face, her mismatched eyes sharp as diamonds, cutting through him. "Perhaps it would be better to trust someone. These are my people. They will not turn me over to my brother."

Demacharon hardened his fists, and he spoke in a firm voice. "Listen carefully. If you want to live, you must do precisely as I say. Never tell anyone who you are. Never speak anything of the life you knew before, to anyone, understood? You are no longer a princess of Aenya—you are Noora, my servant, and you must speak, act, and think accordingly."

"Noora?" She smiled. "Why Noora?"

"My sister," he answered matter-of-factly. "She died when she was eight."

"How awful. What happened?"

"Typhoid fever."

"Nothing like that exists in Tyrnael. No one ever dies of illness, I mean. The Zo saw to that long ago. They changed our bodies somehow, made us immune."

"But you were sick as a child, very near Skullgrin's domain. Your father's hair turned white with grief. Or is that only a faerie tale?"

"For cycles, I could hardly lift my head from my pillow. Having seen nothing like it in their lifetimes, the healers were at a loss for what to do, which is why my father called for his emissaries to search for cures beyond the Crown."

A thought suddenly occurred to him, a clue to unraveling the mystery of the city, which he had believed, until recently, to be a place of myth. "*Noora*," he addressed her, "before the late king sent for healers, had there ever been foreigners in Tyrnael? Men like me?"

"I don't . . . I don't really know. My life was lived in the tower, always."

"As a servant, Noora? Working the kitchens? Is that not what you mean?"

"What? Oh . . . of course." She closed her turquoise eye and nodded. "But we're fugitives both. So, by what name shall I call you?"

He scowled, but did not answer.

"Your short name, perhaps? Or do you expect me to believe that your mother called you by your full name? 'Demacharon! Dinner's ready, Demacharon! Come to the table, Demacharon!' Truly?"

His mother was a memory from another life. When he tried to conjure her face, only his wife emerged, who morphed into his son. But for the first time in many years, his family came to him without pain. "I was called Dimmy."

"Really?" She caught her mouth, watching for onlookers, as laughter pushed the tears from her eyes. "All right, Dimmy! Nice to meet you, Dimmy!"

Annoyed, he studied the people as they took to their seats, and in a short time, the amphitheater was filled with hundreds. Faces were obscured by shadow, shawls or masks. Those he could make out possessed the same indistinct features, men and women in their middle years, of average height and girth. He did not doubt their love for Radia, but theirs was an innocent civilization. Protected for aeons from invasion, illness, and even the ravages of aging, they were unused to cruel realities and likely to be weak of spirit. Zaibos would cow them with little effort and they would surrender the princess. But he and Radia needed someone. Alone, without supplies or transportation, they could not chance to cross the mountains of the Crown. All their hopes rested in finding outsiders.

The lights dimmed and not a murmur could be heard. From his bouzouki, the bard produced a set of dramatic notes, as a man in a strange pink hat addressed the crowd in a booming voice. "Long ago, before the time of the Zo, the world was a dark place, inhabited by Men of the Snake." Shapes glided across the dimly lit stage, figures wearing serpent masks and scaly costumes of crepe paper, with long winding tails that swished at the pull of puppeteers hidden in the rafters. As the flamboyantly dressed narrator receded into the background, so did the shapes become increasingly distinct. Demacharon could not help but groan. Groups of naked men and women bounded on stage, spilling ribbons of confetti blood as 'snake men' slaughtered them one by one. Nothing resembled the reality he knew. The fighting was too tidy, the killing devoid of the suffering, the gruesomeness, the chaos and confusion that made killing abhorrent. Yet the audience was delighted, clapping wildly. Even Radia, who professed her hatred of violence, sat enthralled.

The opening of the final act impressed even the Hedonian, if only in regard to the stage props and their arrangement. Every piece was meticulously recreated, from the golden cymbal representing the sun to the stone blocks of the arena to paper cut-outs of snake men sitting opposite the theater. The Prince of the Septhera was an amalgamation of actor and puppet, but the man playing Batal was miscast, lacking the musculature of the fabled hero. Watching the choreographed battle, Demacharon was tempted to march on stage and show the actor how to properly hold a sword. If the true Batal had been so destitute of charisma, he thought, mankind would never have rebelled against their masters, nor formed the Zo civilization. By the time the actor playing Batal cried out, "Men of Aenya, you lose no freedom when you are free to fight!" Demacharon could not have been more relieved to see the curtains fall, despite the thunderous applause.

"Wasn't that amazing! I think I'd like to be an actor now."

He turned to her, unable to hide his displeasure. "No."

The narrator returned to the stage, thanking the audience and muttering something nonsensical regarding the importance of history. He concluded by naming several performers scheduled to come on after intermission.

As the lights brightened, the people began to mingle, and again he scanned the room. Two men were seated at a table across from them, undoubtedly fish-out-of-water. How had he missed them before? The first would likely draw attention anywhere, for he was quite large, with a round belly and a strong upper body. On his head, he wore a metal cap topped by a wheel of spinning blades, and a reddish braided beard covered his face. Seated next to him was a tall, gaunt figure in green leathers, his narrow waist held tight with belts of daggers, darts, and quarrels. All but his chin was concealed by a hood. That they were foreigners, Demacharon would wager a leap from the Compass Tower. But outsiders could also be spies, and he could not afford to be trusting.

"Wait here," he said to Noora. "And do nothing to draw attention. Understood?"

She nodded and he was off.

Accosting the pair would have been awkward in any place, as he did not know their custom, but he felt confident that they, too, were strangers in a strange land.

"Greetings and salutations, my good men. Might I have this seat?"

The bearded one looked up from his pint and shrugged. "Can't see what's to stop you."

The round table was not built for three. He sat closely, noticing the leaner of the two, a boy with a smooth face and fine hair, and emerald eyes the color of his hood. He could not have been much older than the princess.

A tense silence blanketed the table as he waited for the strangers to reveal something of themselves, but he quickly became aware that they awaited the same.

"I am guessing you two are not from here."

"You might say that." The bearded man looked strong enough to wrestle an ox, and despite his companion's unease, stared confidently into Demacharon's eyes. "And you, I'd wager, are a further way from home. Do I lie, Hedonian?"

Demacharon grew tense. If they were in league with Zaibos, to present himself could pose a danger. "How did you know?"

"Your gladius," he answered matter-of-factly, "and that smug, ugly mug." His large frame shook in a bout of sudden laughter, as he thrust his meaty hand to embrace the Hedonian. "Relax! We're all guests here, right? They call me Davos the Tinker. And my timid friend here is Ecthros."

"Ecthros, son of Xenox," he piped in.

They did not seem like enemies, but Demacharon remained apprehensive. "For now, call me Hedonian."

"Terrible what happened to your home," Davos said. "Who could've imagined, an entire city swallowed by the Sea? Doomed by the gods. You were lucky to be abroad."

"I wasn't," Demacharon replied. "I watched the waters rise, saw countless men drown. My wife was among the lost." It was not in his nature to be forthcoming, but he needed their trust, and to learn whether they could be trusted.

"That is half a world away," Davos remarked. "Come to think of it, you're the first southerner I've seen in Mythradanaiil."

Demacharon's confidence was renewed. Of their identity, there could be no doubt—

only outsiders called the city by that name. "You're well-traveled, but I cannot place your accent or attire."

It was true that Davos wore a mishmash of textiles, a shirt and leather vest, and form-fitting pants. "Oh, I am from everywhere and nowhere. The place I call home is always moving, see? My ship is the *Cloud Breaker*."

A ship! Fate smiles on us today! And yet, he had never known a vessel to traverse the barrier, the glacier separating the city from outer Aenya. After almost a year of searching and finding no way through or around it, he had been certain that the passage to Tyrnael was blocked. With nothing but a tent and a tinder box, Demacharon had made every effort to cross over the mountains, and if not for the aid of a kind hermit, would surely have perished in the snow. At last, after cycles of treacherous terrain, and having nearly lost his nose to the cold, he gazed with pained eyes upon a verdant valley, and the shining city at its heart. He could not chance to take the princess by the same route. His only hope was for a mount or a caravan.

"So, you're saying that your ship made it through the pass?"

"We're here, aren't we?"

"That may be to my good fortune, for I am seeking egress from the city, south of the Crown."

Davos stared at him, as though trying to guess his need. "Few men wish to leave Mythradanaiil, once they find it."

Demacharon began to grow impatient. Behind him, the host was announcing a talent search, urging anyone from the audience with a modicum of skill to take the stage.

"I must attend to an urgent matter. Take us with you, and you'll be greatly compensated."

Davos leaned forward, the table creaking under the weight of his hands, the browning tulip at the center drooping lifelessly. "My crew burdens my ship as is. Not sure I can take another. Either way, we won't be leaving port for at least three cycles."

"That's thirty days. We cannot wait that long."

"Don't have much choice in the matter. See these performers? They're foreigners, most of them. I brought them here. Years ago, anyone coming over the mountains got sent packing. I tried, again and again, to set up trading arrangements, but they didn't care for what I had to offer. Then it hit me, like Strom's fire—these folk were starving to learn of the outer world. They didn't care for spices or fabrics. They wanted culture, entertainment! It's become a bit of a fad now, dressing up like bird men and whatnot, and it was all my doing. When the show runs its course, we'll be off, and not a day sooner."

Demacharon receded into his chair. Good commanders planned for every eventuality and he was failing in that regard. He did not even know what the princess had brought in her satchel, but he could bluff. "I can double your profits. In gold."

Davos laughed. "I hope you're not suggesting tearing up the streets. I'd do that myself if the punishment wasn't death. No, Hedonian, in this city I deal in trinkets and baubles. I sell treasures from Tyrnael for a hefty sum—a rich man will pay more than its weight in gold if he's convinced of its origin."

Davos was a trader and a sailor, but otherwise an enigma. What could entice such a man to deal? As he mulled over his options, his attention was broken by subtle clapping. Someone was ascending the stage, but he did not care to look. "I can offer you my servant," he said at last. "She's young."

"I've no need of that!" Davos exclaimed. "I've a wife with children, and I am an honorable man."

"Wait." Ecthros sat up with interest. "Is she pretty?"

"Quiet, boy!" said Davos, smacking the side of his head. "Forgive me. My nephew thinks always with his member."

"In truth," Demacharon went on, facing the young man, "she's the prettiest girl you've ever—"

A girl had broken into song, her voice impossible to ignore. He could see it in Ecthros's expression, the stirring in the eyes, the marveling. Davos, too, was captivated by it. But to Demacharon's ear, the voice was as familiar as it was shocking.

I sing the Goddess that is in all,
who gilds the wheat and sun born rye,
who, in dreaming plains we seek her call

In the greenwood, in the elms that fall
from sundered root to shaken ply
Her eternal verse brings breath to all

In the hornèd moons that nightly rule
her silver sisters dance the sky
and from dreaming plains attend her hall

Even in the sore and weeping gall
there is the ballad which brings release
there is the Goddess of great and small

In streams deep and mountains tall
from lover's rage to felled knight's wreath
Zoë sings her song, who is in all

Do not dread and shrink from winter's pall
or of Luna's chill bite be dismayed
For Zoë, dying, sleeps in snowy shawl

And Springs born to sing the gilded corn
so broken hearts are once more allayed
when mourning moons break to Sun of Morn

At the start of her song, Demacharon's blood had run hot with rage. The princess had not only endangered herself but everyone in the theater. It did not matter whether they recognized her. Every attendee witnessing her whereabouts became an accomplice to her escape. But as the last, soulful note echoed from the walls of the amphitheater, his heart was lulled. The people gathered there that day continued to sit in their chairs, bound in silence, as if by some magic force. Did they know her? He could not be certain, for the shadows were deep and her mismatched eyes glittered from the stage like distant stars.

"Never in my life . . ." Davos murmured, wiping a tear with a strand of his beard. "Who . . . who is she?"

Demacharon seized upon the question. "She is with me. And she needs to get out of this kingdom."

"Well, why didn't you say so before? A girl of such talent is worth the extra trip! We'll leave by the morrow."

The Princess of Tyrnael descended from the stage to the clamor of approval and adoration. The audience members were so busy bringing their hands together and bowing to the princess—some actually reaching out to touch her arm or shoulder, that no one noticed the preternatural transformation in the space until she and her protector were long gone from the theater—a small parting gift that would capture the imagination of the people for decades to come.

Every flower on every table was in full bloom.

10

Bastion

His name was Bastion, but everyone called him *The Bard*. Bastion went about his days peacefully, unencumbered by anxiety or doubt. And yet, he could not explain the alien emotion building inside of him, causing the hairs on his arms to stand and his neck to sweat. Never in his one hundred and twenty years had he known true fear, not until that morning, when soldiers burst into the theater, rearranging chairs and tables, tearing down curtains, shattering props. Their black burnished armor, emblazoned with a fist and morningstar, had taught him the meaning of dread. Who were they? And where were the protectors of the realm, the knights in gold and white, who wore the sigil of the bucking unicorn, among whom he could count his son? These other soldiers refused to answer his questions, and at last, he was forced, needlessly at the point of a sword, into a small room to be questioned.

This is a mere formality, he told himself, taking small comfort in that he was permitted to keep his bouzouki on his person. But the stringed instrument echoed terribly in the confined, hard space, and his trembling fingers were unable to find a tune. A city built upon ruins was one of vacant rooms and lonely passages, and now here he sat on an empty cask, with little else to do but stare at the door ahead. Long-ago emptied wine racks lined the walls, enough for hundreds of bottles—it was a shame, because a swig of fermented grape would have greatly settled his nerves.

The door opened with sudden force and Bastion found himself standing as if preparing to run from a predator. A shadowy figure stooped under the lintel, the dim lamplight painting a monster before his eyes, a blood-red hulking thing, with narrow points of iron gouging lines through the brittle walls on either side of him. Bastion clutched his heart as if to catch it from leaping out, only moments later recognizing the iron face for a mask, but the revelation offered little comfort. What kind of man would choose to don such armor, in the heat, at peacetime? He might have been an actor, playing the role of the Dark God, but his costume would never be practical. The horns alone were as long and sharp as pikes, and just as likely to kill.

"Be at ease," the man said, laying his helmet between them. "And sit down."

Bastion did as he was told, holding fast to the small table in front of him, for use as a barrier. "For what do I owe the honor of your visit, my lord?"

"The honor is greater than your knowing," he replied. "I am Zaibos, son of Anabis, King of Tyrnael."

"You . . ." Bastion could not believe what he was hearing. "*You* are the prince?"

"I am your king!" he growled.

Bastion's unspoken fear took a sudden form. The man across from him exuded power. His voice alone rattled the spine, and his eyes were dead and terrible, like a fish after it has been caught and is gasping for life. "K-King Zaibos," he squealed, bowing his head against the table, then falling clumsily to the floor. "Forgive me my ignorance, if I had but known—"

"Quit your quailing, and return to your seat!"

Zaibos was the elder, but only the adopted son of Solon. The throne was not his to take, unless some awful fate was to befall the princess. "my lord, your good sister, has she—"

"Humble yourself, bard! I ask the questions and you answer! Understood?"

Zaibos's unwillingness to speak of Radia confirmed Bastion's worst imaginings. If she were merely lost or had relapsed into sickness, why not speak of it? "Naturally, my lord. I am yours, here to serve you. If there is anything you wish—"

"A great number of people gathered here today—performers and . . . singers."

"Yes, indeed, my lord. *The Festival of Ages* is taking place as we speak. A celebration of diverse cultures held but once a year, when outsiders arrive—"

"You take part in these festivities?"

"I am but a simple minstrel, my lord. I play the bouzouki. Would you like to hear it?"

"I would not have my time wasted. Music is a useless talent."

Hearing his life's work insulted in such a manner, Bastion found a measure of courage and grew bold. "Useless, my lord? I beg your pardon, but I think not. Music is in us all. It speaks to the soul, inspires us to dream. To hope."

His heart drummed as the silence between them grew heavy and thickened with dread. He expected Zaibos to strike him, but the man who called himself king did not rise in anger. "So I have heard. The whole of the city is abuzz with rumors, of a beautiful singer, who causes grown men to weep."

"Ah, I see!" Things were beginning to make sense now, for the eloai girl was a wonder to hear. Doubtless, the Compass Tower wished to have her voice at court, perhaps to sing before the princess. "For one hundred years I have practiced my craft, carried melodies for singers in the thousands, but never with anyone so fair! She sings with the voice of the goddess, she does!"

"Her voice does not concern me. Did you notice anything else? Something particular about her?"

"Particular, my lord?"

"Her eyes, you fool. Did you see her eyes?"

"In truth, I remember not."

Zaibos stood, a terrible noise issuing from his armor, from the plates at his knees and elbows. "You wish to deceive your king?"

He cringed, hiding his face behind his hands. "I beg your mercy, my lord. I do not recall—"

"The most beautiful girl in the world stands beside you, and yet you do not recall her face?"

"The theater was dark, and my eyes are not what they used to be."

The wooden legs of the table, scraping across the stone as Zaibos shoved it aside, made a terrible sound. Now nothing separated him from the monster. He moved away, his spine hard against the wine rack, and reached for his instrument. Perhaps it could protect him in some way, inspire pity in his assailer.

Zaibos spoke again, but without anger. "So you do not know who it was in your theater last night?"

"I know only what she told me. She is an eloai, named Noora."

"Stand up! Stand and take your instrument. If what you say is true," he said, "you are free to depart."

The bard stood warily, clutching the bouzouki's round belly against his own. "My lord, I was honored by your visit, and by your grace take my leave." He turned to face him, king or monster or prince, bowing repeatedly as he backed through the doorway.

"Wait."

"My lord?"

Zaibos did not answer. Instead, he replaced his helm, and called loudly, "Captain Mandos!"

A man entered the room, a knight whose cuirass and pauldrons were of burnt, blackened steel, the crest of the fist and morningstar etched across the breast. "My King?"

"Have you questioned the witnesses?"

"I have, my lord. The singer was dressed as an eloai, but some recall her as having peculiar eyes, each of a different color. Some claim it was the princess, Sire."

"Radia!" Bastion gasped, unable to hide his delight, knowing that he had stood, albeit unknowingly, in her presence. "The Princess of Tyrnael was here! She sang for us! If I had but known—"

"There is more," Mandos said. "A fair number swear that some enchantment befell them. I find their testimony dubious, but they claim that the flowers themselves turned to hear the girl, as though she were the sun itself."

Bastion winced as Zaibos's mailed fist dropped upon his bony shoulder. "So, this girl was not who you claimed. And now your deception has been exposed. Do you know the penalty for treason in my kingdom, bard?"

Bastion wanted to protest, to plead for innocence, and he could feel his lips move, but no sound would come forth.

"Seize his instrument."

Mandos tore the bouzouki from his arms, and in that moment of resistance, his fingers played awkwardly across the chords, making an awful tune. That sound, that tune, would haunt him until his last day. But all that he now knew was that he had been intimidated, insulted and robbed, and his fear turned to fury. "How dare you! My father gave that to me, as his father to him. You cannot have it."

"I did not say that I wanted it." With a single swipe of his gauntlet, Zaibos split the stringed instrument asunder, and it fell from Mandos's grasp in splinters. Zaibos then commanded the captain to retrieve the table, and to lay the bard's hands upon it.

"My lord, might I interject?" Bastion detected a quiver in Mandos's voice, a hesitation, but he pressed on. "It is quite possible that the bard is being truthful. Only a handful of the people I spoke with noticed the girl's eyes, and fewer still claim it was the princess."

The mask was incapable of movement or a change in expression, but somehow Bastion knew that under his helmet, the self-appointed king wore the same, perpetual scowl. He could see the truth of it, for Zaibos's true face was not the one of flesh and blood beneath, but the outer visage of iron. In his years as a minstrel, traveling between the outlying kingdoms, Bastion had met with such men, if only briefly—men incapable of compassion, whose hearts were black and soulless and deaf to the music of the gods.

"Captain, I did not ask your opinion."

"No, you did not, my lord."

"Question my commands again, and I will find some new use for you, understood?"

"I do, my lord."

As the morningstar was brought into the room by another soldier, the captain pressed the bard's hands down against the table. All the while, Bastion could see the turmoil in his eyes. "You're no wicked man," he told him, "so do not be afraid. You will find your path in the netherworld."

Mandos gazed hard at him. "Don't waste your breath, old man. It won't make things any better for you. Now move from that chair and the king will have your head."

Zaibos took up the morningstar, palming the ball of spikes in his mailed palm. "And now I will teach you the folly of music, for it is a weakness, a thing for women and birds, not men. The only instrument a man need know is that of his weapon. The only chord a man needs strike is that of his enemy's throat."

Bastion did not cry out, but by the time the pain came lurching into his brain, his hands were no longer recognizable, a shapeless mass of tissue and blood. His once nimble fingers, which could move with such skill and conjure such beauty, were twisted at every wrong angle, the bones protruding through the flesh broken and shattered. Pain could be endured, Bastion knew, but seeing the mangled mess beyond his wrists, all courage and pride went from him, and he whimpered, again and again, "How will I play? How will I play now?"

"Do you see, Captain? This man dared to contest me and was given a lesson. From great suffering comes strength. Remember that, Captain."

With the aid of another soldier, Mandos carried the bard tenderly from the room. What Bastion remembered from later that day was a haze. Blood was pooling from the pulverized ends of his arms, making his head light, mercifully dulling the pain.

Like a corpse, he was brought into the street. It seemed that all Tyrnael was gathered there, circling a great fire, but what was being devoured he could not make out. People marshaled to his aid, lamenting the man they knew and the music they would never again hear. The Zo, in their time, might have restored him, but their wisdom was lost to the ages. Their healers could but lend loose garments, scarves, and belts, to staunch the blood, and offer balms from the aloe tree.

Across from the theater, a newly-erected scaffolding stood, flanked by soldiers. Bastion looked for his son among their ranks, but could not make out their faces. The fist and morningstar was upon their hearts, and was flown from their sarissas, and from every rooftop. Only Orson he recognized, who stood on the platform over the gathering. He was known for speaking to large crowds and was now clearing his throat, preparing to read from a scroll he held in his quailing hands.

"King Zaibos, son of Anabis, Sovereign of Tyrnael, does decree the following: The Cosmos Theater is hereby closed. Music, singing, dancing, as well as any general celebratory action, are hereby outlawed. Ahem. Secondly, all standards, symbols or sigils of the bucking unicorn are hereby abolished—anyone found displaying or aiding in the display of any such emblem intended to represent or that may be interpreted to represent the old regime, which henceforth shall remain unnamed, will be found guilty of sedition and forthwith meet their end. Thirdly, anyone harboring, willingly or unwillingly, the traitor known as Radia, also known as Noora, or harboring knowledge of the whereabouts thereof . . ."

From the scaffolding, Zaibos watched, never stirring. The king was a golem of iron, and made no appeal to win the people's hearts, nor any attempt at persuasion or deception. Fear was an all-encompassing palpable reality, the like Tyrnael had never known. As he watched the mass of stunted faces, Bastion grew angry, despite the agony in his limbs and the weakness in his head. He listened for any voice of protest among the silent, but when it came, he was at once filled with remorse.

The girl could not have been more than six, and her tantrum sounded above the roaring flames. Her mother's eyes went wide with terror, as she bent to shush her child, urging her to let go of the banner the girl clung to. Between them and the fire stood a soldier. Bastion watched him turn to face the pair, begin to move towards them. It could have gone in a bad way. Mother and daughter could have been made into an example. But the boy in the blackened mail was gentle, easing the tasseled hem from the little girl's palms. And as the last banner fell upon the flames, the girl stayed to look, as the gold-embroidered unicorn shriveled and turned to ash.

11

Davos

The city slept blanketed by the turquoise moon. Blue-green light limned every walkway and light post. Windowed walls formed narrow alleyways, with wooden frame trusses crossing between, laden with doves and laundry. Chimneys could be seen rising from vaulted rooftops, drawing swirling gray shapes upon a starlit canvas. Noora could not resist peering through the multicolored panes of glass into each home, fascinated by every little thing, from the food on the tables to the brass chamber pots, from tapestries to blazing hearths. But with every step, she envied her companions' footwear. The sun had disappeared and frost glazed the streets, and icy water sloshed in the spaces between the cobblestones. Eloai did not wear shoes because they did not go out after eclipse, and the night seemed colder than when she had slept blissfully on the grass without a thread of covering. With inflated pride, Ecthros had offered his green cloak, but it did little to fend off the weather.

If she could only huddle by the hearth not two steps from her eyes, but Demacharon would not hear of it. He insisted they keep to the streets—it was not a proper thing to knock on strange doors in the dead of night. One more taboo to add to the list. First, she had to wear clothes, and now they could not seek shelter from her subjects, despite that she and their fellowship and the families in every household were of the same human family, and more so, fellow living beings. Why was Demacharon so blind? But it was not only him. The nature of existence remained invisible to most, especially to people like her brother. From the smallest sapling to the greatest wakefin, everything to draw breath was of a singular essence, like a flower that only she could see.

"No time for daydreams, Noora," Demacharon urged, as the fat man and his skinny friend followed, stealing from shadow to shadow. "Hurry along."

Noora. Right. I have to think of myself as Noora now. She held tightly to the circular clasp fastening her cloak, stumbling over numb feet. "You are still angry with me. I can feel it."

"Angry? How could I be?"

"Oh." She mulled over his reply, adding, "You are being sarcastic again, am I right?"

He rounded on her forcefully. "Ra—! Noora . . . do you have any idea what could have happened? Because of what you did?"

"Someone could have seen me, I know. So what? Perhaps I wish they had. No more hiding. I am their true heir. We cannot outrun the truth forever."

"It was not the proper time!" He pulled her behind a wain of casks. Further on, the street broadened into an open square. "Besides, I specifically told you to do nothing that might draw attention. What you did was the exact opposite."

"Oh, Dimmy, have you never had the impulse to do something out of the ordinary? To dance in the rain or chase rabbits round a copse?"

He squeezed her wrist until it hurt. "No."

"Then you've forgotten what it is to be alive." She freed her arm from his grasp. "You simply can't go suppressing such things or you'll die inside. It happens slowly and you may not feel it until it's too late, but a man can walk and talk, yet be dead to the world. Maybe it's happened to you already. Maybe that's why you're such a miserable old codger."

"Misery is not my concern. If you want to go on singing in the days to come—if you want my protection—you'll set aside such childish notions. Good men have given their lives for you, and because of your foolishness, more innocents will likely die that could have been spared."

"I . . . I didn't think." Noora could feel the tears rushing behind her eyes, but held back, lest she be thought a child.

"Exactly. You never think."

"Now you're being mean." She bundled Ecthros's cloak in her palm, patting the wetness from her eyes. "Don't do that, Dimmy. You must do as I command, remember? And I am commanding you to be nice to me from now on."

"That," he turned to face her directly, "is an impossible request!"

Ecthros was scowling now, as was Davos, who was looking over his nephew's shoulder. "Hold up, commander! I think it's time we had a say in all this, eh?"

"Enlighten us."

"Well, I just think . . ." Ecthros swallowed hard. "I agree with her. You could be a little gentler. And who's to say what harm will come of her singing? Eloai or no, you can't treat people this way."

Davos pulled him aside. "Get your cock out your brain, lad. This here's no servant! I knew it from the start who she was. Wouldn't have agreed to help you both if I didn't. Never you fear, though—I've loved this girl since I sat on my father's knee, rapt by the old man's story."

It was evident by the look on his face that Ecthros did know of the myth of the ailing princess, and looked on perplexed, until Davos leaned into his ear. "You mean to say—" he started, the whites growing about his green irises, "that this here's the pri—" Davos jabbed him in the gut, "—vate escort, eh? Wow. That's really something."

Despite their show of devotion, Demacharon grew tense. "Don't be afraid," she said to him. "These are good men. I feel the goodness in their hearts."

"Before the order of your execution came to pass, did you pry into your brother's heart also? Or those of the praetorians sworn to protect you?"

"That was different! I was naïve then. There happened to be a darkness I could not perceive. Or did not wish to," she added softly.

"So there's the rub," Davos cut in. "Zaibos has instigated a coup, which is why we've been running about half the night keeping to ourselves."

Demacharon studied the man's round cheeks and reddish beard and small glittering eyes. Trust seemed a rare commodity in such times and he was disinclined to give it. "If you must know, the Knights of Tyrnael have changed allegiances and become traitors to the princess—the whole lot of them. Our only chance is to get out of the city. Which is why I came to you."

"Port is two blocks over," Davos assured him, "and the *Cloud Breaker* and all her crew will be expecting us. Just wait until you lay eyes on her, Hedonian. She's a majestic sight! By morning, the princess will be out of harm's reach."

"No!" Noora assumed her most regal posture, but shivering in Ecthros's overlong cloak, she felt she must look less the ruler and more a damsel of fifteen. "You told me nothing of this! I cannot flee from my people and leave them to that—that monster. I belong here, where I can do the most good."

"If you remain here," he said, "you die here. Zaibos is as resourceful as he is ruthless. He will give no respite, show no mercy, nor lay down his arms until you become an example. Once you're gone, none will dare to oppose him. For his plans to come to fruition, the dynasty founded by the Zo must end with your demise."

She stared, one by one, into the wells of their faces. Who were these men? Strangers all, she thought, becoming acutely aware of her father's absence, wishing for his familiar voice and counsel. To abandon the city would be to abandon the one person she could truly call a friend. "I must go back. For Larissa."

And she fled.

"Stop!" Demacharon called out to her, but she did not heed him. "We've come too far, Noora! You'll never find her!"

"I can tie her up in a net if you think it best," she heard Davos say, as the three of them pursued, with Demacharon adding, before she could escape earshot, "There's nowhere for her to go. She'll tire and she'll think."

Noora crossed from house to house, a fire burning in her bosom. She had lost so much in so little time. Her father. Her throne. She could not endure losing her only friend. Even at such a distance, she might feel some dim beacon of Larissa. Moving blindly through open courtyards, rounding fountains, pushing past hanging signs, her heart spread across the city in search of the one she cared for most, and on she followed, into unfamiliar moonlit passageways.

At last, there came a feeling of familiarity, of greeting a loved one after a prolonged absence. Larissa was near. Noora could feel her presence, emanating from a great cloud of pain and sorrow. Never had she sensed such emotions in her servant and it made her rush forward all the faster.

"Radia!"

Larissa was calling from an alley. But she was drained, her voice dredged from the depths of the lungs, weighed by a thing Noora did not at first recognize.

Fear.

The eloai's familiar silhouette took form as Noora rounded the corner. But it seemed odd that her childhood playmate was not running to greet her, was not moving in the least, but merely stood amid the passage, waiting. Moving closer, Noora could see the strange way in which the body was positioned, the arms and legs stretched apart like the limbs of an insect caught in a spider's web.

"H-He made me cry out..." Hints of blood colored Larissa's lips and the rims of her eyes, and the moon shone on the tears accenting her cheek. "Go," she urged.

"Larissa! What's happened to you?"

Breathing hard, the eloai pleaded, more forcefully than before, "Get out of here! He's close by. He wants you!"

Noora heard the warning but could not bring herself to leave. Dread seized her with every step, noticing how Larissa was suspended. At certain angles, caught by the moon's light, the strands became visible, gleaming about her wrists and ankles.

"I have to get you down from there."

"Don't!" She made a slight gesture with her arm, and it cut into her flesh, drawing lines of fresh blood from palm to elbow. "I can't be moved." There were many more gashes, Noora could see, from earlier attempts.

"Who did this to you?"

No answer came.

A red puddle formed beneath Larissa's feet, and there, Noora saw the box. It was meticulously crafted in cherrywood and alabaster, a treasure worthy of her bower, but undoing the latch, she found it empty and featureless, but for the two round holes set into its recess, where grapes might be fitted, or things of like proportion, and a hollow at its center large enough for her fist.

Demacharon arrived at that moment, pulling Noora down as the wall next to their ears erupted. Debris was in her hair, whitening her fingertips, clouding the air. She could see the cracked and cratered mortar and the dull gray orbs embedded in the wall. The attack was meant for her. If her protector had not come when he had, she might have been finished.

Already, her Hedonian protector's gladius was drawn. Davos stood at his side, wielding a ludicrous weapon between his sausage-like fingers, a sword so broad it could double as a shield, with a point curved like a spoon. Third in line, Ecthros crouched defensively, taking aim against imagined threats with the miniature crossbows fitted to his wrists. But there was little room to maneuver and too many places for the killer—or was it killers—to hide: an open window, a shadowy alcove, any one of the trusses above. Death could come from any direction, but only a pervasive silence filled the alley, and they waited.

"Assassins," Demacharon shouted, "show yourselves if you would die honorably!"

"Aye!" Ecthros joined in. "We don't fear you!"

Despite the boy's assertions, she could easily sense that Ecthros's emotions neared panic. His terror wrapped itself around her, blinding her as though she were staring into the sun. Yet, she also felt compelled to act—she could not allow them to die for her, not as she had let the guards fall in the Compass Tower.

Climbing to her feet, a rush of air sounded from the rooftops, followed by a metallic echo. Demacharon had been swift, calculating the direction and moving in time, so that his sword took the place where his heart had been. The iridium ball cut a hole through the bronze blade but lacked the force to punch through the adjacent wall, thudding against the cobblestones to roll under Noora's eyes.

"He's on the roof!" he cried, and turning to the others, ordered, "Stay with the girl!"

Davos moved without hesitation and fell on top of her, losing his hat. She could feel his enormous gut, pinning her to the ground, offering a measure of security with a great dose of awkwardness, during which time Ecthros, seized by youthful passion, began to shout, "By my life, no harm will come to you, princess!" He then abandoned her to follow Demacharon.

The aged commander moved deliberately, his body flush against the wall, his eyes fixed on the balustrade overhead. The boy was faster but reckless, leaping between windowsills.

"Get back here, you damn fool!" Davos said in a loud, hushed voice. "You'll get yourself killed!"

"I can do it!" the boy called down. "I've been preparing for this moment for my entire life." As Ecthros clamored over adjoining rooftops, breaking shingles against the stone railings below, a flock of frightened pigeons took to the moonlit sky, casting winged shadows across the alley. Startled, the eager young warrior spun like a top with his arms outstretched, crying out, "Tornado shot!" Crossbows sprang, buzzing from his wrists, sending quarrels everywhere and nowhere.

Davos, still lying over the princess, could see nothing but the street. Concerned for his nephew, he lifted his neck for a better look and a roll of fat knocked her chin into the stones. She shouted, and he backed into the wall, begging for pardon. Glad to be free of him, she managed to regain footing, when his ruddy cheeks started to turn white. With a sudden jerking motion, his hand flew to his neck, and Davos started to scream. Noora could sense the intense needling pain, but she was much more attune to his fear and confusion, his helplessness.

"What's happening? How can I help you?"

He was nearing paralysis, rocking in agony along the ground. "My back!" he managed between clenched teeth. "Get it off! Something in . . . my back!"

It had the appearance of a white pearl just beneath his skin, a welt made by the thing biting him, scurrying down his exposed neck until it disappeared under his armor where she could not get to it. To watch a man suffer, and do nothing, was beyond her capacity. Compassion demanded that she tend to him.

Though the assassin remained ever-present in her mind, she did not sense him, nor the silver blade in his palm, cutting through the skin and tissue and windpipe until Larissa's anguish caused Noora to turn and see her friend opening her mouth to shout, to warn of the danger. Only red came gushing from her lips—blood in place of words. Despite this, Larissa's inner thoughts conveyed to Noora, at that moment, that she did not lament dying, having been a loyal friend, but that now was the time for the princess to run, to run away as fast as her legs could carry her. It was a powerful mix of love and fear louder than any scream, loud enough to turn Noora to face the blade poised to enter her spine, to cause her to flee as the killer advanced. And as she fled, Demacharon was on him, gladius flashing, repelling the long dagger. Gradually, he forced the assassin back along the corridor, toward the body of Larissa. From a distance, Noora watched them with fascination, but could not keep her eyes from drifting to the horror suspended beyond. Hoping beyond hope that there may still be some life in her friend, she burst into a run, but Ecthros came into her path. Twisting free of him, Noora made for the combatants and the wire mesh, until Davos caught up with her, snatching her up like a toddler. His arms pressed painfully into her ribs, but he suffered the more. She could still feel his agony, the numbness in his bones.

"Your friend is gone," he murmured. "Won't do no good chasing after her."

She did not need to see it to know. Larissa's emotions were no longer—there was only a void, a great gnawing emptiness. The shock radiated through her nervous system, until her very fingertips ached with the thousand-thousand days and infinite might-have-beens that could never be, robbed from her in an instant. If only for that instant, she knew what it meant to hate and to desire harm in others.

Larissa.

She sobbed in Davos's arms, repeating the name again and again and again. It sounded over the rooftops, rousing neighbors from their beds, and those who slumbered deeply dreamed of dark and mournful places.

Ahead of them, swords resounded, where Demacharon engaged the assassin.

"We should help him," Ecthros remarked.

"If only we could, lad," Davos answered, "but this girl is bound to go and do something stupid. But don't you worry none. If our Hedonian friend isn't up to the task, you'll get your chance. I say, our assassin couldn't have picked a better trap. Too damn narrow for three of us to fight, otherwise I'd give him what for!"

"Right." Without another word, Ecthros took up an arrow from the quiver at his hip and was off. Noora watched him go out from whence they came, but her attention was immediately drawn to the duel not ten paces away. Of those faithful to her, of those she could call friend, only Demacharon remained. Could she suffer to lose him also?

"Villain!"

"Insults will not avail you," the assassin replied. "You waste your breath."

Demacharon's gladius flew wide, shattering a potted plant, showering them in soil and ceramic. "I've killed men like you by the score! Better men! Stronger men!"

"There are no men like me," he answered, lunging forward like a serpent and retracting, expanding the distance between them.

"You think to escape me!" Demacharon cried. "To cut our throats in our sleep?"

"Rest assured I am here for the princess. I am not being compensated for your lives but will take them if you hinder me."

One man would give his life to save her or die in an attempt to murder her, but Noora understood that every life was deserving of compassion. Even the death of her childhood friend could not sever that connection.

They battled down the alley, their blades becoming shadows in the hands of giants, until she could only hear the ringing of their arms, every clash resonating in her heart. Fear, much to her surprise, gave way to hot-blooded fury, and the thrill of battle. She could feel the intensity between them, and she was ever more alive because of it.

The assassin pulled a second dagger and Demacharon's eyes filled with blood, flowing from a gash in his forehead. She only knew this because she could feel the stinging and burning on her own brow. Her champion was blinded, enough for the other to break from combat, to cut a path through the razor mesh. Larissa's body slumped to the ground, freed of her deadly bonds at last, allowing her killer to flee.

Demacharon gave chase, to the end of the alleyway and out into an open courtyard. The assassin pivoted, arm wide, hand clutching a sling. Dusk had yet to fall, and the turquoise moon bathing the city only hinted at the deadly contours speeding toward him. The first missile broke through the trunk of a cherry tree, littering a fountain with leaves. The second vanished into the night. But the third found its mark, knocking the gladius from his hand and punching into his rib.

Methodically, the assassin walked toward him. "Whoever said I was escaping? I intend to do my job. Tonight, if possible."

"Have you no honor?"

"Honor? I know not of honor. I was born without it, you see, for I am an abomination." He freed his dagger, making a deadly noise. It caught the moon's glow, illuminating the Zo runes etched onto its surface. "There is one law in this world, Hedonian, one ethic, one code—kill or be killed. Do you see the writing on the blade? Do you want to know what it says? I will tell you, as I've told all my victims, 'There is one god and he is Death!'"

Demacharon fell silent, not with fear but contemplation, until the silence was broken with his pitying laughter.

"Why do you laugh when you know that death is imminent?"

"Your so-called code . . . do you imagine you are the first to spout such drivel? I might have said as much in my youth. Kill me and take what pleasure you can, for you do not know the place that awaits you. That awaits all men like us. I have seen it, assassin, and it is to be feared far beyond death, beyond what mortal men can imagine. Go on, if you will, and free me from this burden of living. I will wait for you, as those below wait for me."

There must have been something in his tone, a sincerity, a gravity to the words to give the assassin pause. But it was short-lived. As the blade came down, Demacharon tugged at the hilt at his hip, and Severetrix rounded in a flash, singing a high note. The assassin stumbled away, holding the bottom half of his halved dagger, and before he could reach for another of his death-dealing tools, an arrow clacked behind him. He turned to the young archer at the opposite end of the courtyard as two more arrows climbed into the air, but none hit their mark. By the time Ecthros nocked his fourth arrow, the assassin was nowhere to be found.

"Who taught you to shoot? A blind man?"

"Well," Ecthros said, panting, "my father did. Xenox. He was the greatest archer in the world! Me, er, not so much."

"You'll learn."

The boy lent the Hedonian his arm. "You're hurt!"

"It's nothing." He dug three fingers into his body, with only a wince, and the ball dropped to the ground, slick and red with his blood. "Like pulling out an arrow . . . a big fat arrow."

With her praetorian out of harm, Noora turned to the shadowy spot, her feet becoming wet and red as she approached the body. Blood bubbled from the opening in the neck and pooled behind the head, turning the half of Larissa's peplos crimson. Noora caressed her maidservant's ankle, thinking of all the times Larissa had washed her own feet. Had Radia been a worthy friend? Had she shown her eloai adequate compassion?

"My dearest Larissa. I am so very sorry."

Demacharon was standing over her, nursing the wound in his side. She could feel his disappointment. "Do you see now? Do you see why we cannot stay here? Every moment you remain in Tyrnael, we endanger its people."

"But . . ." Noora wiped her eyes and he came into focus. Running felt like surrender. These were her people and Zaibos was stealing them away. Her heart was against it, but she understood his wisdom. Either way, she dared not disagree with her protectors, not now, not when so much life was at stake. Slowly, she nodded, offering a hand.

Davos soon joined them, having found and replaced his spinner hat. "It was a spider, damn you! Shook it out of my pant leg!"

Ecthros cringed. "Blimey, that assassin's got some nasty tricks. Next time I'll stick an arrow in his ass. Oh, begging your pardon, princess."

"No one is to call her that, ever," Demacharon said. "When you think her name, you think Noora, got it? Now, daylight is almost upon us, so we'd best hurry."

Noora stood but did not move. "What of Larissa? We can't just leave her."

"There is no time."

"She deserves better than this!"

"Yes," Demacharon said, his voice momentarily soft. "But we don't all get what we deserve."

Ecthros lifted his cloak, from the spot where Noora had left it, draping the body in green. "We can do this one thing, at least."

It was the last she would see of Larissa, for the alley was growing warm with light, and shouts of command could be heard some distance away.

12

Krow

It was a cold sunrise. Morning light broke in patches of yellow and gold from behind a wall of iron-gray clouds. By the time they were gone from the alley, a cold drizzle was glazing the streets. Demacharon could not remember such weather in Tyrnael. It seemed to come suddenly and from nowhere.

They moved in silence, distancing themselves from the patrols, from the din of armor and shouts of "I think they went this way!" After a passing, the high-walled neighborhood became unrecognizable and Demacharon could see the city for what it was. The towering geometric hills built millennia before had been, in recent centuries, repurposed for housing.

Tyrnael stood upon the remains of an older city, as that city overlaid the grave of still another. It was the peak of a hill, atop which dead and forgotten civilizations were buried, as someday, those now living would go unremembered. Evidence of long-extinct peoples could be found everywhere, if one cared to look. The world's oldest thriving city was a hodgepodge of anachronisms. Streets were repaved countless times, the occasional hole exposing the layers, and walls rebuilt with newer materials and kerosene lamps, and shingles added to rooftops where open courtyards once stood. Newer doors enclosed ancient archways, and windowsills supported by fresh mortar contrasted with the mossy, tired stone beneath. And somehow, despite the passing of aeons, a single chain remained unbroken, linking the unfathomable past to the age in which they lived. The last link in that chain was a fifteen-year-old girl forced to flee from her people, with three strangers bound by a common purpose to protect her.

Did they see in her what he had? Did they harbor the same torments in their dreams? Demacharon could only guess at his newfound companions' motivations, as well as the assassin's. He had been waiting for Radia in the alley, yet how could he have known, unless his captive, Larissa, had been forced to divulge her mistress's secret. Using Noora's ability to feel pain, the assassin could lure her anywhere, into a trap Demacharon could not prepare for. All the more reason to run, far and away, to where people could not exploit her. He had not wanted to deceive her, but she would not have agreed to go willingly. In the hands of Zaibos, Tyrnael could very well fall to chaos and ruin. Even if it were the last bastion of the Zo, a land fabled for peace and immortality and light, and very much worth fighting for, his allegiance was to her alone, for she was more important than anyone could know, more than she herself imagined.

"How much further?" Demacharon asked.

Despite his belt size, which could loop around the three of them, Davos moved tirelessly and with surprising speed, not slowing even to answer. "Nearly there! Don't you worry. See the calamari?"

"Damn," Ecthros remarked, "now I'm hungry."

"You're always hungry, nephew—*Maelstrom Mouth*, they ought to call you!"

Boulders in the tens of thousands served to hold back the river. The sound of rushing, crashing water reminded him of the *Coast of Sarnath*, where Demacharon would stroll with his wife to watch the Sea, and where he had found his son, murdered.

Tents had been erected all along the promenade, their wooden frames painted in rich blues, fresh squid set to dry across their tops. But the wicker chairs stood empty in towering stacks. The sun was still breaking like an egg yolk across the horizon, and only the early morning fishmonger was about with his creel of fish, which was sure to remain fresh in the unexpected chill. The scent of spices made Demacharon's stomach protest. For how long had they gone without a proper meal?

Passing the tavernas, they came to a stony bulwark, which dropped a short way into a crop of rocks at the river's edge. Bobbing and groaning against their moorings were vessels of every kind, from dinghies no longer than a man is tall to fifty-oared longboats. The river was more violent than the Sea he knew, and the sun colored the water in murky browns and greens that turned to foamy white where it pummeled the rock.

"Which one is yours?" Demacharon asked.

"You take me for a fisherman, do you? I'm a trader by trade! Come on, you'll see!"

They followed the water's course, where sails became indistinct from clouds, and masts overlapped to clutter the sky. Southward, the river expanded, changing to gold as it followed the horizon to meet the sun.

"You there! Halt!"

Had his lack of sleep and food enabled the soldiers to approach without his notice? Their armor was blackened steel, and a morningstar was carved into their breastplates. Demacharon stood motionless before the two men, shielding his eyes from the glare, awaiting their accusations.

"Where are you four headed in such a hurry?"

Before he could respond, Davos leapt in front, the blood rushing to his cheeks. "And what business is it of yours? Can't a man be free to go about where he pleases in this kingdom?" It was distraction enough that they did not study the girl in their midst, who was hiding behind her satchel.

"I'd watch that tone of yours. You speak to the king's men!"

"The king! Bah!" He spat on their greaves. "I recognize no king. There is but one proper ruler in Tyrnael, and that be the Princess Radia, may the gods watch over her and bless her."

With his eyes on Davos, Demacharon fingered the hilt at his side. He did not want this fight. Not now. Not here. It could only draw attention. But if forced, it would end quickly.

"Haven't you heard?" the second soldier replied, who sounded younger and timid. "There's been a coup. Talk like that is bound to get you killed, foreigner or not."

"Well, then," Davos replied, brandishing his belly like a mace, "if that's the case, you'll no more see the likes of me! I'll take my wares elsewhere! Never to be back! Come, crew," he urged, motioning with his mitten of a hand, "let's find us some better place to set up shop."

"Wait." The first soldier pushed back, as the other drew his sword. "Who's that girl? Tell her to come forward."

Demacharon tightened his grip. Severetrix could take both their heads in a single swipe, but it would mean breaking his oath to the princess.

"That girl?" Davos repeated. "She's my niece, from my hometown in Yefira, if you must know. Begged me to take her on a trip, she did, to see the fabled city. I'm afraid she found it a bit of a letdown, with all you people running about asking stupid questions."

The first soldier freed his sword, poking Davos in the belly. "I'll have a look anyway. Bring her forward."

Demacharon's eyes burned through the gorgets covering their necks. They intended to draw blood, but seeing the princess would make them hesitate, if only for an instant. *And then they'll be dead.* Suddenly, Noora's hand was on his, holding him back.

"No." It was her first word since leaving the alley. Sickened with mourning, her face was ashen. "There will be no more killing this day. I won't allow it."

Noora lifted her gaze to meet the soldiers' eyes. "I am the one you seek. I am True North, Radia, daughter of Solon, fifty-fourth descendant of the Zo, Princess of Aenya. You obey my brother because you fear him. I can feel it in you. But should you do his bidding, should you bring me to him, the act will follow you. It will follow you all the rest of your days, for you know his cruelty, and what he means to do to me. Obey what is in your hearts. Stand aside and let me go my own way."

His helmet removed, the soldier looked to be young, but his face was deeply lined. For a long while, he stared at her, and at them, with anguish. Demacharon studied him like a predator its prey, his palms growing wetter, his heart seeming to beat once, and after a moment, again.

The soldier fell to his knees, thrusting his sword into the ground, and with some hesitation, his companion did also.

"Your Grace, forgive us."

"Join us." She reached out to him, her hand small and delicate, like a porcelain doll's hand beside his mailed glove. "Swear fealty to me."

"W-We cannot, your Grace. I have a wife and a boy of three. And this," he said, turning to the second soldier, "is my only brother."

"Then," she said, "tell no one of this."

"Your Grace." He stood, donning his helmet in a rush. "More men are coming. Zaibos knows you are here. Go! And may Sargonus speed you with a mighty wind."

Did anyone see them? Merchants, or fishermen? Would the soldiers be betrayed? His sudden concern for the two men, whom he was prepared to slaughter only moments ago, surprised him.

"How did you know they would let us go?" he asked Noora.

"Easy," she replied. "If given a chance, people are generally good."

"I wish I could believe that."

"I know you do."

The *Cloud Breaker* was of mixed design, not as sleek or elegant as a warship, nor as bulky as a merchant galley. A single skeletal frame formed the hull and keel, like the ribs of a wakefin, with curving beams of cedar stretching from bow to stern.

"Krow!" Davos shouted. "It's me, Krow—lower the gangplank!"

The creature peering over the gunwale gave Demacharon pause, for he was not human, and there was a history between his people and theirs. Though as narrow in the shoulder as Noora, the avian stood taller than Ecthros. Short black feathers covered him, and black, glittering eyes the size of lemons bulged from between his cheekbones and long, hooked nose. Avians were not known to wear clothing, but for minor ornaments wrought of gold and silver, but this one wore a green shirt and a red scarf about the head. Known also as bird men, avians could fly, catching the air in feathery membranes that extended from their wrists and ankles, but Krow's body exhibited only the frayed ends of wings. The bits of exposed flesh and torn feathers reminded Demacharon of a soldier who has lost his arms.

Davos boarded first, leading Noora, and the others followed. She approached the avian immediately, staring with the wonder of a small child, despite her weakened state.

"I've never seen anyone like you before."

"This here's my first mate," Davos explained. "Krow, Noora. Noora, Krow."

He extended a slender palm, touching her lightly on the shoulder. "I am honored, Noora." His voice was multifaceted, deep yet shrill, as if some tiny bird was nesting in the back of his throat.

"Alright, introductions over," Davos said. "Now make haste! And if you don't know what to do aboard a ship, stay the hell out of the way!"

"This is unexpected, Captain. Where's Orson and the rest of the troupe?"

"Delayed!" He was turning the capstan, lifting the chain and anchor, a job for two or more men. "We're going to have to leave them."

"Are we in trouble, Captain?"

"You could say that."

Krow drifted across the deck on taloned feet, making for the center mast. Ropes needed to be pulled and yards of canvas unfurled. Demacharon aided with the rigging, proving himself adept at knots, as Ecthros ran down stern to some other task. Everyone found something to do but Noora, who was clutching at the rail to keep her balance.

The *Cloud Breaker* pushed from the stony quay, slowly navigating between the tall rocks. Once clear of the shallows, the great sails dropped, swelling to fullness. The wind lashed their faces with something between rain and ice. Demacharon planted one boot up on the jib-boom, looking out across the gray and black waters. The Potamis was the lifeblood of Aenya, running down from the Crown of Aenya to the Sea like a great spinal column. All the rivers in the world branched out from it, but like no river in the world, the Potamis was too broad to see across from one bank to the other. If Demacharon had not known better, he might have thought he was sailing out from home.

To Demacharon's dismay, several smaller craft slipped from port at the same time. They were painted black, but for the standard emblazoned upon their sails, the crimson fist and morningstar rippling in the wind. Despite some Tyrnaelean styling, Demacharon recognized the basic design of the penteconter, an oared warship built for speed and able to accommodate fifty rowers. No galley could hope to outrun such a ship, and certainly not at such proximity.

"We're being chased!"

"They won't catch us!" Davos called back from the wheel.

"Look, I've sent entire fleets into battle, and I am telling you, they will overtake us!"

"Not *my* ship! Where we're going, they can't follow! Krow—hard to port! Bearing south by south!"

The *Cloud Breaker* pitched suddenly. Demacharon held tight to the gunwale as Noora, oblivious to the goings-on, fell into Ecthros's arms. "I am a bit woozy," she admitted. "Never been sailing before. But I've read all about it."

They were moving toward the center, where the current was strongest, and the *Cloud Breaker* responded with disapproval, lifting high into the air and crashing down again with enough force to bring them to their knees. The pursuing vessels followed course. Demacharon could see their archers on the bowsprits, fires in their bows like yellow points of light in the haze, but they were overzealous, unaccustomed to warfare. At such a distance, the wind could only steal their arrows, though Ecthros was already responding, wasting shots of his own. It was not their arrows that he feared, but their swords. If boarded, the four of them could not hope to take on fifty, much less the other two crews. And here, on the Potamis, there was nowhere to hide.

"Dead ahead, Captain! The *Sundered Coast*!"

For so long, Demacharon worried over Zaibos's men, that he failed to consider what had nearly killed him when he first arrived in this place. Now, that danger loomed high above them, in the form of a chain of mountains that rose from the morning haze with awful clarity. At its base stood a glacier, a solid white mass, surrounded by a thousand-thousand icy daggers that protruded from the water like prehistoric teeth. Sailing through this region could only mean death. The hull would be ripped apart, and they could not hope to swim in such waters.

"Krow," Davos cried, his tin hat spinning furiously in the wind, "are the burners ready?"

"Nearly, Captain."

"Make it now, Krow!"

"I am only one avian, Captain."

"That's no excuse!"

Demacharon could hear the popping and crackling echo through the floorboards—

tiny icicles breaking against the hull. If Davos's plan was to dissuade Zaibos's men from following, it was not working. All three pentaconters were closing, from three different directions, every oar dipping and gliding in unison.

Translucent islands were sailing past them now, towering over the topmast, threatening to shatter them to timbers. *This is madness.* There was good reason Tyrnael managed to remain hidden for centuries. No captain could hope to navigate such waters, even if some pass through the mountains were discovered.

"Captain!" Demacharon shouted. "I must insist! Bring the ship about or we're done for."

"Never you mind, Hedonian!"

He looked back, seeing nothing but the rolling waves, and thought their pursuers gone, perhaps foundered by the ice, until they reemerged from the top of the surf, thundering down with increased speed and closing near enough to allow him to see the faces of the rowers. It was at that moment that Demacharon considered the unthinkable. As admiral, he would have sent men to their deaths for the mere rumor of it, but mutiny was his only option, the only way to keep his oath to the princess. Men could be fought, nature could not.

Demacharon made for the wheel, but something gave him pause, a roaring as from a blacksmith's furnace sounding three times in succession. What followed mystified his senses. Despite the surrounding glacier, the sound of crackling ice diminished, until he could no longer hear it. And though he could still see the turbulent waters, the ship moved in perfect stillness, as though sailing the most tranquil of lakes.

Krow called down from the crow's nest. "We're rising, Captain."

The icy hills were diminishing, not in actual size, but with distance. In a short time, Demacharon could hide the pursuing vessels with his thumb. The sails, he could now see, were transformed. They were no longer flat sheets of canvas, but round and bulging, and at the base of each mast a flame raged, from within a kind of cauldron-shaped brassier.

Davos nearly tipped over the gunwale in his glee, laughing, smacking one meaty hand behind the other and shoving both palms outward in what Demacharon could only assume to be a rude gesture of some sort. "Try catching us now, you boneheaded bastards! I'm king of Sea and sky! And I shit on your houses!"

True to its name, the *Cloud Breaker* sailed upwards, higher and higher, toward the clouds. From above, the great Potamis River was little more than a ribbon of silver and gold, cutting through a crust of ice and rock, and on through the hills in ever-smaller tributaries. On the starboard side, the city shone like a glittering snowflake, with its towering structures and matrix of bridges, but broken in sections where the bridges had fallen into disrepair, imperfect as snowflakes tend to be. At this height, Tyrnael was no more than a twinkling jewel in a mountain crown, and the Compass Tower at its center, a beacon of pure silver light.

Demacharon could easily see how remote and removed the city was from the outer world. From this impossible vantage, the fabled city looked insignificant, as were all things made by mortal hands, he supposed. Only the land—Aenya itself—could be deemed eternal and omnipresent, and the sight of it frayed his nerves, recalling to him the last time he had stood upon a precipice overlooking the world. He tried in vain to convince himself that some body of water lay beneath the ship, and moved toward the captain, wanting to embrace the man. "I should not have doubted you."

With a jubilant expression beaming from under his beard, Davos looked ready to dance, but the time for celebration ended abruptly, with his nephew in a panic, yelling, "Uncle! Come quick! Noora's been hurt!"

Davos shook his fist and looked to the sky. "Blast, the gods must be cruel jesters to play us so!"

Even Krow was quick to join them, having abandoned his post. Ecthros sat on the floor, Noora's head cradled in his lap.

"She must have swooned," the boy murmured.

But Demacharon knew otherwise. He knew the look of the grim god in a wounded soldier's eyes. Many were the time he was given to choose, the healer or the executioner, the tourniquet or the hammer. If she were a soldier on the battlefield, he would have known what choice to make, and he despaired to think of it. Noora's greenish pallor did not sully her beauty, but she was rigid, like a beautified corpse, and the way her toes and fingers curved, like the branches of a wilted tree, sickened his heart.

Davos continued to gaze at the still body, as though knowing her his whole life. "Has she been hit?"

"I checked," said his nephew, "but there's no wound. She was feeling sickly, unaccustomed to sailing . . ."

"Perhaps it is the altitude," Krow suggested. "You humans are unused to the thin air."

"No. That isn't it."

Demacharon took to her side. Blood still flowed in her veins. He could hear the quiet rhythm of her heart, a receding, shallow sound, and realized that what he long suspected— what he long feared—was true. The day they escaped the Compass Tower, when he had fought and killed the guards in front of her, she had not fainted out of empathy. There was something more, what she dared to keep secret from him, despite the risk to her life.

"No." His voice was drained of feeling. "She is unwell."

Ecthros lifted her up, passing Noora to his uncle, who took her in his arms. "I don't understand. What do you mean, she is not well?"

"I mean to say she is very ill."

Davos eyed him accusingly, as though he were a liar. "Again?"

"No," Demacharon answered, "not again. All those years . . . she was never cured. She's been dying."

13

Radia-M

Grumblestump had met an early end. Diggers discovered his head as they were arriving to work and immediately engaged in bogren kickball. Everyone but Ugh found good sport in this. The diminutive digger never cared for his foremen, yet he abhorred the thought of his own body being used to entertain idiots. Watching Grumblestump's head grow soft, like a lump of clay, and turn black as it rolled from one sooty foot to another only increased his loathing for his kind and his place among them.

Ugh's only consolation was that life was short. The lowest class, to which he belonged, was lucky to live twenty years, owing to violence or mishap or simply malnutrition. If not for the pain, he might have tossed himself into the magma. Warriors could hope to see thirty or forty years depending on their toughness, but even the greatest among them eventually met with fatal arrows, or if maimed, were sent to the Forge to drive workers. Grumblestump lasted a few shifts. Or was it only a few days? None could say with certainty, as the markers of time—the moons and stars and the sun—were mysteries known only to the chieftains. Taking his place was an unsightly creature, even by bogren standards, a brute called Meatface.

Little was spoken as to the cause of Grumblestump's fate, for bogrens detested explanations, but rumor was a popular distraction for those whose entire existence revolved around swinging a pickax. A similar story had been told countless times before, and in every permutation, a fight was involved. In this instance, a disagreement arose over the placement of a pale, and Grumblestump had said something to the effect of, "You remind me of my mother." Meatface, in response, removed his head clean with an ax.

Only hearsay could suggest whether he had been injured in battle or had fallen face-first into magma, but Meatface looked as one might expect given such a name. His nose and lips resembled ground steak, and considering his remarkable cruelty, he could not have been happy about it, being particularly incensed when a digger looked at him a certain way, though none could quite figure what "that way" was.

"Hey, you there! What are you looking at?" he would say, and no matter what the response, the beholder became one with the magma. To escape such grisly death, workers avoided the foreman altogether, until he found insult in this as well. Chosen at random, Meatface demanded a digger look at him, and the cycle of questioning and murdering would begin again. Like everything else in this meager existence, the situation was hopeless. If called upon, Ugh was prepared to stare directly into the foreman's eyes, if only he could manage to find which part of his face were eyes.

Ugh worked furiously to distance himself from his coworkers. Slackers and those of a slower pace often met with the lash, these being the very young or very old, while faster diggers spent time in newly unearthed recesses, far from those who might do them harm. Ugh always followed the path of least resistance, through the loose gravel. Given his size, he could squeeze between naturally forming fissures others would miss, and with his keen eye for rocks, could determine the location of a cave site by the surrounding limestone. Outperforming those who were bigger and stronger gave him a sense of pride. It was the only part of his job he enjoyed. But the threat of this new foreman pushed him harder than ever before, until he found himself in a strange place, lost and alone.

Among the bogren race, diggers are most sensitive to light, but Ugh saw only blackness. He listened for the tinny chime of picks or the roar of pouring magma or the screams of those being punished, to no avail. When he tried to retrace his steps, he was turned around, doubling back to where his pick lay. How did he get here? Had his fear of Meatface worked him into a trance? Or had he unwittingly burrowed into some alcove, the remnant of a riverbed or lake from the surface world?

Frightened and exhausted, Ugh sat down to ponder. A part of him felt relief. Meatface was far away and could not possibly hurt him. Nobody could. Like a worm protected by earth and darkness, he felt snug and secure. In time, he would need to return, for sustenance, and for safety against the many things that hungered in the core layers of the world. The strength of their kind, he knew, lay in numbers. If he were never seen again, it would be assumed he had fallen into the magma. No one would miss him or mourn his passing. Such was the life of a bogren. But if he were to make it back, Ugh would be treated as a deserter, and the punishment was always the same. Magma.

It occurred to him then that how quickly he returned mattered as much as whether he chose to do so at all. As he sat there, paralyzed with indecision, the darkness developed patterns. Shades of black emerged, and he focused his eyes upon them, channeling every particle of light into his eyes. With a pick in hand, he worked methodically, through the darker shades into the paler, until the rugged surface took on dimension. But it was a type of rock with which he was unfamiliar, black and glittering and smooth, from possibly a vast metal deposit, a great find. Or was it? Diggers were never awarded anything but punishment.

He continued to swing his pick, but the surface resisted his blows, and he worried he might have to find another path. Striking again, something yellow and bright caught the light, a single spark in a vast well of darkness.

Gold.

The taste was unmistakable. His kind knew nothing of currency, preferring lead and iron and copper to make tools and weapons, but Ugh loved shiny things. For gold, he would swing his pick until it was broken, and dig his way out with his hands.

Gold was falling in large clumps from above, unnaturally shaped, with edges like those made at the Forge. To his delight, it appeared pure and refined, mixed with few other minerals. Continuing to hack away, he never considered how he might transport such wealth, or how someone of his size could hope to keep it from being taken. All that mattered was the joy of shiny things, until the roof collapsed and a stabbing sensation shot through his pupils.

Ugh forced his eyes to open against the bombarding light, but there was only whiteness where there once had been blackness. Lifting himself from the fallen debris, the rays were streaming down from the opening his pick had made. It could only be the surface world. Though Ugh had never seen it, he knew that food was abundant here, and for sake of his stomach he braved its agonizing brilliance.

The whiteness receded, giving shape to his surroundings. Light was everywhere, pervasive, punishing him from all directions, but he could not make out its source. It was neither from fire or magma or even glowing fungi. The space was vast, like a cave, and yet all the surfaces were flat and angled. The longer he stood there, his eyes adjusting to the luminous flood, the more things came into focus, and the less he understood. Everything was wrong, unnatural, from the tall rigid bones between floor and ceiling to the green leafy things overhead. What he saw all around him lay beyond his capacities of comprehension. Colors, more varied and vivid than he thought possible, brought life to refined, sharp-edged shapes. If he were to return to his warren, he would not have been able to say where he had been.

"You're a funny looking thing."

Startled, Ugh turned to the strange creature beside him. About his height, it resembled a bogren, with two arms and legs. The shape of her skull and the pitch of her voice suggested she was female. But her eyes were too small, and her nose and lips seemed to extend from her face, and her skin was a pale yellow like fire and, like everything on the surface world, she was smooth. But what fascinated him most were the bizarre, gold ropes falling from her head, hanging along the sides of her face. Did it grow from her skull? Or did she wear it like a kind of helmet?

"Do you want to play with me?"

"Play?"

"You know . . . *play*? Haven't you ever played before?"

Though she was not speaking his tongue, he could somehow understand her. "Is that like digging?"

"Well, I dug to Shemselinihar once, but that was just in my imagination. Hey—look what I can do!" She lowered her head and moved it in a circular motion so that the gold ropes started to spin. "Whoa . . . I'm dizzy."

"I don't think I can do that."

"You can do whatever you want to do. That's playing."

"Whatever I want?" Ugh had never heard those words arranged in such a way. "I don't understand."

"You will!" She seemed excited, hopping on one foot. "I can show you. You can be my friend."

"What is a *friend*?"

"A friend is someone you can play with, silly."

"Who are you?"

Her lips spread apart and her cheeks lifted to reveal a brilliant set of teeth, and he recoiled, afraid she might bite him. "My name's Radia. What's yours?"

"Ugh."

"Ugh? That's not a name. I'll call you Oscar. Come on, Oscar!" He stared at her open palm and again grew afraid. The surface world seemed a strange and terrible place, where the light hurt his eyes and the spaces felt wide and unprotected. There was nowhere to hide! And what was this *play* she spoke of? A kind of torture? Was a friend more like a worker or something worse?

When he went to take her hand at last, she flickered, like a flame that goes out and is rekindled, and his hand passed through hers as if it were made of air. "Oh, sorry about that. I'm immaterial. It means you can't touch me. But we can just pretend, OK?"

The word "play" remained a perpetual mystery to him, involving a series of tasks without any discernible goal, but he obeyed the female creature as if she were his foreman. He supposed that playing might be similar to things bogrens did for merriment, like kick-head or lava jumping, except that on the surface, the chance of pain or death did not figure into the activity or present itself as a goal. Among his many duties were hopscotch and leapfrog, and something Radia called dancing, which was so strange that he feared for his sanity. Another game involved guessing what Radia was looking at, which reminded him of his old foreman, and caused him to quake with fear. Would he be punished for answering incorrectly, thrown into the awful source of light—the "sun" as she called it—which burned with greater intensity than magma? With increasing dread, he failed several attempts to guess *fish*, but she did not hurt him. Instead, she taught him of the creatures that lived their entire lives submerged in water, and of the birds that moved without touching the ground. Ugh found the latter difficult to believe, until she led him to another part of the castle, where the little winged creatures threaded through the bone-lined openings in the walls. They were the size of his hands, and the blue of their feathers dazzled like sapphires, but their incessant twittering made for awful noise.

When his stomach started to speak, Radia showed him to the outside, to a place she called the "garden" where the green was abundant, and that was when he discovered the awful source of light, a forge of white magma hanging high above them. His eyes were pained to look anywhere near it, and under its glow, Radia became difficult to see, which frightened him, for he thought she might disappear altogether and leave him alone. Together in the garden, they chased grasshoppers and butterflies, and she made bogren sounds when he chomped into them, which made him laugh. Humans did not eat bugs, she told him, but colorful orbs hanging from tall roots, which were sweet and turned to water in his mouth.

When his shift was over, the light flowing from the walls changed from fiery orange to magma red, hues reminding him of home, and after a time, to a violet fungal-like glow that did not hurt his eyes. At this time, Radia bid him her farewells, promising to "play again tomorrow" before disappearing, and he went over to where two walls met, to sleep. In the morning, he welcomed the light, despite the pain, knowing she would be waiting for him.

With each passing day, Radia revealed more of her world, and always new games to play. She "prettied" him up with wigs and makeup, and with the many dresses she kept in her mirrored room, but Ugh found that he did not like this game in that he looked nothing like she did. What they both loved most was to pretend. Ugh acted like Meatface, barking commands and waving his fist, but she just watched, quietly and with a solid face. His impression of a bogren dissolving in magma also failed to amuse her. But when he became a worm, squirming on the floor with his arms flat against his sides, she laughed and clapped, guessing it on the first try.

For Radia, the choice of animal was infinite. Life was far more diverse and abundant on the surface, and after seeing a bird for the first time, Ugh did not doubt the existence of other creatures parading beyond the castle walls. For passings, he sat listening, as she recounted each of their names, and he laughed when she brayed like a mammoth or charged him on all fours like a tiger. Some animals, she told him, were too small to see, like the eight-legged tardigrade. But her kind knew enough to paint them.

Something powerful was overcoming him, transforming him, delighting him—so much more than food ever had. Days passed before he could give the emotion a name.

Radia.

She was everything bogrens were not. In her mismatched eyes of violet and turquoise, he was an equal—if he were ever to fall into magma, he knew she would never laugh at him. The life he had known as a digger struck him as unthinkable now.

He had but one thing to fear upon the surface world—a monster he stumbled upon, after Radia introduced him to "hide and go hunt". Ugh liked this game because he was small and could easily conceal himself. It was not unlike what he had done underground, time and time again, to avoid bullies. Except that he trusted Radia not to eat him when the hunt was over.

Their first games ended quickly, when he hid behind the bone-white support structures called *pillars*, or behind the foliage that hung from the walls, but over time he sought better cover, exploring deeper into the castle. Most rooms were vast and empty, except for some odd-looking objects he could not identify, either in name or purpose, and frescoes portraying beings similar to Radia. No place was forbidden, at least not that he had yet encountered, until he discovered a stairwell.

Down and down he went, to a deep place, and at once a sensation of fear overcame him. Something large moved just below him and it was not of Radia's kind. The creature stood as tall as a horg but had flesh the color of coal. It walked on four legs, like a unicorn or an ox or a nereid, but with two arms and an upper torso, and a cranium the shade of fire. Whether it lived in a cave or a room, Ugh could not tell, for its dwelling was cluttered with forged things, some round and others square, which were neither weapon nor armor nor any tool he knew of. Most of these things were meticulously engraved with symbols, and the monster spent all of its time in a kind of trance, staring at these symbols.

"That's Nessus," Radia said, appearing next to him.

"Is he like you?"

"What? No!" She made a funny face and stuck out her tongue.

"Does he eat bogrens?"

"I don't think so. I'm not even sure he eats. He just stares at that door all day, and then gets mad and breaks things, and says things you shouldn't repeat in polite company."

Ugh looked for anything resembling a door but could not find it.

"It's right there. Look where I'm pointing, Oscar."

What she showed him in no way resembled a door, at least not to his eyes. It was a great slab of gold, forged in the shape of two great birds with feathers of fire, their wings touching at the height of the room. If it was a door, it didn't seem to lead anywhere, except to the other side of the room.

"Can't he just walk through it?"

"No, silly—it's a *Fantastica Gate*! Sometimes it opens and you can see twisty mountains like ice cream and trees like big balls of cotton . . . well, *that* place I liked, but most are downright scary. It's like looking into someone else's dream. But Nessus can never step into it. The gate won't let him and that makes him mad."

"What about you? Can you go through it?"

Radia chewed on her gold head ropes, or braids, as she liked to do when she was thinking. "I don't need to. *I* can play pretend! Which reminds me . . . Found you! Now it's my turn!"

"Fine, but no disappearing!"

For many cycles, they played and ate and wished each other good dreaming, and if Ugh possessed the words to describe his feelings, he would have told her that she made him happy, and what's more, that he loved her. But his kind did not possess such emotions, and so Ugh came to believe that he was no longer a bogren, that by some magic he had been transformed into a human.

One evening, after long passings of laughter and general bliss, Ugh became frightened by the strange noises suddenly bursting from Radia. She sat between the inside and the outside, under the flickering blue jewels that came out when the great sun forge went away. Since his coming to the surface, Radia had never caused him any sort of pain, until now. It could only have been some human weapon, for Ugh could feel its effect on him, his heart twisting painfully under his ribcage. But taking a seat beside her, he realized that she might also be in pain, for the sounds she made reminded him of screaming bogrens when they are tossed into the magma. But what could be hurting her? It was her face, he realized. Someone or something had broken it and the water inside was leaking through her eyes.

"Who hurt you, Radia?"

"No one has, Oscar. It's me. I've done a terrible, terrible thing."

Ugh looked confused. Had she thrown one of her own into the sun forge? No. Radia was incapable of cruelty. He was certain of that.

"You'll never forgive me, Oscar. Never."

"I don't know what *forgive* is, but I'll give it to you, if I can find it."

"Oh, I doubt that, honestly. You see, all these days, I've been lying to you. It's not in my nature to be dishonest, but I have. You see, Oscar . . ." She flickered as she smothered her face with her sleeve. "My name's not really Radia. Now that I think of it, I don't even have a name.

Ugh wanted to reply, but did not have the words, so he waited for her to continue.

"It's all that monster's fault, the one you found the other day. He wants to know everything about everything, so you know what he does? He takes things apart. Want to know how the tulip grows? Take it apart. Only, when you do that, the tulip dies."

Before coming to the castle, Ugh had never seen a flower. Radia was the first to show him the countless varieties and to teach him their names. "Do you want a flower? I can bring you one—"

"Oscar!" She sounded annoyed. "I am telling you a story here, so just listen, alright?"

He nodded.

"One day, King Solon heard a baby's cry, and when he went out into the garden, there she was, alone in a patch of ilms. The king wanted to know where she'd come from, to understand, so he took the child to his artificer. Only, Nessus couldn't take her apart like he wanted—the king wouldn't let him—so he made a copy, a simulacrum. That's what I am. It means I don't really exist. Do you know how awful that is, to not really exist?"

"Would it help if we played a game?"

"That's just the thing." Her eyes leaked profusely now, and Ugh could see clearly through her to the opposite wall. "I can't play with you anymore."

"B-But why?"

"There was only so much power."

"Oh."

"Do you forgive me? For lying to you? Please say you do!"

"You do?"

"We've had so much fun together, and you've been such a good friend to me, Oscar. Always remember that, even if I can't. I have to go now. Goodbye."

She flickered away, leaving only the echo of her voice, and Ugh strained to make sense of what he had heard, and after giving up, crawled into his corner exhausted. The following morning, he waited, but Radia never emerged. He waited for her all the next day as well. And the next. When he could no longer count the days, Ugh realized that his friend would never again appear. And that is when he learned the terrible truth of the outer world. In abandoning his former home, he believed he had escaped pain and cruelty, yet they were just as abundant on the surface. Except that here, in this place, the pain penetrated him much more deeply than he had thought possible.

14

Lyr

The placard outside the door displayed a winged-serpent, with chipped and faded letters that read, *The Moontalon Inn*. Like most places within the inner-city, the walls were part of the terraced superstructure left over by the Zo. It was once tenement to a lord, but how often ownership had changed, none could say. Now it served as a tavern, a favorite spot for Hugo and his fellow men-at-arms to drink. Tapestries lined the room, recounting the tale of the Batal. Every child knew of the story, but Hugo could recite it by word. His earliest memories were that of his father, singing of the fabled hero.

According to legend, Moontalon was a great black dragon whose wings could eclipse the greater moon. It was a vain effort by the Zo to create the most superior of beasts, and an affront to the Goddess. In the form of the phoenix, she selected a young boy to become her champion, to rid the world of all such abominations. At first, the Batal mistook the dragon's tail for a winding stair, and its eye for an emerald set into the wall, but then it lurched, drawing its immense size to his attention. The hero could scarcely hope to slay the monster, with its scales like armored plates, but he found a way. Jumping down from a hanging stalactite, the force of his fall was enough to break through the dragon's skull, his two-hander impaling its brain.

Hugo never gave the story any serious thought, believing it was fanciful nonsense. Though not one for heroes, he held his father in great esteem, marveling at how the bard worked the bouzouki.

He sometimes envied the life of the entertainer, but Hugo had no talent for it. Serving under the royal family seemed the next best thing—a nobler profession he could not ask for. He was especially fond of the inherent fellowship between men of arms. Only now, the gold and white he had worn since manhood were taken from him, to be melted down. Black and crimson replaced his old colors, a fist and morningstar in place of the unicorn. Even a layman could see that their new suits were crudely fashioned, the joints so stiff that patrolling the streets became an exercise in endurance. And as he did not gleam whitely in the sun as before, Hugo could feel its fire, cooking him in the afternoon. So it was with utmost relief that he found himself at the end of his patrol at the *Moontalon Inn*.

Servant girls bustled from table to table, trays of mead, bread, and roasting meats balanced atop their heads. Despite his diminished instincts, he enjoyed watching them, the curve of their bodies showing beneath their silk livery. But today his brain was a jumble. Feeling the coarse hammered-iron of his helm beneath his fingertips, he wondered at its purpose. War had not visited their homeland for millennia. The Zo had seen to that, having moved mountains to keep the city from invasion. Apart from the occasional tourney, his old armor was ceremonial, a way to honor the ruling family, a dynasty of fifty-three generations. Now, he could not push from his mind the banality of his station. By what authority did Zaibos command him? By what right did the Usurper rescind his oath to the ruling heir? Before the last cycle, he had been sworn to protect her.

Two men, their faces obscured by visors, were approaching his table, rather too quickly for his liking, but he managed a calm demeanor. He did not wish to draw suspicion, though everyone was looking jumpy these days. Hugo recognized the elder of the pair as he doffed his helm. The other was lean-faced, his head poking like a turtle from under his cuirass, a boy who could not have been more than a year in service.

"Hail, Hugo!"

"Greetings, Galen." Seeing as though he was not being given a choice in the matter, he added, "Feel free to take a seat."

"Don't know if you've met," Galen said, setting his helm to cool against the trestle table. "This is Lyr, Kaleb's grandson. Remember Kaleb?"

"How could I not? Dozed off at his post, broke his back. Fell thirty feet, I hear. No disrespect, lad."

"None taken, sir." The boy fidgeted nervously, uncomfortable in his oversized shell. "We thank Zoë he's alive. I inherited his mail, which I was wearing, until they changed it, that is."

"An honorable man. Always did what was right."

Lyr offered no response. But that was not unusual. Looking up from his swirl of mead, Hugo saw that there were few empty chairs, out of less than a hundred. And yet, a disquieting silence pervaded the inn, though he knew that it was symptomatic of the city as a whole. Since the coming of Zaibos, people spoke in hushed tones and with nervous glances.

"Hey! Hey, you there!" Galen's voice boomed. "Eloai-girl, could we get something to drink here, if you please?"

She was plain enough to look at, with a broad nose and curly brown hair, but her buxom frame gave them an eye-full, straining the lacings of her chiton as she bent to accost them. "Apologies, my lords. What will you be having?"

"Cold mead for me and the lad," he answered, "and a third for my friend here."

"That's quite alright," Hugo said. "I've an early morning ahead."

She turned and trotted off, but just as soon as she could disappear behind the counter, Galen was calling after her again. "Eloai-girl! Come help me out of this breastplate, will you?"

"Be right there." It was another girl, hurrying with a flagon to an adjacent table, where a crowd of merchants debated the changing economy in angry, muffled outbursts.

"Why so few today?" he asked no one in particular. "I've not seen more than four eloai-girls in the place."

Hugo sat tiredly up in his chair. "Why must you do that, Galen?"

"Do what?"

"Treat them so. They're not so different than we are."

"Well, they're certainly more pleasant to look at, but I'd hardly call them our equals. We've been bred to defend the kingdom, and they've been bred to deliver drinks."

"That may be so, but you needn't call her eloai-girl."

"Why not? That's what she is, isn't she?"

"They have names, also."

"I don't know her name," he said matter-of-factly.

"Did you ever bother to ask?"

The portly girl returned with a chalice in each hand. Galen choked it down, caking his mustache with froth, as the second girl tugged at his leather side-straps, and Lyr wrestled with his lobstered gauntlet.

"Let me help you," Hugo said to the boy.

"No, it's quite alright. I've got it."

"Are you sure?"

"Have one of the girls do it," Galen remarked. "That's what they're here for." He motioned at the servant, who continued to yank until the halves of his cuirass came apart. He wore a purple doublet chased with silver underneath. While precious metals were not difficult to come by, working them into an item was another matter, and his was a garment fit for an aristocrat. It was not a wonder he treated eloai in the way that he did. Doubtless, a few of them served in his household.

"I really do hate this new armor," Lyr said, his gauntlet hitting the table with a thud. "What was wrong with the unicorn, anyway?"

The inn went quiet again, and even the servant girl rushed off, as if remembering something important. Hugo and Galen could only stare.

"Did I say something wrong?" the boy asked sheepishly.

Galen raised a hand as if to smack the back of Lyr's head. "Take care how you speak, lad. Times have changed."

His eyes grew wide. "I know that. I was just saying—"

"Don't be saying."

"But I meant no disrespect, honestly—"

"Never mind what you meant," Galen pressed. "A loose tongue will get you killed. Or worse."

Hugo looked on, sipping from his chalice.

"No worries." Galen smiled, smacking the boy with a meaty hand. "We're all friends here, are we not? No words leave this table tonight." He turned, biting his two fingers in a siren-like whistle. "Hey, eloai-girl, we've had a long, hot day and we're hungry."

Despite the man's assurances, the boy shared no other thoughts. But his discomfort was evident. He looked trapped in his irons, bound by fist and morningstar. The tension broke when the food arrived. Salted pork simmered in onions and peas under a garnish of basil. Alongside it, the eloai served bowls of bread drizzled with olive oil and clumps of feta. The aroma reminded Hugo of his stomach, helping to set his mind at ease. Galen tore into it with his fingers, like a man starved for days, but the boy did not eat.

"You've got a heavy head, Hugo. Care to unburden it?"

He glared at Galen from his empty mug. Considered calling for another. "Not really."

"Surely, you must have a say in all this."

"A say in what, precisely?"

"All this. What's been happening. Everything."

"If I didn't know you better, Galen, I'd suspect you were goading me into revealing something."

"Why? Have you got something to reveal?" He laughed and stuffed his mouth. "Come now. Feel free. We're all friends here."

"Want me to say my armor is uncomfortable? Well, I won't deny it. But that's hardly a secret. Don't think you can find anyone who will tell you, straight-faced, how he prefers it."

"That's an easy one," Galen admitted, "but there's a lot more that's going on, and we all have a say in it, one way or another."

Hugo turned his mug over. "I think you're right, Galen. I think I'll have another."

"Take Radia, for instance," he went on. "How many fishmongers you think were at the docks that day, when she boarded that ship? How many do you think saw her?"

"I really do not know."

"Don't play dumb with me, Hugo. We've known each other how long? Ten years?"

"It was early morning," he conceded, choosing his words carefully. "Probably not many. They likely took her for a grocer."

Galen did not bother looking up from his dish, but continued devouring the pork, leaving nothing to his apprentice but the pink on the bone and a few charred scallions. Lyr did not appear to have much of an appetite.

"Who patrols that area, anyway? I seem to recall you holding that position once, or am I mistaken?"

"You're not," Hugo said, after a long quiet. "But I did not see her."

"Unfortunate," he intoned, still not looking at him.

"In what way?"

Galen seemed to be hiding behind his smile, his eyes like small polished shields. "She's awfully fair. The Princess. There's no one else like her. Or so I've heard."

"A face to melt the hardest of hearts."

He nodded. "Indeed."

Lyr snatched a piece of bread, nibbling on the hard, outer crust. "You know what I heard? I heard that the king has spies positioned everywhere. Anyone among us—"

"Don't believe everything you hear, lad." Galen wiped the grease from his fingertips, took up his helm, and stood abruptly.

"Going somewhere?" Hugo inquired.

He glared, his face cold, impassive. "Eon is long in the sky, and my bed awaits."

"I've never known you to be an early sleeper, Galen."

"It's the wife," he said. "She's been going on about that. All men are as eloai to their wives, or don't you know?"

Hugo threw a smile at him, a facade of his own, but Galen could see through it. His friend was far better at this game and he knew it. "I'll let you know when I take one."

"Ha! Until then, my good man. Enjoy your freedom."

His armor was put away, sent home by Vanessa, one of the servant girls. He wore a cloak in place of it and was glad, for in all his days, he could not recall such a biting chill.

The night was crisp, and the wynd behind the inn dim with shadows, the moons masked by towering walls. Without a lamp to light his way, it would be a labyrinth to navigate. But he did not need to know his destination. He would follow the clink of poleyns on greaves, the splat of heels in puddles, wherever they might lead. Hugo needed to know where his friend of ten years was off to, because Galen lived to the right of the inn, and upon exiting the tavern door he had turned to the left.

His quarry was a silhouette, a fitful motion in the darkness, turning narrow passages broad enough for a single cart, occasionally climbing a stair to a higher tier. He knew the city well enough, perhaps better than Hugo did. But if Galen was aware of his pursuer, he showed no sign of it. In his loose-fitting cloak and undercoat, Hugo moved without a sound.

Rain started to fall, gentle as mist, dampening his forearms, coating his garments with a wet sheen. The shadowy figure turned onto a broad promenade, bright with lanterns and the turquoise glow of the greater moon. From here, he could take any route, but only one led to the Compass Tower. And the king. Galen went north, and he went after, producing his dagger from its sheath. His prey was no longer a silhouette, but a man bound in armor. The pace quickened, and Hugo knew that Galen was onto him.

It soon became a chase. Galen tried to lose him in the side streets, but Hugo was wise to it. The hunt led them to an abandoned part of the city. The buildings were far more ancient, their rooftops and columns having long ago failed, crumbled under the weight of time. A stony framework was all that remained—odd, triangular shapes of what once were walls. There would not likely be witnesses here. But what did he purport to do upon catching him? Murder his friend? Over the most nebulous of suspicions?

The people of Tyrnael aged slowly, and illness had been conquered millennia ago by their ancestors, so that death was a mere specter, waiting at the far end of more than a century. The act of killing straddled the divide between truth and fiction, an event for historians and storytellers to mull over. Or so it had been, before Zaibos, before the Usurper had come to shock them out of their complacency.

A missing brick, flooded by rain and thereby imperceptible, sent Galen hurling down. But the sound that he made was not what Hugo expected. It was not the voice of a seasoned soldier, but the shout of a frightened boy.

Hugo advanced, his dirk tight against his bosom, just as Lyr caught his gaze. Galen, who he thought he had been trailing, was nowhere to be seen. In the dark and in the rain, he had been following the boy the entire time. "You? I thought—"

"Hugo? Why were you following me?"

"Why did you run?"

"I sensed someone was after me and got scared. I'm sorry."

"No, I owe you an apology." He lowered his weapon, shamefaced. "It would seem, with the way things are, everyone has gone a bit crazy."

"I understand," said Lyr, getting to his feet.

"Do you live around here?"

"I—um—no." Hugo could not make out the puzzled look on his face. The boy was turning in place like a dog chasing its tail, his fingers poking the creases of his armor.

"Have you lost something?"

"Nothing important. I'll find it on my own."

"No, let me help. It's the least I can do."

"Really, it's quite alright. I'm sure it's around here someplace."

Hugo saw it first, a small piece of parchment caught between the wind and the remains of a fluted column. It was damp about the edges, but the writing at the top was legible.

To Captain Mandos. My report, as follows:

He continued to read in horror, as the boy tried frantically to snatch the paper away. It was all in shorthand. Words Galen had spoken. And his own. The boy had to have scribbled it while he was doffing his armor.

"You?" Hugo cried. "You're the informant!"

"I-It's nothing," he murmured. "Just something the captain asked me to do. He said I'd get a promotion, a secure position in the king's regime."

Hugo crumpled the paper in his fist. "I ought to gut you here and now. But I suppose you're too stupid to know any better. No one is safe in this kingdom—not you, not anyone. Zaibos is a monster. He cannot be trusted. Whatever hope you might have had for a future went out with the princess."

"That's—that's high treason, sir."

"Treason it is."

The boy stared at him for a moment, thinking. "Aren't you afraid, sir?"

"I am. We all are. But what I fear more is to do nothing, to say nothing. What is happening in our city, to our people, we cannot let it stand. If we do, we lose everything our forefathers fought to defend. All of it."

The rain was falling cold and hard now, like a gray veil separating the man from the boy. A yew tree growing out of the ruined wall offered a modicum of shelter.

"Did you see the princess at the docks, then?"

"I suppose there is no point denying it. Good men were made to suffer and die, because of the choice I made. Had I betrayed her, we might all be sharing drinks tonight. Then again, I will never more hear my father play, and the king is to blame."

Sounds of rain filled the space between them. Lyr was at a loss for words, his face ashen, focused on the blade in Hugo's hand, which he had brandished without realizing it.

"Are you going to kill me, sir?"

"Do you want to be killed?"

The boy chewed on his lip, uncertain how to answer. "No, sir."

"Then you will go to Captain Mandos, this very night, just as you planned. But you will be delivering a different message."

"What should it say?"

"I will tell you."

15

Ester

---

*N*o one can stop me.

He crept into the light from the underside of the ship, from where he had been waiting and listening. His surroundings were otherworldly, and his heart raced with uncertainty, with fear. But fear was a tool like any other, could be used and manipulated, and for the strong served to sharpen the senses. For someone like Larissa, it only crippled and enslaved. She had been like a sheep under his control, providing him with all of her mistress' hopes and desires, and weaknesses. If only those buffoons had not shown, his quarry's heart would now be in a box, and his mother restored.

You gave me everything, mother. I owe my very existence to you, and for that, you were made to suffer. For bearing an abomination, they marked you as they did me, and you became as that which you bore. But I will repay you this debt. I will restore the years stolen from you, and then, what a sight you will be! To sing again on the stage! To be adored, as you once were, for your beauty and your rare voice. Everywhere they will know your name again. Ester. Ester. Only a little time now and you will be made young again. I am aboard their ship and they suspect nothing, and no one can stop me.

He pulled himself over the banister, listening intently, but the crew was nowhere about. Silent as an owl, he glided across the deck, without so much as bending a plank.

The light of day was no more and the sun deep in the greater moon, but it was not as dark as he would have liked. Tyrnael was beyond sight, so that there was not a wall or tree or a rock to cast a shadow, to shield him from the turquoise glow. Opposite the moon, the stars made him turn in wonder. He never imagined there could be so many, like grains of brilliant sand dashed against a velvet sky, whereupon the constellation of the dark god, Skullgrin, smiled upon him.

Still, there were places enough for him to hide. He needed only the width of a mast, a spool of chain, a heap of netting. Most of his victims were dead before seeing his face. To kill was a simple endeavor. Children learned to do it at a young age, when swatting a fly or crushing a grub under a shoe. The difference between an assassin and a thug was planning. When his designs fell into place, it happened in a matter of heartbeats, a quick thrust to the neck from behind, or if witnesses were present, a quarter-moon incision severing the jugular. The princess would die this way, in her sleep. Imagining his kills beforehand was a matter of preparation, but it also gave him a thrill, to picture her blood washing warm over his palms and her waking to recognize her killer, if only for an instant. The panic in the eyes, the awful awareness, the sudden shift of fate, there was no greater sense of power than in that moment of death when death was in his hands.

The fools thought she could be stolen away, hidden, but she will be delivered to Skullgrin. No one can stop me now.

To him, assassination was a dance between predator and prey, and the movements of his quarry so predictable they just as well could be rehearsed. People fleeing for their lives were certain to seek aid. Like herd animals, they believe themselves safe in numbers, and who better to help an outsider—the Hedonian—than an outsider? And where better to find help from beyond the city than the Cosmos Theater? Everyone in Tyrnael knew where the foreigners were docked. Eros was like a germ embedded in the brains of his prey, knowing their every thought and instinct, which is why no one ever managed to escape him.

The flying ship had taken him by surprise, no doubt, but served his purposes nonetheless. Any situation could be turned to his advantage, and now, sailing the clouds, the crew had let their defenses down. Already, Eros could hear the captain snoring. Without a sound, he removed his dirk from the sheath in his boot, and advanced. The blade was smaller than the one he had lost, but four inches sufficed to sever the princess's porcelain throat and release her blood.

High on the mid-mast, on a small round platform, the avian creature slept. Eros could silence him with an arrow, but chose discretion, moving down a short ramp to the cabin door, and producing a vial from a side pocket. He doubted whether the slumbering fools would hear him enter, but water and metal did not mix, and he remembered how noisy the hinges had been when the captain went in and out. A dab of oil and the door opened without warning.

The passage was narrow, broad enough for a single man. If any were to wake, his blade was sure to meet their throats. Only one thing concerned him. The Hedonian was a dangerous foe, despite his age, experienced at killing like no other man he knew. Before finding where the princess lay, he needed to seek him out.

The captain was face down in a puddle of drool, a bottle of celebratory rum in hand. The boy slept on the floor in a corner, clutching a lute. Perhaps he had hoped to serenade the princess? Eros moved on, as they were both too drunk to be a threat.

A plaintive cry came from the adjacent cabin as he passed, causing him to leap against the wall.

"Astor! Don't you recognize me, son . . . Astor! Astor?"

He crouched, fearing discovery. But there was no one else on board, no one named Astor, at least.

It was a familiar voice, yet more pitiable than he would have thought, coming from such a man. *The Hedonian is*

165

dreaming. Another advantage. *The spirit roams far from the body and will take time to return.* But Eros took no stock in chance, approaching the quarter door and wedging it shut with the broken haft of his dagger. It would not hold long, but a splintering door would make a great sound in such a cramped space. *When he wakes, he will find his princess dead, and me gone. What awful dreams then, Hedonian?* Eros smiled, imagining the scene, the floor awash in red, pooling from under her door, staining their frantic feet. The store of blood in a single body never ceased to amaze.

He turned every knob, watching for traps or alarms. But there were no bells behind her door, nothing to alert her protectors, not even a locking mechanism. Truly, they thought her safe. Between the Hedonian's nightmares and the captain's incessant, wall-rattling snores, Eros grew at ease. Who could hope to stop him now? No one. Already, his thoughts were turning to the much greater challenge of escape.

The princess's cabin was small and poorly furnished. Only a single window, silver with the moon and stars, illuminated her head on the pillow. It was a sad, pathetic end for one so renowned, for the ruler of the greatest and most ancient of cities, for one born in a tower seen from a day's journey, and who slept in silk and ivory.

Perhaps, her demise at his hands was fitting—she, the highest of the highborn, and he, the lowest of the low. She and her ancestors were to blame for making him what he was and condemning his mother to a life of ostracism and isolation. With her death, and Zaibos's rule, might the marks be lifted? Could abominations throughout the kingdom find acceptance? Perhaps a man and woman could again join in the flesh, one body to another, without fear of condemnation, as his mother had bonded to his father. Or woman again know the pangs of birth and the wailing of babes, bearing their children as his mother bore him, without judgment, without the accursed Committee.

Blade in hand, Eros approached her cot and knelt beside her. In the streaming moonlight, her hair shone like pure silver. It did not please him to destroy such beauty. But death came for all, to the lovely and the grotesque, the innocent and the cruel. But like the flower that is cut when it is still blooming, so it is better to shear the life of a maiden, so that the memory of her beauty remains. That is what he told himself, as he nudged her braid aside to reveal the soft flesh, poised to thrust his blade into her spine. Skullgrin was near. He could feel the dark god swelling within him, waiting for the assassin to deliver the sacrifice. Even if the Hedonian were standing in the doorway, there was no possibility—no time—to stop him. Nothing and no one could. Life and death were in his hands.

But why did he hesitate?

Still sleeping, the princess turned on her other side, and Eros recoiled as he saw her face. His dirk slipped noisily to the floor, and he stumbled backward, slamming his back against the edge of the swinging door.

By Skullgrin, how? How can it be?

He trembled, horrified by what he had been about to do. But the reality was beyond his scope of reason. Shutting and opening his eyes, thinking he was mistaken, fooled somehow, he again approached her bedside.

No. It can't be.

A single tear rolled from his eye, as she slowly opened hers. Standing a mere breath's length from her, he saw upon her face none of the fear he had imagined. Only pity. A deep, all-consuming sorrow for the monster he had become.

"Mother!" he wept. "Mother."

The alley had been dim, but in the brightness of the stars, the resemblance was unmistakable, uncanny. And yet, she was not the tortured woman he knew, the prisoner sitting at home, the face worn by time's many regrets. No. This was the mother of his youth, the singer in the murals, the girl he hoped beyond hope to resurrect.

Noora continued to stare, empathy radiating from her mismatched eyes, and Eros fled from the room, and from the demons that pursued him.

No one can stop me! No one. No one . . .

He ran out into a raging storm. Raindrops fell hard as stones against his brow and neck. Blinded, he found the rail with his gut and retched over the side.

No one can stop me but myself.

16

Amalthea

Sunflowers rolled over the hills and towards the horizon in a continuous blanket, reaching with open faces to drink the light. Other flowers beckoned provocatively, with open skirts of pink and orange, and stamen tongues of violet. Winged creatures of all sizes flew and buzzed about her, collecting pollen, spreading seeds of rebirth. Across shades of undulating green and in the woods hugging the valley, along the peaks where the snows broke and tumbled down to feed the land, there was the ebb and flow of energy, of life. She could feel it in her skin and deep in her bones, the eternal striving to exist, to draw breath, from simple organisms too small for the naked eye to the sail-winged airwals that dimmed the sun as they flew overhead.

"You still don't know who you are, do you?"

Noora or Radia—she was unsure of her name—gazed into the starry eyes of the magnificent white creature. In all existence, no greater beauty could be found, none more divine. No greater harmony of muscle and bone and sinew. Even in the way she stood, turning her head and swaying her tail, there was music. Her coat was like the halo of a star, her mane like foam against a rocky shore.

"Amalthea," she said. "I remember you. For a moment, I'd forgotten myself."

"What you remember is but one life, the fifteen years of your human host, which is less than a blink of an eye to me, and to cosmic time. There is more, much more you must discover. If you do not recognize your true nature, we may all be lost."

"We? Who is we?"

"Everyone and everything striving to know itself, to exist, to live."

She looked about her, perplexed. Try as she might, she was unable to recall a single memory from before the sunflower fields. It was as if the universe, time itself, was created for this one moment. What she did know was the sights and sounds and smells, that filled her with a sense of well-being and clarity. But touch, more than any other sense, made her feel the most aware. The wind carried vapors and spores and pollen against her pores, and brightly-lit butterflies tickled her neck. Her bare soles drank the soil like the roots of a tree and she could taste every nutrient. Hazily, as if from a dream, she remembered clothing and shoes, but to hide as humans did seemed abhorrent to her now, like saddling a unicorn.

"Where am I?"

"You are in the womb of Aenya, the most fertile ground, and the birthplace of the ilma. Over the ages, it has gone by many names, but the humans of today call it after themselves, Ilmarinen."

"How did I come by this place? Did you bring me here?"

"No, but this is where I expected to find you. Your presence is potent here. When your companion, Larissa, released me, I searched for you, from the highest peaks to the deepest trenches, but I could not feel you, because you've forgotten yourself. Now you must remember. We all need you to remember, or all is lost."

"Larissa . . . I remember her. She loved me dearly. But when I think of her, it's like looking through a different set of eyes, that are mine yet somehow not mine. Does that make any sense? What's happening to me? Help me to understand. Please."

"It is the poison coursing through your material form, the poison you've fed upon since you were young, that has trapped you and kept you from fully becoming what you are. It is the reason we have never spoken until now. This lapse in your consciousness has been fortunate."

"You speak in circles. Why? Can you not simply tell me who I am?"

"I could, but it would not avail you. To know a thing only by its name is to know nothing about it. You must recognize the truth within yourself, but I can help you do this. I can show you, if you will come with me."

She ran her hand along the unicorn's mane, which was like silk, but strong as the hardiest of ropes. Like a lover leaning into a kiss for the first time, she knew what to do, how to straddle the unicorn's back and hold to it with her thighs and fingers. Amalthea rushed forward with the suddenness of a gust of wind. Off they went, powerful muscles flexing beneath her, the field of sunflowers becoming a blur of white and yellow, vanishing behind them.

She watched the foothills looming before them. Effortlessly they climbed, until they were looking over a rolling green landscape with veins of blue and sheer slate rock all around them, and then higher to a snowy pinnacle, and down again through the river valleys to lands beyond, their speed ever-increasing, the unicorn's hooves touching faster and softer, until they were skimming the ground. Tangled vines and towering timbers of vast woodland rushed toward her, just as quickly becoming a mere spot of emerald in the rear of her eye. They ran the beaches of the One Sea, kicking up sand and saltwater, and cut paths through temperate forests and vast fields of grain, into the wild places of the world, riding side by side with the striped ziff and the green tiger and a herd of proud mammoths. Wherever they were seen, they were shown reverence, from the domestic beast latched to the plough to the bright soaring phoenix to the fish hopping from the waves to catch glimpse of them. But where humans gathered, in their high-walled cities, they were rarely noticed, and even then not recognized, but by young children who looked for wonders.

Only once, Amalthea rested, atop a high place overlooking a landscape of fruitless cliffs and deep gorges.

"This was once a bountiful land, teeming with fish and crustaceans, with birds and wakefin. I myself grazed and took shade upon the islands here, but only stony peaks remain. *Ocean*, it was called. The lives of men are short, and their memories shorter still, and no mortal creature can remember its beauty."

Raising a hand to her brow to shield her eyes, she looked out across the tortured terrain, a surface of ceramic scale under the sun, and could feel no living thing. "What happened?"

"The Zo," Amalthea answered, "they'd forgotten you."

Without further explanation, they were off, racing at impossible, senseless speeds. She could feel the wind snap her hair against her flesh, but there was never any pain, nor fear. Beyond the scorching wastes, they came to the eastern hemisphere, where deeply-shadowed ridges basked under perpetual moonlight. Even here, where the land had not known sun for untold ages, life found its way, in neon ponds of algae and tree-like mushrooms, and volcanic depths hidden far below. But she could sense the great time of dying that had been, and the countless extinct forms layering the earth, and a sadness she could not place welled up in her heart. It seemed that, to spare her the pain, Amalthea moved even more swiftly through these lands, over tops of mountains to the North, where ridges of ice mirrored their passing. Turning South, they met shadowy jungles and marshy fens, and lakes and riverbeds and hilly grasslands, until meeting the Sea again and crossing to the opposite shore in a blink. On they flew, through sunshine and rain and sleet, surpassing the speed of day, the sun and moons and stars rising and falling like pendulums, dawn and dusk breaking like lightning. The world wheeled beneath them in a rainbow of hues and textures as the stars stretched into lines of blue fire. When she could not imagine moving any faster, Amalthea's pearly horn blazed silver and white, and they exceeded the moons, moving faster than light, faster than Time itself.

All was still. Quiet. The stars were points in the sky again and the world was no longer spinning. "Where are we? This place looks familiar." She recognized the flowers and the shapes of the hills and the mountains beyond. "We circled the world a dozen times so you could bring me back to where we started?"

"We are elsewhere," she answered. "A place, as you understand it, exists as a temporary state. The mountains are shorter than before and have moved considerably. I sometimes sit for millennia, watching them migrate, like great big turtles."

"I don't understand."

"Countless chains of life have come and gone. In the western hemisphere, life swims in the Ocean. Look up, and see that the greater moon is but a distant light, a pale wanderer among the stars. We are in the epoch of the four seasons, when there were summer and fall, winter and spring."

She somehow knew those words. The ancient names for the seasons were used by the Zo before the coming of the greater moon. "We are in the past?"

"Yes, though we are not meant to be here. It is a gross violation of the governing laws of the cosmos, but I wanted to show you something. Something significant."

She dismounted, feeling a bit woozy, and followed the unicorn on numb legs through a field to a gryke of flickering light. It was a fire, she realized, coming from a cave. The entrance was tall enough to permit Amalthea, the roof grazing only the tops of her ears. The surface was yellow limestone, smooth and cool to the touch, creating a shelter ideal for human habitation. She followed the shadows cast by the flame, ducking under stalactites, to a deep niche, where a great number of strange creatures gathered. They were not so unlike humans, but for the dark hair covering their bodies, and less pronounced faces. Their jawlines were broader in relation to their skulls, which were both smaller and less rounded than hers. But she could see the young among them doing what children do—laughing and wrestling—as the fathers were skinning kills or drumming goatskins with femur bones. The mothers sat clustered together, making pigments with berries and bugs crushed in pestles, using hair bristles to paint animals on to the rock wall.

"Who are they?"

"Ancestors. Look there," the unicorn said. "This is a momentous point in Time."

In one corner, a young female was nursing her infant. But the child was different than the others, with its dark skin exposed.

"Does the hair come later?"

"That is what the mother is hoping, but it is not to be. Her daughter has been born with a special gift, the power to shed heat faster than any creature on the planet. When she comes of age, this little human—the first of its kind—will chase ziff to exhaustion, providing sustenance for the entire tribe. Her name is Ilma."

"Why bring me here? Why show me this?"

"Because, there is something else you must see."

Amalthea directed her gaze to a sepulcher adorned on all sides by depictions of four-legged animals and fruit-bearing trees. Within the rock, a crude idol could be seen, a pregnant female made from a boulder, with broad hips and enormous breasts and a rocky, misshapen head.

"She is called Yobaba. She makes the seed sprout and the herd appear, and what's more, she gives the gift of change. Do you recognize her?"

"I . . . I am not so sure."

"Much later, she will change, and go by another name, Zobaba."

A sick feeling came over her at that moment, and she fled from the cave. Oceans of memories crashed against her consciousness, threatening to extinguish any sense of identity she possessed.

"Please, Amalthea, take me far from here. I don't want to see any more."

"As you wish. But there is one last thing you must see. Perhaps then you will come to enlightenment."

They were moving again, the mountains rolling under them, only now they seemed to be growing lighter, ascending. Wisps of cirrus swirled and flashed and thundered. And she rode upon the sounds, the fury and the lightning, higher into the ether. Far below she watched the clouds drift and coalesce and break apart. The world was round and orange and ringed by white, an egg she could fit in her arms, in her palm, a seedling on the tips of her fingers.

Where was Amalthea? Gone. She was alone in a cold vast emptiness, alone but for the stars. They were spread all around her, and she felt she could reach out and gather them, but they came to her instead, each with a lantern in hand or a glittering crown or a fiery gown. They were dressed in storms and skirts of ice, with hair like rivers, and skin like forests and granite, their vulvas birthing fish and birds and species undreamed of. Many were human. A far greater number were not.

They were dancing, she realized, a million-million star women, all in a great circle of unimaginable proportions. And she was but one of the dancers. They were her sisters, she knew. Her sisters all.

17

Orson

The sky was not gray, nor heavy with rainclouds, as one might expect. If not for the pillars of smoke, the sun would have shone in blinding gold over the city. But an unmistakable pungent stench filled the air, and the falling grey ash flecked many a house. Intrepid hearts huddled before the hill, but none among them were so brave as to utter a word of protest. There was no recourse to survival but obedience.

In speech after speech, the people were told of the great folly of their ancestors. They were like children, Zaibos told them, ignorant to the meaning of suffering. Even death, the greatest driver of life, had been kept from them. For in those instances when some man or woman did upon hundreds of years expire, the true face—and power—of the Taker was never seen, as the bodies were quickly and quietly borne away, to be forgotten. Ages ago, the Ancients labored to relieve all mankind of suffering, but in so doing, robbed from him his courage and strength of will. So did Zaibos explain the weakness of the people of Tyrnael. Several magistrates, members of the Committee, voiced dissension, questioning his right to govern, and these were the first to demonstrate the king's message. They were marked as subversives and met with immolation, their bodies blazing on what came to be the *Hill of Lamentations*. And Zaibos became known by many names—Tyrant, Usurper, *Lord of Agonies*—but to most, he was simply the *Monster King*, for he was never without his crown of spikes. Even the few that knew him became convinced, that the brother of Radia had been transformed, for who but a demon could dispense such cruelty?

Only the silent were safe, those who did not question, the weak-willed eloai, and the aged. But it was the men-at-arms, many of Zaibos's own forces, who proved the most rebellious. Possessed with the idealism and bravado of youth, they refused to cast down the white and gold unicorn and were among the first to burn. And yet those who adopted the *Fist and Morningstar* met with worse fates. Unwilling to set fire to the square where those loyal to the princess were barricaded, the black-armored rebels were routed, and the loyalist families delivered to the hill. But of the forty defectors who survived the skirmish—boys between seventeen and twenty—Zaibos had other plans. On that day, bundles of pikes were cut from the surrounding wood, their ends sharpened to a point, to be driven by hammer the whole length of the body. It proved more effective than fire, for as the king himself made clear, when the outer flesh burns away there is little pain. When the poles were erected, bearing the bodies of the rebels upon them, less than a dozen still lived, having endured the impaling.

Three days after the princess's departure, and the hill became known as a place of horrors, of bloodied and charred corpses, a feast for birds and insects, and its effect on the city was engrossing. Words went unspoken, among them *Radia* and *princess* and *unicorn*, but also *loyalist* and *dissenter*. Even the young were forbidden to speak of the things they once knew to be good, nor could a child submit to his or her imagination in the drawing or painting of a unicorn, lest they be disciplined by their kin.

But mercy could not be vanquished entirely from the city. Those impaled were secretly incinerated, so that among the charred anthropoid shapes, mothers failed to recognize their sons, or daughters their fathers, and in some small way, hope was kept alive.

When Tyrnael was broken, when there could no longer be found a single shred of gold on white, or any object large or small resembling a unicorn, the king's attention turned to the princess and those loyal to her, for his cruelty could not be sated. And silence was no longer a protection.

"Where did she go?"

The first to die were those most obedient to him, the crews that gave chase to the *Cloud Breaker*. They could only relate what they had seen, that a ship lifted miraculously into the sky, as though carried up by the gods. Fifty oarsmen recounted the story and were summarily executed, but when the second crew related the same tale, Zaibos no longer doubted. The third and fourth crews were spared, if only to search for her, but none could say how one was to seek a ship that flies.

"What is this ship? From whence did it come?"

The line of questioning led to the harbormaster, to his inventory of vessels, and the *Cosmos Theater*.

All these stories Orson knew, for rumor and fear spread from mouth to mouth in equal measure, and grated in his brain like a millstone, until his head ached with thought and his body quivered with constant dread. Despite his own assurances, he knew they would be coming for him, and this was the day. From his hiding spot, Orson peeked through a fold of fabric and watched faceless knights in charred-black cuirasses break into the theater to ransack it. The search went on for passings, until Mandos, the king's hand, remarked that the rolled-up curtain looked pudgy. Orson had only to keep silent, but after repeated blows to the body, he gave out a yelp and the curtain unfurled to produce his fat self, hidden inside. Without a word of accusation, Orson was forced into chains and taken down from the bannister to an awaiting wagon.

But for the tendrils of ash reaching into the sky, it was a clear, cloudless day. The ride to the hill had been short, and his heart nearly failed in seeing that place. His enormous weight overcame him and his knees buckled, but his captors brought him again to his feet, forcing him up by the spikes of their morningstars. In the distance, Orson could make out the semblance of a man, stiff and black and featureless. Even now, the figure seemed to be shouting to the gods, his final expression hardened like baked clay, only the whiteness of his teeth spared from the blackening flames.

The horrific spectacle threw Orson into a panic, making him throw aside whatever dignity he possessed. "Please! I-I am but a mere entertainer! I care nothing about your politics. Why should I? I am a total stranger to this land."

They said nothing to him, and their helms concealed their faces entirely. Together they crossed the field of bodies, the brittle, flaking limbs like the boughs of dead trees, trees deformed into mockeries of men. By the time they reached the upper part of the hill, Orson was gasping, the stench blinding and choking him. But he was not led to a pyre, nor did he see any poles about, affording him a glimmer of hope.

"Tell me one thing, at least. What is to become of me? Is it the fire? Or . . . or the other thing?"

"We've run short of stakes," Mandos said to him, as if discussing some mundane matter, "so we've devised something new."

"S-Something new?" The thought of this unknown torture filled him with even greater dread, though he could scarcely imagine anything worse than a pike, forced up through the genitals. Before he could give it any further thought, two soldiers turned him about so that he faced the other way, and they proceeded to strip him bare, shredding his clothing with their gauntlets. Being forced onto his belly was a discomfort, but bearable. With his cheek to the ground, his breathing came in quick, nervous gasps, and as the armored men tightened coarse ropes about his wrists and ankles, he forced himself to think on other matters, distancing his mind from the awful reality he could not escape. He focused on the grass between his eyes and the clover brushing his nose. An ant was crawling along a single leafy blade, and he pondered its rich red hues, its enormous mandibles. *How oblivious we are to this single ant, as we are to it! This is the forgotten wisdom of children, who will crawl upon their bellies to explore this alien world, this place of miniature monsters, that in later years becomes invisible to us. Oh, what a thing for a play! The actors could dress up like ants, and . . .*

Fallen leaves crackled in his ears. Alarmed, he strained to lift himself to see above the sward, momentarily forgetting his bonds, but the ropes did not slacken and his lips and nostrils fell suddenly and were caked with dirt. The sound of encroaching boots magnified until he recognized Mandos by his voice and by the dull black sheen of his greaves, but the second pair, stained like dull blood and fire, ornate and sharp-rimmed and monstrous, could only belong to the one he most feared.

"Wake up!" Mandos was kicking him again. The knight seemed to delight in tormenting him, repeatedly burying the tip of his boot in Orson's belly. "The king will question you now."

"I hear speak of a galleon—a *flying* galleon. What do you know of this?" It was *him*! The sullen voice, what he had so often heard in speeches, was unmistakable.

At that moment, Orson did not consider who he might betray. Rather, he was relieved to know the answer. Perhaps, if he were to offer it quickly and concisely, some measure of clemency might be shown to him. "It is the *Cloud Breaker*, my lord—the ship upon which I arrived. See, I am merely a humble visitor, a performer! I come bringing merriment and . . . and laughter!"

"Lies," Zaibos intoned. "You've come to plunder. To tear up our streets."

"Never, my lord! I would never—"

Mandos's boot came at him again, much more forcefully, and the pain was all-consuming, rendering him unable to speak or even breathe. His collar was shattered. A second kick collapsed an organ.

"I know why you are here!" His voice was inhuman, reverberating through the chambers of his monstrous helm. "My sister was naïve, allowing your kind to infest us, to germinate like a plague in our sacred city. Now she has fled, gone into hiding, like a rat. She cannot be allowed to return, you see, with her idealistic notions, and your inferior blood. I must know where your ship has gone."

Orson could feel the tears lining the sides of his nose. He was weeping like an infant, fearing to utter a word. But to remain silent, he knew, was to bring pain, and so he addressed the king, sobbing, "H-How could I possibly—"

Another kick and the taste of iron and blood mingled on his tongue. This time, it was Mandos who spoke. "We know you are an actor, and to deceive is your profession, but the king is no fool! Answer him. Tell us where your ship goes to moor. Give us a name!"

An icy realization ran the length of his spine, briefly numbing his agony. They were asking about home. *His* home! Gods forbid the Monster King step foot on the shores of his birthplace, where his brothers and sisters, nephews and nieces slept, ignorant to this nightmare, to the things transpiring upon the *Hill of Lamentations*. Green vistas opened in his mind, soothing his misery, for though he was powerless to escape his tormentors, he might protect his people from the same fate, if only he could muster the strength to silence himself, like the tragic figures of the stage.

"That, I'll never tell you!" He wished to have said something profound, for bards to recite when his story is told, but his mind was shattered with pain and he could conjure no other words.

"Perhaps you fancy yourself the hero," Zaibos said. "You may believe that someday, someone will find inspiration in this show of defiance. But let me assure you, you are no Batal. No one will sing songs for you. No one will lament your passing. You will die here, upon this hill, and no one will remember you."

The king stepped away, and Orson recognized a third man, not a soldier, but by the looks of his leather shoes, possibly a merchant or a trader. "You are the fat man, the jester," Zaibos went on. "You are here to make us laugh, to amuse me, and do you know what best amuses me?"

Long wet strands weaved across his naked back, something syrupy, sticky and sweet-smelling. The sensation, to his befuddlement, felt strangely pleasant. But there would be more, he knew, and it frightened him.

"Wh-What are you going to do?"

No answer came, only the sound of a large cork, and the timid voice of the merchant cautioning the two armored men. Another sensation followed, things being dropped onto him, minuscule and nearly weightless, like raisins. But they were *alive*, moving now, crawling across his skin, tickling him. There was no pain, until the first bite. It was like a needle dipped in fire.

"Fascinating creatures," Zaibos intoned. "Radia would have loved them, but she would not approve of what they do. You see, the wildwood ant makes its home in a tree."

The pain was more than Orson could handle. His spine and shoulders were afire, worse, he was slowly being eaten by countless mouths. And he realized that he was screaming and could do nothing but scream.

"It is a hardy species, a survivor, which is why I so admire it. For when an invader, like yourself, comes to eat of its tree, the ants gather to defend their home. They do not befriend the invader or try to understand him. No, the wildwood ant attacks, paralyzing the muscles, so its enemy cannot flee, and then they feast. A wild boar will disappear entirely in a matter of days."

Orson was screaming. Orson was begging for death.

"I will not spare your life, nor end it, but I do have water. Water will scatter them, if only for a moment, and in that reprieve, you will know bliss, in the abating of your pain. So I ask you again—where is your home?"

18

The sudden sound of crackling ice forced Demacharon to halt and rethink his steps. Dropping to his knees, he could feel the cold penetrating his palms as he brushed at the snow, revealing the slick surface beneath. A spider web of lines spread out from his boot, threatening to engulf him and the crew in icy waters, but there was no sign of the saboteur.

Davos stood beside him, breathing great sighs of dismay, surveying the expanse of white that stretched into the unknown, a landscape of snowy peaks and glittering crystal and the translucent blue of the frozen inlet upon which they stood. To the north, a wall of ice and rock dominated the view—the sheer cliffs of the Crown of Aenya, surrounding and hiding the lands of Mythradanaiil. West and eastward, the terrain was impossibly uneven, marked by toothy hills and deep ravines. Southward, the fjord let out onto rushing, half-frozen waters. To take a ship, any ship, through it, posed a great many risks, but they lacked other options.

"Looks like we're stuck, Uncle," Ecthros called out.

"You think?" Davos shouted.

Ankle-deep in sludge, with picks in their hands, Ecthros and Krow bent under the bow of the *Cloud Breaker*. The galley sat moored in place, leaning against its starboard side where it had run aground, its exposed keel rising through the permafrost. "It's icing up faster than we can thaw it," he complained.

Despite all their shoveling and hammering, they could not so much as budge the vessel. Davos cursed himself and the ship with every blow, until Demacharon could see that exhaustion had set in. His nephew kept hacking away for another passing, until he too began to slow.

If Demacharon was to protect the princess from would-be assassins, it would mean *moving*, and soon, for a man like Zaibos would not give up the pursuit. But he was at a loss for what to do. Born at the equator, in view of the palms that swayed along the One Sea, he was unused to polar climates, and could only guess at the thickness of the ice or how much weight could be safely put upon it. Never had he led his armies so far north, yet he was not oblivious to its dangers. Before his arrival in Tyrnael, he had challenged fate in ascending these very mountains, and yet he was alone at that time, with nothing to lose but himself.

Giving in to the cold, Krow and Ecthros trekked from the ship to join them on the ice.

"It's impossible . . . there's no way," the boy huffed, stuffing his hands into his green cloak.

"What I told you a good century ago!" Davos's glare was sobering, despite his windmill hat spinning crazily in the wind.

"It was worth a try, wasn't it? What else would you have had us do, O Captain of Mine?"

"Watch that tongue, boy! I'll have no sassy talk on my ship, nephew or no."

"But we're not on your ship now, are we?"

The *Cloud Breaker* was grounded, in an alcove between the mountain and where the mountain broke apart to join the river. But to abandon the ship was folly. Come nightfall, they would be dead, frozen in their sleep. Unless they could climb to the opposite side of the mountain, where—rejecting all that he knew to be natural—the land was green and warm, a paradise now ruled by a tyrant.

"Is there no way to take her up again?" Demacharon asked the bird man. "Flying would serve us well about now."

"Unfortunately, our saboteur was thorough. He shut off the burners and cut a gash in the sails, accomplishing just enough to land the ship, but not kill us."

"And there's no way to repair it?"

"The sails are delicate work, light as silk but stronger than tanned leather. Only my people know to make such materials. Only in Nimbos can she be made whole."

Ecthros turned to the avian, his cheeks reddening against the wind. "What I don't understand is, why not kill us? Cut the sails completely and let us crash?"

Davos shook his head in protest. "And how in the hoary hells do you suppose *he'd* survive the crash? He must have wanted to get away."

"On foot? You're not supposing he could fly? He must have gotten up there somehow."

"The secret of flight is known only to our people," Krow remarked, a hint of pride escaping his hawkish facade.

Davos eyed him incredulously, his red beard flaring like a torch. "So the saboteur was one o' you? I think not, my friend. And do I have to mention what none of you've bothered to notice? We should be halfway home, yet here we are, right where we damn-well started! Seems the bastard turned us around in the night. He knew what he was doing, alright."

"None of it makes sense," said Ecthros. "If he had wanted to deliver us to Zaibos, why not take us all the way, right into the city? Why drop us here?"

"Perhaps he lost control, cut the sails too soon," Krow suggested. "He couldn't have known how to pilot such a ship."

Unable to tolerate their chatter any longer, Demacharon stepped forward. "Let's not forget why we're all here. *Noora*. The assassin—and make no mistake it *was* our assassin—was on board, in her very cabin. He could have killed her at any moment, and we'd never have been the wiser, but she's untouched. Why?"

Ecthros clenched his fist. "If he's out there, I'm betting he'll return! Maybe he's gone to bring Zaibos! Or he's watching us this very moment, plotting something wicked." He marched forward, moving further onto the ice, attacking shadows with his aim.

"Come back here, boy," Davos called. "We've no time for your heroics!"

"But he must be around here someplace," he argued, sliding an arrow against his bow. "He *must*—"

CRACK!

It was Demacharon who lunged, pulling the boy to safety. "Get back! The ice—!"

"No need to trouble yourself," Davos replied calmly. "If the ship didn't break through it, we sure won't, though I've got a few pounds to lose for sure."

A great distance off, across the blue-white inlet, a crackling could be heard, an echo in answer to the first. Defying reason, the ice was breaking apart, a fracture line running through the ground like a bolt of frozen lightning, dividing the icy shelf. The surface upon which they stood rose and twisted, multiplying into ever smaller segments, and there was no thought but to run to the imagined security of the ship.

They had no time to turn back, to see the dreaded thing approaching, yet all could sense it, some unnatural force at work, something massive and powerful. The ice was breaking in snaking, zigzagging patterns, as if something was swimming just beneath the frigid waters below, disturbing the frozen surface with its immensity. As they reached the hull, the cold air rushing painfully into their lungs, most of the plateau was gone, leaving a precarious periphery upon which to hang. Davos grabbed Ecthros by the hair, pulling the boy's leg from the icy sludge and dragging him up toward the *Cloud Breaker*, but the ship was loose and pulling away. Demacharon, all the while, screamed his dead sister's name, reaching to where the princess slept, as water sloshed between him and the ship.

"It's out there." Krow regained his composure, and was facing away from them, peering through the flurry with his keen hawk eyes, to where the surface was bulging and roiling. "My people call them *crawlers*."

In the direction where the avian pointed, the ice was of a different shade, a hard crystalline white, but also organic— *alive*. Demacharon instinctively tugged at his gladius.

"I have him!" Soaked and shuddering, Ecthros stood against the gunwale above them, steadying his bow. His arrow climbed into the sky, but the wind stole it away.

A wave lifted the *Cloud Breaker* free, and Davos and Krow clutched at the rope ladder to join the boy. With aching bones, Demacharon came last, tumbling over the rail in a heap.

As it surfaced again, they could see it in its entirety now, a crustacean-like carapace with multiple legs and pincers formed entirely out of—or camouflaged to mimic—ice crystals. With an undulating motion, it swam at them, each insectoid section submerging and reemerging from the water. Ecthros trained his arrows upon it, one after another, and each vanished to no avail.

"Steer us clear!" Demacharon shouted, but Davos could only nod as the crawler latched itself to the hull, its mass rocking the ship as it began to climb. Everyone recoiled to the safety of the upper decks, except for the captain. With his enormous spoon-sword drawn up to his shoulder, he lunged forward, catching the rail with his gut. "Have at it, crew! Looks like we're having lobster tonight!"

Demacharon steadied himself and watched as Davos made for its eyes, the glassy bulbous cluster centering its body, but his blow fell short, and with the lurching of the hull he nearly fell overboard. Unfazed by his show of courage, the crawler regarded him with indifference, bearing its whole weight upon the galley, casting them in the shadow of its multifaceted grotesqueness. The ribs of the galley strained under the pressure, its long beams creaking and groaning, until the *Cloud Breaker* was tilted nearly onto its starboard side, and the crew lost footing, sliding into the crawler's awaiting maw.

Demacharon held to the mast, Ecthros found purchase in the rigging, and Krow drew long gashes into the floor with his talons to stop himself, but Davos fell between its pincers.

"Uncle!"

Its crab-like claw clamped about his waist, to squeeze the life from him, but the captain's spirit could not be shaken. He cursed and spat at it defiantly, and Demacharon knew then what he had to do, dropping onto the crawler's face, or what he deemed its face, *Severetrix* in hand. The Zo blade cut between the narrow unshielded joint in a single swipe, spattering the deck with a yellow briny substance, and the claw fell away, carrying Davos with it.

With a thundering crash and a burst of water, the ship righted itself, as the crawler slunk over the edge. Demacharon could only assume that it was badly injured and that it possessed no vocal cords with which to scream. Picking himself up, he rushed to the gunwale, finding Davos free of the claw and clinging to an ice flow. He looked more perturbed than frightened. To Demacharon's dismay, the crawler was not retreating. Despite amputation, the instinct to feed was paramount, and it was now circling, making again for the captain.

"I'll save you, Uncle!" Ecthros cried, nocking three arrows in his bow and loosing them simultaneously. The one closest to his pinky fell on his toe and the top arrow never left the shaft, but the third took flight, missing the creature by a wide margin.

Demacharon glowered over him. "You ever hit anything with that bow?"

The boy's face soured and his limbs slackened, but he gave no reply.

"What on earth are you doing? This isn't a game—this is war! Arm yourself, soldier!"

The creature was low in the water now, its eye-clusters half-submerged, as it moved toward the drifting fat man. Davos's reddish hue was dulling, turning shades of blue. Clinging to a chunk of ice and kicking to stay afloat, he was utterly defenseless, and the crawler was gaining. Demacharon considered their options, but no strategy presented itself. In war, the battlefield was everything—it meant the difference between victory and defeat, but here there was no ground, only freezing water and a rocky inlet no sane sailor would dare enter. Should they even manage to turn the ship about, the *Cloud Breaker* was without ram or ballista, or arms of any kind.

But the man in the water went unnoticed. Even with its many eyes, the crawler was moving blindly, seeking the large mass occupying its domain. It reminded Demacharon of two things—a fast-approaching trireme, and a charging bull. "Hold on to something—it's going to ram us!"

"What's all the fuss?" Her voice was deep with sleep, and calm, too much so given their predicament.

"Noora!"

She was standing in their midst, oddly still, the violent swaying of the deck seeming to not affect her. "I fell out of bed—"

"Noora, you have to get away! The crawler . . ." It was a futile warning, for there was nowhere to go, no safe place to flee.

"It's going to be alright," she assured him. Slowly, she walked to the edge of the ship, her bare feet padding softly, her eyes glassy. Was she even awake, or merely walking in her sleep?

As she raised her arms, the waters became calm, transforming into a placid, silvery lake. Even the wind was silenced, and the crawler no longer charged towards them. Noora appeared to be looking through it, her gaze arresting its movements. When she lifted her hands again, its enormous claws snapped at the air, mirroring her movements.

Demacharon ran up to her side, dumbfounded.

The crawler immersed itself beneath the sludge and disappeared, but it was some time before she became aware of him, blinking hard and fast, as if she were waking from a dream.

"How did you do that?"

"Do? Do what?"

"The creature, it was like a puppet, and you were pulling its strings. How did you do that? Were you in command of it?"

"No," she whispered, "nothing like that. But for a moment, I felt . . . this is going to sound impossible, but . . . I felt as if I *was* the creature."

The crew formed around her, equally astonished, then Ecthros and Krow remembered their captain, jumping into the water with a length of rope to retrieve him.

"You should not stay out here any longer." It was the only thing Demacharon could think to say. "You'll catch your death of cold with what you're wearing."

"It doesn't bother me. Not now, not yet," she remarked. "Later, perhaps I might feel it." She was looking away, half-watching the man and the avian wrestle their captain onto the ship, Ecthros ribbing his uncle about his weight the entire time, until the captain hit the floor like a sack of potatoes.

Krow was the first aboard, lending his captain a feathered hand. "Are you well?"

"That depends on my ship—" he spat, hiding his trauma with bravado. But as she caught his eye, Davos was taken aback, suddenly finding the strength to get to his feet, clasping her small shoulders in his hands. "Princess . . . we thought the worst!"

"Give her some space, will you?" Ecthros barked. He turned to face her, timidly adding, "Can I get you anything, my lady? A warm blanket, perhaps?"

There was much that needed saying, but as a former admiral, Demacharon knew that this was a time for action. "Davos, we mustn't tarry. If she's still seaworthy, we must get the *Cloud Breaker* moving. That monster did us a favor—let's not waste it."

"Agreed." Krow took swift action, tugging expertly at the knots. "Won't be long before the ice hardens again."

They went to work, all but Demacharon, who could not bring himself to leave Noora's side, though their avenue of escape narrowed with every breath. He watched as she continued to stare out at the water, wanting to embrace her, to shield her with every thread of his being. For days, he had thought of nothing else, fearing he had failed her. His helplessness angered him, in guarding against a threat he could not see. What was the nature of her illness? Was she keeping it from him, or did she not understand it?

Sails snapped tight, swelling to fullness, and he could feel the bones of the galley stir. The *Cloud Breaker* was cutting through the drifting ice, and the familiar sway of a ship at sail lulled him like an infant in a cradle.

"Hedonian, tell me about the Sea, your home—could you describe it to me?"

He was in no mood for idle talk, but this was Noora, he supposed, earnest as ever, and he wished not to discourage her. For a time, he considered her inquiry, wishing to give answer, but after several false starts, he settled with, "I am not the man to ask. I am no bard. My sword is my instrument. What I must say, I write in blood."

"Try," she pressed him, gently. "Try for me."

He closed his eyes, searching for a memory, but the one that came to him was like a gauntlet gripping his heart. "You can smell the salt in the air, long before you come to it, and something about that scent fills your soul with wanting. The roar and crash of the tides, and the cackling sea birds—it is like a rush of the familiar, reminding you that no matter your actions, our feeble attempts to master our fates, the world continues to flow, oblivious to our petty concerns. To look upon it, to really see it, is to see home, the place you are most at peace, but just so, it is an eternal stranger, teeming with mysteries we can never know."

Noora did not speak or turn to face him, but continued to stare out at the frozen waters.

"Forget it," he said after a pause. "That's utter nonsense."

"No. It comes from your heart, and there is truth in it." Her voice was a murmur, heavy with contemplation. "I saw it, Dimmy. I sped across the Sea atop a great white steed, swift as the gale, the spray nipping at our heels. And yet, I've never been to the great water. Does that make sense? Can it be that I was dreaming?"

"I do not know."

"That is where you saw him last, was it not? Your son? He was killed beside the Sea, murdered, and what murdered him came again in force, and Hedonia was lost, washed away forever."

"How can you know that?"

"It is like an old rhyme . . . something ancient, that has always been and will be again, just as you and I have stood here, for eternity, two characters from a story. Your son, I did not know him, yet you call his name in your sleep, and as you were telling me of the Sea, I sensed a great loss in you, coupled with the memory."

Demacharon did not wish to speak of this, not now, when there were other, more pressing matters. But the pain he struggled to bury surfaced suddenly. "You know nothing about me. You're just a child, thinking the world to be like one of your storybooks. What do you know, truly? Life is cruel and ugly, princess, and the face of it has been hidden from you. What happened in the alley, to your handmaiden, *that* is the reality, the ever-present threat the common man faces day after day, until meeting the Taker." The release of his anger felt empowering—he could be strong, he would not break.

"You sound almost like my brother."

"Yes. Well, we are probably not so different as you imagine."

"I don't believe that. I can't. There is goodness in you. I feel it."

"You feel only what you want to, same as the rest of us. If you were to look within . . . if you only knew, you'd run far from me."

"You don't know that." She was staring into his eyes now, her violet and turquoise pupils shimmering, wet with tears. Did she possess the power to see into his heart? To see his sins? "Everyone can be redeemed," she murmured.

He turned, unable to face her. "There is no redemption for me. I have my duties and you have yours. Ask no further into my past."

Davos stood at the wheel, stern-faced and with firm hands, wrestling for control. At the topmast, Krow searched for sinkers, directing his captain clear of the jagged islands dwarfing their vessel. For passings, they navigated the treacherous flow, the prow plowing through the ice, the river breaking apart and coalescing in their wake. But the greatest threat to their lives lessened at the close of day, and it was not long before the *Cloud Breaker* escaped from the inlet to join the broader waters of the fjord. Reaching the narrows of the Potamis, Davos wiped his brow and eased his grip, no longer having to fight the wheel. For days they sailed without incident, following the river's course—the lifeblood of Aenya—a southerly wind filling their sails.

The cabin was dim but for the light of the moons streaming in through the windows and the single brazier casting flitting shadows across their faces. Ecthros was fingering his lute, as expertly as he might the strings of his bow, singing snatches of half-remembered ballads. Tales of heroism and undying love spilled from his lips and, beside him, Davos strained to follow the melody, his red caterpillar eyebrows twitching with every missed note, but after three mugs of ale, the captain joined in the song without complaint. Demacharon and Krow watched on in silence, exchanging the occasional bemused glance.

"Lady, come out, come out, lady . . . You and I, we'll have a baby . . . Don't you believe that I'll be true?"

"With lyrics like those," Davos said, adding a burp, "don't be expecting her to go anywhere near you!"

"But she's been in there all day!" the boy complained, setting aside his instrument. "Why won't she come out? I only want to talk."

"Because you're a buffoon, that's why. You think the *Princess of Tyrnael* would ever fraternize with a common ship hand such as yourself?"

"No, it's more than that," he answered. "Something's upset her. I can tell."

"There's no greater mystery in all the universe," Davos remarked, pausing to take a swig, "than a woman. Better men have tried to navigate a woman's heart, but all've failed."

"What of Kiki?"

"What about her?" He wiped the foam from his beard and topped his mug again. "Gods know what goes on in that woman's head. Stopped trying to figure her out ages ago. But I love her all the same. Best do what they ask without troubling your head, eh? 'Wife of misery, life of misery,' that's what they say!" He raised his mug suddenly, soaking his sleeve and forearm. "A toast . . . to women! They steer us crazy and yet we adore them still!"

"Here, here," the avian agreed, less than enthusiastically. Demacharon, leaning over the table, was last to join his mug in the toast.

"Don't let him fool you," Davos muttered, turning from Krow to Demacharon. "He's a true romantic, that one, more than you or I. Did he ever tell you his story?"

The bird man leaned away, looking to depart, and if not for the feathers hiding his face, Demacharon was sure it was would be turning crimson.

"Captain, I'd rather you not—"

"Oh, be a good sport, now! It's a good tale! Besides, we're all friends here. There's no greater bond than 'twixt those who've fought and faced death together, and we've certainly shared our share of peril now, haven't we?"

"If you insist, Captain."

He dropped a burly hand over the bird man's slender shoulder. "Ah, there's the spirit! Now then," he began, leaning close enough for Demacharon to smell the alcohol on his breath, "long before joining my crew, Krow was a right regular bird man, living up there in the clouds with all a' rest, doing whatever it is bird men do. But Krow here had a secret, he did, a real hankering for all things human, and from time to time came soaring down to spy on us and our ways. One day, as he's out and about, doing his usual perusing, he spots himself a lovely village lass. Never saw the girl myself, mind you, but she was buxom as they come, with great flowing hair and dark eyes. Or so was told me. Down comes Krow, flapping his arms, black feathers falling this way and that, scaring the girl half to death. See, she'd never seen his like before, and being from a tiny village, was innocent to such wonders, so she quick takes a fancy to him. Thing is, she's a married woman—but does that stop the two love birds? Far from it! When Irene strikes the heart's sails with love, well, there's not a power in all the universe that'll change ye'r course."

"But, Uncle, what of you and Kiki? You'd never—"

"Shut up, boy—I'm telling a story here. Now, where was I?"

"The gusts of love," Krow answered, with considerable irritation.

"Right, right. Turns out, less than a year later, wife pops out a baby boy, a *feathered* baby boy, if you gather my meaning. The husband, mad as all hells, nearly strangles the poor young girl, and the babe, too, right in their beds, and he would have done so too, if not for Krow, who comes a swooping in—"

"I really didn't *swoop* in," Krow interjected. "There was just a small window—"

"No matter. So you come *barging* in, fight off the husband, and deliver mama and newborn to safety. Problem is, those other bird folk sitting up in their clouds, catch wind of this and are none too happy. Krow is excommunicated, see, and his wings are torn from his body."

Demacharon seemed to notice the bird man for the first time, his dark feathers turning gold in the torchlight, his semi-human, hawkish facial features difficult to discern. "You have my sympathies."

"If not for the captain and his crew," Krow answered him, "who found me, I might not have survived. The captain is a generous man, and I am deeply indebted to him."

"Pish posh! You've paid your debt many times over. Truth is, we're family now, just as you and Noora are."

Demacharon wanted to run from the cabin, to escape these people for whom he shared no affections, but who dared to call him family. But there was nowhere to go. He emptied his flagon, steadied himself in his chair, and spoke not a word.

"What of you, Hedonian? Ever know the shackles of wife and child?"

He glared into that fat drunken smile, and Niobe's pallid countenance flashed before him—those pleading brown eyes, forever accusing. "No," he answered at length, "I've no family to speak of."

"Tell us a story, then! Surely, as admiral, you've witnessed aplenty, and have got a great deal to share."

"Some stories are better left unspoken."

Davos dragged his chair closer to his, nearly touching him with his beard. "Every man's got a story, and you ain't leaving here till you share yours."

"So that's the way it is, eh?" Demacharon rose, balancing himself on his feet, the floor shakier than he remembered, and his chair fell noisily behind him. "That's what you want from me—my story? So we can all bond and sing our virtues? Am I some shelled thing in which you think to find a pearl, sailor? There's nothing here," he cried, pounding his sternum, "yet you insist that I sit here and mewl like a whore, as if you might understand, as if a drunkard captain and his lovesick nephew and a cripple of an avian have any capacity to know me, to absolve me of anything!" He was yelling now, raging without knowing what he was saying. Yet something propelled him forward. "See here, captain, I am not one of you, nor shall I ever be, so keep your stinking breath far from my face, and we'll all get along better, I assure you."

Davos stood, his chair falling hard, his fists raised. Ecthros was already tugging at his arm, pleading restraint. "You've saved my life once, and for that, I won't throw you off my ship. That's *one*, Hedonian. I won't tolerate another insult."

"Calm yourself, Captain," Krow interjected. "The ale speaks for you both. Besides, he has not taken to bed in days. I watch him in the night, pacing the ship." Addressing Demacharon, he added, "I suggest you return to your quarters. Find sleep, if you can."

"*Sleep?*" he laughed, but he felt the energy flow out of him, and thought to soften the moment and to mitigate the hard words he had thrown at Davos, which he already felt himself regretting. "I am not so blessed as the dead to know such peace. But there is a tale I would share if you'll hear it."

"Well!" The captain slapped his knee in triumph, downing another mug. "Let's have it then!"

Demacharon tried to think where he might begin, but his head was throbbing and his mind in a whorl, and it seemed he had spent his last bit of energy in an angry outburst. "Have you ever heard of a people called the *Fel*? No, don't answer, I know you haven't. No one has.

"We'd been marching a full battalion, a company of ten thousand, far to the north, through the hills of Gasamen Naar, beyond the tributaries of the Nìr Waden. A good many hailed from Hedonia, but most were conscripts from surrounding colonies. At any rate, we were a year out from anywhere any man could call home. Our mission was multifold. We were to establish outposts for future settlements, find trading partners perhaps, but more than anything, we wanted to know what was out there, to fill the empty spaces on our maps. In all the world, there is but One Sea, or so we believe, but we wondered if there could be more, waiting to be discovered. Likewise, we were curious to know if there were other, foreign empires, about alien coasts, as rich and renown as our own. It was an exciting prospect.

"There was a cartographer in our ranks, drawing hills and valleys with every new horizon, naming places we were just discovering after myths and legends. But the soldiers grew more restless by the day, fearing the unknown that awaited us, wanting to return to the map they knew. 'We'll march off the face of Aenya,' they protested, but the officers knew better. I assured them that the world was a sphere and that there was no danger of falling from it. And yet, there were perils to consider. The further we marched, the longer and hotter the days, and the shorter our supplies. We were in want of water, and cycles from the tributaries we had passed. Our only hope was to find some new source, another Potamis circling opposite the world, or turn back with nothing to show for our efforts. With each new dawn, we found nothing but arid hills and brush, for as far as our scouts could recount.

"Starvation was already setting in. Two of my men were killed squabbling over scraps. Others succumbed to sickness, never waking from their tents. Rumors of desertion spread throughout the camp and I was forced to take harsh measures. Perhaps too late, I gave the order to turn back.

"We could tell by the stars that we were headed east and south, but the land did not conform to our maps. Lost, hungry, and frightened, we met with the *Fel*.

"At first our scouts could not discern whether they were human. They met us in bands by the hundred, naked but for the white and blue mud caking their bodies, and the animal skulls obscuring their faces, femurs round as my fist protruding from their chins. They beat their breasts, jumping and hollering like beasts, rattling weapons of bone and spilling their blood. We were horrified, but sought peace. Our emissary, a learned linguist and historian, returned upon his horse missing his head. After that, Dagmar, my first lieutenant, suggested we circle round them, but the passage to the south would take us through unforgiving hill country, and we would be losing days, if not risking injury. It was my second officer, Marcus, who noted that the Fel had water, and food. The decision proved simple to make. At first light, we armed ourselves for battle.

"I prayed, to all the gods in our pantheon, that the Fel lay down their arms, see to reason and surrender peaceably, but they were a stubborn lot. They fought bravely, no question, but fell like fools upon our swords and spears, dying just the same as any man, despite their monstrous appearance. It was our most complete victory, yet the battle haunts me still, for by the evening of that day, we counted forty of our dead and more than a thousand of theirs. The following morning, we raided the village of all that they owned—livestock, grain, pots of rainwater, but reports returned to me of that which I most dreaded. The Fel were taken, down to the last man, but the women and children remained, hiding in huts of mud and dung. I took counsel from my officers, as to what was to be done—abandon them to fate or deliver them as slaves. I chose the latter.

"We marched for the Nìr Waden, with as much water and livestock as we could carry, hundreds of women and children in tow. The cycles came and went, and I did what I could to prevent the mistreatment of the captives. But a camp of thousands is no easy thing to manage, and there were rapes, and many women took their own lives, and the lives of their children also. I remember the constant wailing, from the infants and their mothers, but I found solace in knowing our destination, in that we were taking them to paradise, *for better to be a slave in Hedonia than a king in the wild*, they say. And yet, it seemed that day would never come, and that the constant thirst would drive us to cruelty and madness.

"One night . . ." Demacharon swallowed hard, choking on the words he was about to speak. "I summoned my first lieutenant, offering him a drink of wine from my provisions. It was all I could do to ease the burden I was to saddle him with. He was an honorable man, Dagmar. 'There must be some other way,' he kept saying, but I reminded him of our creed, 'Do your duty, and do not question.' He was never the same after that . . . I could see it in his eyes, but gods know he understood me, understood what had to be done. It was us or them, you see.

"It was to be done quietly, if at all, I urged, a quick cut across the throat, and remember, the mothers first, always the mothers!" His voice was trembling now, breaking at the syllable. "The children are young and won't know what is happening, but the mothers . . . I made him swear . . . dammit if I didn't make him swear. But the gods are deaf and blind, it seems, or they take no pity on men, for some of the families were awake when the men came into their tents, and their piercing cries swept through the camp. The begging, the desperation—in any language it wounds the soul—and the whole of that night I sat in my tent, trying to justify, to myself, what we had done. Come dawn, I took up a spade, to help in the digging. In a mass grave, we piled the bodies, without ceremony, the last of the Fel. Four days out, and we arrived at the Nìr Waden. There would have been enough water for us all.

"My duties fulfilled, we returned to the capital, parading in the streets like conquering heroes, but I can still hear them in the night. I can hear them begging, pleading for their lives. I can hear the screaming. You wanted a story, Captain—well, there's your story." No one spoke, but Demacharon did not wait for them, nor did he care to gauge their expressions. What others thought of him bore no consequence. He found his quarters, five paces from where he had been sitting, and stood silently before the dimly lit room. After five mugs, he felt lightheaded, but it was the nights without sleep that were affecting him, so that he clung to the doorway for a moment. Tugging at his shirt, he worked his way to his bed, every bone aching, his eyes remaining open through force of will. And like a drowning man, he held fast to the chain securing his cot to the wall, and there he waited, fighting the tug and lure of sleep.

. . . faces press upon mine, swallowing me whole, and in that last moment, I recognize the source. A city. By the gods, the light is a city!

The bed was a pit, he knew, and deep within its folds a yawning abyss, waiting to devour him. His gladius was mounted to the wall, and he regarded it with cold contemplation, fingering the brass pommel. This was his only escape, the only way to end the struggle.

They wait for me . . . why do I make them wait? I should never have reached for the light, I am undeserving of it, but it's too far now. We're days from the city . . . days from the light . . .

In that moment of darkness, Demacharon felt a presence enter the room and stand behind him, her hand warm and soft upon his tortured shoulder. Turning to face her gleaming, mismatched eyes, so uncannily like the moons, he found that he could not speak. How much had she heard? How much did she know?

"It's alright, Dimmy," she said. "I'm here."

Wrought with despair, he broke at her feet, and wept in her arms.

19

Bloodsnot

Ugh was staring at the ground in what was, as of late, becoming a more familiar emotion, though his species had no words for *wonder* or *fascination*, or anything approximating such feelings.

Worms came in many shapes and sizes, he knew, most no bigger than his little finger. But a rare few were immeasurable, for by the time anyone could measure one, the worm would have already eaten them. *Devastation worms*, his people called them, or *wyrmaks*. When diggers worked the tunnels, where the hard dirt had laid undisturbed for ages, there was always the danger of waking such a creature. Wyrmaks were drawn to subtle vibrations in the earth, but being both blind and deaf, they relied on organisms falling haphazardly into their mouths for sustenance. Imagining such a scenario, the little digger came to understand how he had been separated from his crew, and why now, after returning from his long absence, there was no trace of them but pickaxes and decomposing bodies. The evidence was everywhere, from the circular tunnels left by the wyrmak's wake, to the crusted purple mucus coating every rock and body part. The workers were in such disarray of blood and bone and tissue, he was unable to recognize anyone, or guess how many had managed to escape uneaten or uncrushed.

Earlier that day, when Ugh decided to return to the underground, he did so with great reluctance. *Shirkers will be thrown in the magma*, he recalled, and he was not looking forward to the possibility of such an agonizing death. But what else could be done? There was nowhere in the world for a lone bogren to go. Only Radia could love a hideous, worthless creature like himself and, after some time, even she had abandoned him. Bogrens did not mix with those not of their kind. However crude his species, Ugh belonged to them.

Upon his arrival, he expected to be apprehended and marked as a shirker, but there was no one about. Fearing the return of the wyrmak, Ugh assumed the tunnel to be abandoned. With this unexpected twist of fate, he considered his actions as best he could, without straining his brain in the process.

Bogrens held no stock in recording their history or improving the prospect of their communal lives, and therefore did not take census of their number. If he could make his way to his hovel without being seen, he could pretend that he was never among Meatface's crew. Even now, he might chance to cross paths with some dozen laborers, clearing rocks for a new passage, but he would need a tool to escape suspicion. Only one pick not yet dissolved by mucus remained, but the corpse to which it belonged was stubborn and refused to let go. Tugging and tugging, Ugh became annoyed with the dead digger, until the twig-like fingers broke away with a snap, and he stood over the body with the tool held high, like a warrior standing over a kill.

"Ay! You there!"

Ugh turned rigid, torn between playing dead and running away. Slowly, his eyes adjusted to the dim recess, where a large figure was fast approaching—not a foreman, but someone of even greater stature. Paralyzed with uncertainty, the diminutive digger watched the imposing figure come into focus. He was nearly twice Ugh's height, with arms of corded muscle and shoulders made even more immense by the scaled pauldrons armoring them. Robust chains jangled down to his genitalia, and he wore a crude helmet of spikes. But it was the warrior's face that most startled Ugh. It looked as if someone had split his skull down the middle and stitched the two halves together with small iron rings.

"Ay, *you*! Whatch you doin' ere?"

"Me? I am, um, am . . ."

"D'you kill 'em?" His brain could be seen pulsing from between his eyes and nostril, and the damage must have affected his powers of observation, Ugh thought, for he did not seem to notice the wyrmak-shaped hole in the wall, nor did he take into account the half-eaten bodies. Bogrens were known to be cannibals, in extreme cases, but were never so messy or wasteful.

To lie or tell the truth? With little time to mull it over, Ugh's instinct spoke for him. "Yes!" he asserted, "I killed them, alright."

"Hrmph." The warrior grunted, snorted, and grunted some more, and Ugh could feel the mutilated wheels of his brain torturously turning.

"That's right. I chopped them all to pieces! Tell *me* what to do, will they? See, this foreman comes bellowin' at me, so I whacks him in the head. Whacks him good, till all his brains spills out, and then the others come by, saying I can't be doin' that. So what do I do? I hacks and slashes them too, till they don't bother me no more."

"You done good!" the warrior said, without an ounce of doubt. "I'm Brainbash. You come with me now. See chief."

Ugh quailed. "Wh-What? The chief? Why?"

Brainbash put a hand on his shoulder, in a gesture of goodwill, and the two bogrens took off, through the labyrinth of tunnels, toward the bright orange expanse of the Forge. On rickety scaffolding and narrow rope bridges, they crossed one overflowing pool of magma after another, reaching finally across the Great Abyss, its countless alcoves rising above and stretching below them. The oaf leading him stomped clumsily over the decrepit beams, never regarding the weakening structure twisting under their feet. Perhaps, it would have been best for the latticework to fail, for then he could watch the warrior thrash as his body dissolved in the lake of fire, and Ugh could perish with a smile. He preferred this to whatever fate awaited him.

By the few workers present, Ugh could tell that it was early in the day. As always, great simmering cauldrons were being winched up from hot glowing pools, and magma poured into molds, and the whole of the chamber rang with the familiar clamor of chains and pulleys. Hammers fell and sparks sparked, but Ugh could not see the results of their labor. The artisans he envied, those who cut images into the breastplates and shields and helms, were nowhere about.

Beyond the Forge, Ugh and his escort came to a series of steps cut into the rock, a place he had never seen before. They started to climb, carefully, for though the rock was sturdy, the footing was narrow.

After a dozen or so passings, the Forge shrank to a yellow glow no bigger than the palm of his hand, and they arrived at a broad alcove, with a great roof of hanging stalactites. Warriors busied about, testing their weapons on one another and shouting obscenities, and bullying whomever was deemed the weaker. Several large humanoid shapes squatted in a dimly lit recess—the stone idols of some great chieftain, perhaps—but then one of them turned his way, making him leap with fright.

"What are those things?"

"Har! Never seen un, eh? Them's horg—just bitches really. It's the bulls you got to watch for."

"Oh, right."

They came to an immense door with iron rivets and rings. With a grunt of acknowledgment, the doors were slowly pulled apart by a pair of muscled guards, and what met his eyes was what every worker dreamt of, but could never hope to witness—the place of plenty, the chieftain's horde. Everywhere he looked, there was an assortment of objects, piles and piles of them, things he could not name and others he could only guess at—pots and pans and chairs and tables, moth covered chests and shattered mirrors, hills of skirts and shawls and undergarments, mountains of shoes and bangles and tiaras, children's clay figurines and tin soldiers and broken rocking horses. Above all this ramshackle, overlapping tapestries stretched from corner to corner, the vague standards of nations come and gone.

Organization, design, symmetry—these were foreign concepts to bogren, even for a chief. What mattered was the total sum possessed. Whoever owned more, owned greater status, no matter the relic or their condition.

Seated against the wall, in a pile eroded beyond recognition, Ugh noticed the chief. A human skull was strapped to his head, wearing its own crown of gold and jewels, and the chief's hand gripped a scepter made from the bones of an arm, and upon the arm's skeletal fingers, affixed with wax, were rings of emerald and sapphire and topaz.

Ugh waited quietly, for the chief was digging a fingernail into his nose, a nose of considerable girth, resembling a leech that was choking on his face. He was going at it with such determination that the little digger did not dare to interrupt him.

Brainbash, however, was not so apprehensive. "Bloodsnot! Ay! Look 'ere, will ya!"

Bloodsnot turned his head with a snort, drawing blood and mucus across his breast. "What'd you bring this digger here for? Ain't he supposed to be digging?"

"This lit' guy kills hisself his fo'man as well's 'is whole crew."

"You sure about this?" Bloodnot replied. "You seen this with your own eyes?"

"Sure did. They's all dead."

The chief shifted in his throne, a few items of the stuff comprising it rolling down the sides, as he glared at the diminutive digger. "Looks mighty puny to me. I shit bigger shits than him. You sure you're sure?"

Brainbash grunted in the affirmative.

"Look here, Brainbash, we're all knowing you're none too bright, yet you keep coming round here wasting my time. Bogren's gotta be smart, see? So, I says we test the little shit," and turning to the group standing by the weapons, added, "Give him something to fight with!"

Ugh yelped, too terrified to object.

But the chief, with his immense nostrils, must have smelled his fear, saying, "You wants to be fighting, right? Join the Master, in the Overland?"

"No! I'm no . . . I'm not a warrior!"

"Well, if you ain't no warrior, you'll be dying a whole lot quicker."

It was apparent that the chief did not believe Ugh's story, nor was he concerned with shirking workers. Nothing mattered to the warrior caste but battle, and the little digger's certain death was sure to be entertaining.

"Who's he fightin'?" another one asked, gripping his hammer eagerly.

"Eh . . ." Bloodsnot intoned, "How abouts you, Brainbash? You brings him, you kills him."

He agreed, raising his double-headed ax as Ugh scurried away. Already, the warriors were forming a circle about them, crossing iron with iron, their gleaming eyes lusting for blood. Someone dropped a morningstar beside him, its spiky head impaling the ground, the pommel rising above his head. He could scarcely hope to lift it, let alone wield it, and considered calling for a *time out*, to appeal for a weapon he might manage, but they were all in a fervor and would not listen. Even now, Brainbash's ax was coming down. Ugh tugged at the morningstar with every ounce of his might, but the weapon was heavier than he was and did not budge, and in another instant, he was fleeing for his life, ducking under thighs and over feet.

Brainbash pursued, insisting that his opponent remain still—fight or die—but Ugh was not about to oblige him. Round and round, the two circled, Ugh taking advantage of every obstacle in the room. Brainbash stumbled noisily over pots and platters, slipped on books and brooms, and banged his toes against helmets and anvils. Everyone was laughing heartily, and judging by the timing of their uproars, Ugh sensed that it was not directed at himself, but the one chasing him.

Brainbash was a disgrace, owing to his injury, someone to be hated and mocked. A single swipe and Ugh's arm would be torn from his shoulder, or his body split from skull to belly. But the insults kept coming, which was enough of a distraction to keep him alive, and Brainbash was fast becoming tired. Each swing came earlier and slower, until Ugh felt some measure of pity for the brute. Finally, the bumbling warrior stopped, heaving and wheezing, his brain pulsing, and Ugh considered that he might survive the day if he could be but clever. Returning to the morningstar, he waited, teasing his would-be killer, and when Brainbash came lurching, the little digger tipped the weapon over. Iron spikes skewered the warrior bogren's foot and, hugging his ax as one might an infant, he toppled onto his face.

Ugh knew that the battle could not officially end until one of them lay dead, but he did not wish to vanquish his opponent, not in such a way. Seeing him prone, face-down in the dirt, elicited only pity. It did not seem right to bash what was already bashed, but what choice did he have? He surveyed the room for a weapon, anything to do the deed, when something peculiar caught his attention. The metal fasteners holding Brainbash's face together were popping off, one by one, and rolling across the floor. His gray matter was spilling out and he was no longer stirring. Every bogren, chief included, erupted in a guttural cry of triumph. It was the greatest show of status one bogren could bestow upon another. His victory was theirs.

Ugh's life changed considerably after that day, for he had achieved what he had not known possible—the feat of moving into a higher caste. Chief Bloodsnot renamed him, *Brainsplitter*, and he was given a mace, the smallest in the armory and created specifically for him. Warriors from other burrows, who did not know his story, liked to mock and threaten him, thinking him easy prey. But when those who had watched him dispose of Brainbash came to his aid, regaling his would-be tormentors of his triumph, Ugh's standing grew, until none dared molest him. Sometimes he was made to spar before the chief, but always in jest. Once, a bogren cut him with a knife, and Bloodsnot became so enraged, he sent the warrior into the horg pit to be devoured. The chief took it upon himself to stitch the gash in Ugh's forehead himself, and it left a scar that Ugh wore with pride, as a mark of his newfound status. But what most excited him were excursions to the Overland, where food was ever abundant, and where, owing to his small stature, he was assigned to a mount, a blue *bandersnout* the size of a dog, which he named Dippy.

A digger no more, Ugh lived in a haze of wonderment, unable to fully accept his good fortune. And yet, after much food and drink, he fancied himself a warrior, and would even boast of his prowess, despite never having killed another bogren directly. Memories of Radia, and of the beautiful murals of life forms and the bountiful gardens he had found so arresting, faded like a dream from his mind, and his heart. This was where he belonged, he told himself. His only duty was to attend to the chief, to scratch out a boil or dispose of a snot rag, a paltry price to live in such comfort. And every night, he fell asleep with pleasant thoughts, chanting a mantra of sorts. All is well and good now, all is well and good . . .

Ugh was suddenly awake. Someone had smacked him in his sleep and run off. Was this a joke? Sitting up in his cot, rubbing the soreness from his cheek, he wondered who had hit him, and why. Rising to investigate, he peeked out into the main burrow to see the warriors rushing to and fro.

"The Master! The Master!"

He tried more than once to ask what was happening, tugging at thighs here and there, but there was too much bustle, with no one stopping to answer. As before, Ugh felt invisible. Fighting a tide of bodies, he worked his way to the chief's hollow, but Bloodsnot's pile was devoid of his buttocks.

With no one to inform him, Ugh decided to follow the crowd, to the ladders and the pulleys and the ramps leading to the Overland. Tethered to a small stake, he found Dippy, and he hastily mounted the beast and rode out to the clearing where bogrens trained for battle.

All the warriors he knew, and many more that he did not, were gathered in this one place, perhaps having advanced from every warren in existence. They were as numerous as the workers below, each a giant in his eyes, except for the bogrens he despised, who were smaller even than he was, the gray, spindly *Outcastes*.

Before joining the warrior caste, Ugh had not known such creatures to exist. The Outcastes dissected corpses, studying each organ to divine its secrets, sewing dead limbs to living bodies in grotesque mockeries of his kind, making bogrens with multiple arms and legs and heads. Thankfully, such abominations did not live long. But the Outcastes' primary duty was tending to the horg, a species from the far reaches of the dark hemisphere, brutish mountains of fat and muscle, with long yellow tusks. Ordinarily, horg could not be tamed, but the intelligent gray wretches found a way. By removing the top of the skull and hooking a series of delicate strings to the horg's brain, the Outcastes could manipulate the brutes like puppets, controlling each arm and leg as if their own, the tamer effectively merging with the tamed.

Ugh could not explain the reason, but watching these hybrid monstrosities roaming the field, their masters saddled upon their necks, infuriated and disturbed him. Yet no other bogren shared in his disgust. They remained as oblivious to the Outcastes' cruelty as the diggers who laughed when the scaffolding would collapse to drown his coworkers in magma.

"Humans!"

Climbing atop a fellow warrior's shoulders, one who knew and respected him, Ugh searched across a field of heads, to where the Master stood upon a hill. He was as commanding a presence as ever, with his blood-red body of iron, and broad crown of horns. But it was the eyes that most intimidated him, or rather, the hollow vacancies where eyes should have been.

When the Master spoke at last, his voice came booming across the gathered, now-silent crowd, and settled about Ugh's ears like a physical force.

"Long ago, the humans drove you underground, into caves, and into the lands of the Great Moon, where nothing grows. They took all the food for themselves, leaving nothing for you. For too long, bogrens have fought tooth and nail to survive. Well I say, no more! No more groveling! No more hungering and wasting away! The time has come, for bogrens to rise, for bogrens to live above and humans below! Follow me, my faithful, and I will lead you to the promised land, to a land of plenty, with enough food to fatten your bellies for all time! Follow me, and together, we will kill the humans!"

"Kill the humans!" The gathering roar rippled through the masses like thunder.

"Kill the humans!" the Master wailed, raising Bonecrusher to the moon, twirling the ball of spikes by the chain so that the air rushing through its myriad cavities caused it to whistle and whine.

"Kill the humans!"

Ugh continued to watch, as the Master was accompanied by two others, their bodies shining, black and metallic. All the years he had seen the magma poured into concave shapes, he never bothered to question for whom they were being made, for bogrens did not often wear plate armor. Now he knew.

A naked body was brought forward, knees bloodied, dragging between the two suits of armor. Ugh could not be certain, but this particular human looked to be obese and was devoid of hair atop the scalp. Perhaps the hair had been removed, in the process of some torture, for the man could scarcely twitch. He was dressed only in his blood, and as he was thrown onto his face, Ugh could see what little remained of the man's backside, where the ants had already begun to devour the bits of skin and muscle tissue clinging to his spine.

"Kill the humans!" they shouted, descending upon the fallen body.

They painted their maces and their axes, and every murderous tool in their possession, in human blood, with every voice joining in the chant. Except his own.

20

Liana

Noora could see the blue sky and drifting clouds from the small port window in her quarters and, if she relaxed her focus, it almost felt as if she was sitting at her dresser in the palace, her bejeweled comb in hand. Her hair was not prone to tangling, but brushing it was part of her morning ritual, something to start the day. With her handmaiden gone, she was learning to care for these things herself. With long, lazy strokes, she drew the comb down to her waist. Sometimes, she found petals in her locks, pink and white and yellow, that were carried in through the window as she slept, but she could not imagine from what land they originated or how they could have drifted so far. All the while, she pined for Larissa and her father, and all the people she would never again see.

In many ways, Noora felt lost, in that she did not know where she was or *who* she was. Her sense of identity was as open as the window posing for a mirror. Having witnessed the death of her praetorian guard, the murder of her closest friend and the fall of her father's kingdom, she knew she could not hope to remain the same young girl. The innocence of youth—

that which made the world magical—had been stolen from her. And even her name was changed.

Better that, as *I don't feel much like Radia anymore.*

Then there were the dreams, which could come at any time, whether she was sleeping or awake. The unicorn and the Sea, and the countless sisters composed of light circling a great ellipse of stars, seemed so senseless, and yet she felt profoundly changed, as though she was and always had been something more. Even after waking from her coma, that feeling lingered, a sense of oneness with the Cosmos. The dread and panic of the crew were her own, but the monster was also a part of her, as was the wind and the sun. A curtain had been drawn away to reveal the true inner workings of the world, and it frightened and confused her, in that she did not know what to accept as real, and what to believe was imaginary. Such fears, however, were not entirely unfamiliar. She was given to *fever dreams* after first falling ill, when she would run around the palace completely naked, awash in the belief that she was a unicorn. But her father had always been around to catch and console her, when the fruits of her visions turned sour.

Across from the porthole, her satchel lay open, its contents lost amid the folds of her bedsheets. Reaching across the tiny room to replace her comb, she could not but notice that her veins showed starkly. They were like vines under the skin, giving her arms a pale green hue. How much of her body looked this way? She was afraid to disrobe and look, but could no longer ignore the mounting evidence, the dreams and hallucinations and the swooning, and now the discoloration of her skin. Her illness was returning in full force, but Dimmy and Davos and Ecthros could not be made aware of it, lest they fall into a despair she was powerless but to share. Late in the day, she would join them for supper, and always she ate briefly, in the hopes that they not notice her complexion, or think it a trick of the moonlight. But she could not hide indefinitely.

With every passing day, the captain's excitement grew. She could hear it in the way he carried on about his family and the beauty of his homeland. From beyond her cabin wall, his singing voice resonated, and Ecthros's lute missing every other note. Shortly they would arrive, and there was nothing left to be done, but that which she most hated.

Throwing herself down, she pulled the jewel-studded box from her satchel and opened it. Inside, six corks fit tightly into their respective slots. She tugged at one of them and a crystal-shaped vial came loose. It was roughly the length of her finger and tapered to a point, and when she let it go, the vial floated up into the air like a bubble, weightless over her palm. But the beautiful crystal was a ruse, she knew, to mask the awful substance it contained. Nothing in all the world could taste as bitter and putrid. Even now, she was filled with revulsion, as bile started to rise in her throat. She remembered being eleven and pleading with her father night after night. The cure was worse than the disease, she had insisted, and was also changing her. *Yes*, the memory was clear, but why had she said that last bit? What had she meant by it?

Before she could contemplate further, three brisk taps came at the door.

"Noora! Wonderful news!" Ecthros stood outside her door, sounding more excited than usual. "We're coming into port! Shouldn't be long now! Be there before the cock crows. Look out your window! I'm headed to the deck for a better view." He did not wait for her to reply, stomping up the stairs noisily.

Tossing the cure aside, Noora scrambled over the cot to the opposite wall. The view through the window was awash in green. An unbroken line of hills filled her vision, speckled with white walls and blue doors, where sheep and goats and other livestock grazed. She wanted to scream, to stick her head from the porthole to be consumed by the wind, but the opening was too small, so she rushed to the door, only to stop at the sight of her outstretched hand and the growing sickness under her skin.

You can't go out and play unless you take your medicine. Her father's words rang in her ears. Groping blindly, she found the vial and popped off the cork. The potion was odorless, but she

215

could hear the vapors escaping, hissing, curling to corrode her fingertips. *Liquid death.* Yet she could not deny its effectiveness. *No more dreams or delusions. No more unconsciousness.* With eyes clenched, she brought the crystal to her lips, tipping the oily blackness over the back of her tongue to blot out the taste, and resisting the urge to choke it back up.

Outside, the waters were calm but the wind wrapped about her briskly, filling the sails and undoing the work she had done with her comb. She watched the coast drift dreamily by, as though she were astride her unicorn again. Krow was tugging at ropes, trimming the sails to reduce their speed, as Ecthros and Demacharon stood by the capstan to prepare the chain and anchor. Everyone was busying themselves, and all she could do was look out, dumbfounded by this strange new shore, the scent of distant flora waking her to new sensations, rousing her to life.

Morning climbed ever higher to gild the land, the unseen sun rising in a haze from between the hilltops to kiss the innumerable little peaks the water made all around them. The river flowed in patterns of aquamarine, dashing against the rocks with a distant roar, forming an ethereal mist that seemed to hang perpetually in the air. Even where she stood, she could feel the cool wetness condense over her eyelids. Where the shore lay flat and weathered smooth, the river gushed inland, washing over countless stones and pouring out again, the land and water like two lovers never quite at peace.

"*The Hills of Tororo!*" Davos proclaimed, as if the scenery were a painting of his own making. "And the river here is called *Nasica.*"

The *Cloud Breaker* continued its winding course through the hills, the captain holding to the coast with a firm grip. With time the river narrowed, enough to see both sides in greater detail, and Noora surmised that at some point the ship must have veered away from the main vein of the Potamis.

In another passing, homes came into sharp focus, whitewashed and dome-shaped with rounded chimneys.

Yellow and red flowers could be seen on windowsills, and undergarments flowing from wires, and she spotted a child chasing a kite. The piers consisted of a wood and stone lattice, meticulously crafted and maintained. Dinghies and dhows cavorted between dock and tether, despite their lack of sails, their hulls brimming with netting and weights. But there were no other galleons but the one coming into port.

Noora went to stand beside Davos as the ship sidled the shore. From here, she could make out the tall swaying grasses, a sweeping green sea rising to the hilltops. From every peak, in every direction she looked, towering windmills stood, their blades spinning in unison. It only made sense that they take advantage of the wind, which only intensified as they neared the riverbank, making her braids snap like blindfolds across her eyes.

"Is it always so breezy?"

"This?" He guffawed, his cap audibly whizzing, a wonder that it did not fly from his head. "A mild day for my people!" he said, and turning to look at her, added, "Welcome to Yefira."

More than a hundred people were gathered to meet them. She could sense their excitement and eagerness, yet they stood with patient smiles, from toddlers clinging to mothers' arms to elders on canes. Richly colored clothing and broad hats appeared to be the fashion, for women especially, though the younger boys—fishers' sons by the looks of their tanned and peeling shoulders—stood shirtless under the pier holding to the pylons, knee deep in water.

Davos shouted and waved, and as the ship drifted into place, he gave the command to drop anchor. Krow lowered the gangplank, and the crew rushed to disembark, herself included, but Demacharon cautioned her, "Walk close behind me and try not to draw attention to yourself."

Davos, in contrast, became the focal point of every eye, and almost at once he was attacked by three young girls. They seized him by his arms and thighs and the fat of his gut. Peals of laughter erupted from his large frame, shaking the children, and he spun them round in his arms like a merry-go-round, until they were all quite dizzy and collapsed in a heap of hysteria.

"*Girls*! Seriously! Get back here!"

Judging by her appearance, Kiki was an unassuming woman, stout and broad-hipped with a striped bodice looking to burst with buttons. She shooed her daughters away, but one look from her husband was enough to melt her austerity.

"My lady." He embraced her hand with a kiss and lifted her in his powerful arms despite her protests.

"No, Davy! Put me down at once!" Her cheeks reddened to match the hollyhocks in her hat. "Not here!"

He did not seem to hear, pelting her with kisses. "Let them look! What do I care, when I've been so long away?"

"Whatever are you talking about? You're home early. And where's the rest of your crew?"

"It's a long story, my dear, and all will be told, at supper. But first!" He proceeded to introduce his wife and children to Demacharon. The oldest of his daughters looked to be thirteen. She was plain-faced like her mother, tall and lanky, with a sprinkling of freckles about the nose. "Athalia," he said, "named for my grandmother." She nodded timidly, adjusting the fit of her dirndl. The ten-year-old was tanned like a sailor and barefoot, with chestnut hair tied up in a messy knot and green, mischievous eyes. "And this is Niah, our little troublemaker," he went on, but she did not notice what was being said, showing more interest in her clogs, one of which she seemed to prefer wearing on her hand, while poking up from the other shoe, Noora thought she saw the ears of a rabbit. Liana was four and only too happy to make acquaintances, calling herself "Flower" and mumbling a litany of questions too quickly for anyone to understand. Her face retained the roundness of infancy, but she gazed long at her father with knowing, pale-blue eyes, and in her silvery blond hair she wore a crown of blossoms.

"The gods saw fit to bless me with three girls and not a single son," he remarked, but Noora could sense no resentment in him, only love, the like of which she had not felt since her father was alive.

Other children came around—Niah's friend, Miya, who was older yet dressed in more faded colors, and two shirtless boys, Colin and Tobias. The latter was the younger sibling of Ecthros, and Tobias made it no secret that he envied his brother, inquiring after his adventures before they had even finished embracing. Ecthros was more than obliging, relating how he, with expert marksmanship, warded off an ice monster, while Tobias stood perfectly still and wide-eyed, hanging on every word.

Their patience exhausted, the crowd turned aggressive, pushing to talk to Davos as if he were the most beloved man in Yefira, and yet their concern was only for their wares, for the treasures they hoped to procure from the fabled city. He appealed for a measure of calm, but their questions were relentless.

"Daddy! Daddy! Listen to me! Daddy? Would you listen to me!" Liana was shouting and jumping in place.

He dropped to his knees, waving the people off. "What is it now, my Flower?"

"What did you bring me?"

Noora could sense her hope. She was too young to understand the trouble, that her father should not have arrived so soon, and his regret was palpable, even to those without her power.

"Liana, you have to understand that Daddy—"

"You didn't bring me anything?"

"Well, I didn't quite say that, now—"

"But you promised, Daddy! Promised meeeee!"

Everyone in the crowd nodded in agreement, much to Davos's annoyance. And his daughter's eyes began to glisten. Despite his genuine affection, he did not know to navigate the heart of a young girl. But Noora was closer to her age, familiar with the ways of children, and with childhood games. It would take little to help her to forget.

Noora bent to meet the girl eye-to-eye. "Hello there, Liana. It's wonderful to meet you."

"A princess!"

Davos rounded suddenly, and Noora saw the look of alarm in his eyes. Even Demacharon looked perturbed, suspicious.

"You brought me a princess!" the little girl gasped, her unhappy tears sweetened with joy. "Oh, she's so pretty, Daddy! But why are your eyes different from one another?" It was a straightforward and innocent question, without a hint of ridicule.

"Well, Liana, when the gods made me, they took a bit of light from the greater moon and a glowing patch from the smaller moon, and they fashioned my eyes in two different colors."

"Really? Are you telling the truth?"

She cupped the girl's hands in hers, feeling the entwining warmth. The other children circled them now, joyful looks upon their faces. Like them, Noora sensed what the grown villagers could not. There was something special, magical about herself, evident only to children.

"Do you want to play with Hazel?" It was Niah, holding a tan rabbit in her arms.

She looked to Davos for help, and he to his wife.

"Who is this girl, Davy?"

"This is my, um . . . cousin's daughter. Noora."

Kiki knew better than to push the matter, dismissing the children, and off they went, hand-in-hand with the strange girl from the land of myth.

In the days following their arrival, Noora made many new and wondrous discoveries. Yefira was a hamlet of no more than a few hundred, without a man or woman who did not know his neighbor, a place where every mother kept a watchful eye on every child and no two people crossed paths without a friendly word of greeting. Building a home was a community effort, and should anyone happen to fall ill, it was to the consternation of the whole. Poverty and misfortune were not uncommon, but adversity was shared, and it brought the people together in ways Noora did not see in Tyrnael. In Yefira, one could find welcome in any home, no matter the time of day. Likewise, in such climate, the children were free to explore the limits of their homeland, from the grassy foothills to the rocky riverbanks, to the gradual slopes overlooking the countryside.

Houses were spread far and apart, built at the whims of their owners. The line of hills ran north and south, and families could be found on either side, but it was from Davos's windmill home that Noora and Demacharon first discovered the marvel of Yefira.

If Noora had not known better, she might have thought the tiny village perched at the edge of the world. Overlooking the eastern slope, opposite the Nasica, the whole of Aenya dropped into a boundless gorge. The river running to the village ended there, the falls disintegrating into the ether. A gray haze during the day prevented her from seeing across the divide, and at night an eerie darkness hung over the chasm.

As for the drop, Colin loved to scare the girls with fateful tales of boys and girls, who did not listen to their parents and played too closely to the edge. "And they are falling *still*," he loved to say, gripping their hearts with terror. Though such fears were common, it could not dissuade the daring from living on the very edges of the great gorge, their homes clinging to the rock face, an engineering feat that came with its own set of challenges, from the stairs and ladders needed to reach level ground to the continual updraft carrying hats and kites and pottery into the sky. Colin and Tobias and Niah loved to throw things into the current to watch them sail up and away.

But the more clever and intrepid Yefirans could be found venturing along the gorge in small flying boats, or *whirlydinghies*. They came in every shape and size one could imagine. Davos had informed Noora that the creators of these craft spent years designing and testing, and were always discovering some better method of achieving flight, from wings of canvas and bamboo, to balloon sails filled with hot air, to configurations of propellers. It was no longer a wonder to Noora, after seeing an assortment of these airborne machines, that such people could produce a flying galleon, the first in many centuries to reach Tyrnael.

At supper, Davos told them of explorers who navigated the gorge, traveling many years through many lands, only to circle about the planet and come again home. Since that time, he said, it was known that Aenya was a sphere, and that the gorge did not end. Another legend dealt with the *Great Bridge of Laenkea*. Only a single pylon remained, a stone ruin overgrown with vines, of the bridge built by the Ancients, that long ago spanned the gorge to the dark hemisphere. After the Great Cataclysm, the bridge was thought to have collapsed. Demacharon, in hearing the tale, was quick to point out the logistic impossibilities of such a monument—arguing that such a structure would have to cross the length of an entire village or more to reach the opposite end—but Davos maintained the truth of it. "After all, the Zo were believed little more than a myth," he said, "until I went in search of the fabled city and found it."

For Noora, it was the people that fascinated her, their customs and cuisine, their songs and their stories, whether based in history or imagination. Most of all, she loved the children. Her favorite games were tumbling and flying kites and chasing Niah's rabbit, and teasing Colin and Tobias, who labored incessantly over their whirlydinghy.

One morning, the girls led her into a wooded grove, over a trickling brook of moss-covered stones that poked above the water, to a shady copse where a gold cocoon the size of her fist was hanging from a branch. There they stopped, brimming with wonderment.

"It's a chrysalis," Noora explained.

Liana looked at her, puzzled. "What's that?"

"Well, it's like a little bed, for a caterpillar. When the caterpillar grows up, it makes a cocoon, where it curls up and goes to sleep. Then the caterpillar dreams of flying, and after days and days it is reborn, with gold wings that glitter like fire, which is why we call it a *fireflutter*."

"Can we open it now?" Liana suggested. "I want to see!"

"We mustn't do that," Noora said, "or the caterpillar will be hurt, and get very grumpy."

"But why?"

"Because, well . . ." Noora was forced to think. "Because of Nature, that's why."

"What is *nature*?"

"Nature? You mean you don't know? I can't imagine what your mother's been teaching you if you don't even know that."

"We learn washing and sewing, mostly," Athalia admitted.

"And cooking!" Niah added, clutching her rabbit tight.

"Oh, but there's so much more to living! Just look around you. Nature is the reason we're here, why the trees reach for the sun, why the birds sing and the bees buzz in the flowers. She exists in every living thing, *and even in you*," she poked the little girl's nose, making her giggle, "and as part of you. Without her, there'd be nothing to this world but, well, dust and rocks."

Athalia, tucking her dirndl under her legs, sat in the tussock, as did Niah and Liana. "Tell us more."

"Alright. Well, in my country, we call nature *Zoë*, but she is also called *Alashiya* or the Goddess, sometimes the Green Goddess . . ."

That night, Noora sat at supper, across from Davos and his daughters and Demacharon. Kiki crouched by the chiminea, a peel in one hand and a poker in the other, stoking embers under a pan of bread.

"And then he jumps up and shouts, 'tornado shot!'" He brushed the tears from his eyes, choking with laughter, as the girls watched him with wide, attentive faces, soaking up his every word. "I tell you, he's a good lad, but one of these days he's gonna get himself killed!"

"Well, you know that nephew of yours." Despite her size, Kiki moved in a spritely manner between the kitchen and dining table. One moment, she was throwing scallions, salt and cumin onto the meat, the next, removing the bread from the pot-shaped stove and serving roast potatoes, onions and tomatoes under their noses. For dessert, she prepped two kinds of cheeses, one crumbly and white, the other soft and yellow. "He just wants to be like his father, gods absolve him—believes every crazy story the people say about him."

"So what happened, Daddy?" Liana interrupted. "Did you get away?"

"Well, what do you suppose happened, my dear? We're sitting here, ain't we?"

The sounds and smells of cooking made Noora's mouth water but seeing the meat on the table soured her stomach. She recognized the neck and shoulders of the animal, and could not help but recall the bleating of the lambs from earlier that day. Davos's livestock was well-provided for, with ample feedings and freedom to roam, but she could not bring herself to digest what, that very morning, could communicate with her its feelings.

The tale continued, without mention of Larissa, Davos pausing only to fill his mouth with food and drink. Noora sat without eating, unable to focus on any one thing. Even the joy that seemed to flow out of the children felt muted, remote.

"Are you alright, Noora?" came Demacharon's soft voice.

She leaned against her chair, trying to quiet her stomach, fearing she might vomit. "I'm fine, Dimmy. If you would excuse me, I need to go lie down."

She found her way to Athalia's bedroom, the place she slept, and after making certain that no one was looking, reached for her satchel, removing the last crystal vial.

What will I do when they're gone?

For a long while, she lay on Athalia's bed, holding the vial tight against her bosom, listening to the sounds of Davos's home. She could hear the clink of dishes being stacked and the creak of the windmill turning on the roof, and the music of the wind chimes set in the doorway. Demacharon and Davos moved out onto the porch, engaged in some debate, while Kiki insisted the girls prepare for bed, much to their displeasure.

"I want a story," Liana implored. "Can Noora tell me a story?"

"Perhaps. If she's up, and if she's feeling well enough."

But before Kiki could leave Liana's bedside, Noora came around from the adjacent room. "I'm here."

"Are you sure? You've been looking a bit pale as of late, my dear."

"Please. It's all I can do to repay your hospitality. And besides, your children are precious to me. How could I say no to them?"

Kiki answered with a smile and a touch to Noora's shoulder, before departing.

"I want a story about a princess."

Noora perched at the edge of the bed. "Have you heard the tale of Radia? The Princess of Mythradanaiil?"

"Tell me again," she murmured. "Daddy tells it to me, but you know the real story, I bet."

"I do. Now listen. Long ago, in a faraway land, there lived a wise king who was just and generous to his people. But despite his wealth and power, the king was forlorn, for he possessed no heir, no child he might care for and love. With longing in his heart, he prayed to the Goddess, Zoë, for seven years and seven cycles, asking for a child, until one day he found a baby girl, alone in a patch of sunlight in the garden. He named her Radia, and there was much rejoicing in the land—dancing and feasting and tournaments. As the years passed, Radia grew to love music and art, and reading from the great libraries of the Zo. All that knew her loved her, but no one so deeply as the king. No father was ever so devoted. Though her family was small, Radia was very happy.

"Or so it was until her eleventh birthday, when she fell deathly ill. Fearing for her life, the king never left her bedside. Physicians from throughout the kingdom were called to restore the princess, but she only grew more sickly, and so the king sent for the wisest of healers from all the known kingdoms of the world. Seven arrived, one from Kratos and one from Nibia, two from Hedonia and three from far off

Shemselinihar, but each of the seven was mystified, and the princess slumbered ever deeper and nearer to the netherworld.

"Grieving for his daughter, the king became terribly ill himself, refusing to eat, sleeping in fits and dreaming of that dark place of the dead. When, at last, he left from his daughter's bower, he was as an old man, bent and white-haired. Two men aided him to his throne, upon which the king made one last proclamation:

"'Whosoever should deliver my daughter from death, shall I bequeath my very kingdom, and all its vast wealth, in recompense.'

"None answered the call, but known charlatans, who were turned away at the palace gates. Until, one fateful day, there came a wizened sage from an unknown kingdom. He went by the name of Anabis, and of his worldly possessions, there was but his satchel of cures and a young boy.

"Anabis promised to save the king's daughter but did not ask for the throne in return. He wished, instead, for two things only, to become court advisor, and for his son, Zaibos, to be adopted by the king—"

"Noora?"

"Yes, Liana?"

"Did the princess become well again? I know that she did . . . but I would like to hear it from you."

"Of course. Anabis was a great wizard, you see, with the powers of the Ancients. He concocted a potion that the princess was to drink once a cycle, and from then on, well, everyone lived happily thereafter."

As Noora crept to the door, leaving Liana to her dreams, the girl called out once more. "Noora? Was he ever mean to her?"

"Who?"

"The brother. Zaibos. Was he ever cruel to Radia?"

She thought back on the day they met. Noora was sitting up in bed, the awful taste of Anabis's potion lingering in her mouth. Her father came into the room, looking younger, the color already returning to his face, and then he told her of a surprise.

"Your brother," was how he was introduced.

Noora remembered a boy nearing manhood, underfed, scrawny, a mop of dark hair covering his eyes. To her father and everyone at court, he was unimposing, a timid, simple-minded child, who rarely spoke. But to Radia, he seemed a body of empty space, devoid of emotion. She had never met such a being and it frightened her. When she was well enough to leave her room, she led him to the garden, hoping against all odds to inspire him with its beauty. There, near a bubbling fountain, they spied a chrysalis forming from the flowering branch of a tree.

"Isn't it beautiful?" she said. "Soon it will become a fireflutter."

But Zaibos was not impressed. He wanted to know how it worked, and he shattered the cocoon with a rock and laughed when she wept, calling her weak.

Liana still waited, fighting the heaviness of sleep.

"The brother had become a prince," Noora said at last. "And that made him self-important, made him believe that his life mattered more than the lives of others."

"One last thing." The little girl's eyes were half-closed, and her voice heavy with sleep.

"Yes, my flower?"

"Was the princess, you?"

Noora only smiled, and left the room, shutting the door softly behind her.

21

Skullgrin

E ros had wanted to wait before stepping out from under the awning, but there was no sign of the downpour ending that night, and he could no longer delay from unloading his burden.

The storm was more than a simple downpour, unnaturally heavy and freezing. Tyrnael was growing colder and wetter by the day. He could hear the drops pelting the cobblestones and windowpanes, feel the door frames growing softer. Streets had become streams, splitting into smaller tributaries where the ground was elevated, washing down steps and into pools. The people kept indoors, but there was no joy to be lost, for the men of the *Fist & Morningstar* were put off, offering the populace a welcome respite from the king's reign of terror. Eros did not know the cause of the changing climate, but a feeling suggested some meaning behind it.

The rumors spread even to his town, and to his ears, that the true heir to the land was lost and, most likely, dead. But the king would not be so easily satisfied. Should Eros fail to return with proof of her demise, his spies would continue their search, beyond the Crown if need be, and the princess could not hope to hide forever. Zaibos would never rest until her heart lay in his hands, and so Eros had no other choice, but to do the awful deed he had done.

He pressed on through the storm, tugging at the straps of his shoulder bag, passing between the flickering window-lined streets, occasionally drenching his eyes to find his way to the Compass Tower. The rain beat his cloak relentlessly, beading along the brim of his hood and filling his boots with murky water. Every layer of his clothing felt damp and cold, the moisture somehow seeping into his bones. Sheets of it obfuscated the air, and despite his careful footing, his ankle twisted where a stone was missing.

But on he treaded, alone, climbing terraces and crossing bridges. Not a single soul was out to suspect him, to accuse him. And all the while, a voice murmured in his head, again and again.

I had to do it. There was no other way. All for her . . . everything for her. Nothing else matters. I had no choice . . . I had . . . no choice. No other way. Dammit, why won't the rain stop?

Eros reached the gardens, where the downpour could be heard beating against the trees and trickling from the branches. Following the golden path leading to the palace gates, he reached the base of the hill and stood there for a moment, catching his breath. All around him, melted snow from the Crown of Aenya came down in torrents, joining the Potamis River, the sound of waterfalls merging with the deluge in a roaring symphony. He turned again to ascend the steps cut into the rock. The storm was less oppressive here, a mere drizzle at the foot of the Compass Tower. He welcomed the reprieve but was still shivering, unable to conjure even the memory of warmth.

Ice was in his bone marrow, had been for days, since risking the impossible heights of the Crown. Never once had he considered turning back. He would return home or die in the attempt. It was not only to save the princess, an idea which came later to his mind, but to seek answers. He climbed the whole of the night, knowing that if he were to rest for even a moment, he could not hope to wake. If not for his rage, his burning desire to *know*, he would no doubt have perished, as so many adventurers before him. At last, clambering on hands and knees, he gazed upon the wondrous expanse of Mythradanaiil, a green valley ringed by jagged white, and there, with the sun's light on his cheeks, he collapsed into a deep sleep. He was in Dis the following day, with a knife at his mother's throat, begging, weeping. The beauty she once possessed had long departed. She was like an outsider now, grown haggard. He could see it as never before, and yet it was not age, but society that had made her so.

'There were two,' she had said, 'and I could not bring myself to let them do it—to brand the both of you. I went to the cliff, to the very edge, and let her go. It could just as well have been you. It was an act of faith, a blind sacrifice, for no mother can ever be made to choose between her children.'

Those words haunted him, but no more than the nature of his father. 'He was a stranger,' she said, 'but if you must know, he seduced me. What more can I say? He was handsome and spoke with such eloquence, a true poet. His eyes were like inkwells, and he wore only black, but for a white skull collar of some horned beast.'

"State your business here!"

Eros lifted from his trance with a start. In the gloom, the guard was almost invisible, but for the gleam of his helm.

"You take your position too seriously, methinks," Eros said to him. "What dread enemy do you imagine storming the walls of this castle, in this weather no less?"

"I am in no mood for games, stranger. Speak plainly or return to your home."

"I have no home, at least one to which I hope to return. But if you insist, I am here for Zaibos. You see, he has asked me to kill someone, and I am here to deliver."

The guard was visibly shaken, questioning him no further and allowing him to pass. It seemed a strange thing to trust an assassin, but the people of the city were unaccustomed to such things, he supposed, and disarmed by the mere mention of murder.

The stonework became more intricate as he ascended, the banister on either side of him inlaid with patterns of beryl and lapis lazuli. Great burning urns of onyx illuminated the highest tier, the rain falling like a diamond mist between the furthest arch and the front gate. It was awkward entering this way. Eros was a creature of shadow, having learned to survive by not being seen. At any moment, he expected a trap to spring, or an ambush. But there was only a pair of guards to greet him, their halberds crossed to impede his advance. He could not see their faces, but they sounded young and apprehensive and tired, weighed down by their pauldrons. Until recently, the role of palace guard was ceremonial. Neither their fathers, nor their fathers' fathers, had ever needed to kill, and he did not doubt how effortlessly he could end their lives if need be.

"I come bearing gifts for the king."

They did not argue, which only served to increase his anxiety. Was he expected? Being watched? Followed? *No, that is impossible.* Zaibos had his spies, but Eros was no commoner. In his long murderous career, never did he draw suspicion. Still, he sensed that something was amiss, though he could not explain the reason.

He had not thought what to expect upon entering the palace, but the deathly silence unnerved him. Every child knew of the music that filled the halls of the Compass Tower, from harps whose strings stretched entire rooms, to handpicked choirs of heavenly voices. Travelers crossing under those hallowed gates marveled at the sound, an ethereal melody to stir the deepest recesses of the soul. Even from Dis, he could remember hearing the music, and it never failed to lift him from his darkest moods. Now, even the storm was silenced by the walls, and if not for the echo of his footfalls, he might have thought himself deaf.

He made for the atrium, where fluted colonnades stretched in all directions, and mosaic windows met vaulted ceiling hundreds of feet above, but he could only imagine the awe they once inspired. In the lattice of shadow and torchlight, the inner courtyard was like a tomb, a ghostly remnant of happier days.

There were none to greet him but servants, eloai busying about with brooms and pans, seemingly oblivious to the recent transformations. Asking around, he found the great stairwell of the Compass Tower. It spiraled along the inner wall without a guardrail, vast and open, like a tunnel standing on end. Though imposing, it was not the ascent he feared, but being exposed. If things did not go as planned, he would have nowhere to run, but down.

Halfway to the summit, and he could see the fires below like burning wicks, and a flickering glow above leading him upward. He continued to climb, ignoring the ache in his thighs, and was startled by the sudden silhouettes stretched across the steps. They were alive, he realized, a dozen young girls, perhaps more, stripped bare or in tatters, their peploses clinging to their bodies. He recognized them, by their simple features, as eloai. What was Zaibos doing to them? He did not think to ask, nor bother to help, proceeding on to the throne room.

The walls here were open to the sky, but Eros could see no sign of rain, only rolling clouds, dark and violet. A ring of guards stood at the far reaches of the circular room, standing upon a great compass etched into the floor, their armor gleaming black and orange in the torchlight, their halberds tall as three men. Banners stretched down all around him, the black fist and morningstar against a blood-red backdrop, and for the first time he wondered what the sigil represented. How was the hand holding the ball? Were the spikes passing between the fingers or did they penetrate through the palm? He supposed it did not matter. It was an abstract image, meant to induce fear. Moving further into the light, his heart quailed at the raised dais and the statuesque form of Zaibos watching from his throne. The king was fully armored, his helm ablaze with horns.

Why is he wearing that, even upon his throne? Has he renounced his humanity entirely? Or does he expect a battle to erupt at any moment?

Eros crept forward, guarding his thoughts as if the king might enter his head to tear the truth from it. All the while, Zaibos spoke not a word, forcing him to wonder whether a living being sat before him or a statue.

"I have delivered upon my promise," he said, waiting, watching the faceless mask stare in silence. "My King," he tried again, "I have done as you have asked. She is no more."

"Is that so?" he replied stonily. "Show me."

"I have it here, my lord." Eros dropped to his knees, fumbling with the straps of his pack. After what seemed too long a time, he removed the decoratively carved box, lifting it before him like something fragile and precious.

"Her heart?"

"It is here, my lord."

"And her eyes?"

"Both of them. The blue and the purple."

Zaibos shifted in his chair, ever so slightly, waving his gauntlet. "Bring it to me."

A guard moved from his post and Eros noted his armor. Or was it a she? Unlike the guards below, with their burnt and beaten plates, this suit appeared as if it was crafted from volcanic glass, each piece tailored to the body, every angular joint fitting with precision. He doubted the finest blacksmiths in Tyrnael could have forged it.

Zaibos held the box in his glove, its lid hanging open. "Your cruelty cannot be doubted, assassin."

"I do only as I am contracted—no more, no less." It was all that needed saying, but when he should have remained silent, some foolish part of him added, "I do not delight in the torment of others, as some do."

The king rose and stepped forward, a giant in his armor, a terrible cacophony of metal upon metal following his descent from the throne. "Tell me, when you killed her, was she aware? Did you . . . smell her fear? Did you look into her eyes in the moment of death? How long did it last, before she was still?"

Eros stepped away as the king advanced. His eyes fixed on the guards. Could he hope to slip between them? "It was quick, my lord. I am not paid to torture."

Zaibos stood at the base of the platform, his daemonic visage gleaming in the fire. Opening the box, he removed the eye and held it like a peeled egg between his mailed fingertips, the dull blue iris staring back at him, accusing him. Eros watched intently, desperate to gauge the king's expression.

"You speak as though you do not approve of my methods. You think me evil, and yet we all do what we must, to get what we want. Only . . . I do not understand what it is that *you* want."

Eros could feel his legs swell with pent up action, yet he could not flee, not without implicating himself. "I . . . I do not know what you mean, my lord."

"You are a murderer, Eros. You know this. I know this. But what I cannot fathom is why . . . why kill *two* women, when I asked only for one?"

Eros palmed the hilt at his side, his other hand in his vest. "I still don't . . ."

Zaibos closed the gap between them, coming within reach. "Was it difficult, assassin? The heart was easy, any swine will do, but the eyes! A turquoise-eyed girl cannot have been difficult to find, but violet? Why go through all this trouble to deceive me?" The box fell against his greaves, the eye rolling away, the heart deflating limply at his feet.

Eros stood his ground, staring directly into the slots of the king's mask, tightening his grip on his tools. "You are mistaken, my king. It wasn't two women. I could not find a girl with blue-green eyes, but there is a butcher I have hated since I was a child. He made me kill a dog, you see, a beast that I pitied. The other, the violet eye . . . well, that belonged to my mother." He cried the last word, hurling himself away as three iridium balls exploded from his palm. One sailed past the king's head, but the other two found their marks, embedding between the spikes of his breastplate. Zaibos collapsed in a heap of iron.

Eros was on the floor, his shoulder aching, but the king was finished. Perhaps now, the guards would let him be. Surely, no one in Tyrnael owed allegiance to this madman. And yet, the guards continued to close about him, their spears lowering.

"Hold!" he cried. "The usurper is slain. What has he done for this kingdom, to earn your loyalty, but betray its rightful ruler?"

They hesitated, but did not right their weapons, their helmets turning beyond him.

"They are the Silent," a familiar voice remarked, "my praetorian guard, and they cannot answer you, for I have removed their tongues."

Eros watched as, with some effort, Zaibos pushed himself to his feet, and the iridium orbs dropped from between the spikes of his cuirass. "You think yourself so clever, assassin, and yet what are you? A glorified peasant, an outcast, an abomination! I stand upon the shoulders of gods, for such were the Zo, gods among mortals! My armor was forged ages ago, in the fires of the sun, and is part of me now. Nothing can kill me, least of all, you!"

Eros retreated, an eye on his enemy, the other searching for an escape. But the circle was shrinking. He could not hope to slip past them without being skewered. His only chance was to fight, but he was not one for combat. Everything he did was calculated, to assure victory, but in meeting Radia he had lost his way, and it would cost him his life.

"Bring my weapon," Zaibos commanded. "I am going to enjoy this." A small gray creature emerged from a shadowy alcove. He delivered the morningstar with considerable effort, but in the king's hand, the ball of spikes could just as well have been weightless. "Bonecrusher," he said. "A simple name, given by the simple minds who forged it."

"Bogrens," Eros murmured. "You're using them. Tyrnael isn't enough for you, is it? You want the whole world." Perhaps if he kept the king talking, used his vanity against him, he could think a way out of this.

"And why shouldn't I? The world is my birthright, for it belonged to our ancient ancestors. *That* is who we truly are, still—we've only just forgotten. The coming of the Greater

Moon robbed us of our glory, and we have been sick ever since, cowed by a dynasty ill-suited to govern. Solon and his forefathers were a sickness. In this, and *any* world, one law governs survival—the strong devour the weak!"

Without warning, Bonecrusher came at his face, a spike grazing his ear, and Eros fell further back, the hilt of his dagger growing moist in his palm. The morningstar was heavy, easy to evade, and against any other opponent, he would have found an opening. But the pieces of Zaibos's armor fit too perfectly, and even then, he could not be certain whether some layer of protection lay beneath, a shirt of chain or gambeson.

"Look at you now. You are ready to die, and who has done this to you? Radia has infected your mind, but I aim to cure it, to expunge this world of her kind!"

Keep talking. Waste your breath.

And yet, as if fueled by his own rhetoric, the king began to move with greater speed and grace, the morningstar becoming a blur. Eros could feel the rush of air jostling his hood, could hear its deadly whistle as he crouched to avoid it.

"Zaibos . . . it isn't what you think."

The spikes came down again, cratering the floor. "Why then? What did she say to sway your hand?"

"She means more to me than you know."

With sudden rage, the king charged, every piece of him deadly, from the horns of his helm to the arm-length spikes thrusting from his pauldrons. But Eros was ever beyond reach, in a perpetual orbit, feinting a stab in the groin and abdomen, and slinking away again.

"Do not toy with me!"

Despite his enormous strength, the king could not keep up the attack. It was the assassin's only advantage, and in a short time Zaibos grew visibly weaker, and Eros began to consider his chances of survival, when something sharp cut into his shoulder blades and he jerked forward, nearly losing his head.

The Silent were moving in, narrowing the area of combat, and if not for the king waving them off, they might have ended his life then and there. And at that moment Eros realized what he should have long known. Zaibos was not a man of honor and would make use of his guard if necessary. His only chance of escape necessitated killing him outright, and quickly.

The tiles indicating *south* erupted, and the king strained and cursed, to release his weapon from the floor. It was enough time for Eros to lunge forward and clamber up his body. The spine was free of spikes, and there he planted his feet, and in his fists he held fast to a short piece of razor wire. A single tug would suffice to sever the neck. He had performed the maneuver a dozen times, against cuckolds and card cheats, their heads rolling from their bodies without fail, but the wire could find no purchase, no opening, sliding between the chin of Zaibos's helm and the gorget about his neck. When the garrote snapped from the effort, Eros hit the floor. The impact dazed him, and he could feel the hard edges of the king's gauntlet digging into his shoulder, the force crushing him.

"Now you will tell me the truth!"

Bonecrusher became a reddish blur in his periphery as his head exploded. Agony devoured his senses, radiated to every limb, blasted from his eyes and ears. He was in utter shock, unable to conjure a single thought, but pain. When his vision came into focus, he could see the bits of skin and tissue and teeth, saturated in pools of black and red. It took him some time to realize what had happened, to recognize his blood, strewn halfway to the wall. He could only imagine how he must look. The left side of his skull was missing. He could feel the air rush into the cavity where his cheek had been, sense the tender mass of lip and gum hanging from his face, and his jawbone, affixed to his head by the slightest sinew.

"Why did you betray me? What is so special about this girl, that people are willing to sacrifice their lives for her?"

The voice was difficult to make out, for he was both partly deaf and blind, and his entire being throbbed with pain. But when he tried to push through it, to answer, his tongue could only waddle like a fish inside his mouth, and the sounds that came from it caused him to shudder, and to hate himself even more.

"What is the matter, assassin? Are you having some difficulty?" The morningstar clanged to the floor, as Zaibos reached his mailed fist into Eros's mouth, taking hold of his hanging jawbone. The assassin could not help himself—a muffled, inhuman scream escaped him as the connective bone and tissue holding his face together started to crack and crumble. With a single motion, Zaibos tore his jaw clean from his face.

Eros could never have imagined such extremities of pain, let alone surviving it. He wished for nothing more than to curl into himself and shut his eyes to the world, to end his miserable existence.

"Do you see the power that I wield, assassin? Men will do anything, give up anything, to escape their own misery. There is no greater truth in the universe. You could have stood beside me, doing unto others as I am doing to you, but you chose a different path. *Her* path. Why?"

His body was growing cold and numb, and it excited him to think that the Taker was coming for him, to set him free.

Death is not cruel, but the most merciful of gods.

A sense of serenity washed over him then, as he looked beyond the feet of his killer to the steps of the dais, where the glazed eyeball remained, and he recalled the look in her eyes when she saw him. The resemblance to his mother was uncanny. Even now, with all that he was suffering, he knew he could have done no differently.

Turning to face the Monster King, Eros answered with a guttural sound, the words sounding only in his head.

I couldn't do it. She is my sister.

22

Niah

---

elp me, Baba! Help me!
The words pound inside my skull, scream from my
eyes and ears, consume every part of me and become
me. It repeats, endlessly—I run and run, but we remain a
nation apart, him a black speck on the edge of the water. Try
as I may, with every stitch of my being, and still I cannot reach
him. Never in time.

I gain no traction, my feet slipping in the sand, and with
each step, my legs grow heavier. I am being dragged under, am
sinking. Daring to open my eyes, I take full account of my
surroundings. Marble colonnades and rotundas spread about
me in ruins. Tatters fly in place of banners, and pediments
lined with gods sit broken, black lichen caking their surface.
The Sea lifted against us, a swollen giant from the depths of the
world, and every soul was lost to its waves. I am certain of
nothing else, yet my son remains, his shouts tearing me
between dread and hope. On my right, opposite the city, a
wasteland stretches, an eternity of rifts and tortured cliffs. All
the water—the Sea entire—is turned to fog, and angry clouds
entomb the sky. The fleets have surfaced from their graves,
their ribs cracked, their sails moth-eaten shrouds. And every

man who ever sailed the waters is among the drowned, laid bare for my eyes to witness and my heart to despair, their clean-picked skulls becoming the foundation of the Seafloor, their broken bones comprising the white gravel coast that keeps me from my son.

Still, he calls my name, beseeching that I answer to my duty as a father, and suddenly that impossible distance shrinks to nothing, and I am already too late, powerless to change his fate. The scaly creature is upon him, digging its webbed claws into my son's handsome face, tearing out his eyes, and still he calls for me.

Unhand him, monster! I cry, but my son no longer fills the space beneath the monster. Now it is the Fel girl, a child's body rent apart, but when she turns to me, I see my wife, wrestling beneath that slimy, writhing form, and those jagged teeth. *Niobe*! I shout, but she cannot see me. For I am not there. Was never there. I am nothing. The dust of the dead consumes me, and I wish only to surrender to oblivion and forgetfulness. But then something wakes within me.

It is a singing, a glowing hope in the void. I am like a ship under a moonless sky, drawn to a lighthouse. From up on high, beyond that deathly pale, there is a fiery firmament, like morning shining into night.

It was never a city. I know that now. *She* is the light . . .

"Radia!"

Demacharon was alive and breathing heavily, and it never failed to surprise him. Where was he? Niah's bedroom, of course. His sheets were cold, damp, and he could feel his hand tremble against his brow.

One of the worst mornings yet, he thought to himself, and he was suddenly overcome by a sense of abandonment, realizing that she had to have left the house while he was sleeping.

Since arriving in Yefira, Davos and his family had lavished him with food, and provided him and Noora a place to rest, at their own expense, and risk. Had Davos not sworn to keep the princess's identity secret, he would have been certain that Kiki was aware of Noora's birthright. Noora was only too eager to discard her peplos, in that the garment reminded her of her handmaiden, and with little hesitation agreed to a selection from Davos's eldest's wardrobe. As for Demacharon, the boiled leather of the legionnaire was superfluous in such a land, where there were no armies, no wars. And at Kiki's insistence, he took to borrowing clothes from when her husband was, as she put it, "a slender man," though he doubted such a word could ever have been applied to him. Even now, he felt loose in Davos's old tunic, the sleeves falling well past his knuckles.

Demacharon found Davos by the kitchen, watching Kiki through the window as she hung bedsheets on a line out in the garden. Davos looked upon her in such a way that, had they not three children already, Demacharon might have mistaken them for newlyweds.

"Where's Noora?"

"Ah! Up at last, eh, Dimsby? Is that what you Hedonians do? Sleep half through the morning?"

"My apologies. Peaceful slumber eludes me."

"I've noticed. We all have, come to think of it."

"Listen, I don't wish to be a burden, so if you'd permit me to seek lodging elsewhere—"

"Pish posh!" Davos waved his hand as if to swat a fly. "Nothing could bother me more than your departure! You are guests and shall remain so."

"But . . . we can't possibly stay here forever."

"And why not?"

"Your daughters . . . we're taking up their rooms."

He laughed, turning back to the window to admire his wife. "The girls don't need rooms! They're tough, like me! What they need is . . . Well, what they need is *her*. They're all so terribly fond of her. I can't possibly separate them."

"But it's a small village. Noora could visit any time she wanted."

"True, but you know how it goes! People move away, say they'll write, visit, but do they ever? My mother lives a passing's climb from here yet I haven't seen the old bat in half a year. Besides, I'm sworn to the princess just like yourself, and that's a lifetime appointment. Can't keep an eye on her if she's halfway cross town, can I? Far as I'm concerned, I've earned myself a fourth daughter. Seems the gods like to bless me that way, with an endless supply of girls, and a good thing, that."

"That reminds me . . ." Demacharon said with a pause, uncertain how to proceed, "back in Tyrnael, you said something peculiar. You said you'd known the princess since you were a child. I know your intentions were noble, but what you told me . . . could not possibly have been true, and you must be aware of that."

"Are you suggesting that I lied to you?"

"Not exactly. However—"

"Davos, a liar? I've never once lied in my life!"

Demacharon distanced himself a step, surprised by the sudden outburst. Perhaps he had chosen the wrong words. "Davos, the girl can't be more than fifteen, and when were you last a child? Thirty-five, forty years ago?"

"I could explain myself to you, but you wouldn't believe me if I did."

"I know you're an honorable man, Davos. Perhaps you misspoke, or meant something other than—"

"I always mean what I say!" he barked, slamming his mug on the kitchen table. "What do you take me for, some kind of shyster?" It was enough to catch his wife's attention, but he just smiled and waved her back to work.

"Try me," Demacharon implored. "I've seen no shortage of impossible things in my day, and may yet believe you."

"I can't say I understand it myself. All I can do is tell you what I know, and what I know is that time—*time* itself, that is—doesn't play by all the rules up there."

"What? You mean in Mythradnaiil?"

"Aye. When I first arrived from there, everything felt a bit off, but I couldn't quite put my finger on it. The crops were all out of season, and I could swear that my littlest had grown a good thumb or two. So I went to Kiki and asked her straight out, 'How long I been gone for?' and she looks at me as if I were a loon, and says to me, 'You've been drinking again, have ya? You know well as I how long you been gone.' So I asks her again, and she tells me, she says, 'About three cycles. Missed you dearly, too.' And I went into a rage, telling her, 'Kiki, I ain't been gone more than three days, much less thirty!' We had a fight after, on account she didn't like my tone, and I slept in the barn come nightfall. Was a cold night, too."

"I . . ." Demacharon wanted to say something, but didn't know how to word it. "I'm sorry, but I really don't follow you."

"Let me put it another way. On my next voyage out, I bring with me a hollyhock seedling in a pot, Kiki's favorite, knowing that, come a cycle or two, the thing should grow up to my knee. So a year goes by, it's my third trip out, and I expect to come across a full-grown bush. Know what I find? A single twig, no taller than my ankle."

"That . . . that doesn't prove anything. It could have been a different plant."

"Come now, Dimsby—I'm smarter than that. I used my own pot, with a kind of pattern they don't make in Tyrnael, and I hid it well. Lest someone found it, removed what I'd planted, and replaced it with something else. It was the same one."

"There could be any number of explanations. It might be the weather, or the water."

"No," he insisted. "My wife logged the days I was gone in one book, and I in another, and I can assure you, *time* slows down in Tyrnael. Damned if I know the reason, but it does. But you were right about one thing. I haven't been a boy for thirty-odd years. For Radia? Couldn't have been more than half a decade."

"But wait, it still doesn't add up. If you were the first man to discover Tyrnael, how could you have already known of her?"

"First man from Yefira," Davos corrected. "Who can say, truly, that of all the people who've walked this planet, that I was the first? There've been others, I've heard, brave mountain explorers, like Leminkaynan of Kalvala. But I do know this—

Krow's people never lost contact with the city. They can fly, most of them anyway, so the Crown of Aenya is no barrier to them. Bird men don't often converse with outsiders, but it happens, and there are no wings so swift like those of a great tale. Think of all the stories you've ever heard, of a beautiful princess somewhere, imprisoned in a tower. Do we not all share a similar tale? Have you not read the like in your land? Perhaps as a bedtime fable to your son or daughter?"

Demacharon did not know what to think. Hazy memories surfaced in his mind, of a princess in need of rescue, variations on the theme practically infinite. Could there be truth to it? Did every such myth originate from Tyrnael, born of some historic event? If so, how did the passage of time play a role? He had spent a good year in the city, familiarizing himself with its inhabitants and their customs, proving his skills to ascend to the rank of praetorian. If what Davos said was true, how much time had elapsed in the outer world? Had the floodwaters yet receded from Hedonia? Did refugees still pour from its ruins? And what of Zaibos? The usurper was no doubt seeking the princess still. Was the lengthening and shortening of time a blessing or a curse?

"Where is she now?"

"Noora? She ran off with the girls, to the sugar fields, I think."

"What? Why? How can I find her in that?"

"Now don't get all screwy, Dimsby. She's safe. We're all safe here."

"In this world, no one is safe." Demacharon made for the doorway, when he came across Kiki, nearly toppling the basket from her head.

"Where're you off to in such a hurry?"

"Sorry, but I must find Noora."

"Won't you have breakfast, at least?"

"When I return, perhaps."

"Alright, then. She took my blue scarf and hat. Remind her to bring it back, would you?"

Demacharon wasted little time, rushing past neighbors who shouted cheerful greetings after him.

In Yefira, most of the crop came from a garden, or small family-owned plantations, interspersed between individual houses. A few ran north along the foothills. Other farmers made use of the steppes, growing more rugged vegetables above like napshins and rutgebarrows. The sugar fields were on the outskirts, facing east, like a fence dividing the villagers from the Great Chasm.

After a short trek, Demacharon stood before a wall of green, fronds sprouting from the tops of the sugarcane like disheveled hair. A person could easily get lost in such a field. He rushed in, realizing he was without armor or weapon. Even here, he could not dismiss the possibility that Zaibos's agents could be lurking, and he would be powerless to defend against them. Sugarcane swatted at him, pushed him in directions he did not want to go, and all the while he listened for the sounds of children at play, but there was only the wind knocking the stalks together, the buzzing of cicadas and the melody of a distant wood thrush. Having lost his direction, he started to look for a way out. He had never been a scout, after all, and navigating the land was a far cry from finding his bearings over water.

Something blue caught his eye, swaying like a flag. He followed the color to a lone scarf. What he assumed was the princess, wearing Kiki's straw hat and sundress, was a bundle of plants, which could only mean . . .

Bursting through the row to the opposite side of the field, he paused to let the wind hit him, taking in the view. To the north, a series of green hills sloped downwards, dropping suddenly off the edge of the world. Southward, a river tumbled toward the gorge, disappearing in a thunderous spray. She was lying in a bed of heather, her arms wide, as if to embrace the sky, her hair tributaries gilded by sunlight.

"Noora, by Zoë, what do you think you're doing?"

"Oh, hey, Dimmy. I'm cloud gazing."

Demacharon had known the finest captives, exotic beauties brought to him from throughout Aenya, and yet he could not help but shy from her exposed body, feeling as if he were looking at his daughter. And yet, in that glance, he noticed how more robust she had become, fuller in the hips and bosom, less a child and more a woman, and it turned his mind to what Davos had told him about the strange passing of time.

"Noora, you know you can't be alone out here, so far from the house. How many times have we talked about this? What if . . . what if something were to happen?"

"Things are always happening, Dimmy. *Life* is happening, all around you—you're just too busy worrying to notice."

"And what about your clothes?" he went on. "What if someone were to see you?"

"Everyone has seen me already. Just the other day, the neighbors did for sure. It was such a beautiful day . . . I couldn't help myself! They didn't complain, nobody did, so I've decided to give it all up."

He could feel his blood vessels constricting. "Give up what exactly?"

"Wearing clothes. The Goddess never meant for us to hide, not since the Cataclysm, anyway. That seems to have ruined everything, the way things were made to be."

"Noora!" he shouted, forgetting himself. "You must take the world as it is, not as you wish it to be! Get dressed at once."

"Or you'll what?"

"Noora, not everyone sees things the way you do. There is great wickedness in the world, cruelty and . . . evil."

"I don't believe in evil."

He was stunned to silence. How could she say such a thing, after all they had seen and done, after the massacre of her guard and the murder of her handmaiden? "Then, you are still a child . . . a poor misguided child, and I was a fool to think otherwise. Someday, these crazy ideas you have will cost you, and when that day comes, I won't be around to save you."

"And who will save *you*, Dimmy?" Her mismatched eyes focused on his, disarming him. "Tell you what—lay down beside me, and I'll get dressed," she said, adding, after a pause, "And don't forget, I outrank you."

Realizing he could in no way control this girl, he took a knee by her side. "So, what are we doing?"

"Not like that," she said, tugging at his belt. "Down all the way."

He could hear the grass crumpling under his weight. "This isn't safe . . ."

"It's perfectly safe."

"I feel ridiculous."

"I'm sure you do," she said. "Try to relax."

Something was pinching him in the leg, and he smacked it impulsively. "Dammit, ants!"

"They don't like you."

"Noora, just tell me what it is you want me to do, so we can stand up."

"Look at the sky!" she exclaimed. "See it?"

He started to protest, without even bothering to look, but there it was, plain as the mount he used to ride into battle, and the more he relaxed, the more the cloud came into focus, creating the image of a perfectly-shaped horse.

"In Campania," he murmured, after a time, "where I grew up, we used to love to do this." Something deep within him, long buried by tragedy, welled up to the surface of his mind, a host of memories, childhood friends he had not thought of in decades, the faces of his father, and mother. He tried to suppress his yearning for what could never be, but was not quick enough, and his eyes started to dampen.

"Look, Dimmy, a hawk! And there! A rabbit!"

Every animal seemed to appear just as she was pointing them out, and Demacharon continued to gaze upward, watching the heavenly parade, surprised by his imaginative capabilities. But he soon began to doubt himself. The images formed by the clouds were too well-defined, as if an artist was using the sky for a canvas, and water vapor as a medium. The cloud did not merely resemble a rabbit—it *was* a rabbit.

He found it all so very unlikely, impossible even, and yet there it was, spread before him in spectacular detail. "Noora, are you . . . are you doing that?"

"Doing what?"

A sound flitted through the sugarcane, a fast-moving animal or person, and Demacharon was on his feet in an instant. "Quick! Get dressed!"

To his relief, she responded immediately, snatching Kiki's straw hat, the one he had pulled off the stalk, to shield her bosom, leaving the tunic to drape against her thighs.

Now the sound of shifting stalks was drowned out by wailing. Niah came crashing through, and froze upon seeing them, her face awash in tears, a ball of gray pressed against her heart. She made several attempts to speak but was choked with sobs. Demacharon stood within reach of her, but Noora moved more quickly, taking Niah into her arms.

"What is it, Niah? Are you hurt?"

The Hedonian squatted beside them, repeating, with impatience, "Tell us! Have you been hurt?"

Dumb with grief, the little girl relaxed her arms, so they could see what she was holding. "Why?" was all she could say, in a small whimpering voice.

Gently, Noora transferred the limp weight from Niah's arms into her own, and ran her fingers over the rabbit's backside, massaging its floppy ears, but its eyes remained closed and it did not move.

"He won't wake up," Niah explained. "I tried poking him, giving him some red cabbage—his favorite—but he just sits there. Athalia says he's dead. Is that true, Noora? Is Hazel dead?"

"It would seem so," Demacharon answered. "What happened?"

"Father tried to get him out of the house the other day, but Hazel got scared and scratched his arm, and father dropped him. Mother says he broke his back and that . . . that it'd be better that he not suffer, but I just couldn't . . . I put him next to me in bed, got him all cozy, read him a bedtime story, but this morning when I got up . . ." She started to weep, and dropped to her knees.

"Death is the way of things," Demacharon murmured. "It's something you must learn to accept, if you are to grow into a woman."

"Does . . . does everything die? Father and mother? Will they die as well?"

Demacharon glowered. "You mean to tell me your parents never—?"

"Please, Dimmy," Noora said, pushing him aside. "She's only a little girl. This is no place for a legionnaire."

Niah lifted her glistening eyes, and Demacharon could see the hope in them, as she gazed upon Noora. No, not Noora, *Radia*. It seemed that the princess had the same effect on everyone. And he was moved also, despite the countless cruelties he had witnessed on the battlefield. *The Taker visits all—even our little creatures—and leaves us to our woes.*

"Is it true, Noora? Will I die one day? And if that's so, why is it so?"

"Come with me," she answered, taking the girl into the clearing, and cradling Hazel in her lap. "Let me tell you a story, and perhaps then, you will understand."

The girl nodded quietly, eager to listen. And Noora began to tell her tale, stroking the rabbit's soft mane all the while,

Long ago, in a great castle, there lived a prince and his beloved princess. Together they lived happily for many years, until, one fateful day, she fell deathly ill. This was the time of the Red Plague, and many who lived in the kingdom perished from it, including the princess. With his father's blessing, the prince called upon artisans and masons, to build for her a monument, and there her body was laid to rest. To preserve her beauty, a graven image was fashioned, cut from the finest stone. For seven days and nights, the prince never left her monument, but on the morn of the eighth day, his sorrow turned to rage. He wished to know why Skullgrin, the god of death, would take from him that which he most loved in all the world, when they were still so young and had been so happy.

And so, that very evening, he set out to find Death, to ask him. But it would be no easy task. The king, his father, begged that he not go, fearing that the young prince, upon finding his beloved in the Underworld, would never wish to return from her side. The prince, however, could not be dissuaded. Many books he read, and he sought counsel from many learned sages, until coming upon the Dreaming Mountain, where the hidden grove of Hpnos led him far beneath the earth's surface. There, in the darkest depths of the mountain, the prince crossed the Veil of Sleep, which separates the waking world from the dreaming, and where he laid himself down and slumbered, and dreamed through the lands between Life and Death until reaching Lethe, the River of Forgetfulness. Here he joined the crew of a many-oared vessel, a sunken warship from ages past. Following the river's winding course, they arrived at the Gate of the Underworld, and the Realm of the Dead.

And yet his journey was far from over. Across the Plains of Apathia, he journeyed on foot, where the shades of the dead are said to roam, restlessly and forever, until at last, he reached the Castle of Dreadfulness. He cowered before the walls of teeth and bone, and a terrible sadness filled his heart as he looked upon the moat filled with the tears of all the people who have ever lost a loved one. But upon entering that awful place, the prince was surprised, for what came out to greet him was not a scary god with a skull-like face and horns, but a very old man, so feeble and decrepit that the prince could not help but pity him.

"Who are you?" the prince asked, thinking that the god must be elsewhere.

"I am he whom you have long sought," the old man answered. "I am the Taker, Skullgrin. I am Death itself."

"Tell me then, if you are who you say, why is it that all things that draw breath must die?" He asked this, rather than inquire after his beloved, for during his quest the prince had learned the meaning of compassion, and that the extraordinary pain in his heart was not unique to him, but common to all people in all places throughout history.

"That is a thing I cannot tell you," the aged man answered, "for it is not a thing that can be told." At that, the prince became furious, but he fell despondent, for he knew that he could not challenge Death.

"But," the god went on, "I see that you have traveled a great way and are weary, and so you may stay in my home until you are rested. And as your heart is pure, you may watch and listen, so that you may yet attain the answer that you seek."

The prince spent many days and nights in the company of Death, and was surprised at how kindly he was treated, so that, after a short while, he felt neither bitterness nor animosity toward his host. The old man offered him tea and bread, and together they sat and spoke on many subjects. But the prince was most amazed by the man's young daughter, who was unlike any of the denizens of the Underworld he had met, for she was bright and playful, and the sight of her filled him with joy.

The prince then noticed something even more remarkable. It seemed to him that the old man grew sicklier by the passing, as his child grew taller and ever more beautiful. After less than a cycle, the child was fully grown to womanhood, but Death was unable to rise from bed. By now, Skullgrin little resembled the one who first greeted him, his flesh like parchment, and his eyes hollowed and yellow.

Seeing that his time was nigh, the prince asked of his daughter, "How can this be? Truly, if he is Death, how is it that he himself can die?"

"This is the way it has always been," she answered him. "Whenever I come into the world, he begins to fade. For I am Life, Zoë, daughter of Skullgrin. You see, as Death is the end of Life, so is Life the end of Death. I cannot exist without him, and he without me. When Time comes to take him, for Time is greater than either of us, I will go into my bower and give birth, for I am with my father's child. He will be my son until I pass away, and the cycle will begin anew, as you found it when you first came here."

It was then that the prince realized the lesson Death had provided for him. He bid farewell to the goddess, and in looking back upon that place, he saw that it was not like what he had first seen. For only to those arriving does the castle appear dreadful, but to all who depart from it, it is a tower of pure golden light.

When, after these seven years sleeping, the prince awakened, he headed straightway to his father, to preach to his people what Skullgrin had taught him, so that those who listen might celebrate the Giver, and dread not the Taker.

Niah waited for more, watching Noora intently, and said nothing.

"Did you like the story?" Noora asked finally, gently stroking the rabbit's ears.

"Yes," she nodded, though her face, still wet with tears, looked uncertain. "I . . . I think so. I mean, the prince and the princess were never together again?"

"Nobody really knows," Noora replied. "Never is a very long time."

"I still miss Hazel," she said at length. "I know they make babies, so I can get another rabbit, but still I miss him."

"I know you do. I can feel it." Noora closed her eyes, slowly wiping a tear from her own cheek. Demacharon, watching from a distance, could see the connection between them, the empathic bond.

"I just wish I could play with him, just for one more day."

Noora lifted her hands from the gray ball of fur, and her face eased into a smile. "You may yet," she murmured. "Take a look."

Hazel was blinking, brushing the crust from his eyes, and with a sudden jerking motion, he glanced this way and that, as if waking from an unpleasant dream.

The little girl screamed, stealing the rabbit into her arms. "Noora! Look, he's alright! Oh, thank you, Noora. Thank you so very much."

Far from being crippled, Hazel dashed from Niah's arms, into the sugarcane in a zigzagging pattern, and the little girl was quick to pursue.

Demacharon caught himself, overcome with wonderment, and emotions he did not know he possessed. Niah's delight was infectious. And without having spent the last few cycles as the princess's escort, witnessing all manner of impossibilities, he would have surely been awestruck.

"You know, I was ready to skin that rabbit. I know a dead animal when I see one."

She stood, looking demure, slipping her tunic over her head. "He was only sleeping."

"Noora . . ." he wanted to search her eyes, to gauge the truth from them, but she turned away. Perhaps she did not know herself what she was capable of. "That was a good story. One of your myths?"

"No, not at all. Prince Kormin is my great ancestor, eighth descendant of the Zo."

"Noora, you can't possibly believe all that. It's a fine tale for children, but what the prince witnessed, if any of it is based in reality, can only have been a dream."

"You don't believe in gods?"

He sighed, weighed by what he was about to say. "In Hedonia, we venerated Sargonus, killed and conquered in his name, trusting in whatever the High Priest told us, believing the babbling of mystics and the writings of the Prophet. Yet where was Sargonus when the Sea came crashing into our city? Drowning everyone who worshipped him? Or for that matter, where were the gods of the savages, of the Fel, when we slaughtered them? Myths, fairytales, religion, they are all the same, humanity's way of coping with the great burden of existence. Never, in all my journeys, did I see any evidence of a god or gods."

She stared at him, her face impenetrable, and he could not tell whether she was in agreement, or judging him. "What is it you believe, Hedonian?"

"I believe . . ." he started, as if the thought had never occurred to him, "I believe in people, and that what we do to each other matters into eternity. But also, well . . . I believe in *you*, Radia."

23

Esse

Three women stood in a parlor, their needles and thimbles moving swiftly and precisely. Reams of colored fabric spilled over their toes, awaiting embroidery. Half-finished banners lay rolled in corners, needing thread, and along each wall articles of clothing were piled in neat squares, ready for customers to take away. Moving about the center table was an ordeal, as the women could not take three steps in any direction without hitting a wall. But over the years, they had learned to manage the cramped space. There were no windows here, only aging tapestries giving the illusion of the sun and moons, or a stepped garden in bloom, or the Compass Tower on the skyline. A single narrow slot, built into the wall, gave notice of the outside world. Requests from throughout the city were dropped in through here.

Before the new king seized control, the three seamstresses met these requests with delight, for, being eloai, they were born to love labor. Now, slips continued to fall throughout the day, beyond their capacity to answer, each one calling for the same item.

Shrouds. Shrouds for the dead.

Esse was the youngest of the three. When she was born, her abilities were assessed by the Committee, and by age nine she was delivered into the company of Madame Latima. In a way, Latima became her mother, as eloai commonly attached themselves to their superiors. With Vasila, a girl two years her senior, she was as close as any two sisters could be. For ten years, the trio worked at sewing and mending, and even though many larger companies of seamstresses could be found, the very best work came from their skilled fingers. Their tapestries rivaled the greatest murals in the land, and their tablecloths and tea cozies were as delicate as a spider's webbing. The clothing and finery they produced came to be a mark of status among the highest born. Nobody quite understood the secret of their excellence, but for them, it was no mystery, for they toiled tirelessly and without ego, and loved their work more than anything in life. At least, that was how it had been before the new regime came into power. Now, there were no curtains to be made, no ceremonial gowns for aristocrats coming of age, only sheets, simple coverings to hide the dead. Or their remains.

Naturally, Latima, Vasila, and Esse could not hope to thread a needle without embarking on a bit of good-natured gossip. The words that passed between them fueled their efforts, made the tedious aspects of their work go unnoticed, but lately, there was talk of one thing, and one thing only.

Before Zaibos, only the very decrepit of Tyrnaelians, nearing three hundred years, were known to die. For fatal accidents were uncommon, and sickness and murder not known to the people but in legends. Now death was an everyday occurrence, and no citizen was immune to it. And yet the greater distress was not the frequency of lives cut short, but the unnatural causes behind it. Terrible, unimaginable things, things Esse shuddered to think about.

"You know what I heard," Vasila started, jabbing a needle into the seam running between their hands. "I heard the king found something worse."

"You don't say," Latima replied, continuing to work without pause.

"Seems like most folks don't quite feel the fire, was the smoke that got them, breathing it in and all."

"Well, that's a relief, a small relief anyway."

"I suppose so," Vasila added, with no less enthusiasm. "They suck it all in through the nostrils, dying of asphyxiation. I think they do it on purpose—"

"Is that so?"

"So as so," she answered. "So what's the king go and do? He finds all this out and comes up with something new. No more burnings, he says. Much too easy a way out. So he visits this blacksmith. You know the one, with the scruffy beard and goggles, always smelling of ashes?"

Latima nodded in the affirmative. "Unpleasant fellow, that one."

"Well, the king asks him for a way to burn traitors without creating any smoke."

"Really?"

"Oh, yes. So the blacksmith, he sets himself to working, making this cast iron beast, a mammoth I think they said it was, or a saurian, doesn't really matter . . . And so the blacksmith shows up before the king with this thing, and it's basically a big oven, but for roasting people, you see."

"How ghastly," Latima casually replied, her fingers never slowing. "I can hardly imagine—"

"You're telling me!"

Esse, who could not help but listen to the exchange, suddenly slammed her hands against the table, making the needles jump and a spool unravel from table to floor in a long ribbon. "Stop it!" she screamed. "Just stop it! How can you two just go on like that? Honestly?"

Vasila turned to her, perplexed. "I don't get you, Esse."

"You two just sit there, rambling on and on about the worst things! The very worst! This isn't some storybook—these things are happening right in our own city, in our very homes!"

Latima lowered her gaze, her spectacles slipping to the tip of her nose. "What would you have us do, my dear? It's not as if we wish these things should happen. It's just the way it is."

Esse got to her feet, huffing with frustration. "I know that. But it's no good talking about it!"

Vasila looked suddenly afraid, her eyes darting about the room. "It isn't . . . forbidden, is it?"

"Don't be silly," Latima chided her, carefully examining the stitching as if nothing could be of greater importance. "These walls were built by the ancestors. Nobody can hear us."

Esse did not want to argue, partly because she did not know how to, and partly because she could not explain her feelings to herself. All she knew for certain was that she wanted to be away from the room and the women in it.

A single stairwell led out from the parlor and down to a kitchen and to the beds they shared. Their home and place of work were built long before any of them were born, and they could only guess at its original tenants, or to what purpose the structure once served. Features from ages past, like the small space set in the wall, remained a mystery to them, but as the air began to change, in a way that made them shudder and bring their lanterns closer in the night, they quickly surmised its function. It was a place to make heat, by fire, but the eloai did not have the means or the knowledge to work it properly. Even when they managed to get a flame started, flakes of frozen water fluttered down from the sky to put it out. Their only recourse was to create thicker fabrics, an odd thing for them to do, for clothing had always served to convey status, or to adorn its wearer, but never to protect one from the elements. Now Esse went to the hook on the wall, to don this kind of protective clothing, when Latima's voice rang out, "Wherever do you think you're going?"

"Out! Where else, Madame? I am going out!"

With her multi-layered peplos wrapped about her, Esse abandoned the room. She could feel the cold penetrating the masonry, hear the frightful wind beyond as she ascended, the stairwell brushing at her elbows on either side.

The small arched door blew open onto a narrow parapet, and to a bridge extending into the gloom of night. Looking below, she could make out the walkways crisscrossing the city, connecting every tower and terraced structure. Every path converged north, towards the stone giant rising from the horizon. Despite the troubled times, the Compass Tower looked as it always did at this time of day, a silhouetted lance against the turquoise moon. She leaned against the railing, finding peace in her solitude, piecing together the fading stonework tessellation at her fingertips. Nothing in the night suggested danger or any awful thing. Watching her breath expand, holding her layered peplos tightly in an attempt at keeping warm, she tried to conjure a happy memory, but every last one had flown.

Esse hated the cold, but more so she hated being afraid. How quickly her world had changed! Before the new king had taken the throne, her greatest concerns regarded misaligned stitching and finicky patrons. Before the soldiers in black, her imagination could never conjure the thoughts now seated on everyone's lips. More than anything, she was tired of not knowing what to say or whom to trust. Anyone could be an informant, and the slightest insinuation, a wrong word or insincere expression, could be treasonous. One woman was burned alive for alluding to the princess's beauty, or so Vasila told her. Of course, nobody knew for certain whether such stories were true. But the effect was palpable. Rumors abounded, spreading from mouth to ear like a sickness, creating a perpetual dread. And the people did not risk leaving their homes.

"Excuse me? Miss?"

Esse spun to face the voice, having been certain she was alone, and a shout caught in her teeth. A man was standing on the walkway, but in the dim light, he appeared no more than a tall shape.

"Forgive me," he said. "I did not mean to startle you. Is this the residence of Madame Latima?"

Her heart was telling her to flee, but the bridge was too narrow for more than one to cross at a time, and the only other way was back through the doorway and into the house. "It is," she said with hesitation. "If you have a commission, you can drop it through the slot."

"I do have a job in mind, but I fear it cannot be delivered but in person."

As the man shifted his posture, Esse could make out a second shape, a smaller man standing behind him.

Why were two men needed for a single order? And where would a pair of peasants be going in the dead of night? It did not make sense, unless he was not what he claimed to be. The king's watchmen, on the other hand, commonly moved about in pairs, as a lone soldier could not be trusted to follow orders without a second to keep him in line. Distressed by these thoughts, Esse started to tremble, and to backtrack, her hand clumsily reaching for the door.

"Please, don't be afraid! I wish no harm upon you!"

"Are you a soldier?"

"I am, in fact, on the Night Watch, however . . ." He paused, her apprehension evident.

Esse could feel her heart, like an angry prisoner in her ribcage, and it became more than she could control. The floor pitched like the deck of a ship, exchanging places with the sky, and her arm latched onto the railing, but it was the soldier that saved her from injury.

"Are you alright? Miss?"

"I've done nothing!" Her breathing came and went and came again, her voice escaping when it could, and yet she went on, forcefully, "I've done nothing! I've done nothing!"

"Poor creature," he murmured, but she could tell it was more for the other man to hear. Turning back to her then, he added, "Tell me, do you still enjoy picking berries?"

She could feel her eyes grow wide, catching glimpse of his face from under his hood, and her memory stirred. "You!" she murmured, her sense of dread waning. "How is it you know me? That was . . . ages ago," or so it felt in that moment, "and I am just an eloai."

"An eloai, yes, but one with many talents, I am told." He lifted her in his arms, bent under the doorway, and continued down the stairwell. From over the man's shoulder, by the glow of the sconces set in the stairwell, the second man came into view. He was much older, garbed in an awful tattered cloak, with sleeves tailored too long for the fingers. She watched him turn and slam the door with his foot.

From the parlor below, Latima's voice drifted up. "Esse, it does no good to go marching off in a fit, in the dead of eclipse, and how many times have I told you never to slam that door . . ." But in seeing a man enter, with Esse limp in his embrace, the old woman quivered into silence. And just as quickly, she straightened her hair and spectacles, as Vasila rearranged the knitting table.

"My apologies," Latima said. "We were not prepared for visitors, not so late in the day. Now then, to what do we owe the honor?"

Esse lowered herself onto her chair, as the young man pushed the hood back from his face. He was not at all difficult to look at, she thought, with his square jaw and high cheekbones, despite the days of growth on his face, and tired, heavyset eyes.

"It is I who should be apologizing," he said. "Never would I think to disturb you on such a moon, was it not urgent."

"Terribly urgent!" the older man added.

Latima studied them as if to measure them for outfits. "Well," she sighed, "we are here to serve, is that not so, Vasila? Esse?"

"Oh, certainly, Madame!" Vasila offered at once.

"Madame." He addressed her like a performer taking the stage, "My name is Hugo. And this is my father. I am—I should say, rather—we are in urgent need."

"Yes, yes, you said that already. Whatever could you be needing?"

"Well, you do . . . sew, do you not? Am I not," he glanced around, eyeing the needles and the thread, "am I not in the right place?"

"Of course," she said, "of course."

"Excellent." He rubbed his hands together. The old man, standing behind him, coughed and cleared his throat, but spoke not a word.

Fiddling with the thread in her hands, Latima looked impatient. "Well? Out with it!"

Esse and Vasila gaped in horror.

"What we need is . . . I mean, what we've come here for is . . ." He glanced about the parlor for the dozenth time. "Forgive me, but is anyone else home? Below, perhaps, who might hear us?"

"No," she asserted. "Go on then. Tell me why you're here. Or do you wish me to guess?" Latima could be as intrepid as any woman, and Esse did not doubt she could stare unflinchingly into the face of the king.

The old man stepped forward, nudging the young officer away. "Banners. Flags. We need a good many, as many as you can make."

"How many, precisely?" Her voice grew hard, and deliberate, as if she were understanding something Esse did not.

"Hundreds," Hugo answered sheepishly, "if possible." An absurd request, Esse thought, but Latima looked unfazed.

"That would take, well, a good long while, and we've much work already. We couldn't even begin until . . . a good cycle or two from today."

"No," Hugo intoned, "you don't understand. We are in desperate and immediate need."

Latima sat in her chair without moving or speaking. Esse and Vasila exchanged glances between themselves and the two men. "Perhaps," the old seamstress murmured, pushing her spectacles into place, "if we knew the nature of the work you required. Are you, um, opening a business?"

"That is . . ." Hugo started, his eyes nervously scanning, his voice dropping to a whisper. "This won't be so easy."

"Is it some sort of a pattern? A sigil perhaps?"

He nodded.

"An animal?"

"Madame, I insist you speak of this to no one. In fact, I must have your word."

"How do I know," she said, "that you yourself can be trusted? What if you have come to investigate us?"

Vasila balled up in her seat, tucking her feet under, a crochet needle hard in her fists. "Investigate us! For what? Madame, what is he talking about?" Esse, all the while, was too afraid to speak, her eyes peering timidly over her knees.

Hugo turned slowly to his father. He was looking exhausted. "Show them, Papa."

The old man lurched at them, almost stumbling, his face marked like a dry riverbed.

"My name is Bastion, but they call me the Bard, or so they did, once. Two hundred long years I worked at the Cosmos Theater, until *he* came. Look here . . . look what he did to me!" He raised his arms, and the sleeves bunched against his elbows, so that they could see the mass of flesh that was once his hands and fingers. Esse steadied herself in her chair, trying not to swoon again. "He said I was useless! That music, *all music*, was useless! Ninety years, I play the bouzouki! Ninety years, I give the world beauty, and now look at me! You know I asked that shit that follows him like a puppy, that Mandos fellow, 'How will I play now?' and you know what he says to me? Do you know he says? 'Why don't you learn to play with your feet!' Ha!" He was laughing, and in the same instance, sobbing.

"Papa, I think that's enough."

"I can't do anything now! My poor son has to feed me, must wipe his own father's ass!" The old man folded like a dying blossom, hiding his face in shame, and tucking the cauliflower stubs growing from his wrists beneath his cloak.

Hugo turned to each woman, his eyes clouded, pink. "You see I have every reason to despise him, for what he did to my father, and for what he has done to so many others. I know you are afraid. You have every reason to be. But fear does not rule our hearts. Fear cannot sit the throne of Tyrnael. Rest assured, I speak for a great many . . . not just soldiers, but for bakers and butchers and smiths."

"I understand you," Latima remarked, her voice laced with dread, but also something more. "But you still have not told me what you wish of me, and my girls."

"You, Madame . . ." Hugo was beseeching them, not only her, but Esse and Vasila also, "what you can provide us, will be our rallying cry, for when she comes back."

"Treason!" Vasila seemed to finally get it, and was now pointing accusingly. "I know it when I hear it! Treason! We should . . . we should report you!"

Latima held her in check with a glare. "Shut up, Vasila!"

Esse was still quivering, but something in Hugo's face, and in his tone, gave her reason to hope. The feeling was far better than any she had known in a while. "Yes, shut up Vasila," she said, finally finding her voice and, at that, the girl bunched deeper into her chair and covered her ears, as though not hearing could save her from the words being spoken.

The old seamstress removed her spectacles, weighing them between her fingers. "Some say, she is dead already."

"No. Two men working at the docks watched her board a ship, a magic trader. They saw it ascend straight into the clouds."

"A flying ship? What nonsense!"

"I've known these men since I was a boy, know them like brothers. If they say she flew up into the sky, that is what she did. But she will return. I know it."

"And how can you possibly know this?"

"I have faith."

Carefully, she set her spectacles atop the half-finished funeral shroud, considering the corpse with which it was to be entombed, weighing the dangers against the outrage. "Young man, I ask you for the last time, what do you ask of me?"

"We do not speak of it. But allow me to show you." He leaned into the light, his belt buckling against the table, and lifted his shirt.

There, leaping gracefully over his navel, was a white beast. A unicorn.

24

Hazel

Farmer Maggot's crop was finally beginning to sprout, with orange carrots and green cabbages and white ollyps, and Hazel could hardly contain himself. With anticipation, his claws gathered clumps of damp earth, his ears twitched, and his eyes roved from front to back. The farmer was nearly blind, and his dog had been put in the ground some time ago, after it had stopped running. Hazel's only real obstacle was the large rooster that liked to strut about the field with his chest held high. The wild animals that did not have humans to feed and groom them, like Hazel did, often made the mistake of underestimating Maggot's rooster. Sensing no predators, they assumed the crop was safe to approach, but did so at their peril. Yet Hazel thought himself swifter and cleverer than they were and did not doubt he could escape a flightless bird, however ferocious. And though he was not hungry—Liana made certain of that—like all young rabbits, he longed to stretch his legs and to test his instincts, to explore the green, wide-open spaces.

He watched the farmer stroll sluggishly between each row of dirt, a rusted canteen hanging from his crinkled fingertips, the man squatting occasionally to fondle a stem or crush a weevil from an exposed root. Hazel's lithe body grew tense as the man's footfalls died away, and the little bell above the lintel rang out and the door slammed shut. If the rooster was anywhere but in his pen with his wives, Hazel's long ears could not detect it. Discerning no other danger, he raked his paws under beam and post in a flurry of movement, working his snout beneath the soft soil and pulling himself under. Once on the other side, he paused for threats, and finding none, reached the crop in two great leaps. His nostrils twitched, taking in the earthy scent of growing food, his two front teeth laboring over the leafy crown of a budding carrot. He did not much care for the taste of orange food, but enjoyed the sensation of pulverizing vegetables in his mouth. Adjacent to the carrots, a series of ollyps tantalized his eyes, their heads bald and pale and white-purple, like human babies being born from a bed of curly jade bulbs. He leapt from one row to the other, seeking the ripest ollyp and peeling its outer layer to get to the tastier, yellow rings inside.

Hazel chewed his way to contentment, his mind settling into oblivion, as he was wont to do when deep in consumption, until something made him stop. He waited, listening, a long sliver of ollyp hanging from his furry snout, not knowing the reason for the interruption, only that his body was tensing up again, and that his senses had become more acute.

What was that sound? A creaking of hinges, but smaller, less heavy than the door Farmer Maggot had stepped through. His ears twisted toward the field opposite the house, to the sounds of human footfalls, grains striking the ground, the scuffle of claws and beaks. Hazel was never one to ignore fear, even when he did not know the source of it. He started to run as the rooster rounded the corner. A furious gleam shone in the bird's beady black eyes, his green-blue feathers flashing as he propelled himself forward. Hazel made straight for the fence, but the rooster was already upon him, threatening violence with each terrible squawk, recalling the terror imposed by his distant ancestors. Hazel pivoted and turned away, but the fence was too tall for him to jump, and the rooster was guarding the only exit, the small tunnel Hazel had made earlier. Frantically seeking a way out, he darted back and forth as the rooster relentlessly advanced. His hooked claws were long and sharp and could tear eyeballs like grapes from the vine. Hazel had seen the result of such an attack before, in the disfigured face of a fox that once chanced upon the henhouse looking for an easy meal. The animal survived, never to go near Maggot's place again, but Hazel did not wish to end up like the fox. He very much hoped to keep both his eyes.

If a rabbit cannot run, he will hide, and, eager to lose the frenzied bird, he dashed into the crop, leaping over carrots and cabbages and rutgebarrows, kicking dirt into the rooster's beak. Forming several figure S's in his wake, much of the field was pulled up and away, which impeded the rooster's passage, and Hazel settled on a soft patch of earth, where he thought he detected the remnants of an old burrow. Desperately working the ground with his paws, he dove nose-first into the newly-formed aperture, scurrying under the clumpy tilth where he hoped to dig his way to freedom.

His claws did not have far to go, as the surface he stood upon gave way again, and Hazel dropped into a space further below, wads of dirt and plant matter toppling down along with him. Slowly, he lifted his head to eye his surroundings and turned his ears to potential danger. A dark tunnel stretched before his nose and receded far behind his tail. Surely, he would have no trouble evading the rooster now. But as he started down the passage, a sense of unease caused him to tense up again, and his nostrils to shiver. He did not feel safe, though he knew not the reason for it, and the further he moved through the underground path, the more agitated he became. This was not a rabbit warren, he realized, for the dirt did not close in around him. The tunnel was broad enough for a young human to stand, and he felt vulnerable in it, as he did above ground, except that here he could only expect to run in one direction.

Hazel continued onward, the occasional briar root dangling overhead, worms writhing along the curved dirt wall, ants busily repairing the earthwork sections that were lost, until a shaft of sun finally led him out and into daylight.

He did not bother to think more on the matter of the strange, enormous cavity. Having had enough adventure for the day, he now longed to feel the warmth and security of his human again, and in so wanting, dashed toward the house on the hill, the familiar windmill slowly turning, groaning noisily about its axle as it always did. But Niah was nowhere to be seen.

The morning had brought rain, and where grass gave way to damp earth and soft clay, the ground remembered the trespass of children. Hazel followed the impressions of young human feet across the vale, dashing from thicket to tree stump, from the corner of a barn to the shadow of a wagon wheel. Gradually, he made his way down the slope of Yefira, toward the lowlands in the east, where the world ended.

The three sisters were with two shirtless boys Hazel vaguely recognized. They gathered near a great chestnut tree that was leaning over the drop. Athalia, the tall one with the freckles washing over her nose, sat with her blue and white dirndl folded under her knees, with her back against the tree's gnarled bark. She was listening to Niah talk, who was wearing her wooden shoes on her hands, and whose face was twisted into a scowl. The boys were responding with unhappy noises of their own, and although she stood a head shorter than either of them, Niah was staring them down, cowing them into a submissive posture. Hazel, being a rabbit, could not understand the meaning of the sounds they were making, but could sense the tension rising in the air, the potential for danger prickling the hairs of his ears. Perhaps she was upset that Hazel had gone missing, and was asking after his whereabouts. She was likely worried about him, more than usual given his recent return from the long sleep, from where he knew rabbits rarely—if ever—returned, and Hazel started to feel guilty.

With quiet little hops, he edged closer to the gathering, to avoid getting stepped on, when he spotted Liana, the youngest of the sisters, climbing the tree. Her dress, the one with tiny yellow primrose flowers sewn into the fabric, billowed around her ankles as she clambered, unsteadily and on all fours, along the bough. Suddenly, the taller of the boys turned angry, strutting within reach of Niah. He reminded Hazel of the rooster, making a lot of noise with his chest puffed up. Whatever Niah was saying to him, he was not approving of it, and now Athalia moved to intervene, getting to her feet and waving her arms. For the rabbit, it was all very confusing, for there was not a vegetable within scent's reach, and what else was there to fight over but food? He crept closer, ducking so low that the tall grasses closed over his spine, continuing toward the gnarled chestnut roots. Liana, all the while, teetered along the branch toward a solitary nut, which was dangling precariously over the drop. The boy was now holding Niah's forearm, his fingers turning pink about her wrist, and she was shouting, frantically twisting her body to pry herself from his grip. Hazel wanted to dash over and bite his toe, but he was not a dog or a fox or a rooster. His teeth were hard and could draw blood if threatened, but he was unable to do anything but arch his back under the high heather, watch and shiver.

Liana remained oblivious to all but the chestnut, sidling ever nearer to the object of her desire, occasionally losing her grasp as the tree limb dwindled in her embrace. Here the wind gushed from the depths of the underworld, up and into her face, making her hair dance and her eyes shut, and blowing up her cheeks like the sails of a whirlydinghy.

Athalia reminded Hazel of a rabbit. Even for her age, she was taller than the others, nearly reaching her mother's height, but was slow to action, uncertain of herself, nervous. Like prey. Niah was of a different species, it appeared, as she swung her arm about in a wide circle, her fist in her clog. The boy let go as her wooden shoe smashed into his face. His nose was bunched together, like a trampled bouquet of cauliflower, and was turning colors, and water started leaking out of his eyes. Now Athalia rushed to him, to stare closely into his face, with a melancholy, pitying look. The shoes went clacking to the ground, and Niah was biting her lower lip, walking softly backward, away from the weeping boy and his friend and her sister. Hazel considered making his presence known at that moment, the tension having subsided, when sounds of groaning and snapping sounded from above them.

"Liana!"

The tiny girl came crashing down, still clutching the broken branch, the momentum carrying her down the slope toward the end of the world. She rolled sideways, dead leaves and bark shavings catching in her hair, and Athalia moved after her, more rapidly than Hazel knew the girl could move, swift as a hare fleeing from a wolf. Niah came next, and the two boys. Everyone was calling Liana's name, their voices shrill and frightened. But someone had built a house into the cliff face below their feet, and Liana landed onto its rooftop. When, finally, they managed to pull her to level ground, they made angry sounds at her. Hazel could not comprehend the reason for this reaction. Niah was safe. Was laughing even, but her sisters' faces had changed to a reddish hue, and were becoming wet from the water shedding from their eyes.

Niah watched the boys slip down to their father's workshop, and when they were gone from sight, she remembered to snatch up her shoes, as Athalia started in on her usual speech, mimicking their mother's exasperated tone with annoying accuracy. "Liana! What in the Goddess's name were you thinking?"

Liana, looking at the grass, could only shrug. "I dunno."

Niah's older sister crossed her arms defiantly. "What do you mean, you don't know? You don't know or you don't want to say?"

"I dunno."

"You could have fallen into the gorge!" she scolded. "Is that something you want? To fall and fall forever, until you die of old age falling? Because that's what'll happen to you, you know."

Tears started to form in the corners of Liana's eyes, and in a long, slow motion, she drew her arm across her nose, leaving a trail of mucus to harden against her cheek. "I dunno," she said again after a time, having contemplated the question, but with nothing more to say.

"Did you ever stop to think what would happen to me? Or to mother? If you went over the drop?"

"I—I dunno!" Liana said with finality, sobbing as she wrestled with her words.

Niah could not stand to hear any more. "Come off it, Ath. She's learned her lesson, obviously. Won't ever do it again. Right, Liana?"

The four-year-old wiped her nose the other way, drawing a yellow streak across the opposite cheek. "I dunno."

"Liana!" Niah shouted. "Seriously?"

Athalia busied her fingers about the little girl's scalp, picking the brambles still tangled in her hair. By the end of it, Liana's head would look a frizzy mess, and their mother would be needing an exhaustive explanation, but the toddler, having shed enough tears to satisfy them, turned at last to Niah, saying, "So did you find Hazel?"

As if summoned by its name, the fawn-colored rabbit emerged from the surrounding thicket, bounding into her waiting arms. "Hazel!" She pressed its slim form to her bosom and nuzzled its ears with her nose, which poked up from the crook of her elbows. "Where in Aenya have you been?" she asked in all earnestness, as if the rabbit could offer her some detailed account.

"This is all your fault!" Athalia remarked. "If you weren't so convinced Colin had tossed him over, we wouldn't have almost lost Liana."

"Don't be ridiculous, Ath," Niah shot back. "We didn't lose Liana. And, well, when I told him how Hazel had come back to life, Colin called me a liar, and I just thought . . . I thought he'd done something mean, because he didn't want to look stupid when I'd show him."

"But, Hazel didn't die *die*," the little girl said softly. "I mean, Radia said he was just sleeping."

"I thought so, too, but did you see Baba's face? He turned white as a shade when he saw him hopping around."

The moon was growing in the pale turquoise sky, and the sun was merging into it, melting across its rim in shades of oranges and reds. Time had snuck past them unawares, and Niah jerked her head up in alarm, her rabbit following with its ears. "It's eclipsing!" she cried. "Baba's going to kill us."

"Wait," Athalia intoned. "I'm almost done with her hair."

From the base of the gorge to the peak of the hill, Niah drew her gaze, counting the hundreds of domiciles climbing up and over the slope, a warm light flickering one-by-one from every window, a gray ribbon swirling from every chimney.

Whatever questions her mother was bound to have did not trouble her, but for Baba, Niah had a weakness. Because he was too often gone, too long and far from home during his merchant voyages, and even now her heart ached to think on him, worrying.

"Baba is going to come searching for us. Leave her hair and let's go." Niah started up the hill, not bothering to look back, squeezing Hazel against her bosom. "Promise you'll never run off like that again, alright?"

25

Ecthros

Noora stood beside her borrowed bed, where Davos's eldest, Athalia, used to sleep. Her jeweled box lay open on the mattress, full of empty vials. She had drunk the last of it days ago, but had yet to tell anyone of her condition, or of the cure she so desperately needed. Would she swoon again? Fall into some eternal slumber? Strangely, she did not feel sick. Her only symptoms were the occasional dream world interloping into the waking world, and the green tinting of her skin. What would Demacharon say if he noticed it? He would be angry, she mused, and yell. But everything he did was out of love. She had no doubt. She could feel it.

"Mom!"

A scream came through the wall from around the hall. Liana was frightened again. Every night, she complained of monsters under her bed, insisting they were tunneling beneath the house, that she could hear them shoveling and hammering. Noora offered to share her room, but Kiki would not have it.

"It's time she learned to sleep on her own!" her mother had said.

"But mom, they're under the bed, I swear!"

Noora could feel the girl's dread. It was entirely genuine, and with Anabis's potions spent, her empathy was more acute than ever.

"Liana," Davos hollered, "come sleep with papa tonight. I'll keep you safe from the monsters."

"Nonsense!" Kiki never failed to voice her displeasure. "Don't you dare encourage her, Davos! You always make me out to be the villain!"

"You know I love you, *flower patch.*"

Despite her mother's admonition, Liana sounded ecstatic. Noora could hear the pitter-patter of feet as the little girl rushed to her parents. And when all was quiet again, Noora sat in the dim light against the bed frame, alone with her thoughts.

Soon I'll be green as a leaf, and what will they say then? Dimmy and Davos would not abandon her, she was certain of that, but what of Kiki? Village folk tended to fear that which they did not understand, and for all Noora knew, her disease was contagious. Would she be forced to live elsewhere? It saddened her to contemplate, for she had never been so happy since living with Davos's family.

TCK!

She looked out the window, but the sun had long since gone away, and the moons and stars poured dimly from a quilt of clouds. But something had made a sound, like a woodpecker gently rapping its bill against the side of the house, and she very much wanted to see a woodpecker.

She waited by the window, for what seemed a reasonable amount of time, watching the fold of the windmill pass in and out of view, and sat back down.

TCK!

And there it was again, and again she pressed her nose to the window, peering out. Nothing. Was this some new symptom of her growing illness?

TCK!

No. Something was definitely stirring, a slight way beyond her windowsill. Determined to its discovery, she parted the drapes, lifted the latch on the frame and pushed, encouraging the wind to swirl into the room.

"Psssst!"

A boy was standing below, hissing like a cat, the percolating moonlight netting the space around him in shifting shadows.

"*Ecthros*? What . . . What are you doing?"

"Noora!" He simply stood, stunned by his success to conjure her. "I wasn't sure if this was the right window."

"Did you need something?" she asked, her voice soft, coy.

"Well . . . I just wanted to see you."

"Wait right there." She gathered her gown from around her ankles, raised one leg over the windowsill, and started down from the ivy.

"B-Be careful!"

It was a short way to the ground, from the second tier of Davos's windmill home, and she did not fear injury. On she climbed, trusting her feet and fingers to the vines. The wind, all the while, played peekaboo with her gown, lifting it up and around her shoulders, translucent silk painted with tiny silver stars.

"What is it?" She was nose to nose with him, sounding giddy, like a child awake far past her bedtime.

He tried to speak, but her beauty was disorientating. She could feel the effect she was having on him, his needing her like a sunflower that turns toward the sunshine. But there was also fear and doubt, love and desire, crashing against her like the tide against the beach.

"Well . . . I really hoped that I could, you know, see you for a bit. I've missed you, Noora."

She smiled and immediately felt him, dying a little. Since last seeing him, he had become so frail, like a leaf on a dying limb. Had he spent the last few cycles pining for her? Was he eating? Sleeping? Doubtless, she could destroy him with a word, but Noora could think of no kinder thing to say, except, "If you wanted my attention, why didn't you aim for the window?"

"I was!" he exclaimed, all wound up with nervous energy, "but I kept missing. I'm not a very good shot, not with a bow, not even throwing stones."

"There are worse things than being a bad shot."

"Anyway . . ." He was studying the grass, wishing he could hold her face in his gaze, without her seeing something in him he did not wish her to see. But then, after an uncomfortable silence, he added, "I wanted to show you something."

"Is it finished?"

"Colin and Tobias fitted the rear axle earlier today, so it's all done, and I wanted you to be the first to see it."

"I'd be delighted." She reached for his hand and the rocks he was still holding dropped to the ground.

They stole into the night, like schoolchildren playing hooky, answering to the summons of the moons and the call of the great tectonic chasm. Shoeless, she trod over dirt footpaths, between fenced-in daffodils and hyacinths and chrysanthemums. The village was falling asleep. Curtained lights were winking out one by one as they ran, and where they stopped to rest their hands atop their knees, they could see the chimney smoke diffusing over a starlit sky, from the hearths that kept the villagers cozy in their beds.

Ecthros watched her sharp, misty breathing, and she sensed the way his heart failed a bit, swelling in the estimation of her beauty.

"I'm such a fool!"

"Why?"

"You'll catch your death out here. I should have brought something for you to wear."

"It's quite alright. I love nights such as these, when the air is crisp and cool. It makes me feel alive." She twirled in place, and the stars on her dress orbited reverently, as if she were the core of a galaxy. "You could say I'll catch my life out here."

"You're so very clever. Fair and clever."

"Really? Demacharon doesn't seem to think so."

"What? He thinks you're ugly?"

She started to chew her braid, like she did when she was nervous, but could not keep from smiling, and laughing. Something about him made her feel normal, and she desperately longed to feel that way, to simply be Noora, not Radia, just another daughter from a no-name village.

"So, where is it?"

"Oh. Right." She followed him to a dimly lit edifice, where he lived with his brother and mother. The ground was hard and rocky, and she could feel each pebble between her toes, impressing themselves into her soles.

At the rear of the house, rows of turned dirt offered nothing but dead twigs, the remains of a neglected crop. She stood brooding over it, feeling the tug of things longing to come into being, to grow, until Ecthros led her away by the elbow.

The shack attached to the back wall was a dilapidated mess of hastily assembled boards, all tilted to one side, with a single door leading in and a single window looking out. Here and there were tools, a hammer of stone and twine, a bellows for smelting rivets, and a saw with rusted teeth lying in a bed of clovers.

"My apologies," he said, "next time I see Colin and Toby, they're gonna get a harsh word from me."

"Not too harsh, I hope."

"Well . . ." he sighed, "not judging by the mess, what do you think?" He pulled a tarp away from an area she had not noticed, situated between two trees, to reveal a kind of shallow catamaran, fitted with two chairs and an arrangement of miniature windmills, or propellers, as Ecthros called them. Lying off to one side, fastened to its base by a length of rope, there was a fishnet and what looked to be small round sails.

She moved to examine it, when a cloud passed from the face of the moon, unveiling the creature painted on its nose. "A unicorn? It's my favorite animal in the whole wide world!"

"I know," he said sheepishly, "Colin wanted a tiger, and Toby wouldn't shut up about his phoenix, but I wouldn't give them an ounce of oil—what we got from Tyrnael—if I couldn't name it, and do the unicorn, of course."

"What did you name it?"

He lifted his eyes to gauge her reaction. "*The Radia.*"

"You . . . you really shouldn't have." She laughed. "I mean, it's flattering, but—"

"You don't like it? Please tell me you like it . . . *Please.*"

She rolled her eyes. And smiled. And his heart throbbed. "All right, I'll give you permission to keep it, under one condition."

"All that I have to give, my lady, is yours."

"Take me up."

"You want to take a ride?"

She nodded.

"In this?"

"Why ever not?"

"Are you not seeing this clutter? The boys'll be lucky not to lose their lives come morning. I mean, I wasn't planning on getting in it myself."

"Well, why not test it, together? You brought me out here for an adventure, didn't you? And you just said you'd give me anything."

"Certainly, I would, but . . . I just didn't think you'd wanted our deaths." He frowned. "Very well. Grab the other end of this."

They carried the whirlydinghy on poles. Ecthros lifted from the front, which was more difficult, having to navigate his footing in the dark of eclipse, as Noora followed from the rear. It was surprisingly lightweight, given the length of the frame, but trundling over the hilly terrain was no easy task. More than once, she scraped the edge of her foot, or tripped and fell ankle-deep into a gryke on the path.

When the land sloped downward, their movement came easier and quicker, and she knew they were nearing their destination. At night, the chasm was a river of sheer darkness, a starless sky set into the ground, as if the gods had run out of material at the onset of creation and there the world was left unfinished.

They headed toward the ancient ruin at the edge of the chasm. It was taller than any windmill in Yefira, a broken arch reaching across the void. They climbed the broken slabs of stone, dark green with lichen, each one immense, impossible to move by any means known to men. Carrying the skiff to its top was an ordeal. Every time it slipped to the ground, the frame threatened to splinter and the assembled pieces to break away, and Ecthros could be heard cursing over the howl of the wind. She considered surrender, but he was determined to please her, and she did not want to disappoint him.

When they had it at last, she rushed to the edge of the ruin, to peer directly into the darkness, but his hand shot out and seized her. "What are you doing?" In the torrent of air, he had to shout to be heard.

"I just wanted to see."

"People have fallen doing that. It's the darkness. Sometimes, it pulls you in."

The wind was more powerful here than in any place in Yefira. It swaddled her, lifting her dress, and making her hair come alive. "If it's so dangerous, why are we launching from here?"

He went over each part of the skiff, hand and eye, testing the strength of the frame with his boot, pulling at ropes and retying knots. Removing the sack about his shoulders then, he uncorked a bottle of kerosene. "Well, it helps to have the wind with you when you take off. It's strongest over there, at the center of the drop."

"So, this ruin, it was built by the Ancients?"

"So they say," he said, pouring the oil into the twin burners. "In Yefira, we call them the Bridge Builders of Laenkea."

Noora looked to the sky. The constellations, the eyes of gods, were staring down at them as fate unfolded. "Some say the Ancients built bridges to the stars. Wouldn't that be nice? To visit the stars?"

"Well, if I can just get this flame going, we'll be partway there."

When he wasn't watching, she tiptoed to the edge, hoping the ruin did not collapse further. Gazing into the chasm was like going blind, or seeing death, and she became suddenly frightened, turning away to the East. "If this was a bridge, where do you suppose it went?"

"To the other side. I guess."

"Oh." She laughed. "Is that sarcasm?"

"I don't know. Maybe."

"I think so. Dimmy taught me all about sarcasm."

There was a sudden *whoosh*, and she could see the orange and blue glow, illuminating the green cloaked boy beside the shallow boat. Now, Ecthros was rushing about, the fishnet and sails in his hands. "This is the hard part," he said. "Have to make sure the whole thing doesn't catch fire, or it's all downhill for us."

Quickly, he turned the knob on the burners, shortening the flame to a blue hiss. The netting was floating above the whirlydinghy, keeping the inflated sails in place. Stepping away, like a sculptor judging his masterpiece, he assessed every component. She could feel his eagerness and excitement, but overpowering every other emotion, his longing for her remained.

"I sure hope this works."

"It'll work," she assured him.

"How do you know?"

"Because I'm feeling so up!"

"Now who's being sarcastic? Come on. Help me with this."

"But I wasn't—" She was pouting, but he could not see her face with her braids knocking about. The skiff was almost weightless, only scraping the ground, but he needed her to lean it away from the wind, to the drop point at the broken end of the bridge.

A rush of dread passed through him as he pushed the nose, crudely painted with a unicorn, over the edge. The sudden updraft caused the frame to shudder and the front end to buck, but they kept their weights on it to keep it from flipping.

"There's a good chance we could die here, you know!"

She reached out, touching his hand, and she could feel the fear drain from his body. "We won't. Not today. Trust me." And without a further word, she folded into the back seat.

If Colin or Tobias had been with them, there would have been somebody to shove them off, but there was only the two of them, and he could not leave her alone in a craft she did not know to maneuver. Before Noora could even consider the problem, he was pushing her into the chasm.

She closed her eyes, overcome by anticipation, and there it was, a sudden, abrupt drop, sudden even as it was expected, and in that same instance the wind came slamming under them, rattling the floorboards, as Ecthros clamored over her and to the front, clinging with desperation to the floating fishnet. Air was rushing all around, the skiff seesawing from side to side, the chasm undecided as to what to do with them. Everything was happening too quickly to comprehend or control. Her heart was jumping into her throat and crashing down again and back and every wrong way. She wanted to say something, to ask him if they were going to alright, but the air was screaming and the wind was in her eyes, blinding her with tears. And yet, she did not know regret, for all her senses were awakened, intensely focused, alive. For when death feels imminent, she knew, life does also. What followed was the realization that they were airborne and flying. The whirlydinghy hit a powerful updraft, and they were being lifted, higher and higher.

"We're flying!" Ecthros shouted, hooting with triumph.

They drifted with the current, where the air was calm, thin. She knew she should be freezing, her nightdress barely containing her body, swirling like silk in water, but there was only the thrill of flight.

"It's so like a dream!" she exclaimed, her arms embracing the sky, when a horrible thought came to her. "I sure hope I'm not dreaming." It was hard to tell, sometimes, given her condition.

"What are you doing back there? Are you even helping?"

"What do you mean?"

"Start pedaling, will you?"

Noora had never pedaled anything before, but she found where to put her feet, and figured how to rotate the flywheel, which in turn moved a chain to spin the gears of the propellers.

They managed a good rhythm, kicking in sync, as far below them, the chasm snaked about the world, a gaping nothingness black as ever, as above them her hair was ablaze, with a million-million stars and planets. She tried to stand in her seat, to the gather the light like fistfuls of diamonds, but quickly reconsidered as the skiff started to sway.

"The universe!" she bellowed, with a joy known only to few who have lived.

"What about it?"

"It's so very big!"

"I don't like it," he admitted. "It makes me feel small. Like, like we don't matter, like nothing we do matters."

"No, no, it's quite the opposite, really," she said. "Don't you see? It's us. *The universe is us!*"

Ecthros pulled a lever, and a frilled rudder unfolded from the bottom of the craft. Tugging at it again, like a tiller on a boat, they banked west, toward Yefira.

"Thank you, Toby!"

"What's that?"

"I was so worried about her being airworthy, I'd nearly forgotten about steering," he called over his shoulder.

"Can we fly over the village?"

"Can't see why not. We've got enough momentum."

The whirlydinghy passed back over the broken bridge. It was like a toy block, left by a child. On they went, soaring over glittering foothills until the whole of Yefira emerged like a cache of hidden toys. She could see the warm glow from the windows, like a nest of fireflies in a hollow, the wisps of gray rising from thimble-sized chimneys, the plantations neatly arrayed like handkerchiefs, and the river, catching the moonlight like a glassy serpent.

She considered how small and delicate the village truly was, a cradle of innocents sleeping unawares, and a dark mood came suddenly upon her.

"Can we fly lower?"

He twisted a knob, shortening the burner to a lick of blue flame, and the world expanded. They were soaring over pines and sycamores, and a frightened herd of sheep, where a man with a pipe spied upon them, his mouth agape. He was both a shepherd and the night crier, Ecthros explained, but with never any danger to report, was mostly a shepherd. She greeted him with a smile and a wave, but as they were drifting dangerously low, they took to the sky again, and the shepherd shrank to a dot.

She could have soared the whole of the night, had their burner not spat and sputtered, its fuel spent. The rudder had also formed a tear, so that they were forced down upon some random shelf overlooking the village.

Ecthros crouched by the skiff, cursing. "I have more oil to get us moving, but with no way to steer, we might just get blown over to the dark side. If I only had some twine . . ."

"*Ecthros*," she murmured, in a way that caught him off guard, "come sit by me."

He took a last look at the broken rudder, shrugged his shoulders, and turned to her. "I really shouldn't complain. She kept us aloft a good long while. Better than I hoped, really."

"It's a good name," she admitted.

"Could you make it official, then? Being that you're royalty and all?"

"Oh. Oh, yes. Of course." She walked adjacent to the whirlydinghy, her shoulders thrown back, her braids combed behind her ears. "By the right of my forefathers, I hereby dub this ship, *The Radia* . . . How was that?"

"Great," he said, with all sincerity, "that was just great."

"Oh, good." She smiled. "I've never done that before."

Tucking her starry gown beneath her, she sat back against the boulder, her knees tight against her bosom. Ecthros followed nervously, their bodies nearly touching.

"Hope your brother doesn't mind . . . that we stole his skiff."

"Tobias? Nah. Ever since we were little, since Papa didn't come home, he's looked to me, for guidance, and encouragement, that sort of thing."

"He thinks the world of you, you know . . . the way you do your father."

"How can you know that?"

"I am an empath. I know what people are feeling. All the time. It's like everyone—every living thing—is a part of me."

"Really? Do you know what I'm thinking now?"

She offered him a weak smile, which was, for him, no less potent. "It isn't like that, silly. Thoughts are complicated things, that get in the way of feelings. I think . . . that's all people ever try to do . . . make words for what's in their hearts, but it never works out right."

"Maybe," he said, "if we were all like you, there wouldn't be any wars, or any evil."

She smiled. "Perhaps."

"Xenox, my father, was a great adventurer," he said after a time, "traveling all over Aenya fighting evil, and championing the downtrodden, from here to Shemselinihar. He could shoot three arrows from his bow at the same time, and never miss his mark. He could split an oncoming arrow, mid-flight, with one of his own. No one could best him." He was animating with his hands, drawing invisible bowstrings, tracing the trajectories of his father's arrows. And then his voice became sullen. "We never learned what happened to him. That's the hardest part. I think he was surrounded. By a thousand enemies. Or it could have been a dragon."

"You wish you could be like him."

He answered with a murmur, too low for her to hear.

"You're afraid to fail," she added, "afraid you'll never be able to replace him. That is why you miss."

"D-Do you really think so?"

"Stop trying to be Xenox. Just be Ecthros. Next time you grab your bow, aim from your heart. You can never be your father, but you can be better."

"Well, I can't be any worse."

They looked at each other, and the sincerity was too great to bear, and the laughter brought tears to their eyes.

"Noora, I'm really happy we could do this." He garnered the courage to rest his hand upon hers. "Whenever you're around me, I feel like, I mean I'd like to . . ."

"You'd like to kiss me?"

The way his heart was quivering, she would have thought they were in the skiff again, careening from the edge of the bridge. She was thankful, at least, for her own anxiety, lest she drown in his.

"Kissing is often a prelude to sexual intercourse," she said matter-of-factly.

He jerked his hand away, looking confused, almost hurt. "You say that like you're reading it from a book."

"I *did* read it in a book. I had to. There's no sexual intercourse between men and women in Tyrnael."

"Oh."

"But . . . I don't think that's right."

"Oh?"

"I think I'm going to change all that," she said softly, "when I go back."

"So you're going back?"

She looked away, to the sleeping village at her feet. "They're still my people, Ecthros. And they are suffering. I can sense it. Even from here. Demacharon won't let me; he thinks we can hide forever, but—"

She stopped. And stood abruptly.

"Noora?" She could sense him sensing her alarm. "Noora, what is it?"

Without bothering to look at him, she rushed to the lip of the shelf, crouching over it. He was quickly beside her, but could not fathom it, the enormity of what was happening.

The air surrounding Yefira was blackening, rising in thick, sooty, billowing columns. Barbs of orange and red were spreading out across the fields, out along the gabled rooftops. But it was the steady movement below that gripped her heart with fear. Shadows were amassing from the North, South and West, a marching multitude like colonies of termites, its angry iron hue glimpsed by countless flaming torches. And they were descending, down upon the still slumbering populace.

"By Zoë!" he cried. "What is that?"

"My brother," she said. "He's found me."

26

Thulken

Embers were falling all around her like snowflakes set aflame, and fireballs whistled down from the sky like hail, igniting rooftops near and far, turning trees to raging torches. There was never a day in Yefira that was not windy, and Noora recognized how this feature quickly spread the fire from neighbor to neighbor.

On bloodied feet, she stumbled through the midst of it like a lost child. She could feel the wail of every living thing, the dying throes of the plants, the panic in the animals and villagers alike. So many emotions. Too much for her to bear. Once a source of insight, her empathy was crippling, and she needed to shut it off, will herself to callousness.

A choking haze poured from every opening, wafting over footpaths between smoldering gardens and filling her lungs, until every breath came like a knife to her chest. Blinded by smoke and tears, she was no longer able to find her way. Like a wilting tulip, she wrapped her arms about herself and folded into her knees. Inert upon the ground. Powerless to think. Only to feel, and suffer.

"Noora?" Someone or something was calling her, a voice from another world, an echo from across a tunnel of dread and despair. "Is your name Noora?"

She tried to focus, but could only nod mechanically. He looked familiar, but her mind was a jumble of suffocating sensations.

"Are you hurt? You're looking sickly, a tad greenish, I'd say." He was an imposing figure, larger than Demacharon or even Davos, his fingers encircling the wider part of her arm.

"I'm fine," she said, but could not keep the quiver from her voice.

"Name's Thulken. Colin's grandfather. Ecthros was worried. Sent me to find you."

"Ecthros?" A tinge of guilt threaded its way to the fore of her consciousness. "Is he alright? I didn't mean to run off like that, I just couldn't—"

He shook his head, hushing her, his ash-white beard shaking along with it. "He went to find his brother. They're fixing up the skiff, hoping to get her airborne, get a look-see as to what's been going on."

"You mean you don't know?"

He shook his head again.

"Davos!" she cried. "Take me to his house. Please, hurry! I only hope I can find him!"

They battled through the smoke, Noora crouched behind his immense frame, as families rushed from their porches on either side. By the time they reached the outskirts of Yefira, nearly all the people had left their homes and gone to safety. And yet, others still wandered about in confusion, shouting names of loved ones, as, elsewhere, families watched everything they had worked to build the whole of their lives shrivel and turn black, clutching whatever meager belongings they had managed to rescue.

The windmills were built on the upper slopes and hilltops and went largely unaffected by the onslaught. Only a single fold had caught fire, and as it turned, Davos stood with a bucket in hand to douse it. Seeing him there, alive and struggling, she fled from Thulken's shadow, but was stopped suddenly by Demacharon. With or without her empathic abilities, she would have known that he was furious.

"Where were you?" He was shaking her by the arm. "I thought you'd been taken! I thought he'd got you!"

"You're hurting me," she said.

He looked torn, over whether to strike her or cry. "There's no time to pack. We have to go. Right now."

"Wait!"

She twisted free and looked to Davos, who was still cursing the flames that were spreading along the beams, and she watched as three frightened girls sped into his arms, their screams muffled by his embrace. She yearned to join them, to run to him also and call him father, and his daughters, sisters.

"We can't leave them," she implored.

"We can and we will."

Kiki was the last to leave the house, a wicker bread basket tucked under her arm, as though caught in the middle of some chore. She looked about in a daze, and seeing the smoke and embers rising from her village, she began to weep.

Noora matched Demacharon's determined stare with her own. "Don't you see? *We* did this to them. By coming here. We're responsible."

"No one is responsible but your brother," he shot back. "We cannot be made to pay for his misdeeds."

"It doesn't matter," she said. "We have to do what we can. To help."

"I gave my oath to protect you, not them, and that's what I aim to do." He seized her again.

Kiki stood between them now, looking incensed and suspicious. "What in all the gods above are you going on about?" But no answer was offered, and so she snapped at her husband, "Davos?"

He approached with Niah and Liana and Athalia. They were huddled against his large round frame. "I wanted to tell you, flower patch, honestly I did. But I knew you wouldn't handle it well. I just knew."

Her face reddened, holding back an undercurrent of fury, and in that instant, Noora stepped forward. "It's my fault. I made him swear to silence, for my sake. For you see, my name is not Noora. I am Radia, daughter of King Solon, fifty-fourth descendant of the Zo, and heir to the throne of Tyrnael."

The woman was dumbfounded. It was her eldest, Athalia, who spoke, "Does that mean you really are a princess?"

"A princess and more," Radia said to the children.

"I knew it!" Liana embraced her, as did Niah, with Hazel poking from under her nightgown like a tuft of gray fur.

"Never mind who you *were*," Kiki said, with some difficulty. "You're part of our family now."

Radia wanted to answer, to impart a share of her own emotions, but she could only stand, overwhelmed with gratitude. It was a tender moment lost on the two men, for they could not ignore the hill looming above them and the darkness gathering there. "How did he find us?" Davos intoned. "They couldn't have tracked the *Cloud Breaker* when we were in the air!"

"Orson. Or one of his troupe." It was all Demacharon needed to say.

"No," Davos objected. "They were honorable men, *good* men every one of them. I do not believe they could have betrayed us."

"You do not understand what we are dealing with. A man may betray his own mother, given the right conditions. Orson is not to blame."

At that moment, there came a distant roar, followed by drumming akin to rolling thunder. Every voice fell silent, and not a single eye, young or old, could turn from the billowing column claiming the sky. They watched like hunted prey, gauging the motives of a predator, as the stars and moons blacked out, suffused by a dark, unnatural miasma. And upon that singular column, a shapeless pall coalesced into a face, and terrified shrieks rang from every corner of the land, many calling it a *monster*. But Radia knew the face for what it was, the mask with its rust-hued teeth and demon horns, and those vacant eyes swirling darkly as it formed out of the smoke and the fire.

"GREETINGS. I AM ZAIBOS, KING OF AENYA, MASTER OF MEN AND BOGREN, FIRST OF HIS KIND. WHAT YOU HAVE WITNESSED, AND WHAT YOU HAVE LOST, IS BUT A SMALL DEMONSTRATION OF MY POWER, BUT I DO NOT WISH TO DESTROY YOU UTTERLY. I COME HERE, ONLY, FOR THE ONE CALLED RADIA. SHE IS TO BE DELIVERED TO ME AT ONCE. SHOULD YOU RESIST, YOUR LIVES, AND THE LIVES OF YOUR CHILDREN, SHALL BE FORFEIT. I GIVE YOU UNTIL THE FIRST LIGHT OF DAY."

Kiki ran toward the column of smoke diffusing over the purpling horizon, "Never! We'll not give up our own! Do you hear me, monster? We do not bargain with our children!"

"I concur," Demacharon said. "Radia. Follow me."

"Wait." It was Davos who spoke now. "Why must we be so hasty? Let's think this through, at least."

"There's nothing to think about. We're going, at once. Or would you suggest we hand her over to that monster, like a hog to the slaughter?"

"What? No!" Davos was taken aback, insulted, but his rage was tempered by shame, for there seemed to be some truth, however small, to the accusation. "I love her same as you."

"I sincerely doubt that."

"You've only one to lose," he answered, defeated, "but I've got four. My whole family to think of."

Demacharon turned to leave, pulling her along beside him, but Davos chased after, seizing him by the shoulder.

"Unhand me!" Demacharon's arm flew to the hilt at his side. "Or I'll strike you down where you stand!" There was a ferocity in his face, the likes Noora had not seen, not since the day they escaped the Compass Tower, when Sligh and the other soldiers were slaughtered.

"Stop it!" Radia distanced herself from the two men. "I decide. You swore an oath to me, praetorian, but I can rescind that oath."

For a moment, Demacharon appeared shaken, and then he found his voice. "Radia, listen to me. Surrendering yourself will achieve *nothing*. Do you honestly believe that Zaibos will stay true to his word? The instant he gets his hands on you, he will raze this village. Of this I am certain."

She could find no fault in his reasoning, but something more powerful than reason would keep her from abandoning the village, and Davos and his family, to Zaibos. "No, Dimmy," she murmured, as much for her ears as for his. "I cannot run from this. Not anymore. They can't be made to suffer because of me." The tears rolled hot against her cheeks, pooling along her lips and off her chin. "We cannot abandon them like we did my people."

"You're talking nonsense!" he cried. "Now let's go, posthaste, or I'll be forced to carry you."

"You will do no such thing. I am a princess. I rule over you. And I relinquish you from your duties. Go back to Hedonia, praetorian . . . or wherever it is you hail from."

Demacharon watched Davos return to his family, as the orange light of day started from the edges of the greater moon. "Radia," he said, softer now, sounding more broken than she had ever heard him, "there are things . . . I haven't told you."

She waited for him to continue, feeling his armored exterior beginning to break away, to expose the tortured being that he was.

"I came to Tyrnael because of you, princess. When my son and wife were taken from me, I lost everything. All the noble things I'd fought for and sent men to die for, my rank, my titles, the glory of the empire—I realized then that they meant nothing.

"Afterwards . . . I longed only for this life to end. From the peaks of Nimbos, I threw myself, to seek my family in the netherworld. But Death would not have me. I am cursed, cursed with living, forced to go on, and haunted nightly by visions."

She peered into his pallid eyes, almost white in the twilight of morning, measuring the depth of his sincerity and sorrow.

His heart was like a dark chasm that she dared look into, and it threatened to pull her in.

"I remember," she said softly, "on the ship. You were drunk, but you told me of Niobe and . . . Astor. They do not recognize you, you said. And just the other night, you spoke of Hedonia, and how the Sea swallowed it."

"There's more," he went on. "In my dreams, there is a city of pure light. Only by its radiance are the demons driven away. Such grace, I do not deserve, I know this . . . and yet I am compelled to follow it. In my sleep, just as in waking, I was led north, ever north, over the Crown of Aenya and into Tyrnael. The ghosts of the Zo, and every soul who ever lived in that place, walk there still, in the city in my dreams. But only later did I realize my error. For the true light was the tower at its center, your Compass Tower. So I labored to prove myself, rising quickly in rank, to earn a place amongst your praetorian guard. But again I was deceived. For the tower was not the light."

Day crept upon the world, pulling the shroud of night from the crozzled ruins of Yefira. The masses were gathered in pockets, in the low places, and along the hills, for warmth, seeking to quell the dread that stirred in their hearts.

"I still don't understand," she said, a hair above a whisper.

"Would that you did!" he cried, kneading the fatigue from his face. "There is *something* about you. You know this, and I know it. Let's not deceive ourselves. It was never the city or the tower. It was *you*." He lowered his eyes, looking unsure of himself, smaller somehow. "I could not be certain, not until we arrived here, but *you* are that light in my dreams, Radia. I may be . . . an evil man, unworthy of redemption, but if you go, if you turn yourself over to that monster, it won't only be me, who will be lost, but everyone and everything, this entire world. I don't know how I know this, I simply do."

For so long, she had accepted his devotion, trusting him by empathy alone, that she no longer questioned his reasons. Now she understood the truth, and why it was kept from her. Who would have believed that a dream could so perfectly mirror the waking world, except herself, who had known similar dreams?

So much more needed saying, she could feel it like splinters on the tongue, but time was a cruel master. Now, there was only regret and urgency, and of all the things she could have told him, she offered only this, "You're not an evil man, Dimmy. We all deserve to be found. We're all connected. Even Zaibos. He simply doesn't see it. And that's why I must go to him, because if there's anything that can prevent what he intends, anything inside him, I have to help him find it."

A crowd had formed around them now, men and women and children, streaming from the village. Most were simply curious. Somehow, word had gotten out, that the girl that was to be sacrificed was the one who lived in Davos's house. Perhaps, it was apparent, for Noora was a newcomer, and her beauty and charm never failed to leave a lasting impression. To the north and the west, Zaibos's army could be spotted, threatening from the hilltops. They were circling the village, closing trails of escape, advancing to the point that the people could see the glint from their iron and their gray-green, inhuman faces.

"We won't let you leave us," Kiki said to her.

"That's right." It was Thulken, looking adamant, but also frightened. "No one should have to sacrifice himself for the well-being of others. As archon of Yefira, I am charged with the safety of my people—*all* my people. And you belong to us now. We will not bend to the will of tyrants. We will resist!"

"No!" she implored, turning hard upon Demacharon. "There must be no fighting. No blood spilled for me. Promise me this." She pulled up her starry gown, gently placing it in Kiki's hands, and stood, her green-toned figure exposed before the hundreds who had assembled there. "I thank you for your kindness. You're all good people, and I love every one of you, but I should never have come here. Forgive me."

"You've nothing to forgive," Kiki answered, brushing at her eyes, "and I won't let you run off completely starkers."

Radia's laughter was bittersweet. Examining her body then, as if never seeing it before, she remarked, "This is just another layer. It isn't the real me. It never was. Besides, unicorns can't bear to be touched by fabric."

No one in Yefira could say from whence it came, but that the magnificent animal was suddenly among them, gleaming whitely in the morning light. And at that moment, every child from the village—Davos's daughters chief among them—was made to forget their fears, to stare in wonder and delight, while those who were older and more jaded—such as Demacharon—saw only a horse, but a horse of exceeding grace and beauty, with narrow fawn-like features and a mane of flowing curls like wisps of cloud.

"I knew you'd be here," she whispered. "I can feel when you're near, like a mother watching over me, protecting me."

"Climb upon my back," Amalthea answered, "and let us away. Before the hummingbird can flap its wing, we shall cross this planet, where no one will find you."

The green girl shook her head. "But can't you see? Then we will be alone. And lost. And what good will that do anyone?"

"If you go to him, you will die. You must know this."

"I know," she said softly. "Best we hurry."

"Very well," the unicorn replied. "My fate will be as yours."

With slow, deliberate movements, she climbed the unicorn. She did not dread the meeting with her brother, but rather, pined for the loved ones she would not see again, her heart suffused with their lament, with Davos and Kiki, and Liana and Niah and Athalia, and Demacharon most of all. She could feel them reaching out for her, their longing to hold and keep her safe, their despair in her departure.

Having accepted her fate, exhaustion set in, and as she settled down upon the unicorn, her mane became as one with the great beast.

Along the narrow ridge, across the foothills dividing the two hosts, Amalthea raced, Radia upon her, and the ascending sun pursued them, crowning them in a brilliant golden halo.

Zaibos met them at the crest of the rise upon his mount, his blood-red salamander with its six-taloned legs and shard-like teeth. Mandos, his second, was saddled beside him upon a common mare. Only the two were human. The remainder of the force had been called up from the sunless hemisphere and the deep dark recesses beneath Aenya. She recognized the diminutive bogren from her storybooks, their steely eyes now contorted with hate and bloodlust, and, in sparser number, the hulking brutes called *horg*.

"It's been a while, princess," Zaibos pronounced. "The real world, it would seem, has sickened you. And I see also that you've returned my unicorn, whilst coming to me properly arrayed, for a captive. How cooperative."

Mandos dismounted, a ring in his hand, a sword in the other. Giving way to instinct, Amalthea resisted, but Radia calmed the animal with an outstretched hand, and the soldier managed to slip the ring over its horn.

"Brother," Radia addressed him, "I cooperate only so that you not hurt these people. They're innocent and kind. If you have any decency, any compassion in you at all, you will remain true to your word."

Zaibos answered with a gesture, and Mandos pulled her down from the unicorn by the ankle, and she fell to her knees. Bogren swarmed about her, clamping her neck with a collar tethered to a chain.

"Bloodsnot, prepare your forces."

"My lord . . ." Mandos's face turned pale, and his voice to a quiver. "You said—"

"Never mind what I said. Listen to what I am saying!"

Realization struck her, and she began to scream, and to plead with him, having spent whatever strength or pride she possessed. "Don't do this, brother! Torment me if you will, but I beg of you, let these people in peace." But she soon found it difficult to speak, for the bogrens were dragging her away by the throat.

"I *do* intend to make you suffer," Zaibos said, "but in a way that it will hurt you most. Commander!"

"Yes, my lord."
"Leave no one alive."

27

Zaibos

---

awn was still unfolding over Yefira, but morning delivered little but gloom, the light of day obscured by a gray haze. If they had not witnessed the sun break from the greater moon, they might have thought it night. And if not for the fires ravaging their homes, they might have remained snug in their beds, oblivious in their dreams.

Demacharon had stood next to Davos, waiting in long agony, their faces hardened to stone, as Radia and Amalthea raced away, a single white and gold wisp upon the foothills. Even after they had disappeared, Davos and his three daughters continued watching, hoping against reason for hope.

"We've committed a terrible deed," Davos murmured, "the very worst. We should have never let her go. We should have done whatever we could, for there goes all the good in the world."

"Now is not the time for lament," Demacharon answered, "but for action. She is gone. Think upon your children."

Thulken came forward, his face sullen. "Will they go?" But he seemed to know the answer without asking.

"Zaibos would not have brought an army to steal one girl," Demacharon replied. "No. He means to make an example of your village, to cow others into submission."

"What are we to do?"

He turned upon them with eyes of iron, and sensed that every man could feel the weight of it, the strength of his presence, but that it was a cold comfort. "If I know one thing only, it is war. I was bred for it. So if you mean to live to see the coming sunrise, listen well. Before the next passing is out, all hell will descend upon us. Your homes are lost. Abandon them. Your only chance is to break into smaller units and flee, so that, should they give chase, some may be caught while others escape."

"But they have mounts, and artillery," a young man complained, his farmer's hands soiled black. "Many of us are saddled with children, and women heavy with child. Surely, we can't hope to outrun them!"

"We must make do with what we have. Innocents will perish today, but a chance remains for those that are swift and brave and clever. By my sword, I swear you will have that chance," he went on, his gladius gleaming in the gloom, "should every able-bodied Yefiran stand beside me!"

"He's right!" Thulken shook his fist defiantly. "We shall make a stand!"

"Yes, but not you," Demacharon objected. "They will need someone to guide them through the worst of it, whatever may come. Leave the warring to the warriors."

"I can fight good as the rest of you," the archon replied, "but will do as I must, for the good of my people." He looked on bitterly, burning with the desire to defend his homeland, and then his face brightened. "The chasm! The hanging houses! Zaibos will be hard-pressed to find us there. And even if he does, the steps are too narrow for an army."

"That may work, but you cannot hold long against a determined foe. Take the small children, the weak and infirm, those who cannot travel. The rest of you must scatter over the hills, or return to me here, prepared for war."

"How do we do that?" Another voice from the crowd—a young man eager to fight.

"Gather every weapon you can find and every tool that can be used to kill. Farmers, I need your spades! Blacksmiths, bring me your hammers! But remember one thing, we do not fight for victory. We fight for *time*. Every second we delay them, every step we push them back, is another step we give to the fleeing families. Now make haste!"

The hundreds gathered before him started to break away, the mothers with children and the elderly following Thulken westward to the Great Chasm, as the able-bodied and young returned to what remained of their homes in search of munitions. Kiki went quickly and quietly also, back to her windmill, her three daughters tagging behind.

When the two men were alone, Davos turned to Demacharon, saying, "Was a good speech, but I cannot help wondering, is it a fool's hope you've given us?"

"Perhaps," he said, without facing him. "What do I know of your people's readiness for war? Have you a militia? Do you train for battle?"

Davos shook his head. "We've no gold or silver here, no jewels, no mines. Our land is rich in nothing but wind. Until this day, what need had we for war and warriors? We're simple folk, Dimsby, always have been, living off our crop, a few trading in simple goods..."

He turned his gladius from side to side. The Hedonian bronze shimmered, without a spot of blood, but it would not remain that way long. "I've fought more battles than I care to count, and never have I so desired victory, here where I cannot hope to win."

"Truly now? What of your own home?"

"We were not without blame," he answered. "But in this place, there has never been a cause so just. If the gods have any sway in the affairs of men, today we shall see proof of it."

"And if not?"

"Then the gods are cruel and undeserving of our praise, or impotent, and unworthy of it. Or there may be nothing more to the Cosmos, no divinities to judge us, only ourselves, and the consequences of our actions."

These were heavy words, what soldiers often spoke of before the end, and for a while, they stood in the gloom in silence, until Davos turned to him. "This is not your fight, Hedonian. Escape to the hills, if you wish. There's still time."

"Not my fight? Great evil stands at your door. It waits to slaughter you and your people, and we are both men, are we not?"

"Methinks the girl's rubbed off on you."

He stared wistfully, where Zaibos's forces were gathering strength, as if to see her there. "Perhaps."

From the west, a troupe was starting toward them, boys mostly, with hatchets for cutting wood, and saws for felling trees and pitchforks for moving bales of hay. No more than a dozen proper weapons could be found between them, and those few swords and spears and maces that they presented were but decorative antiques from another age. His heart sank at the sight, for they did not resemble an army in any way, but were more like children playing at war. What could he possibly teach them in so fleeting a time? If he had a day, a morning perhaps, to show them basic maneuvers. They had a mere passing—if that—when what he needed was a year. But what came to him at that moment were the words branded to his brain from eight years of age.

"Men and women of Yefira, I will say to you one thing, and one thing only. Do. Not. Hesitate. Killing is not in your nature, and it may even repulse you, but if you wish to keep on breathing, you must learn to suppress it. Never stay your hand, for your enemy will not stay his. Never show mercy, for your enemy will show you none. Strike without deliberation, and always to kill. In war, life and death can be decided in an instant."

He was a commander once more, gauging the readiness of his men. But they were visibly shaken, every one of them. A soldier's fate was written in the eyes, and what he could read upon theirs gave him chills, for of his many talents was knowing, with haunting regularity, which of his men would live to see the morning. *None of them have it. They are too pure of heart. Radia chose this place well.*

"Davos! Davos! Oh, Davos!" Kiki was drowning in panic, it seemed, as she rushed from the windmill, dragging Davos's giant spoon-sword in one hand while pulling Athalia and Liana along with the other. "Oh, it's terrible! Niah's gone! Run off!"

His face turned pale. "What? How? She was right with you!"

She tried to speak between sobs and gasps. "Lost Hazel . . . Refused to go . . . Went looking for him! Oh, Davos! Please . . ."

She passed him his sword and he threw it over his shoulder. "Get a hold of yourself, woman. I'll find her. She can't have gone far."

At that moment, they arrived, thundering from the slopes toward them, thousands upon thousands, their faces grotesque, hate gleaming from under the folds of their brows, a thirsting for blood on their lips. They brandished twisted painful shapes, objects that could not be described as weapons but that looked every bit as lethal. Horg towered alongside them, stomping and swaying blindly, mounds of fat and sinew dressed in chains and rust, and conical helms and ax-headed helmets. Last to emerge were the chariots, with their flaming catapults and smoke machines, their spiked wheels churning the ground. Each was harnessed to a *galumph*, a hairless, muscled beast, awkwardly strutting on its squat hindquarters, spittle hanging from its camel-like snout. But there was one who stood unique amidst the horde—Zaibos, high atop his six-legged salamander, his legions flying in terror before the sound of his morningstar, its many facets funneling and rending the air in a deathly discord.

Demacharon studied their advance, but there was no formation. The bogrens were untrained, undisciplined, and did not expect resistance. They came prepared to slaughter, he realized, and not to battle. He turned back to the villagers. They were terror-stricken, some retreating while others stood frozen. One man was retching on hands and knees as another aided him.

"Davos," he said, "find Niah."

"But—"

"There's no time to argue!" he cried and, seeing that they had nowhere to run, added, "If you want them to live, get them home and barricade the door!" Without pause, he turned to the rest, saying, "Listen. There are far too many to hold back. We must pray they do not circle us. We must keep the enemy focused on where we stand. Understood? You there, with the pitchforks," he pointed, "and you with the spears, form a line, shoulder to shoulder." Even as he said this, he could see the encroaching bogren horde mirrored in their irises, but he would not allow these men to be ruled by panic. Through the strength of his authority alone, he would keep them in order. "If yours is a weapon that is held in *one* hand, get behind the line and wait. As soon as they're in reach, mark my words, and do not hesitate!" As if to demonstrate, he swung around, freed Severetrix from its sheath and, in a single motion, the bogren reaching him first lost its head.

Other bogrens swarmed about him, and just as quickly lost their heads. They stood to his waist and their arms were short, and he cut them down effortlessly, one after another, the two-sword whistling with every strike, leaving them to bleed from severed limbs, opened organs, their skulls halved and quartered. Tissue and bone separated with little resistance, as if he were chopping through reams of blood, the blade so narrow even he at times could not see it, so that his enemies must have thought him mad, fighting with only a broken hilt. And those who broke through the circle of its reach met their end at the tip of his gladius.

On he battled, until the fighting possessed his mind, his actions, his being. No movement was wasted. Every blow a kill. There were days when he could feel his age, in the weight of his bronze plate, in the heft of his weapons, but today was not that day. Gods be praised, he felt stronger than ever he had in his youth.

I am the first line of defense. I alone.

Bodies piled at his feet, serving to fuel their bloodlust, to focus their rage against him. But he could not fend against them all. As they continued to descend, the outliers either failed to notice him or were unable to reach him, and went straggling into the phalanx of pitchforks and spears. The villagers fought clumsily, but were emboldened by their commander, and bogrens started to fall to sons and fathers and daughters, butchered beneath spades and hatchets and kitchen knives.

The defenses were holding, and the more bogrens that were killed, the more fervently the people came forward, raging for the homes they had lost and the loved ones they feared to lose. He could hear them, their hooting and hurrahs, and for a brief time, it seemed the attackers could be driven off. But Demacharon knew better. It was a common enough strategy, one he had employed himself. The first wave was a test, to determine their strength while giving them a false sense of victory. At the very least, they would begin to tire, and annihilation would follow shortly thereafter.

"Fall back!" he shouted. "Fall back, now!"

But it was already too late. The second wave was better trained and with superior arms. They slipped past him, using their dead as a barricade. It was not long after that the wailing began, the cacophony of the wounded and the dying. Demacharon hurried back to the villagers, flanking the enemy front, razing them down with both his swords. But he was powerless to prevent the onslaught. Human blood spilled across his boots, and bodies slumped lifelessly beside him as bogrens crowded round, their crooked instruments falling from one victim to another.

Demacharon called desperately for retreat. "Back to your homes!" Surely, every family had fled the village, or so he hoped. They would make a stand in Yefira, or what remained of it, their burnt and broken houses their last bastion.

He was breathing hard now, suddenly aware of his aching body, as he watched the people fleeing and the bogrens giving chase. And that is when he saw it, the erupting ball of fire.

Behind him, at the foot of the hill, the smallest of the bogrens were scrambling, mounting the giant-wheeled chariots, assisting a mechanism of chains and pulleys in lifting a massive boulder to and from the furnace. In their haste to arm the weapon, a few slipped or were shoved into the flames. There they were cooked alive, before being launched, their crisp and blackened husks hitting the ground in a spatter of ash. If the situation had not been so dire, he might have laughed to see such cruel comedy.

A subsequent fireball plummeted, scorching the earth as it rolled, and he knew their walls—where the people now sought refuge—would offer little protection. He did not know how to dispose of the bogren artillery, only that he had to act, and quickly. Stepping over corpses of man and bogren alike, he pushed his way toward the wheeled catapult. With a whip-like crack, the entire assembly shuddered under the force of its arm, and another stone flew, trailing fire. It crashed into a hill and a windmill collapsed on itself. *Had that been Davos's home . . .*

A horg blocked his way, standing more than twice his height, with lengths of chain extending from its wrists to a pair of crude blades. It moved slowly and deliberately, slaying any in its path with a sweep of its arms. Bogrens fled from its deadly reach, and yet, undeterred, Demacharon pressed forward, closing the distance between them, until the chains caught his upper body and the blades spun uselessly to the ground. With a twist of Severetrix, the links wrapped around him snapped apart, and ducking between its thighs, he opened the monster from groin to belly.

All the while, galumphs cantered into position, and catapults snapped and houses crumbled. The destruction occurring in his peripheral posed a potential distraction, but he fought the urge to look on despair. Another horg came at him, an ax in each arm, tethered by a short chain to a ball of spikes. He found it simultaneously intimidating and absurd, for the duel-weapon tended to swing back around and smack the wielder, and the strange conical helmet worn by the horg limited its vision almost entirely. As the axes came down, throwing a shower of dirt upon him, Demacharon circled, severing the tendons above the creature's heels before raising his sword higher and separating its throat. The corpulent mass collapsed upon the ground and blood bubbled, black and syrupy, over its hideous face. He paused to stare over his kill and calm his heart, and to shake his two-sword clean, when he spotted the catapult, directed at Davos's home. The family, he knew, was still inside. Helplessly, he watched, as the diminutive gray creatures set the stone in place. But before the mechanism could launch, a lone arrow dropped from the clouds. The bogrens panicked, abandoning their posts, as the drizzle became a downpour, arrowheads thudding one-by-one beside them. Demacharon gazed in wonder at the flock of whirlydinghies soaring overhead. Krow led from the vanguard, firing his bow, as did Ecthros from his skiff, with his brother at the helm. At last, the galumph was hit, and the immense beast of burden raced away, the chariot yoked to its shoulders coming apart.

It was enough distraction to make the house. Along the way, he found a blood-soaked spear, and did not question its origin. A horg saddled with a bogren loomed a good distance off. His shoulder was aching, reminding him of too many battles, but experience did not fail him. The spear launched from his arm and dropped through the bogren's collarbone. Without a driver, the enslaved horg went insane, scaring several galumphs, while trampling a dozen of his smaller allies, until colliding, ultimately, with an exploding chariot.

Onward he battled, to where Davos and his family were barricaded, his vision obscured by sweat and a burning sky. Bogrens charged past him, every one of them a murderer, and out of the ether he caught glimpses of Zaibos upon his mount, pacing the stony ridge above.

What is he waiting for?

Demacharon tried to work out a strategy, when a wall of spikes emerged from the curtain of embers. It caught him off balance and he cursed himself. Only by the grace of Fate did he remain unharmed, but the spikes were pressing in, threatening to skewer him. An enormous horg stood behind them, its twisted face scowling from a narrow opening in the moving, shifting wall. He then realized what he was seeing, two massive tower shields joined together, three fingers thick of solid stone, weighing no less than several men, with a dozen prongs protruding from corner to corner like iron rivets. Another improbable weapon, a living siege engine, but this one was terribly effective. His swords could not penetrate, nor could he flank the creature, or even turn to flee, and the horg was rapidly advancing. Stumbling further and further back, he finally lost his footing, landing hard on his rear. There was nothing to do but wait to be crushed.

Hope arrived with a familiar voice. Davos stood with his bladed spoon, as black trickled across the horg's thigh. He hoisted the weapon back onto his shoulder, and rounded the sword again into the monster's knee, like a woodsman cutting into a log. The horg buckled, but did not go down, turning the rim of its shield into Davos's face, knocking him away like a troublesome gnat. But for Demacharon, it was an opportunity. Casting Severetrix aside, he clamored up the wall of spikes like a ladder, and before the horg could notice him, he was leaping from the top of the shield, planting his gladius firmly into its skull. The brute convulsed with a confused grunt, and he rode the body to the ground. A younger man might not have been fazed by the fall, but Demacharon's spine felt misaligned, and a numbing pain was shooting from his elbow to his fingertips. He reached for his gladius from where he lay, but the blade was lodged to the hilt in bone and brain, and would not budge.

Now the bogrens were swarming, like flies over fresh carrion, and his two-sword was down below his feet, beyond reach. He was defenseless, and could do nothing but sidle under the fallen tower shield. It would not take them long to dig him out.

Demacharon watched from under the stone cover, as a great many horg gathered up boulders, to rage at the sky as flying skiffs bore down upon them. Bred from the dark hemisphere, they were mostly blind, and like children throwing pebbles at birds. And in a short time, the pilots became bolder, flying ever lower. Arrows perforated the lumbering beasts like pins in cushions, the whirlydinghies like slow-moving moths fluttering just out of reach. Yet, whether due to arrogance or lack of oil, Krow descended and was caught, and the frame of his craft was ripped to pieces, its balloon sails left to the whims of the wind. The black-feathered avian rolled from the wreckage, but his wingman was less fortunate, split from the waist between a horg's fists. It was then that Demacharon turned away, unable to watch further.

When the wall of spikes was lifted off him, he expected a host of inhuman faces, but what greeted him was a friend. Davos did not look so glib as he had been, now mired in gore, and leaning tiredly against the hilt of his greatsword.

"Lazing about, old man?"

Demacharon was too weary to think of a clever retort. He clasped his companion's hand, and was hauled up, and still in a daze, retrieved his gladius and two-sword.

"Report?"

"Well . . ." Davos sounded uncertain. "I've lost count of my kills. Bastards just keep coming. We've lost a great deal also, but I think . . . I think Thulken got them out."

"And your family?"

Davos whirled around, as if he had lost his direction, and was remembering something awful.

"Davos? Did you get them to safety?"

"I . . . I had to leave them. I'm not proud of it, but I couldn't just stand aside, watching good men die for us. But they're safe. I'm sure of it. Last I checked, they were still holed up in the house."

It was long past dawn, and the fires were going out from the houses and the hearts of the wheeled catapults, lifting the haze to expose the dead. Bogren and horg alike, the bodies were like weeds, despoiling the land. But there were men and women also, and boys newly ripened to manhood, their faces pale and at peace in the stillness.

Out of the shifting smoke, the tower emerged, rising upon a lone hill, its arms slowly turning, creaking against the wind despite its burnt and missing folds.

"Zaibos?"

Davos stared hard at him.

"He was waiting for something, up on that ridge." He pointed, but there was nothing to see but bald rock and brush.

Throwing his sword over his shoulder, Davos started to run, proving remarkably swift for a man of such girth. Demacharon followed as best he could, but his spine was still twisted, and his legs were failing. At every turn, they met resistance, bogrens hungry for battle, but Davos would not be slowed. Heads flew from his blade, and when they came in greater number, he plowed through their ranks with the broad side of his spoon.

"Kiki! I am coming Kiki!"

From a distance, Demacharon could see the glowing cinders under Davos's heels, and the salamander roving his garden, snapping up bogrens like a cat preying on mice.

It was all for the king's amusement, Demacharon realized. Zaibos cared nothing for losses. Whether bogren, horg or human lives, they all meant nothing to him. He had remained upon his hill only to watch the carnage unfold. But with most of the villagers fled, Zaibos had at last arrived, where he now stood, at Davos's door.

Kiki was screaming, as were her daughters, joined in a chorus of terror and despair. All their weight and muscle was thrown against the door, but it was coming apart. With every blow, Bonecrusher pulled the planks away, and she and her children peaked out from the gaps, their faces swollen and wet.

"Zaibos!" Davos cried. "ZAIBOS!"

With the door about to give way, Kiki disappeared, just as her husband smashed through it, carrying Zaibos into the house. Demacharon was a short way behind when the salamander rounded on him. It far exceeded the length and girth of a horse, with rows of jagged teeth and a hissing mouth. He did not know to subdue such a creature, if that was even within the realm of possibility, and could only think to brandish his weapons and cross them in the air. The saurian coiled, but its body remained stationary, its four back legs squatting as if to pounce. From within the house, there came sounds of desperation, the wailing of frightened children and the ringing of steel. It agonized him to hear it, but he could not turn his back on the creature, lest he forfeit his life.

Whirling over his left shoulder, an arrow smacked against the salamander's snout. Though failing to penetrate its scaly hide, it was enough to make the creature flinch, and reconsider what was prey.

"First thing you've hit all day!" he heard someone shout. A whirlydinghy floated overhead, its nose painted white with a unicorn. The craft came so closely, he could almost touch the two passengers.

"That's not true, Toby! I took out some bogrens, I'm pretty sure."

The salamander looked to be mesmerized by the flying contraption, with its spinning rotors and inflated sails. But it was Krow, with an inhuman screech and a wing-shaped sword, that forced the creature to withdraw.

"Go help Davos!" he cawed. "We've bigger beasts in Nimbos!"

Zaibos and Davos were engaged in a deadly dance that tore through the house. The floor was coated with debris, with shards of pottery and cooking utensils, and broken bottles of oil. Across from the kitchen, through the hall, Kiki and the children watched from an open doorway. She was laying over the three girls as if her body could shield them from harm. And she tried over and over to hush them, with soft murmurs, even as she quaked with dread.

Davos fought with more heart than any man he knew, but his blows came to naught, for Zaibos was invincible in his armor. And even as the Monster King taunted him, and threatened his family, he was giving way to exhaustion. The children must have sensed it also, the battle turning against their father, as Niah, huddled over her rabbit, cried out, "Is Daddy going to be alright?"

Kiki tried to reassure her, to reassure all of them, amid the shouting and the cursing and the clanging of metal, and the house collapsing around their ears. Demacharon pushed his way forward, to lend his arm, but the kitchen could barely contain the two of them. Bonecrusher swept the room, singing its deathly pitch, pulverizing chairs, knocking sconces from walls, tearing the stove door from its hinges. Somehow, he had to lure Zaibos to open ground, but Davos could not disengage. He considered leading the children away, but the bogrens were already gathering outside. From the shattered doorway and the windows, he could see them amassing. There was no place to run, or hide.

Seeing his family huddled together, Davos summoned his remaining strength, rushing headlong into his foe with the kitchen table as a barricade. Zaibos tore through it, as Davos lifted his sword, bringing it down with enough force to halve a horg's skull. It could have ended then and there. Zaibos was taken aback, stunned, but with a turn of his head, the horned crown caught the bladed-spoon and pulled it away.

Davos retreated, defenseless and defeated. He looked to his family once more, as the hope faded from his eyes, and the king's morningstar ripped through his innards, exposing the fatty tissue, his intestines unraveling like a bloody spool of rope. Despite her efforts, Kiki could not hide their eyes. They wanted to see. Needed to see it. They did not know, could not know, such evil before now. Davos heard their bawls of pity as he watched his end, as his eyes rolled away into his skull and he slumped to the kitchen floor, a pool of red draining from beneath him.

Niah did not stop.

"Daddy! Daddy! Daddy!" Again, and again and again she called him, the name intensifying with every utterance, until the sound of it became something more than human. Grief itself. Like an earthquake in their bones, unbearable, devastating.

Demacharon knew only that he could not let harm come to the children. He launched himself into the hall, to stand between them and a killer he knew to be invincible.

"Enough, Zaibos! You've got what you wanted. These children will never forget what you've taken from them. They will never forget you."

He did not at once respond, but stood, threatening with his mere presence, Davos's blood dripping red from his crimson armor. When, at last, he spoke, it was with a single word only. "Beg."

"What?"

"Beg," he repeated. "Beg me not to harm these children, on your hands and knees, and I will not."

"If I knew you to be an honorable man, I would."

"Good," he said, "you're learning. Honor means nothing. Right and wrong, good and evil, it all means nothing without the power to enforce it. Power is everything."

"You're wrong, Zaibos. I once believed as you do, but I have seen things, horrors even you cannot imagine. There are other worlds out there, other lives. What we do, here and now . . . it matters more than you know."

"Bah! Your prattle bores me. I will teach you the true meaning of life. I will make you watch as I flay them, layer by layer, from skin to muscle to bone. Make no mistake, they will be alive when they see their own hearts stop beating."

The king was beyond reason, utterly insane, and there was no other course of action, he could see, but for his swords to answer.

Zaibos backed through the hallway and into the kitchen, to make use of his morningstar, as the Hedonian pressed the attack, his knifelike gladius ringing against the seamless armor. But his movements with the blade were only a feint, to keep his foe occupied, as he lunged with his other arm. He hoped, prayed, that the near-invisible blade not shatter. Driving the two-sword forward, into the plated sternum, the impact sent a jolt through his palm and up to his shoulder. At once, Zaibos knocked the weapon from his grasp, and the blade winked in and out of existence as it spun to the rafters. Severetrix had failed to penetrate the armor.

Zaibos could have ended him there, as he had Davos, but chose instead to return to the mother, and her children, to make him watch. Demacharon chased after, wrestling him from the bedroom, his gladius flat against the king's throat.

They struggled through the house, Zaibos twisting like a bull, the two of them smashing through the stairwell and against the wall and partway through the kitchen window. Iron-tipped gloves tore into his forearms, and cauldrons rattled against his skull, and cabinets collapsed under their jarring weight, but Demacharon held fast. He searched for an opening, a patch of naked flesh to bury the point of his steel, but the armor was without flaw, and the long spikes protruding from the pauldrons threatened to skewer him.

Again, they crashed through the kitchen, and tumbled over, slipping on Davos's innards. Before he knew what was happening, Zaibos was stomping on him, snapping his wrist like a twig.

He shrugged away the pain, pulling himself up by the stove, but his assailant was gone. "No, Zaibos! Don't!" It was a fool's hope, to think the monster might listen, but a fool's hope was all that he had.

Demacharon could see him now, standing in Niah's bedroom, his soot-black morningstar in his mailed fingers. But where there should have been weeping and pleading, was only silence, and he knew at once that something was wonderfully amiss.

Zaibos paced the room, two-steps and back, his gauntlet tearing at curtains, ripping apart pillows and dolls made of yarn and clay figurines. The toys, it seemed, were taking the punishment for the children. But where were they? Demacharon was quick to reach the room, but was just as surprised to find it vacated. Zaibos, in his fury, did not even notice him.

Had they gone into hiding? Crawled up into an attic, perhaps? His eyes scanned the ceiling and walls for any subtle crevasses. No, there were no exits but a lone window, clasped shut and surrounded by enemies. All that remained was a postern bed, made for one. Kiki could not have squeezed herself under it, and yet Zaibos flung it against the wall, mattress and frame together. And there, he and Demacharon stared with fascination, into the perfectly round hole in the floor. It was too narrow for an armored king, but an easy fit for a child. Or a bogren.

28

Nessus

The messenger was breathing hard. And sweating. Was it out of fear, or was he exhausted, having just climbed the spiraling tower stair to its zenith? Zaibos could be certain of nothing anymore. Fear was his greatest weapon, but it could also be a nuisance, for there was no one in the kingdom who dared deliver bad news.

His praetorian guard, the Silent, stood true to their namesake, forming a perfect circle about the compass-marked floor, their armor gleaming blackly under a muted sun and moons. Mandos stood on the dais to his right, prepared to receive delegates should he himself not wish to speak. He watched as the sweating man approached, looking startled by the echo of his footfalls and stealing furtive glances at the Silent. Three paces from the edge of the dais, he hesitated, looking uncertain as to where he should stand.

His armor grated against the stone chair as he leaned forward. "Well? Out with it!"

The messenger dropped to his knees. "Forgiveness, Master . . ."

Mandos took a step down with an accusing gesture. "You waste the king's time! Stand up, you fool, and give your report."

Zaibos turned to his right. "I can speak for myself, Captain. Now then, is she dead?"

"Not . . . not exactly, Your Greatness."

"What do you mean, not exactly? She is either dead or she isn't. Which is it?"

"The princess still lives, Your Highness."

"Do you know what I hate?" He tipped his horned helm forward. "Pandering. It sickens me. Call me by yet another title and I shall have your head on a pike. Understood?"

His face grew sallow, and his eyes turned round and white, like eggs about to pop from his skull. "I . . . ah . . . my apologies, Your Grace. Forgive me!"

Zaibos clawed the arms of his obsidian chair, drawing lines in the stone. "Explain this to me—how is it that the heir of Solon still lives, when I expressly decreed that she should die?"

"Well, you see, we've been having some trouble with that. You see . . ."

"Damn your accursed tongue!" Zaibos cried. "Get to the point or I'll have your mouth sewn shut!"

"We can't kill her!" He dropped again to his knees, shivering. "We tried, tried everything, but, well . . . things keep happening, strange events we can't explain."

"Did you try burning her at the stake?"

"That was the very first thing we attempted, but, well, we simply could not get a fire going. At once, it started to rain. You must have seen how the weather suddenly . . ."

"No."

"Everything was soaked, so nothing would light. Then we built a scaffolding, with a tarpaulin to hang over it, and tried again. But a blasting wind came along, the likes you've never felt! We could hardly stand in it, let alone set off kindling."

Zaibos shifted in his throne, the plates of his armor grinding together, serving to increase his irritation. "I suppose you could contrive of no other means by which to kill the child?"

"Of course, we experimented with a variety of methods! We dare not defy you!"

"What else did you try?"

"Crucifixion. We rearranged the scaffolding, to make a cross, but when we put her on it, well . . . the whole structure collapsed."

"Collapsed?"

"We were just as puzzled as you. When we examined the fallen beams, we saw that they were brittle as cycle-old bread, despite us having just assembled it with freshly milled pieces. Termites, we discovered. They'd been eating it from the inside and had hollowed out the wood."

"You must be joking," Mandos interjected.

"Would I humor, er . . . he who sits the throne? We decided to hang her after that, from the bough of a willow."

"I suppose the tree collapsed also?" the captain said.

"No, but it . . . you had to have been there to believe it. The willow, it bent itself down, almost as if, as if it didn't *want* to hang her."

"What else!" Zaibos cried, his impatience building into a rage.

"Drawing and quartering came next, an unorthodox form of execution, I know, but appropriately gruesome, something we thought would be to your liking. We bound her wrists and ankles, and to each of the ropes attached horses. But the animals, well . . . they simply refused to budge. We beat them, with whips and chains, and then a cat-o'-nine-tails, nearly stripping the flesh from their bodies, and they simply lay down to die. The girl was more distraught by their suffering, I believe, than by anything we were doing to her."

Zaibos was standing now. "You mean to tell me, that you and your men went to such absurd lengths, and not one among you thought simply to cut out her heart? Are there no swords left in my kingdom? No axes to remove her head? No maces to cave her skull? How many ways are there to kill a man? A single hand would have sufficed, firm about the throat, to squeeze the life from her."

"We did think of that, your —, er, and we did try. But after all that had happened, with the unexpected deluge and the termites and the animals, the men, they were spooked. Fafnr went to slit her throat, but he couldn't. He said . . ."

"What did he say?" Zaibos stood at the foot of the dais, mere steps from the envoy, Bonecrusher in his hands.

"Fafnr said she reminded him too much of his sister. So we got Tulmus to do it, but the princess reminded him too much of his wife. And . . . it's an odd thing, really, because Fafnr's sister and Tulmus's wife, they look nothing alike, nor do they look anything like Radia. But if you ask me, she's the spitting image of a girl I fancied in my youth."

"Where is she now? What is she doing?"

"We left her on the hill, awaiting execution, per your orders. Last I saw, she appeared to be . . . singing. The same song, over and over."

"One more thing," Zaibos said, moving closer and holding his arms out, as if to embrace the messenger. "Who am I?"

"You . . . you are my king, of course!"

Those would be his last words. Within a few short moments, Mandos would be directing the maidservants to clean the mosaic tile of blood and skull fragments.

Zaibos was furious, and hurried off, but Mandos called after him still. "Master?"

"Yes, Captain?"

"I implore you to reconsider."

He did not face him. "Take care how you speak to me, Captain. I admire your efficiency, but you are not irreplaceable."

"I endeavor only to serve, Master. The people, they dare not oppose your rule. We have made certain of that. But if you kill this girl, their hatred for you may exceed their fear, and that may, in time, undermine all you seek to achieve."

"Captain Mandos," he turned slowly to address him, "do you speak out of loyalty to me? Or for her sake?"

"Master, I've done everything you've asked of me— betrayed friends, murdered innocents, families that I knew personally . . . watched them burn. No one in this world has done so much as I, to prove allegiance to his king. But Radia, she is beloved by all—"

"And what of yourself? Do *you* love her?"

"I did, once. No more. Nothing remains but my duty to the throne. If it is your will, then she must die, but act upon it quietly. Do not make of her a martyr. Let the people believe she has abandoned them, and you will have sullied her good name, and their hatred for you will turn against her."

"No," Zaibos intoned. "She is their last hope. Even now, they conspire against me, cowering in their homes and their taverns, whispering, fabricating tales of her triumphant return, how she will come with an army from the outside to liberate the city. No, Mandos. She will die like the rest, upon the Hill of Lamentations, a traitor for all to see. I will then leave her body as a gift for them, to be paraded through the streets, so there not remain a child or deluded fool believing in her. Hope must be crushed utterly, Mandos, or the people will never learn to obey."

Zaibos knew that no one was so dreaded in Tyrnael as himself. The very mention of his name made seasoned warriors check the dim alleyways about them. And yet, deep in the heart of the castle, there lived someone who frightened even him.

Few knew of his existence. The castle was ancient beyond memory, with doors and passages known only to the first of kings, and to the Ancients who had it built. But of the stronghold's many secrets, one stood beyond others. Fathoms beneath the ground, it lay hidden. *The Star Chamber.* Every mystery known to the Zo, the keys to their knowledge and their power, could be discovered there. And it was in this most hidden of places that *he* secluded himself, the one entity Zaibos feared.

The entrance to the Star Chamber could be reached only through the catacombs, where the bodies of kings and queens and magistrates, and others remembered by history, were laid to rest. Here, the tomb of his father could be found. Solon had it commissioned out of a single slab of quartz, fashioned in

Anabis's likeness. It could not have been more than half a decade prior, but with the strange way in which time behaved outside of Tyrnael, it felt to him like twenty years or more. The stone lid was not easily moved, but Zaibos managed it, revealing the narrow steps leading down.

Uneasily, he descended, lighting the curved sconces on the wall as he went, and the hidden chamber took form as his eyes adjusted to the dimness. There were books and scrolls beyond count, and skeletons of creatures he hoped never to meet, and astrolabes of glass, and crystals diffusing lights and sounds in varied tones, and stranger things he dared not question. Exploring further, he came upon suits of armor, much like his own, and blades too narrow to be seen on edge, and mechanical devices for casting lightning, and orbs containing utter darkness. But what most unnerved him were the golems, giants of flesh and steel, vaguely shaped like men. When they first arrived at the castle, his father had told him that the golems stole men's souls, but the ones in the armory only stared.

None of it mattered much, he knew, but the object at the center of it all, dominating the chamber—two gold phoenixes facing one another, their wings joining to form an arch. It was a gate leading to nowhere, nowhere he could see but the other side of the room. For his father, it went by many names. *The Zo Door. The Fantastigate. The Hub of all Worlds.*

The gate was his father's obsession. But it had not always been so. They had come to the city seeking immortality, convinced that the Zo, or their descendants, could grant it to him. After his dealings with the king, to cure the princess of her affliction, Anabis was given freedom to explore the castle, to learn whatever he could of the Zo. But eternal life continued to elude him, until he went to the stables, and at last discovered the unicorn, a creature that never aged, an immortal being. That was the key. A design plan is contained within the blood of each living thing, his father once explained to him, what he called a creature's *essence*. The Zo knew this. And they learned to mix the essences of different life forms, to transmit the qualities of one animal to another.

In the darkness, a large figure stirred, shaped like a man, but more so.

"Father?" he called at last. "Are you there?"

The figure moved, with an awkward gait for a two-legged creature. In the glow of the golden arch, Zaibos could see him clearly now, the eyes like hot embers, a face like onyx, and a beard the color of fire.

"Anabis?" Zaibos called again.

"You know never to call me that," he answered. "Anabis is no more. There is only Nessus."

It was true, in a sense. The blood of the unicorn had given him more than immorality. His father assumed the beast's physical properties as well, its equine form from below the waist, becoming a creature of myth, a *centaur*. After that day, Zaibos told Solon that his father was dead, and the monster that was once Anabis adopted the name Nessus, forever hiding in the bowels of the castle, in the Star Chamber, where secrets are kept.

"And take that helmet off. You look like a damned fool, wearing it everywhere."

"You cannot speak to me like that anymore," he answered. "I am a king now, the most feared being in all Aenya, and I will be respected!"

The centaur lifted his arm, and with a gesture, Zaibos went hurtling against the wall, books and broken shelves toppling over him. "Stupid boy. Do you think that crown of thorns matters anything to me? You think to impress me with titles, as if they possessed some inherent power? I am beyond mortal customs, more than your feeble mind can comprehend."

He got to his feet, pulling his helmet from his head. "And what have you been doing these past ten years, that any should stare upon you with awe? You've managed to unearth a door, and a useless one at that."

"This is no mere door!" Nessus cried. "You've always been too stupid to see that. The Zo did not perish from this world after the Cataclysm . . . they escaped it! They evolved beyond us, becoming gods, masters of the multiverse! You think yourself superior, but you might as well be king of an anthill, for this world is but a single grain on the shores of The Cosmos!"

"Yes, I've heard this spiel a hundred times before, and still I see you staring into nothingness. Did you ever consider that you may have misread the records? Or that the Zo may have gone insane, as their world was being destroyed?"

"No—no, I have generated power enough to open the gate, but it never lasts for more than a second. You have felt its effects, have you not? The way time slows around it? Did you not leave the city a boy, and return after some passings a man? But in those brief seconds, I have glimpsed worlds you cannot dream of—cities of glass and steel, where immense iron birds drop eggs of erupting suns. I have seen a tower like an obsidian mountain, crowned by a flaming eye, and an ancient wall of ice and stone, standing at the brink of perpetual winter. Imagine, every possible world connected and within reach, through this very threshold, one step removed from infinity! But such marvels are of little concern to children who play at being king. So tell me, what brings you to me?"

"I have the girl. Is she of interest to you?"

He turned his broad horse body sideways, his hooves clopping against the ancient stones in contemplation. "When Solon first confided in me, how he found her in his garden, I was very much intrigued. She was—is—a truly remarkable creature. Her blood contains the essences of every living thing on this planet . . . perhaps every living thing that has ever lived. Life courses through her veins. Even when she was a child, I could see the power growing inside her, power enough to consume her.

"The First Men who walked the world believed that, when the land is ravaged, an *avatar* comes into being, to give voice to nature. For millennia, Aenya has suffered mass extinctions, but when sentient lifeforms are confronted with such fate, they turn to faith, to some greater power to allay their doom.

Only an advanced intellect recognizes that the price of power is often destruction."

"Can she be killed?"

"Straight to the point, eh? How disappointing. But to answer your query, indeed, with time, everything dies. Even the Cosmos itself will someday grow cold, and dark."

"Are you suggesting that I wait? Let her illness take care of it?"

"You really are a dull boy. Hard to believe you are my progeny. I suppose that whore you had for a mother has much to account for. If you leave her to die, her influence will only grow. But killing her should not be a problem. I only ask that you bring me—"

"Her heart?"

"When Solon sat the throne, I was unable to attain it. It is the seed of her power, I believe, and if my readings are correct, it may help me to breach the Fantastigate."

Zaibos gave no reply. For all he cared, his father could remain hidden forever, to rot in the tomb he had made for himself.

"I truly despise you, father."

The Dark Centaur smiled, his face etched in shadow. "I know."

"I sing the Goddess that is in all, who gilds the wheat and sun born rye, who, in dreaming plains we seek her call . . ."

She was singing softly to herself, just as the messenger had said. From the post where she was bound, she was bent like a weeping willow, her feet crookedly scraping the ground, hair drawn over her face and bosom. Zaibos made no ceremony of his approach. He was alone and without his helmet, wanting her to recognize him, the boy she had grown up with, to know with certainty who had been tormenting her.

"I know you can feel me," he said.

"In the greenwood . . . in the elms that fall . . . from sundered root to shaken ply . . ."

"Cease your pretending, girl. Turn up and face your adversary!"

She did not move, as if she were one with the post, a singing tree, the wind rustling through the leaves in her hair. "I have no adversaries," she murmured.

"Don't you, now?" He spat the words at her. "Is this how you delude yourself? That there is no suffering? No evil? And all is right with the world?" He dug his iron-tipped finger into her chin. "You are afraid, of what I am and what I can do, but you can no longer ignore me, princess. It is time to leave childish notions behind, to grow up, and recognize the world as it is."

"I am not afraid."

Zaibos had watched many people be tortured, every one of them feigning courage, a courage that dissolved quickly when the right pressure was applied. But in the girl, he sensed no insincerity. She exuded a quiet strength, a resolve that made him doubt, if only for an instant.

"If you are not afraid," he said, "look here, upon your neighbor."

She was bound to a single post among hundreds and surrounded by the ash-black sculptures attached to them—the morbid remains of human bodies. The figure at her side was twisted in anguish, its limbs frozen in a futile attempt at freedom, pulling against restraints that had long burned away. But it was the lingering scream, scored upon its face, that could not but haunt whoever looked upon it.

"This one here . . ." Zaibos remarked, trailing a finger along a scorched arm, admiring the way it crumbled to delicate ash. "How lifelike in composition, though a little small, don't you think? When the flesh is burned, there is some shrinking, but I do not think this was the case. What say you? Was this once a little boy? Or a little girl? I cannot quite remember."

She jerked away, shuddering. Crows were circling the hill, squawking noisily. One landed nearby, picking at the seared flakes in search of flesh, but all the bodies were charred.

"Come now, have you no answer?"

"... and from dreaming plains ... attend her hall, even in the sore and weeping gall, there is the ballad which brings release ..."

"There is no release from me!" he screamed, cutting her with his fist, stealing a piece from her cheek.

"... Zoë sings ... her song ... who is in all ..." For a moment, he stopped to delight in her hair, streaked red with blood, and in her voice, heavy with unbidden tears. And yet she still found the strength and will to sing.

"Before you die, before I kill you, I ask one thing only—"

"... do not dread and shrink from winter's pall ... for Zoë, dying, sleeps in snowy shawl ..."

"Admit," he went on, "that you think me a monster. Just look around you. Witness what I have done, and admit how you hate me, how you wish to do the same to me, as I am about to do to you, if only you could, if only you had the *power* to."

"I don't hate you," she said, hardly above a whisper.

He clutched her face, that of a broken doll's, between his mailed fingers, forcing her eyes to meet his. "What was that?"

"I do not hate you. I never have."

"You lie."

She looked into him, as if for the first time, her lunar irises aglow, one turquoise, the other violet, vast moons of Aenya.

"When we first met," she said, "I could feel nothing. You were utterly empty, a suit of armor with nothing inside, but I was mistaken. For every life, no matter how cruel, there is a soul, only yours was too small for me to see it, like a mustard seed, malnourished and dying. You asked me to look upon these corpses, but I cannot pity them, for they are already dead. The suffering you brought upon them, however great, is less than the flick of a butterfly's wings to the soul that is eternal, and will go unremembered in the next plane. The deaths you have caused, are as nothing, for whatever lives must also die. But the love they nourished, when they were alive, the husbands for their wives and mothers for their children, you could not steal that away from them, and these things they will keep, forever and ever, until the Cosmos ceases to spin. If you must know, brother, it is *you* I pity most. Everything you have done here is the cry of an infant, an infant wanting nothing more than to be loved."

Zaibos twitched in his breastplate, reaching for his helmet, which was not there. "Stop it."

"The old man, the one you call father, never cared for you, did he? Never once put his arms around you?"

"Silence!"

"Never showed you a bit of tenderness, even when you were ill, or alone . . ."

She was wrong to assume he had ever the capacity to feel. From his earliest memory, he had known that he was different. When people spoke of their emotions, he did not trust them. To him, it was a trick, a way to gain advantage in an uncaring universe. Only liars spoke of sympathy. Upon discovering his mother's corpse, his only reaction was fear, that he not behave as expected. Any child his age would have wept. So, he pretended.

To love and be loved was to be dependent. To be weak. He had always believed this. So why, now, did Radia's words cut him so?

"Enough!" He struck her, harder than before, ruining her face. She would hardly be capable of speech, or singing, any longer. "You think . . . you think I need the old man? Or you? Or anyone!" He bloodied his mailed fists against her, punching and tearing, his metal-tipped fingers pushing through into her sternum.

"I should keep you alive!" he told her, working his glove through blood, and bone. "I should make you watch as I butcher everyone you have ever loved, everyone you have ever known, this entire blasted city if need be, until you admit that you are weak and that I am strong, but you . . . *you*!"

An eerie stillness was in the air. The clouds gathered to watch, but the sun and moons were in hiding, daring not look upon his handiwork. Her hair was slick and heavy, and her breathing shallow, and still she let out, a whimper below a whisper, "And spring is born to sing . . . and hearts allayed . . ."

There her singing stopped. His glove dripped with the vessel it contained, as he turned from her inert body. And the ground beneath him quailed. And the sky turned black with crows.

29

The procession carried on, under a black and swirling sky, where beauty lay in still repose upon heavy shoulders and heavier souls. The people gathered in the streets, funneling in from every hovel and tier and tower, and whomever it was that each one of them loved most, they saw carried on the bier. Sisters saw sisters, mothers daughters, and children mothers. They gathered to hold her in their eyes, as if in the beholding she might tarry, every hand reaching as an infant reaches to be known, if only to be assured that she was lost. And despite the very certainty, the procession carried on.

Even in eternity, even in that dreadful sleep that awaits us all, the Taker could not steal away her beauty—her lips like ripened berries, her braids like sun-gilded wheat, though a pall of lifelessness lay upon her cheeks. And the people seeing her remarked, "Is this the face of one that's dead?" Shouts rang out her name. "Rise!" the people pleaded. "Give us a sign and rise!" But death makes no exceptions, so she did not stand to greet them, nor stir to allay their tears. And ever uneventful, the procession carried on.

A deathly chill befell the land, not of snows giving promise of rebirth, but the bitterness of absent daylight, the sun remote and indifferent and black, hidden behind the moons. It was a blight upon the world, a sickness growing from the root where she was fallen, from where her heart had been cut out. And still, they went on seeking, the princess on the bier, hoping where hope was nowhere to be found, in streets where every eye was turned and faithful hearts were broken. And ever the procession carried on.

In the surrounding dell, the silence was pervasive, for birds knew no cause for singing, and the mammals in their burrows of decay lay down to darkness, whispering not of children that may come, or of any future spring, but surrendering to a dreamless sleep. All was stillness and shadow, but for the crack of timber and hush of falling leaves, the long naked pines standing out like gallows. Wherever leaves unfurled and flowers bloomed, was only shrinking, shriveling. Colors muted, fading into gray, and petals winked, one by one, into death. Still, in distant Tyrnael, the procession carried on.

Across that lonesome sphere, where she was known by other names, they mourned softly her procession. They mourned on dying fields, where rains did not fall, and they mourned her where crops failed to allay the hungry. Storms of dust arose like primordial beasts, to bury the living, and swallow nations whole. On endless plains, devastation moths churned, violent from their cocoons, sweeping homes into the sky. In desert lands, flames devoured what little grew, and mouths went parched by sand-swept riverbeds. On rocky shores, waters reddened, and the fishers' nets were filled with dead. But where the land itself was held together loosely, the world belched magma and hemorrhaged fire, and the living and non-living alike were indifferently consumed. Even where joy runs deepest, in the hearts of expectant mothers, expectation turned to horror and despair. For on that day, no infant was born but born to stillness. And still, in mourning for infant laughter that would never echo, their eyes bent to infant mounds, wives held fast to husbands and carried on.

As they did across the world, so in Tyrnael they toiled and tarried, over earth that would not yield. Yet still, they followed, reaching, ever reaching toward the bier where *life* had fallen, from every roof and window, for every eye to witness, under a swirling cursing sky. And ever the procession carried on.

30

Zoey

Everything was black. Devoid of shape or color. But his skull was throbbing, had been for a long time. It was his only sense of self. Something metallic was pounding in his ears. The world came lurching into focus, but he did not wish it. Oblivion had been comforting. Tranquil.

A long workbench slowly met his eyes, like one a blacksmith would use. But of the man seated there, he could see only broad shoulders and a spine, bent over some task.

The room was small and sparsely furnished. Tools were hanging from the ceiling—

brass tongs, chisels worn to their nubs, a bellows that had seen better days. On the opposite wall, a hearth was crackling, spitting embers. But there was a haze about it all. His mind was still clouded. Spinning. Who had brought him here? And to what end?

The pounding resonated once more, metal on metal, a hammer working a piece of iron. He watched it rise and come down again in the hands of the man whose back was turned to him.

At last, he summoned the ability to speak. "Who are you? How did I get here?"

The blacksmith kept silent, did not so much as shift from his seat.

He tried to move his arms, to accost the stranger, but was unable. Something was binding him to a chair. Ropes perhaps. He could not be certain, as he was still too numb to feel, and looking toward his feet the world went swimming out of focus. If he had been forced upright and was tied down, it could mean only one thing—he was a prisoner, and the man before him was to be his torturer.

"I know what you're at. I know you're trying to intimidate me."

Again, no answer came, no sound but the fall of the hammer and a cacophony of steel.

"Very well. Play on. But know this, I have had more men tortured than you will ever have the misfortune to." He did not know how he had known to say this. It was as if the voice that came from his mouth was not his own, and yet he trusted it. "There's no torment you can devise that I've not suffered worse. You'll never make me beg."

He waited, his breath caught in quiet anticipation, dreading neither pain nor death, and still, to his exasperation, there was no reply. Only the hammer broke the silence, ever pounding.

"You think to break me! To watch me grovel before your master? On with it, then, I grow impatient!"

The blacksmith, or whoever he was, did not speak. He remained dutiful in his task. Was he mute? Deaf? No doubt, something was being fashioned, a cruel device to be used upon him.

"Did you hear me, fool? I said on with it!"

The hammer. Always that infernal hammer. And what could he possibly be making? Tools of torture need not be so refined.

The waiting, the not knowing, the lack of acknowledgment was becoming a torment all its own. And curiosity turned to rage. "Answer me, damn you! Show me what you have there, what tool you think to break me with, for I am already broken and do not fear!"

"Oh?"

"By Sargonus, you speak! You hear me?"

"Yes, I've been listening to your prattling a good long while, but you will not like what I have to show you." He turned suddenly, the hammered shape stretched out in his palms. At first, he thought little of the strange object set before him. Yet the longer he gazed upon it, the more he was unnerved. It was an iron mask, blood-red in hue, with narrow slits cut out for the eyes and mouth. Spikes protruded from the top and sides like that of a steel urchin, or a morningstar. And he realized then what he was looking at. The mask was his to wear. It was the face of Zaibos.

"No," he murmured, the dread beginning to build. "That is not . . . I am not . . . Take that away from me!"

"But this is yours," the blacksmith said to him.

Recognizing the mysterious stranger at last, he found his footing and started backward, knocking a chair behind him. "Get away from me, I beg you!"

"How can you think to escape me? I am always here beside you, wherever you run, wherever you go. This mask you so abhor? I did not make it. *You* did."

Once more, he looked upon the face of his tormentor, and screamed, throwing himself against the walls, but the room was without doors or windows. Desperate for a way out, he clawed at the masonry, until the tips of his fingers bled. His groping hands finally found purchase, in the brass ring of a door he had not noticed, and he flung it open and stumbled on through.

The air on the other side of the door was thick and heavy and suffused with smoke. His breathing came in short, painful bursts. Homes smoldered some ways off, black billowing from rooftops, from shattered windows and walls turned to rubble. And there were bodies. So many bodies. He shut his eyes to them, but they would not disappear.

Men. Women. Children of Yefira. Did anyone remain? A single soul to be saved? He turned from one twisted shape to another, searching among the charred remnants of families, their limbs reaching like branches into the sky. His heart ever sinking, he moved past broken skulls embedded by maces, their screams discernible where the skin remained, and into dark avenues where flies swarmed and the ground was heavy with carrion.

At the edge of sight, he found what he was seeking—the silent vigil of the living. They were watching him, but did not dare approach. Was he to blame? Having brought Zaibos to their homes? He looked directly at them, but they vanished as if they had never been, as if what he had seen was a trick of the light. In their place, there was only a copse on a knoll, resembling a company of mourners, and a twisting pillar of smoke. And yet, he did not fully trust his senses, for he thought he could feel their eyes heavy upon him still.

By now, the villagers must surely be tending to the wounded. But he could not think what else to do, wanting only to lend his aid, and so he continued his search, until he could see, some distance ahead, a small boy lying face down in the dirt. He ran, his chest aching with familiarity, the name of his son like a fire on his tongue.

He collapsed, becoming painfully aware of the scar across his face, the mark given to him by the monster who had murdered his son. He pulled the limp body against his and wept, holding the boy as tightly as one could, as if he were holding his son.

"Excuse me, but what are you doing?"

A girl was standing over him. She could not have been more than nine. There was not a scratch on her. Not a blemish. Even her clothes, a simple white tunic with gold trim, was gleaming.

"Little girl . . ." he murmured, rousing as from a dream, seeing that the dead boy in his arms was not his own, but another of the same age. "Did—did you know him?"

"Oh, I know everyone." Her demeanor was entirely inappropriate, even callous. Her hands were cupped behind her back and she was rocking, to and fro on her bare soles, as overeager children are wont to do.

"I . . . I am sorry," he said, "so very sorry."

"Why should you be? Everybody dies."

Had she any comprehension of what had happened? The death of her village? Perhaps, such tragedy was too great for a child to process, and in this way, her fragile mind was protecting itself. "You shouldn't be here. Where are your parents? Do they still live?"

"Oh, they've gone away. But it's all right. I'm not afraid."

His head was still heavy, perplexed. When he tried to get a better look, to determine to which house she belonged, the midday sun shone about her face, blinding him. He could tell only that she was pretty, exceedingly so, with bright streaming locks of gold.

"My name's Zoey. What's yours?"

"I . . ." The answer sat at the edge of his lips, eager to be let out, but he could not conjure it. Since waking in that small smithy, everything had been hazy. Perhaps his amnesia was a result of some injury, Zaibos's mace to his head? "I can't seem to remember."

"You've lost your name?"

"I don't . . ." He looked at her again, but the sun seemed to follow as she moved, emanating from her face and hair. No, it was not the sun—the light was coming *from* her. She was the source of it. "I do not know who I am, really."

"Hmm . . . that's quite a pickle, I'd say. Looks like you've lost yourself."

"I have."

"Would you like me to help you?" She reached for his hand, and her smile lifted the shackles of his heart, though he could not remember why it had been so heavy to begin with, for the remains of the dead were long vanished from the field and his mind also.

He nodded, resigning himself to her guidance. Hand in hand, they walked, until the village of Yefira was but a silhouette they occasionally turned to look at. The further they went from it, the more the memory of it faded, and after a short trek over the nearest hill, the dead were forgotten entirely, as was the room where he was to be tortured. He knew only that he existed, and that the girl beside him was a source of great serenity. Still, a feeling in him lingered, something remote and indistinct, yet nagging him just the same, like an important task he had yet to accomplish.

They continued wordlessly, the land stretching before them into infinity. Here the terrain was bleak and desolate, cracked and black as obsidian, bestrewn with ash and rocks. To the left and right, rugged hills cut across the edges of the world. Ahead, there was not a thing to be seen, not a tree or twig or fallen leaf. Everything was dull, shades of gray and ghostly remnants of other hues. No birdsong or chirp of insect could be heard, and no rush of wind swept past. Even their footfalls were muted. The silence was so deep, it was as if he had been stricken deaf. Looking heavenward, he saw no moons nor stars. A solitary shape dominated the sky, casting a strange eerie light, a forlorn and chilling sun. But he was numb to the cold, and to every other sensation, for there was only a hollow feeling where feeling should be.

The Plains of Apathy.

He did not know when or how he knew it, only that he did. And as that familiar dread crept into his heart, he found himself holding tighter to the young girl's hand.

"Why?" he asked finally. "Why have you brought me to this awful place?"

"Me? I've been following you, silly! You've brought *me* here!" There was a look of pity in her turquoise eyes.

"I . . . I do not know what's happening."

"Don't worry. It'll come to you." Her smiling face cut like a lighthouse through the gloom.

"Will you help me? Please? I can never seem to get out of here."

"That *is* true. You've been trapped here a good long while. Years, I think. But you can't hope to get anywhere on just one foot."

"What do you mean, one foot? Speak plainly, I implore you. I am in no mood for riddles."

"Part of you wishes to be here, thinks this is where you belong. You can't leave if you won't let yourself go—let your *whole* self go."

"I have tried . . . but something prevents me, and I know not what." Frustration was overcoming him, making him want to scream. The answer was locked in his memory, but it was a lock he feared to open. "By Sargonus, how can I will myself to anything, when even my name escapes me? I am utterly lost, and—"

She hushed him, saying, "You sought me out, you summoned me, and now you're just going to have to follow my lead." Her eyes were brimming with wisdom, beyond her youthful appearance, and her voice was not like that of a child. When he was in doubt, or afraid, she was assertive and knowing, her voice a soothing lullaby. "Take my hand."

Turning from that hellish place, she guided him onto another path, to a place he had never noticed before. *It was to my left this whole time.* He had only to look there to find his way.

He followed her through a narrow mountain passage. Rock walls pressed in on them from either side. But the ground was rich with moisture, and vegetation seemed to sprout up from wherever her bare soles stepped.

Sounds of water rushed into his ears as they rounded a corner and exited the canyon, and a broad hilly landscape met their eyes. The land was barren, but he could see more vividly now. Hints of green gave promise of life beyond, as did the scent of mustard weed and wild lilac. He was a hero, returning with his men from a long campaign, but he was grasping at impressions, still not fully remembering who he had been or the men who long ago accompanied him.

In a short time, they reached the foot of the river. The water, slate-gray from a distance, became clear as they approached, sloshing over rocks, spraying pillars of white against the bank.

"This river goes by many names," she said, bending down to stare into the ever-shifting flow. "It is called *Forgetfulness* and *Lethe* and *Oblivion*. It cuts through every known world . . . every *possible* world. Drink from this source, and it will all be lifted from you. What you were, what you've ever said and done, it'll be like it never happened."

"Why would anyone do such a thing?"

"To lose their sorrows, the slings and arrows of outrageous fortune, why else? He is really very kind, you know. The river flows from his domain, and offers release."

"He? Who?"

"You know who. Death. The Taker. Some call him Skullgrin, but—yech—who came up with that name?" After a pause, she added, "It's funny, if you think about it. So many people afraid of him, when what they actually fear, is me. Take a sip. And it all goes away."

"What does it matter to live, then? If nothing remains to signify your passage through this world? Nothing that says, 'I was. I lived.' Death leaves no trace."

"He gives us another chance, to start things anew, to know a mother's warmth again, to fall in young love again. It is what the Zo forgot, in their zeal to keep him at bay. You'd be reborn, an infant once more—innocent. Isn't that what you want?"

For a long while, he stood quietly by the river, contemplating the dead, watching the ebb and flow of long-passed memories. He longed to drink of it and be finished, but an echo from his past stayed his hand.

"No," he said finally. "I need my sorrows. They make me what I am. And, also, I am bound by something that has yet to be done."

"Is it truly so important? This thing you have to do?"

"It is my solemn duty. Or, at least, I feel that it is."

"Then we must find a way to cross the river."

He studied the water again with fresh eyes. But it was far too deep, too turbulent. "I see no possible way."

"Dig deeper. You must remember who you are if you hope to cross without losing yourself entirely."

"I told you—I can't remember!"

"Can't or won't?" she challenged, stepping before him. "Look to what you hold most dear in life, what you love more than anything in the universe. Look there, and you will find it."

He suddenly became aware of the clothing he was wearing, his trident-emblazoned jerkin, a bronze fibula pinned to his shoulder with a cape of crimson velvet flowing from it. These were the vestments of a Hedonian legionnaire, similar to what any number of soldiers might have worn, but in a pouch about his waist, there was something else, a small piece of driftwood. He held it in his open palm and a shudder passed through him, his heart aching with a sorrow so deep he longed for the waters of Oblivion, and a joy so powerful he willed himself to remember.

"It was . . . *his*. I carved it on campaign. I remember the look in his eyes when I first gave it to him. He was waiting with his mother by the dock. Couldn't wait to see me. Ran straight up the gangplank and into my arms. It's a trireme, a replica of the ship I used to command. It's how he liked to remember me, his father at the prow of his warship. His little fist was still holding to it when, when I found him, where he used to play by the shore. His name was Astor. And mine is Demacharon. I can recall everything now."

"A boat!" she exclaimed. "That's perfect! We can use that."

"This? You must be joking. It's only a child's toy."

"Put it in the water and you'll see! You won't lose it. I promise!"

With some reluctance, he squeezed the tiny replica one last time, and launched the warship from his palm. It plopped into the water, drifted to the top to fight against the current, and just as quickly capsized, swallowed up in foam. Zoey had yet to lead him astray, but he could not help fretting over the fate of his son's—and now his—most precious possession. He watched and waited, the tension growing between himself and the young girl, until it started to happen. Down below, the river was frothing, surging, rising. With a thunderous roar, an enormous structure burst from the surface, half as broad as the river was wide. Water coursed along its sleek black hull, spilling from the rails, pouring from every port and seam. He gazed at it, his mouth agape, denying what his eyes were telling him. It was a full-sized trireme, bristling with oars, a bronze ram at its prow, its white billowing sails embroidered in gold with the trident of Hedonia. A titanic version of what, just moments ago, he had just held in the palm of his hand.

"This . . . this isn't possible!" he murmured, and turned to her accusingly. "None of this is real?"

"It all depends on your point of view," she said. "In this place, physical matter has no substance. Only your thoughts, imagination, are real. Probabilities and possibilities and wave functions, and all that silliness."

"So then, where is this place, exactly?"

"It's a nexus, between here and there and everywhere else. The Zo called it *The Hub of All Worlds*."

"But nothing we do here matters. It's only just a dream."

"*Only* a dream? Every world is the dream of another. And most of the worlds overlap. Why do you agonize over Astor and Niobe, if thought does not matter? If dreams are not real? They matter, because they exist here, in this dimension of dreams.

"Now, Captain Demacharon, will you show me to your ship?"

He was dismayed but offered a reluctant smile. "I would be honored."

If he had not witnessed his son's toy boat rise from the river as a fully-formed warship, he would never have imagined he was dreaming. His callused fingertips ran across the corded fibers of the mainstay, felt along the waxy cedar timbers making up the gunwale. He examined the brass tholes, chipped and faded green by the salty Sea, where each of the oars was fitted. From where did such details derive? His own mind?

Could another dreamer, knowing nothing of the navy, conjure such a reality?

Each of the rowers saluted him, but their faces were abstractions, like unfinished portraits where the paint was left to run. Still, he recognized their voices, the echoes of the dead. People he once knew, drowned many years ago, claimed by Sargonus.

"To your stations, everyone. Prepare to shove off."

He turned to Zoey, standing tiptoe at his side, radiant with expectation. "Where to?"

"We must pass through the Fantastigate. Just follow the river. I'll tell you what to look for."

"The Fantastigate?" He considered asking her about it, but knew that whatever answer she could give would not satisfy him. "Very well."

He gestured for the drummer to begin, and a rhythmic thumping resonated from aft to bow, followed by one-hundred and seventy oars dipping into the water. The sudden acceleration was enough to knock them down, but he was holding tight to the mainstay, his other hand firm upon her wrist. With the wind in his face and the chop of oars in his ears, a sense of purpose and well-being settled upon him, that soon turned to joy. He was living an innocent time, before the deaths of his wife and son, when the rightness of his actions, and those of the Empire, were known with certainty.

Yes. Once, there was this. I was content.

But that certainty was an illusion. Even in life, there had never been peace. Doubt was ever-present. Already, he could hear them, the hushed voices from below. A quiet sobbing.

"What is that? What is that sound?"

He had asked no one in particular, but his first mate stood next to him, right where Zoey had been. "Captain, it's the cargo hold."

"But what could be making so pitiful a sound?"

"Would you like me to silence them, Sir?"

"Them? Who?"

"Don't you remember, Sir? The spoils, Sir?"

"Spoils! What spoils? What are you talking about? Show me."

His first mate shrugged, but did as was told, leading his captain to a trapdoor near the quarterdeck. There was a knotted rope tethered to a hole, and through this small opening, he could just make out the glimmer of their eyes, staring back at him.

"Open this hatch at once!"

As the floor was lifted, the sun washed into the small compartment. An odor of decay and human waste wafted up through the aperture, stinging his eyes and nostrils. Dozens of naked men and women, and even some children, were standing down below. Slaves. There was no room for reclining, or even for so much as squatting. Their ebony skin was patterned with ink, in the tradition of their tribe, but they were emaciated, mere skeletons draped in skin. With the motion of the ship, they were swaying, too feeble but to stare, the light of hope long-faded from their jutting eyes, their mouths drawn open in desperate pleas for water. An infant wept at its mother's teat, sucking hungrily, but she had not the nourishment to give. Some ways back, in the narrow confines of the hull, he caught glimpses of the elderly and the young, propped up corpses gathering flies.

"What . . . what is this?" Demacharon cried. "What have you done!"

"Your orders, Sir. The Boro people. They put up a fight, Sir, and we had to subdue them. No other choice, you said."

"I—I don't remember . . ." Even as he said this, the memory came to him, pounding at the walls of his subconscious, as did the lies he had told himself. "All for the greater good," he murmured aloud. "The good of Hedonia. The Empire. Mankind itself."

The ship was rising and falling with the swell, higher and higher, and crashing down again. He caught himself, wanting to swoon, to retch over the sides. But he was being called. The Boro did not speak the language of the Empire, but he understood them just the same. They knew his rank, and they were imploring him now, to end their lives. To be permitted to die.

"I do not . . . I do not . . ."

Faces dispersed and pooled below him. None of the bodies remained, only faces, their eyes probing, judging, stabbing at him. It was then he could see, that Astor was among them, his skin as black and branded and pierced as theirs. His son was one of the Boro.

Demacharon collapsed into the pit, the hatch diminishing as he fell, the light shrinking until nothing could be seen but a faint star in a gloomy sky. The ship and the river were no longer and he was surrounded. He pushed his way through them, frail bodies folding at his fists, but as each one fell, more appeared. The faces were pressing against his, whispering sins in his ears, and always the staring, accusing eyes. He called his son's name, shouted it, but Astor did not look his way, receding beyond reach.

The Boro swarmed him, pulling him to his knees, tearing at his garments, ripping apart his flesh. Feeding upon him.

Murderer!

Rapist!

Slave trader!

And all while he was screaming, he accepted what he knew to be his fate. For he was a horrid, evil man, no better than Zaibos. How could he have been so foolish, to seek redemption, to believe it could exist for someone like him? At that moment, he wanted only to be devoured, to drown in the River of Oblivion, but even this was too great a mercy. Darkness and desolation enveloped him, until only the voices remained, echoing his sins.

Murderer! Rapist! Slave trader!

His eyes were gone. So how could he still be seeing? What was it? A *light* . . . a glimmer in the abyss? He marveled at its strange beauty, even when there was nothing left of him to feel. And he remembered. He remembered that she was still beside him. She had not abandoned him.

He was kneeling by her bedside, his head cradled in her lap, confessing his sins. Weeping in her arms. Despite everything he had said that night in her cabin, she had not hated him. She had forgiven him. She had even loved him.

Radia . . .

Light blazed against the darkness and his tormentors vanished like shadows in the sun. White-gold permeated his eyes, suffused every part of his being. He stood blinded in the brilliance. The trappings of the legionnaire had fallen from him, and he was naked, a boy no older than eight. It was the same year he had been forced to leave his mother, to enter the barracks and learn the ways of war.

"Who . . . what are you?"

His vision adjusted to the source of the light, which was coming into focus, condensing into a solitary shape. She stepped down from the sky to greet him, a towering woman, with skin the color of green pastures and hair like the crests of a wave, and eyes of two different colors like the moons.

"I am the Goddess," she intoned, "but I go by many names. I have been called Zobaba and Aenya, and Alashiya. The Ancients named themselves after me—Zoë, meaning *Life*. But you know me by another name, don't you?" She smiled, stirring something deep and familiar within him. "The name of my avatar. The name you gave me, after the sister you so love."

"Noora."

The towering being shrank, the hue of her flesh changing like a leaf that has fallen, until a young girl stood before him.

"Radia!" He embraced her as he might a daughter, and did not let her go until the tears flowed freely. "Radia, I knew . . . somehow. I've always known what you were, but I refused to believe."

"How could you have?" she asked. "I don't quite believe it myself."

"It was just a feeling, really, what I was trying to explain that day in Yefira, before Zaibos took you. Long ago, I chose death over life, only to wake in a desert far to the west. Something prevented my abandoning this world, and I knew I had to find that thing. And in the peaks of the Crown, I found you. I have never been a man of faith, Radia. What I did in Hedonia, I did for my people, never for the gods. Or so I'd thought, before meeting you, before swearing an oath to a goddess."

"That's not exactly how it is," she said. "The Goddess is in everything that lives, in every fish and tree and person. Even in you. Radia is my avatar, my voice. I speak directly through her."

"Still, even when I am near you—her—in this plane or the next, the darkness lifts from me, even though . . . I cannot say I am deserving of it."

"The demons of this place are born from your own heart, Dimmy. Each and every night, you have been tormenting yourself. And why should that be so? Because you are a good man. Because you have never abided by the role Fate has given you." She paused, her moonlit eyes penetrating his. "There is no damnation in this universe, nor divine redemption. Only the connections we make, between our lives and another's, the enlightenment that is knowing we are *all* the Goddess. This is what is meant by *love*. And there is no greater power. Zaibos is hateful and cruel, only because he thinks himself apart from those he torments. He is not."

At the corners of his vision, he became aware of two people, a woman and a boy. Lingering phantoms, forever beyond his reach. Staring. Silent.

"If I am not damned . . . why don't they recognize me?"

"You've made yourself invisible to them. But don't feel bad about it. Even in the world above, people are invisible to one another, because they see only with their eyes. They hear, but do not listen. They look, but are blind to all but themselves. Compassion is the true sight."

"But my thoughts dwell only upon them. Up there," he lifted his head, as if to glimpse the waking world, "I have nothing, no one . . ."

"What about me? Don't you care about Noora?"

"More than you know, but—but I'd heard she'd been killed. That is why I . . ." Visions flashed before him, an apothecary, his lips wet with bitter nightshade, a vial rolling under a bed, his breathing coming hard and shallow and then not at all. "I needed to know if the rumors were true, if . . ."

"I'm very flattered, Dimmy, but I don't much care for suicide." Her hair started to swim, as if she were underwater, as butterflies of pure azure light fluttered about the strands. "I'll wake you up now."

"Wait. If you're here, what hope is left for us?"

"I am Life itself, Dimmy. Death cannot hold me long. But the people of Tyrnael continue to suffer under my stepbrother's rule, and it is not in my nature to fight him." She smiled, radiating golden fire, her eyes the moons themselves. "Find me. Help me. I am waiting for you."

31

Mandos

Mandos did not consider himself a man of deep thought. Ever the pragmatist, he was satisfied to do what was expected of him. Always, his mind turned to concrete realities, to food and shelter and matters of survival. Despite the cruel whims of his master, he saw no reason to consider the greater implications of his actions, nor did he take pleasure in the execution of his tasks. He maintained his focus only upon his duties and how best to serve his king.

Only now, Mandos had a problem. He could see it from the banister of the Compass Tower. What had started as a whisper in the taverns, and as a rumor in the barracks, was growing visibly apparent in the streets. Despite the burnings, the endless maiming and torture, and the shadow of perpetual dread cast from the throne, the peasants were rising. At the risk of their lives and the lives of their loved ones, they were fighting back. It was something he would never dare to do, if put in their situation, and was therefore beyond his comprehension.

"Tell me what you see, Captain."

Mandos turned from the bannister. He knew well the voice of his king, the muffled sound reverberating from behind the mask. And still, his heart seemed to fail him, however slightly, whenever his master spoke. *Why does he still wear it?* He had asked himself the question countless times. *We are not in battle. It must be so heavy, so stifling, so hot. If he wishes to intimidate his enemies, who of any significance remains to be intimidated? All Radia's handmaidens, all her sympathizers, have been executed.*

"I see the city, my lord. *Your* city. Glorious, is it not?"

"Pandering will get you nowhere, Mandos. The concern is plain on your face. It's the people, isn't it? They are protesting."

"It would appear so, my lord."

"You need not worry. This was to be expected."

Mandos did not lift his eyes, for he was loath to look upon the mask. He did not fear its physical form, but rather what it represented, that the man within was no more.

Zaibos moved through the archway and into the open air. Bridges stretched the length of the city, threads of gold touching every tower, collapsing on the horizon, an intricate web that long ago encompassed the planet. The people were gathering across it, along the terraced structures, the forested tiers. They were armed with common tools, those of their trade—cleavers, iron skillets, rolling pins, hammers and pitchforks. But a vast number went without, standing against armored soldiers with naked courage, angry shouts and righteous conviction.

"There has not been any violence," Mandos informed him. "At least not yet. I've commanded my men to keep the protesters from the tower, but their numbers are growing, and I fear our forces will be overrun."

"Who is leading them?"

"A man named Hugo, my lord. He was in the Night Watch, a high-ranking official. Many have rallied to his side, peasants and soldiers alike. We did not notice it for some time, because, well . . . it was his job to root out traitors." *And I was a fool to trust him!*

"Perhaps, if he were to be captured, and put upon the Hill of Lamentations . . ."

"That will not do, my lord. The people have taken it over. It has become a kind of marshaling point. All Tyrnael seems to have amassed there. My men can't get near it. They give speeches there, and . . ."

"And what?"

"She is there."

"She? Who?"

"Radia, my lord. It's where they are keeping the body. At the peak of the hill."

Mandos could sense the anger swelling behind the mask.

"Even in death, she defies me! She gives them hope!" Zaibos clenched his metal fist, making as if to strike him.

"There have also been talks of strange happenings, near the body. They've yet to bury her, so she lays on the bier as if in sleep, never decomposing. My informants tell me that even some of her injuries appear to be healing. What's more, witnesses claim a great camphor tree has sprouted up around her. You can see it from here, but for a tree of such girth to grow as it has, it would take centuries. I suspect they planted it in the dead of night, and are calling it a miracle to woo the masses." He paused, doubting his own words, adding, "At least, I can think of no more plausible explanation."

"None of it matters. They will all be dealt with shortly."

The ice in his master's voice alarmed even him, who had done many cruel things, and witnessed much atrocity. "I was not informed of any countermeasures."

"You were not informed because it does not involve you."

"I do not understand. If not I, who—"

"I have sent for Bloodsnot. They did well in Yefira, and should have no trouble dealing with this little insurrection."

"Bogrens, here, inside the city? It's never been done, never in all the ages!" Mandos could not hide his outrage. His tongue was already betraying him, though he knew it might cost him his life.

"Take care how you address me, Captain. You have been of great use to me so far, and I would hate to lose you."

"My apologies, Master. I simply meant to inquire of the people, in practical terms. What happened in Yefira was a massacre. If that should happen here, to your own subjects, who will you govern?"

"The strong, Mandos, the strong! For too long, this city has been a cradle for infants. Without war, without sickness, without death, the people have become soft. They'd never survive beyond the Crown. Now, there will be a cleansing. The weak blood will be washed out, and what remains will make up a new society, the architects of a global empire. We will reclaim the mantle of the Zo, and take this world, all that is rightfully ours."

Mandos stood quivering at the thought of bogrens and horg rampaging through the city. It would be like in Yefira, but a hundredfold, and the people would have nowhere to hide, nowhere to flee. Where the streets gave way to raw earth, there was only ice and impassable mountains beyond. These were his kin, men and women he had known since childhood. The bogrens lived for bloodshed and would leave nothing alive. With this final realization, the truth he had been denying these many cycles could be denied no more. He was a soldier in the service of a madman. No, a monster.

"Do you have something to say to me, Captain?"

Yes. If the people are so weak-blooded, how do they still defy you? It was what he had wanted to say, but Mandos was a practical man, and he knew it would avail him nothing. "No, my lord. All will be as you desire."

Making certain no one was following, Mandos rushed to the stairwell. But to move about in secret was not a difficult thing to do. The tower was mostly empty, except for his men, who kept out of sight in the lower levels, and the Silent, Zaibos's praetorian guard. Occasionally, he might run into a cook or a scullery maid. Someone still had to prepare the meals, do the cleaning and the mending. But they never looked at him directly, and if spoken to, would answer only in the affirmative. *Yes, my lord. Whatever it is you wish, my lord. At once, my lord.* There was a time he might have called them friends. His children had been raised with theirs, and had attended the same schools, and reveled in the same festivals. He remembered their name days, their joining ceremonies, the funerary march of their patriarchs. Now, as second to Zaibos, nothing existed between them but fear.

Few could be counted who had not been made to know grief, and Mandos was largely the cause of it. Under the king's command, he saw to every execution and punishment. The woman who had brought him his roasted pheasant this very day . . . her husband had openly defied the king, and Mandos had given the order to end his life. She never spoke of it, but it hung in the air between them, a dark, brooding cloud.

The tower was far older than anyone could recount, and doubtless, there were secret chambers even he was not privy to. But the steps leading to the dungeons were not unknown to him. While no prisoners were kept under Solon's dynasty, the dungeon had served as a place for storing things best left forgotten, for volatile, explosive powders, and poisons, and materials of dark sorcery.

Descending to the lower levels was like moving into the past and into a darker age. He could see the years rolling backwards in the stone, the gleaming white of the Compass Tower giving way to rough-hewn masonry yellowed with lichen. At the bottom step, he came to a chamber, a ring of braziers burning dimly from above. Manacles were bolted to the walls, and chains hung down like curtains, most of them rusted to a greenish hue. In the center of the room, there was the bronze likeness of a great beast. A hatch hung open from its belly, ashes spilling out if it and into a large black mound between the statue's hind legs. Bones were hidden there, he knew—he had only to sift through the remains. It never failed to make him shudder, remembering the screams that echoed, the agonizing sound blasting from its brass nostrils. People were cooked alive, in a furnace shaped like a saurian, and he had been the one to put them there. Why had he done it? For a greater Tyrnael? To turn the city over to bogrens?

Horizontal bars lined the walls, prison cells adjacent to the furnace. Every cell was unoccupied but for one. The solitary prisoner was not permitted to die. Zaibos had made certain of it. The best physicians in the kingdom had been tasked with treating his injuries, keeping him alive and fully aware.

Looking into the narrow recess, Mandos found it difficult to comprehend what he was seeing. How could such a sack of blood and cloth and stitching, be human? From below his top lip, the man's entire skull was missing, his jaw and teeth and chin, all of it gone. To keep his fluids from spilling out, the prisoner had been fitted with an iron clasp. But it was his cheek that most unnerved him, which was swollen and green and pulsating. Something was alive inside, inside his head, writhing just beneath the flesh. He could see the pustules poking out from the nostrils and lining the cracks in his face. Pain spiders. One bite could cripple a man with agony, and soon there would be thousands, a human face a nursery for pain spiders. How could he have endured their nesting? Stranger still, Zaibos had not ordered it. He could not have, if he had truly wished his prisoner to survive.

"Eros. I know you cannot speak, but if you can hear me, nod your head."

The man in the cell jerked suddenly. His pupils were dead white, like a fish's, after it has been pulled from the water and has stopped flopping, and yet he was awake, staring out through vacant eyes. "Listen carefully, Eros, for there is little time. The spiders in your head, they are about to hatch, and when they do, you will die. I do not doubt it. In fact, I cannot imagine how you've managed to last this long."

The man in the cell stood, looking more powerful and more animated than he should have been. He reached two fingers into a crease in his face, where the iron clasp was bolted to the bottom half of his skull, and with those same two fingers, now wet with blood, he painted a single word on the wall.

REVENGE.

"I can give you what you want," Mandos said, "Zaibos . . . he has gone insane, completely insane. He wants to kill everyone in the city. I cannot allow this to happen. I have friends here, you see. Family." He fished his pockets for a key, and from his belt produced a long dagger. "I've heard stories, that you can get things done, that no man can escape you. You failed the first time, but you were not prepared for such a betrayal. I understand this. Now, if I see to your escape, can you still manage it?"

Eros clambered across the floor toward the front of his cell, like something hunched and broken and far from human, and ever so slowly lifted himself to his full height, his sickly white hands firm about the bars, and nodded.

"Good. But remember, if you should not succeed, this must not get back to me. Betray me, and I'll dig those spiders out myself, and still find a way to keep you alive until you rot of old age. Understood?"

32

Uggy

"**H**ow I'm missing you, Noora. How I wish you were near me. How I long for your . . ."

No, no, that's no good. What rhymes with Noora? Nothing. That's what. Face it, you're as good at songwriting as you are at archery.

With his lute quiet across his lap, Ecthros peered out over the great chasm and into the darkness, hoping for a glimmer of better things to come, anything to lift his spirits. But all that remained were memories, mostly of his flight under the stars, together with the girl of his dreams.

He wanted to be alone, far from the commotion of Yefira—or what remained of it—and the lonely precipice where he was sitting perfectly reflected his mood. But he was also seeking inspiration, to immortalize his beloved in song. He longed to see Noora's face again, if only in his mind's eye, to count every follicle and freckle. But his longing came coupled with guilt, for such thoughts betrayed the memory of his fallen people.

If not for Thulken, who had led them into hiding, into the hanging homes built into the face of the chasm, none of them would have survived. So many were gone, friends and family, but losing Davos pained him most of all. He had been like a father to Ecthros, and it seemed impossible that he should be no more. Surely, Davos was away on one of his voyages, discovering new lands, soon to return with marvelous, never-before-seen wares. His uncle was possessed by life, had embraced every day. How could such a man, who loved the world so fully, be no longer in it?

And still, despite all the tragedy, Ecthros's thoughts were fixed upon a girl he had met but three cycles ago. Perhaps, a young man can only be expected to endure so much sorrow, before he becomes numb to it, before turning to the selfish longings of his own heart. Davos was gone to the Taker. There was no changing that. But for Noora, or Radia, or whatever her true name, hope remained. Zaibos could have killed her the moment she was captured, but did not. For what purpose she was allowed to live, he could not bring himself to fathom. The Monster King was anything but kind, and yet Ecthros continued to hope, to hope beyond reason. What else was there to do?

Forcing the worst scenarios from his head, he looked to the stringed instrument in his lap. The sound resonated from deep within the wood, echoing from the rocks to every glittering home, but where the light failed to reach, the music did not carry. One by one, the notes dropped in pitch over the chasm, growing ever somber, until the melody was lost.

"He's awake! Come quick! Come quick!"

Colin stood at the base of the steps, his hair frazzled by the wind, his tunic disheveled after fitful nights of hard bedding. Without hesitation, Ecthros leapt to his feet and followed. They climbed a good while, moving carefully, for the stones were narrow and uneven and rounded by time, cut into the cliff face by a people who had lived before the founding of Yefira.

Here and there and from remote places all around them, windows spilled into the night, like stars across a wall of shadow. Most of the houses had been abandoned days ago, their wicks smothered, their interiors cold and dim. People too sickly or stubborn to move remained in hiding, the natural rock formation difficult to discern from their places of dwelling. One had to look for telltale signs of life, for post railings and makeshift walkways, an occasional flower pot, a saucer of milk left out for a cat. But a small number of his kin refused to be cowed. The lamps in their windows burned dimly but defiantly, lighting the path for Ecthros and Colin to follow, up and up to Thulken's abode. The archon's door was painted a bright blue, thirty feet below the ground, and the steps leading to and from it were well defined.

Like every chasm home he had been in, the living space was small, limited by the difficulty of hewing through solid limestone. It was enough for a kitchen table for four, a drop-down bed and a simple furnace carved into the corner. His people had chosen the foothills above to build lodgings for bigger families and to plant gardens. After the invasion, he doubted whether they would return, if Yefira continued to exist at all.

Crowded about the room, he saw Thulken and Toby, and Kiki and her three daughters. He also recognized the lean ebony figure that was Krow, and another of the bird man's kind unlike any he had met before. By her willowy shape and bright azure plumage, Ecthros could discern her gender. But he was not there to see them, only the man standing groggily opposite the door.

"You're awake!"

"How long have I been out?" Demacharon looked as if he had just risen from the dead, and sounded no better.

"Days," Kiki answered him. "We thought we'd lost you."

"Kiki." His eyes, yellowed and bloodshot, settled upon her. "I am sorry. I failed your husband. Failed all of you. But you made it out. Niah?"

"She's alright." Liana and Athalia were buried in her bosom, like extensions of their mother. Niah stood apart, with Hazel nestled in her arms, his pink nostrils quivering, his fur rising with every breath. It seemed somehow strange, that a rabbit should have survived, where so many had not.

"The last thing I remember, I was running from that monster, and then something hit me." He winced, discovering the bandages at his side. "And everything went black."

"They got you out," Thulken admitted, turning to Ecthros, and his grandson, Tobias. "Zaibos is not much of a runner in all that armor. He thought to catch you up on that red lizard of his, but Krow and his men kept it at bay. Alas, you were felled by a bogren's bow, and they surrounded you. Had it not been for these brave young men and their flying contraption, the bogrens would have cut you to pieces. We managed to remove the arrow and staunch the bleeding, which was considerable. Our healers did what they could. But we were uncertain. I thank the Goddess you are still with us."

With some effort, Demacharon made it to the kitchen table, slowly lowering himself into a chair. They waited for him to speak, as if he would know what to do.

"Have you ever had such a dream, that even in waking, you did not know what was real, and what was not?"

The others looked on in silence, as did Thulken. The archon had lost everything he was sworn to protect. His once-proud features were like those of a man ripped apart and shoddily rebuilt. Doubtless, sleep had eluded him since the day of the attack.

"Tell us," Thulken murmured. "What was your dream?"

"The images are fleeting, shrinking to nothing as I think of them. I remember an apothecary, and I remember asking him for nightshade. I had wanted to find her—needed to find her— in death."

"Who?" Ecthros asked, though he knew the answer already. Everyone did.

"Radia."

"I don't understand. You sought to find Noora in your dreams? To what end?"

"The Ilmar believe in dream journeys," Demacharon explained, "journeys into other worlds, that are no less real, no less consequential than the one we are now sitting in. I thought such beliefs to be nonsense, the simple superstitions of a primitive mind, but she spoke to me . . . needs me to return to her. Radia is waiting for me in Tyrnael."

"So she's alive?"

"I cannot say. Both the living and the dead communicate through dreams, or so I've heard. It is the middle country between life and death."

"But if she's gone," it pained him even to say it, "how can we help her?"

"Her people, Ecthros. They suffer under the yoke of a madman, and it is my duty to set things right. I made an oath."

"As did I. If you go to Tyrnael, you'll need a good archer. I mean, every good party needs a man with a bow, and I am getting better at it with each passing day."

"No!" Thulken's hands fell heavily upon the table. "We must not get involved. You must remain, son of Yefira, to help us rebuild. I will not suffer to mourn another of my people."

"Staying here is foolish. Zaibos lusts for the whole world! His armies will trample over every blade of grass on Aenya! Make no mistake, he is bound to return, to put us all in shackles. Is that what you want? We have no choice but to lend Demacharon our aid."

"You dare to call me fool? I am your archon!"

"An archon of what? There is nothing here but ruin and sorrow."

"All the more reason you are needed here, to restore what was lost—the more strong backs we have at our disposal, the better."

"You're wrong, Archon-Thulken. How can you suggest we do nothing, after everything we've endured? Zaibos must be made to pay!"

"Such is a young man's heart—quick to action, yet short on wisdom. If you had any sense at all, you would see the folly in this gesture, and take the measured path. Nothing awaits you in Tyrnael but your doom."

"So be it! Better that, than to live to old age as a coward."

"Ecthros!" Kiki admonished. "You go too far."

Demacharon lifted his head from the table, clearing his throat, and everyone fell silent. "The debt you have paid for our coming here can never be compensated. But the boy is right. I have known men like Zaibos. Our history is written in blood—blood spilled by such tyrants. He will not stop until the world is his. And there is another thing also. I am sure you have all felt it. Radia is more than she appears to be, and if we do not act soon, we may lose that which is more precious than even our lives."

"Whatever could that be?" Kiki asked.

"Life itself, my lady. The world we hope to pass on to our children, and our children's children. Therefore, we fight, why all righteous men must fight," he added, turning to her three daughters.

Thulken looked on, anxiously combing his fingers through his beard. "I do not understand. She's just a lass, yet you speak of her as if she were a . . . a goddess."

At that moment, the avian stepped forward, and a silent exchange passed between her and Demacharon. Did he recognize her? She could not be mistaken for any other woman, for she was slenderer than humanly possible. Intricately wrought gold was fitted to her arms, neck, and ankles. Otherwise, she was dressed from crest to ankle in feathers, the wings under her arms shifting in the firelight from deepest blues to gleaming topaz. But it was her eyes that most caught his attention. They were fawn-shaped, as big as limes, wrapping partly about the sides of her face. She reminded Ecthros of Radia, beautiful, but in a strange, nonhuman way.

"Permit me to speak, good archon," she twitted, her vocal cords sounding sharply. "I am Avia of Nimbos, and I wish to tell you of a story rooted in our lore, though you may find it unusual.

"We believe in one whom we call the Ascendant, or Aza. He is the Proto-ancestor, the first of our kind to discover flight, who looks down upon us and our world. Every few millenniums, it is said, Aza descends from Heaven, taking the form of a mortal being to teach us the path of righteousness.

"If Radia is as you say, she may be this One, come again in human form. But if she has been harmed, destroyed even, it would explain what we have been witness to these past moons, what men-kind are blind to from below.

"When Lunestes first devoured Aza, the world was torn asunder, and as you may know, the oceans of the West boiled into the ether, as in the East, the waters turned to bitter ice. Without the Most High One, to guide and protect us from evil, cataclysm ensued. So it comes again, we fear. Crops have been languishing the world over, and famine will soon be upon us, the likes of which Aenya has not seen since the first dark age."

"You expect me to swallow such drivel? I, for one, do not believe the girl was a goddess, or Aza, or whatever else you wish to call her. I know you've been smitten by her, Ecthros, but it takes more than a pretty face and a pleasant disposition to convince me of divinity. Come now, these are myths we're talking, nothing to die for!"

"Myths they may be," Avia answered politely, "but there is wisdom to be gleaned from stories of old, however fanciful."

"Well, *I* am convinced," Ecthros remarked. "For the good of Aenya, we must not tarry here any longer."

Now Krow stepped forward, turning to the boy. "New sails have been fitted to the *Cloud Breaker*. With your blessing, I shall captain the vessel in Davos's stead, and deliver whomever is willing, beyond the Crown and into Tyrnael."

"No." Demacharon started pacing the length of the table. "No," he said again. "Zaibos has an army. What do we have? Myself, a boy with a bow, and two avians, one who cannot fly."

"I'll go!" Colin cut in. "I've always wanted to see Tyrnael."

"Me, too," said Toby.

Thulken scowled at them, and the boys shrank away, swallowing hard.

"What we need is a plan." Demacharon peered through the small window, his face bathed by the turquoise glow of the greater moon. Yefira was quiet, sleeping, but the tranquility was an illusion. Who could doubt the nightmares the villagers must be having? So long as Zaibos lived, none of them could know peace.

"You've commanded the most powerful army the world has ever seen," Ecthros said to him. "If you can't think of a way, nobody can."

A map was pinned to the wall, depicting the length of the Great River, from the Crown of Aenya Mountains to the port of Kratos. Demacharon took it down, flattening it across the kitchen table. They all gathered about him now, and the map, as if expecting some answer to present itself.

"This isn't a battle we can win. Zaibos has every advantage, save one, a weakness we can exploit. Noora . . . she's been right all along. *Love is greater than hate.*"

Thulken was looking no less somber, but the Hedonian had piqued his interest. "What do you mean by this?"

"Six hundred years ago, in Hedonia, a man named Bekkhus claimed the city. He was first commander of the legion. He marched into the Temple, slew the mystics, and put the High Priest's head on a pike. With the full force of the imperial army and no one to oppose him, he declared himself emperor. Like Zaibos, he ruled through fear and intimidation, but the people did not take kindly to him. The more they resisted, the more radical his efforts to maintain control, until the streets were lined with crucifixions."

"So what happened to him?" Colin asked, timidly.

"He was murdered in his sleep, by his own guards."

Thulken took a chair and sat beside him. "You are suggesting an assassination?"

"I am saying there is no other way. We must cut off the head of the dragon. If we were to do this in Kratos or Thetis or Shemselinihar, the people might rise against us, and the throne would fall to the next in line. But there is no second to Zaibos—he has seen to that personally. If he were removed, Tyrnael would unquestioningly support its rightful heir."

"There is wisdom in this, but also great folly," Thulkin argued. "Even if you are successful, you do not know whether

Radia lives to take the throne, and should you fail, the Monster King is likely to retaliate. Your chances of success are close to none. There is no way into Tyrnael but by air. How do you imagine coming down from the sky and into port, without being seen? And should you devise a way, how do you suppose to sneak into the Compass Tower, which is no doubt heavily guarded?"

Silence pervaded the room again, as even Demacharon was at a loss for how to respond. Ecthros, all the while, could feel the anger building within him, matched only by his despair. Zaibos had taken everything from him—his people, his uncle, the girl he loved, and there was nothing he could do about it.

"There is another way . . ."

"Kiki!" the archon rebuffed her. "No!"

She stepped up to the table, fitfully wringing her hands. "You've all spoken your peace. Now it's my turn. You're blinded by remorse, archon—you feel you've failed us, and you fear to fail us again. But we can abandon our homes if need be, find a new place to settle. There're few of us left, and the journey won't be too hard. My girls and I are ready. But someone must take the fight to that monster. And Dimmy has a right to know."

"To know what?"

She turned to her daughters. "Athalia, go fetch him, will you?" The young woman ran through the door and into the night, the wind howling in her wake through the open frame.

After a short time, she appeared again, a mischievous smile on her face. "Please, Dimmy, sir, don't get angry."

"Angry? How could I be angry with—" he began, and suddenly the table tumbled over as he reached for her, and Athalia went sprawling to the ground. Everyone was shouting, but Demacharon was not listening. He moved with a murderous passion, fumbling awkwardly at his side for a hilt that was not there, and with his elbow set firmly, he pinned the diminutive creature by the neck to the wall.

"What is this! Why are you here?"

The creature squirmed and squealed, his bulbous eyes darting frightfully. Even for a bogren, he was small, standing no taller than the Hedonian's waist, with limbs no thicker than Liana's.

"Please!" Niah cried. "Please don't hurt him! He's good! He's good!"

Slowly, hesitantly, Demacharon loosened his hold, but he did not release the creature, not until Kiki tugged at his arm, and pleaded, "He saved us, Dimmy. I don't know why, but he did. Remember the hole in the floor? In my house?"

The bogren dropped to the floor and the girls surrounded him. They were defending him. He was like a fourth child, albeit a hideous, *hideous* child.

"I don't understand. Who is this?"

"His name is Uggy," Niah answered, "but it's not because he's ugly. That's just his name. Please, don't call him ugly."

Ecthros knew what the Hedonian must be feeling. After witnessing so many of their kind murdering the innocent, it was a difficult transition to make. His hatred was deep, instinctive, but there was always a story to be told, to bring about understanding, help curb the violence.

"I don't blame you," Thulken remarked. "I reacted much the same way, when I found out."

"All right," Demacharon said, "but why would he help us? Why would he betray his own race?"

"Ugh no like bogren," he answered. "Work and work below, kill and kill above. Fall in magma. Everyone laughs. And hungry. Hungry every day."

The Hedonian was visibly shaken, Ecthros could see. "Where did you learn to speak?"

"Radia," he replied. "She good to Ugh. She play with me. But then, she go away." The pitiable way in which he said this, gave even the hardened commander pause. Ecthros waited for Demacharon to answer, but he remained contemplative.

"He can help us," Kiki said at last. "We've talked to him. We've learned things. The bogrens don't travel over land. They have a labyrinth of tunnels. That's how they got here, how they surprised us. Uggy, he knows a secret passage, that none of the other bogrens know about. It's how he met her. I believe he can lead you, all the way into the Compass Tower, along a path where no one will see you."

"No. We have to consider an alternative. For all we know, Zaibos may have sent him here, to lure us into a trap."

"He saved all of our lives!" Kiki asserted, abutting him with her flour-caked apron, in a way that Ecthros could not help but admire. "If it weren't for him, none of us would be here. My children would not be here. If I can trust him with my daughters, you can blasted well trust him to lead you to Zaibos."

33

Demacharon

It began with the death of a child.

The city stood divided between those who feared the king and those outraged by his cruelty. Zaibos's forces were ceding more and more land to the revolutionaries, who had taken the *Hill of Lamentations* and the neighboring districts. Lines were continuously being drawn and redrawn, as during the night, sentries on both sides patrolled against acts of treason. Liberty was growing by the cobblestone. Soldiers who had been forced into fealty—shamed by their actions—changed colors from the black and red of the fist and morningstar to the gold and white of the unicorn. With Zaibos's influence waning, dissent spread from hushed tones behind closed doors to impassioned speeches in town squares. Among the most vocal orators was a textile worker, an eloai by the name of Esse, for whom thousands gathered to listen. After every rally, she supplied banners emblazoned with sigils for every trade—a hammer and an anvil to represent the smiths, a bag of flour and a rolling pin for the bakers, shears damasked with leafy patterns for the gardeners, spoons and kettles for the cooks. Simple signage could not reasonably be outlawed and, in this way, Esse with her army of seamstresses managed to mark off the streets loyal to the line of Radia.

At the onset, the protests had been mostly bloodless, the predominant weapons words. But at the center of Tyrnael, where every bridge and walkway converged, where the mountain crowned by the Compass Tower loomed above all, the king's grip was absolute, the highborn families in the terraced structures adjacent to the tower living in perpetual dread. So it was here that the revolutionaries and the loyalists came to an impasse.

It was a brisk morning, the likes of which the eldest could not remember. Not a blade of green broke from the earth, and the trees were naked of leaves and twisted like fingers stiffened by rigor mortis. Snowbanks formed along the alleyways, the tops of the hanging gardens were all layered in white, and the stones in the streets were slick with ice. The ancient capital was no longer insulated by the mountains that surrounded them. What magic once emanated from the city, the eternal spring of the Zo, had long faded. And still, the people gathered, bracing against the encroaching cold, kneading aching palms and fingers, their breath escaping from their faces in agitated clouds. But their hearts were like furnaces, the blood inside stewing. They came with pennons flying, thrice the height of the tallest man, sigils by the dozens rippling defiantly.

Those loyal to Zaibos moved hastily, far fewer in number, but more than making up for it in arms. With shields and helms and cuirasses all agleam in black, they greeted the gathering host. But the king himself did not yet know of the force at his gates, and so the soldiers were free to act upon their conscience. Their hearts filled with remorse, they came not to fight, but to urge the people to disperse.

The revolutionaries stood their ground. The defectors, donning silver and gold, implored the loyalists to turn sides. Many had once been friends, had been brothers, or sons.

Curses were exchanged, and shouts, and what ensued was a cacophony of vitriol. Bodies entwined in angry embraces, and limbs thrashed with kicks and punches. A farmer spat on a guard. Another threw his shoe. Gold bricks were lifted from the street and went flying, breaking harmlessly against the black shields, ringing against obsidian helms. Objects of all kinds continued to rain down until a scream cut through the noise, a sound of anguish fierce enough to give even the most frenzied among them pause. A circle was forming, a mix of people on both sides, all eyes upon two figures, a mother and a four-year- old girl. Cycles past, the little one had thrown a tantrum, when her unicorn banner was taken to be burned outside the Cosmos Theater. Now, her short auburn hair was running red, threads sticking to the cavity where a brick had fractured her skull.

"She will not wake!" cried her mother, the child limp in her arms.

In the span of a single breath, there was utter silence, but for the pleading of a mother. It was the catalyst turning the storm to thunder, and the two sides merged, consumed by a murderous rage. Butchers went into battle with their cleavers, as did bakers with their rolling pins, cooks with ladles, chimney sweeps with pokers. Those without tools used what was in reach—stones and branches and their own bloodied fists. The guards who had not wanted to fight acted to defend themselves, the bodies of their attackers stumbling helplessly onto their swords. And the rioters swarmed in retaliation about each act of manslaughter, twisting off helmets and caving skulls under their heels.

The line was moving closer to the Compass Tower, the mob trampling over the soldiers in black. A small number of loyalists attempted turning sides, but it was too late. The revolutionaries had exhausted what mercy was in them and were now fueled by a need for vengeance. They continued to advance, stealing swords and maces from the dead, and the fist and morningstar retreated to the narrows of the bridge to form a wall of shields. Here, from the rocks and the copses where they had gone into hiding, the king's archers loosed their bows. Pennons fell, poles tumbling from the hands of the fallen, and as bodies started to litter the ground, the rioting host lost heart, scattering into the side streets.

"No! Do not give in! We must carry on!" Esse rushed forward as others pushed past her in retreat. She scrambled over the wounded to reach the side of a dying man. An arrow had punched through his throat and he was gurgling blood. The sigil at his side marked him for a baker. With both hands, she lifted his sign back into the sky, crying, "Now is the time to remember your fathers! Your sons and daughters! All the Usurper has taken from us!" She tugged at the hidden thread running the length of the pole, and the abstract flour and rolling pin ripped along the seam, separating from the layer beneath it. Every bannerman followed her example, their trade signs falling away to reveal another image in gleaming white and gold.

"For Radia!"

They charged, and the archers—their bows pregnant—did not release their volley. Against the unicorn, the sigil of their fathers and forefathers, their arrows could not fly.

Even through his steely mask, Mandos could see that his master was troubled. It was in the way he paced along the rim, studying the battle intently only to steer sharply away.

"They are so much like ants, wouldn't you say?"

Mandos was not accustomed to such heights and did not enjoy looking down, to where the skirmish was unfolding. He preferred keeping his eyes on the white-tipped mountains circling in all directions. More unnerving still, the room was only semi-enclosed, with a curved wall behind the throne and dais with the other half open to the sky.

"You are correct as always, my lord. From here, they do look like ants."

"That is not what I meant. The people of this city are insignificant. They squabble and squirm, eking out some paltry measure of existence, and then they expire, the universe utterly indifferent to the fact that they've ever lived. When you are walking, Mandos, do you concern yourself with the fate of ants? Do you bother to step around them? Or do you crush them under your boot?"

"I have not given it much thought, my lord, but I suppose you're right."

"And yet, captain, would you not give it some thought, should they come into your home? Should you find them crawling in your pantry? In your bed when you are sleeping?"

"I—I would not like that, my lord."

Zaibos moved closer, more quickly than he would have liked, or thought possible in such armor. "If you would not have ants in your home, why then do you allow them into mine?"

Suddenly, Mandos could not breathe. Tears broke from his eyes involuntarily, the pain shooting from his throat to his skull.

The captain of the guard was no weakling. From a young age, he had been trained in the art of battle, and the respect given to him by his men was well earned. But now, he felt as helpless as a child. The king's presence was arresting. Overpowering.

Zaibos dragged him to the edge of the sky, pressing his face to the floor. "Do you see them? Look there. Look at the ants coming into my home!"

Mandos struggled to answer, to pry the mailed fingers from his throat, but was unable.

"What was that? I can't seem to hear you."

"I . . . I . . ." *I have been loyal, done all that you've asked.* That is what he wanted to say. But the king's rage could not be tempered, and Mandos was beginning to accept the inevitable. His decision to turn traitor, to free the assassin imprisoned below, had come too late to aid him.

"Do you know why I have permitted you to live? The men obey you. You are their captain. And what is your duty? Your only duty to your king? Maintain order. Quell rebellion. Even to speak of Radia is treasonous. Yet, here they are, bearing her emblem!"

He turned Mandos's face like he would a puppet's, and from this new vantage, Mandos was made to see more of the battle, the people throughout the city, gathered along the terraced ridges, atop every bridge and walkway, men and women, young and old, eloai and highborn. Their allegiance could not be mistaken. He recognized the gold on white of their standard, unicorns cantering high above the crowds, a pennon for every dozen people. Legions of standard-bearers were marching upon the tower. Where did they get so many? How were they produced without his knowing?

"It is no matter," Zaibos said. "They do not yet realize it, but the great cleansing is upon them, when the weak-blooded shall be washed away. Look to the Eastern Gate!" His face was contorted in the direction of the ancient arch, and dimly he recalled sitting before the equine statues flanking its sides, with a man he once considered his friend, a fellow man-at-arms who had attempted to reason with him. "From this orifice," Zaibos went on, "a purifying iron will usher forth. Only, you will not live to see it, for I've no longer a use for you."

With a single motion, Mandos was lifted by the throat over the rim. He was kicking at empty air, and then he was falling, the world below rushing to greet him, his only thoughts that of regret. Upon his fellow citizens, he had sanctioned unspeakable acts, and to what end? At least, he was allowed one kindness. His death would be sudden.

Ecthros was gasping for air, his fist punching through topsoil and tile fragments. He felt as if he were rising from the dead. Gradually, he managed to grip the surface of the floor, hoisting himself up and out of the hole.

"I thought I'd never again see the light of day!"

Demacharon came up after him. He struggled a bit more, being the largest in their company, but, with a helping hand from Ecthros, he was soon standing in the room. Bogren tunnels were decidedly not made for humans.

"Here Radia meet Ugh," the little bogren remarked.

The pavilion was no doubt built by the Zo. A heavy sensation of time was upon it, years of stillness layered upon every surface, caked upon every stone. The air was thick with memory, the dust of ages glittering in the dreamy light pouring from the cracks in the walls.

"Look there," Ugh said. "A mammoth!"

Flora and fauna paraded about the walls of the room, flowers and fish and birds in faded colors, land beasts etched in stone, every living thing imaginable.

"It must have served as some kind of nursery," Demacharon said.

Ecthros brushed his fingers along the frieze. Most of it was eroded, or obscured by lichen, crumbling into a mossy powder at his touch. Some animals were broken, ziffs with missing heads, trikes with only three legs, ibs with one wing. "Radia never mentioned this place."

The Hedonian did not seem interested in exploration. "She didn't mention befriending a bogren, either."

"Maybe she was afraid of how we'd react. You know her. She'd make small talk with a dragon if you introduced her."

"Just keep your eyes open," he murmured, taking Ecthros aside. "This might still be a trap."

"After all we went through to get here? I think I cooked myself back there a couple of times. Honestly, I'd sooner wrestle Zaibos himself than cross another of those damned bridges. Is a railing too much to ask for? Surely, if the little guy wanted us dead, he'd have pushed us off at any of the hundred or so places we almost got killed crossing. Or he could have just called one of his pals over to—"

"You need to shut up. Listen."

"Sorry."

"It is quite possible he could be trying to win their favor by delivering us to one of their leaders," Demacharon explained. "But they don't like him. That much is clear. I could see the fear in his eyes when we were sneaking around. Lucky for us, we didn't get into a fight."

"I dunno. I would've liked to pick a few off with my bow after what they did in Yefira. Oh, sorry Ugh—I didn't mean you. I guess you're not *all* bad."

"Come, come!" the little creature gestured. He was like an overeager child, showing off his playroom, trying to describe what games they enjoyed, he and Radia, again and again calling her 'my friend.' But the human tongue was difficult for him to mimic, and they understood little of what he was saying.

They followed him to a sunlit archway that opened to the sky. Dusty fountains, a gazebo, and benches cut from solid granite decorated the courtyard, and trees neither of them had seen before, bearing strange golden fruit.

"Are we even in the palace?" Ecthros asked.

"I believe so. There are places hidden behind its outer walls, built before the reign of Solon. It's likely nobody has been here in a lifetime, no one but our friend here."

The little bogren perked up, his head resembling a grinning pumpkin. "Yes! Yes! Ugh friend of Radia's friend—" Ugh clapped his hands together, but before he could finish speaking, a shadow passed over them, an icy voice in answer to Demacharon.

They turned back toward the arch from whence they came, and before fully comprehending the evidence before their eyes, Ecthros was groping for his quiver, as the bogren ducked behind Demacharon's thigh.

At first glance, what stood before them appeared to be a short rider upon a tall, ebony horse, except where there should have been a beast's head was the torso of a man, encased in peels of hammered gold like jagged flower petals. The same dark coat of horsehair that grew over his body also covered his muscled limbs. His deep-set eyes glowed like embers, and his substantial beard and voluminous hair had the look of fire.

Severetrix sang from the Hedonian's hip and into his palm. "Who are you?"

A smirk spread across the creature's lips, but he did not acknowledge the question. "I see you wield a two-sword, a blade sharp enough to cut between atoms. Wherever did you procure such a weapon, I wonder?"

"I won't ask a second time. Who are you?"

"You dare threaten me, in my own domain? I am Nessus. Centaur. Master of this castle."

"What of the king? What of Zaibos? Does he not rule here?"

"That buffoon?" The centaur's expression melted away. "Do you really believe he is in control? True power does not show its face. It remains hidden, behind the stage, from where it can pull at the strings. That armor of his, who do you think gave it to him? And still, the fool insisted on painting it with blood, and adding spikes to it. For intimidation purposes, I suppose."

Demacharon went to speak, but was interrupted by the snapping of a bowstring. Ecthros's arrow cut between him and the centaur, stopping at the halfway mark, as if sticking to an invisible wall. There it remained, inert in space.

Nessus betrayed no emotion, other than curiosity. "Have you ever heard of the paradox of the missile?" He was reaching out, as if to pluck the arrow from the air. "It goes like this: for your missile to hit me, it must first cross half the distance between us, but in doing so, it must cross half of *that* distance, and so on. This halving can go on ad infinitum, which is why you will never be able to touch me."

"Your philosophy won't stop a good sword from going through you," Demacharon answered. "Allow me to demonstrate."

He moved to attack, as Ecthros nocked his bow again and the floating arrow shattered into twigs. What happened next could not be explained. A fiery pain split through his arm, forcing him to drop his arrow and clutch at his chest. Ugh was beside him, face-down in a briar patch, groaning. Demacharon was faring no better.

The centaur's outstretched hand had now become a fist. "This battle, it seems, will be anticlimactic. How do you propose to kill me, when I can crush your hearts with a thought?"

The Hedonian fought to remain on his feet, to raise his sword, but the pain was too great. Ecthros could feel it also, his body shriveling against the cold grip of death. And then, just as quickly as it had come, the agony subsided. When he looked again, the centaur's hands were at his sides.

"No, you will not be dying this day, not by my hand. Take up your arms and be gone. And if you should find my son, be sure to kill him."

When the blood was again free to flow through their veins, the three gathered together, and Demacharon spoke for them. "If Zaibos is your son, why do you let us go?"

"Because he has made a mess of things. By now, I had expected to be elsewhere, long departed from this accursed world."

"I do not understand."

"I will confer with you, but only because I have been in hiding too long, and the isolation has driven me to the brink of madness."

"Make it quick," Ecthros said. "We've a king to slay."

"Very well, I will be brief. I came to Tyrnael seeking the knowledge of the Zo. Learning all I could of their craft, I hoped to find the means to escape death, and after deciphering their texts, I assumed this body, having partaken of the essence of the unicorn."

Demacharon looked on, incredulous. "Wait . . . you're Anabis? The man who cured Radia of her illness?"

"I was Anabis! And no, I cured nothing, because she was never sick. When we arrived, she was in a state of metamorphoses, a state of becoming . . . *more*. The king's healers were baffled by a disease she did not have.

"I admit that I did not fully understand what she was. I still do not. Naturally, the king would not allow me to dissect her, and so I made a simulacrum, a copy, and it taught me enough about her physiology to maintain her mortal nature."

"The vials she was imbibing . . ."

"That was my concoction, yes. I tricked the king, and the princess, into believing she would need the potions to survive.

That way, should they discover my agenda, they would have no choice but to let me be, to continue my studies. That was before. Before the death of Anabis, before becoming . . . *this*."

Ecthros's curiosity was more than piqued. His mind begged for answers, to learn all he could about the girl he loved, and yet he decided to reject the story being proffered. "Why are we even listening to this spiel?" he said at last. "It could all be a lie! Tell us, if you know so much, where is Radia now?"

"She is dead, of course."

"No! I don't believe you!" He lunged at the centaur, prepared for a fight he knew he could not win, but Demacharon was quick to restrain him.

"I can sense how much she meant to you, boy. Young love is a powerful thing. But I did not kill her. Not directly, at least. You see, I thought that I needed her heart to open a door."

"A door to what?" Demacharon asked.

"To *Infinity*. Do you think the Zo, with all their power, went extinct? No. They merely abandoned this petty world. I only needed the *Heart of Reality* . . . or so that is how I had interpreted my findings, taking *reality* to mean *nature*, and nature to mean the Goddess. Fool that I was, I read the text literally. Her heart is nothing but an organ. A pump for blood.

"Therefore, I am releasing you, because I need more time, because my fool son has opened the gates to the subhuman spawn of the dark hemisphere, and they are not known to be a race of letters."

Mandos landed not with a thump, but a crack, his body breaking against the rocks at the base of the waterfall. Every eye facing the tower watched him fall. For his men, it was an ominous sign.

When the last of those loyal to Zaibos had given up the fight, the ground started to swell in protest. People were toppling, pushing into others in the crowd. Confusion gave way to screams. Men and women on both sides lay crippled, nursing severed ankles, not knowing what was happening to them. Elsewhere, faces were being mutilated, and hearts carved out. One gruesome death followed the next, and there came a terror like nothing before known in Tyrnael.

Diminutive creatures had infiltrated their ranks. Moving swiftly through the dense mob, scampering on all fours no higher than Esse's knees, the bogrens at first went unnoticed. They had come from no place she could see, though she watched them now, paralyzed and helpless, as they cut a deadly swath through loyalist and revolutionary alike. They were like children playing at murder, gray and wrinkled and hideous, their curved daggers falling indiscriminately.

"Bogrens are in the city!" someone cried, intensifying the panic.

Now the soldiers in black and red fought alongside those in silver and gold. But the people of Tyrnael had never seen such things. Bogrens were creatures of legend, the stuff of nightmares, stories to keep the young in line. If the king could control such forces, what other powers could he unleash upon them, Esse wondered. The civilians were a simple lot, unaccustomed to feats of heroism, so the highborn and the tradesmen and the eloai abandoned the men-in-arms to flee for their homes. And the bogrens pursued, drawn to the meek by the scent of fear.

Esse was a small woman who had not been bred for anything beyond needlepoint. Her courage spent, she felt herself growing faint, and the banner in her arms becoming heavier. Still, she did not turn from her goal. The people looked to her for guidance. She needed only to reach the bridge to cross into the tower. A moment's rest and her strength would return, she told herself, but at that moment something gray and swift lunged at her throat. She shut her eyes, preparing herself for the inevitable—for what a woman like herself could not hope to escape in such a situation—but when it did not come, she became curious, daring to look into the face of Hugo.

He stood over her crouching form, his faceplate drawn up over his dark eyes, the sword in his hand stained black. A round thing was rolling at her feet, and she shrieked, kicking the bogren head into the gutter.

"Are you alright, my lady?"

"Lady? I am no highborn woman. But I am better than can be expected, given a day like this, thank you."

The bridge was missing, the dashing river spraying whitely against the broken pieces, and enormous creatures were climbing up from the bank. They had flails for arms, with which they swept the ground, hooking anyone and anything crossing their path, whether human or bogren. And, like fallen leaves, the bodies went flying.

Esse could not bear to look upon such horrors any longer. She turned sharply, feeling disoriented, wanting to retch. This was no longer a battle between men, divided by ideological lines, but a massacre, and she had led them into it. They had been prepared for the very worst, but not this.

"Where do we go now?"

"There are other ways into the tower," he said. "We have to climb."

They made for one of the terraced structures forming the avenue, though she was uncertain as to whether they were still invading the king's stronghold, or merely escaping to higher ground. A stairway glazed with ice ascended to a network of minarets and bridges. There was no time to ponder an alternative. She could hear the scamper of little feet at her heels. Hugo bounded onto the promenade, but she slipped on an icy step, catching herself awkwardly. The bogren closed, its dagger plunging between her ankles, tearing her chiton. She tried to regain footing but stumbled again, the thread of her garment caught by the blade. The bogren was clamoring over her, poised to plunge his knife into her bosom, just as its face met Hugo's boot.

As they made to climb the stairs once more, a steel ball came crashing into it, leaving piles of bricks and mortar, and clouding their eyes with dust. Esse did not know what manner of creature she was seeing. The river giants were as ugly as bogrens, but twice the height of the tallest man. Only this one did not have a flail, but a chain about its forearm, and it was preparing for another blow, when Hugo pushed her through a doorway.

They were in a dimly lit room. She saw white-painted lilies and a chandelier swaying over a curio of ceramic figurines. Bits of pottery littered the floor, and more pieces were tipping, shattering every time the walls were made to rattle.

He tugged at her arm, reaching a dining table turned on its side, the legs pressed against the opposite wall.

"We can hide!"

But when she looked to where he was pointing, she found people already concealed, a man and a woman and a little boy holding tight to one another behind the table. They were dressed in their nightclothes, their eyes wide, fixed upon the pounding beyond the windows. Hugo and Esse could go nowhere but the corner.

"We can get through this if we keep a level head."

"Speak for yourself," she said. "I am in way over my head! You're a fighter. What am I? I was born to sew. Whatever was I thinking, giving speeches, thinking I could be more than I am?"

"No," he insisted. "It had to be you."

"Why? I am not learned. I am eloai."

"Because you had more to prove than any highborn woman."

The pounding continued until the wall was shorn away like a sheet of parchment, and the chandelier broke from its moorings, crashing into slivers of glass. But the iron ball lingered, opening like a box, hatching a pair of bogrens. Hugo did not hesitate, making short work of them, dismembering their spidery appendages from their skeletal frames. And Esse simply stood, as dumbfounded as the family in whose home she had taken refuge, before yelling out in warning. The giant in the street was reaching in to grab Hugo. His sword cut a gash in its wrist and the arm recoiled.

"We cannot stay here!" she cried.

They leapt through a side window and into the alley, where a wagon and a bushel of hay broke their fall. Turning, they could see the giant squeezing its belly into the passage. Windows exploded and lantern posts snapped as it came at them. Hugo pulled the brake lever next to him and the two started rolling down the slope, jostling with the wheat, the wagon threatening to tip them over. They crashed through a kiosk of fish, beer barrels, and pickles, until the axle came apart and the left wheel sailed off on its own. End over end, the wagon flipped, and Hugo and Esse were thrown into a mound of snow.

"I never knew life could be this exciting." She was standing behind him, brushing the flakes from her hair. "Better than quilting, at any rate."

"Anything broken?"

She wanted to say something clever, but this was not a time for words. All she could think to do was shake her head.

"I don't think it's following us. Probably got stuck." All was quiet, but the look in his eyes urged caution.

"When we die today," she said matter-of-factly, turning her face towards him, "I think it will have been worth it."

"Don't be so dour. There is hope for us yet."

She was still trying to catch her breath, surprised by how she had managed to remain alive, when the second giant appeared. It was bigger and uglier than the first, its fists coated with the entrails of its victims. They considered running, but the monster was blocking the way forward, and the hill at their backs was far too steep for retreat. There was not even a door to escape through, or a wall behind which to hide.

"Let it take me," she murmured. "My life is worth less than yours."

"Don't be ridiculous. You'll be remembered for a thousand years. I won't." He stood before the creature, his sword firm in his hand. "Run!"

She wanted to move, but her feet were rooted to the ground. Something was not letting her go. It was her own heart.

The giant snatched him up by the legs, rattling him like a worm in a rooster's beak, and his weapon went ringing against the stone. She could not bear to lose sight of him, despite what was about to happen, until a curious thing drew her gaze away. It was a cloud, strung with hanging ropes, moving more swiftly than any cloud should. Emerging from a bank of cirrus, she saw it then for what it was, a ship. *What a marvelous thing to witness before I die*, she thought, when a great bird came screaming into their midst.

The bird was shaped like a woman, with bright azure plumage, and a silvered blade of feathers extended from her delicate hand. She dove past them and up again, driving her wing-rimmed sword like a nail through the top of the giant's cranium. Not knowing what had caused the beast to release him so suddenly, Hugo rolled from its hands, and the bird woman proceeded to twist her sword free.

The three moved through the lower levels, up through the barracks and the armory, where Ugh found an ax, and finally to the upper courtyard, renowned for its hanging flora. At each marvel, Ecthros had wanted to stop, to better impress things onto his memory. He learned what he could from his Hedonian guide, but Demacharon was not native to the land and admitted to scarcely recognizing the place through which they were now trespassing. The trees were little more than skeletal forms, curled leaves girding their roots, their remaining fruits black with flies. As for what flowers once bloomed there, none could guess, for only twigs remained, and cloisters once festooned with the vibrant hues of yellow whin and icy pink bougainvillea had but thorns to show.

"I've heard stories about these gardens," Ecthros intoned. "Was it truly as beautiful as they say?"

"And more so," Demacharon replied. "This was her favorite place to be. She loved to read here and to sing . . . and to dance."

"It breaks my heart," he said with a pause, "to think that I shall never see her dance again."

"You may yet." He escorted them away from that dead place, through a broad arcade arrayed with tessellations of red jasper and beryl emerald.

"But how?" the boy went on. "Death is an implacable warden."

"I thought you did not believe the centaur. That she was killed."

No answer was given, for the boy was uncertain, divided between the hope in his heart and the reasoning of his mind. And so, in brooding silence, they continued, until they came under a great colonnade of figures, each made of gold, and tall as the vaulted ceiling fifty feet above them. They were fashioned in armor of gleaming platinum, with scepters and swords inlaid with sapphire and topaz and lapis lazuli, and precious stones they had no names for, and yet nothing could be seen of their faces, for every one of them was broken at the neck. Headless.

"The Hall of Kings," Demacharon intoned, his voice carrying to the end of the passage.

"What happened to them? Were they like this when you were here?"

"No. For fifty-three generations, Radia's family ruled this kingdom. Solon was among these statues, as was her grandfather, and great-grandfather. Zaibos wanted to erase her lineage, and still, he leaves this—this desecration."

They kept going, the Hedonian commander and himself, a simple trader from Yefira, with a bogren tailing behind them. With every step, they moved back through the ages, from generation to generation. And Ecthros watched in wonder as the trends in clothing and armament devolved, one technique passing away in favor of another. At the far end of the hall, the most ancient kings stood. These were *The Lawgivers*, Demacharon explained to them. The centuries had not been kind to their polished stone robes, and yet, the language of the Zo was intact, set upon the golden tablets in their chiseled hands.

"If such laws were set down," Ecthros inquired, "how did someone like Zaibos take over? Was nothing written to prevent this from happening?"

"Indeed, great tomes were dedicated to the pursuit of justice, and to safeguard against abuses of power, but words themselves are meaningless, if there are none to uphold what is written."

"Alas, if only there were such people . . ."

"That is why we are here," Demacharon answered. "We are those men."

They came at last to the end of the chamber, where they stood under the pediment of an immense gateway. The door was of riveted iron, and so heavy that only four men could move it. To their good fortune, it had been unbarred and thrown open.

"Quickly. We're almost there."

They had expected resistance, in the form of sentries, or at the very least, eloai tending to a menial task. But room after room, they had found the tower deserted. It felt like a temple in veneration of some forgotten god, or an abandoned museum, made to enlighten a civilization that no longer existed. Still, the deeper they journeyed, the greater their apprehension. Surely, Zaibos could not have left his stronghold entirely unguarded.

Ecthros first heard their approach. The chime of mail, the sound of metal on stone, was unmistakable. Three marched forward and stood together, identical in every way, armored like beetles in shimmering black. Their helms were sleek, angular, lacking even the impression of a face. And they brandished strange, twin-hilted swords, long as spears.

Demacharon did not hesitate, his gladius in his left, Severetrix in his right. "Listen to me," he said. "I know you are sworn to your king, but we both know what he is. You once served the family of Solon, as did your forefathers. Look around you, upon this great hall, at this proud succession of kings and queens. What do you owe the pretender who now sits the throne and terrorizes your people?"

They did not say a word, and had Ecthros not seen them coming into the room, he might have taken them for statues.

"I know you are afraid. I know what men like Zaibos are capable of. Perhaps, it is not for your own life that you do his bidding. But make no mistake, your loved ones are not safe. He will see to that. Every remnant, every memory of the past, shall be wiped clean before his bloodlust is sated. But if you stay your hand, if you let us pass, I can stop him. I can end this madness."

There was a pause, and a hope they might see wisdom in these words, and then the guard at the fore lurched violently, Demacharon narrowly parrying the sword-spear by the flat of his gladius. As the two exchanged blows, the others closed in. Ecthros fumbled for his arrows, and in his panic, the first went clacking to the floor. Bow in hand, he retreated further into the hall. They advanced after him, their long swords prodding the air, utterly silent but for the unnerving clangor of their armor. Ecthros managed to slip off his quiver, his arrows fanning every which way, and with three in hand, he ducked behind the platinum heel of Solon's great ancestor. As the sentry pair came about, shortening the distance between them, his cord snapped. The shaft sailed over the left attacker's pauldron and out of sight. Cursing himself, he nocked a second arrow. It rang, dead-center, against the insect-like cuirass, but did not penetrate, the brass tip falling flat.

"That isn't entirely fair!" Ecthros cried, catching a glimpse of Demacharon wrestling the helmet from the man he was fighting, before driving his gladius up through his adversary's chin.

Backed against the base of the statue now, the bladed spears fenced him in. He had nowhere to run, and nothing but his wooden bow to repel them.

"Demacharon! Help!"

The Hedonian rushed into a sprint, but he was beyond reach. Yet at that moment, just as the guard moved in for the kill, Ecthros watched him topple backward, his knee plate shattering and spouting blood. Ugh had come from behind with his ax. Leaping down again, he proceeded to separate the man's head from his body.

They met up, Demacharon and Ecthros and Ugh, and the remaining sentry knew he was outmatched. Dropping his weapon and twisting off his helm, they could see he was little more than a boy himself, possibly younger. And he was terribly afraid.

"We won't kill you," Demacharon assured him. "It's not too late for a truce. You can still join us. Help us to defeat Zaibos."

The boy started to tremble, and finally to weep. He opened his mouth as if to say something, but had only teeth and gums, his tongue having been cut out.

"You can't speak," Ecthros noted. "No wonder you've been so quiet."

The young man's expression changed, to that of gratitude, and relief. He reached out, in a gesture of friendship, and was suddenly lifted into the air as if by an invisible hand.

Ecthros ran forward, stunned by his concern for someone who had, until recently, attempted to kill him. "What—What's going on?"

Like a fly caught in a spider's thread, the guard was squirming high above them, his face turning ever whiter. He was clawing under his breastplate, at the gorget about his neck, his eyes swollen with desperation.

"Can you shoot him down?"

"What?"

"Something has him! Can you shoot him down?"

Ecthros found an arrow, fitting his bow without knowing his target. A spot above the guard's head, he supposed. But before he could aim, the young man stopped struggling and was still, aside from the gentle rocking of his body in the air.

"Razor wire," Demacharon flatly stated. "Nearly invisible."

Ecthros lowered his bow. "Wasn't Larissa caught up in something like that?"

"Indeed."

"Did the king's assassin do this? Do you think he was punishing a traitor?"

"No," Demacharon answered, wiping the blood from his gladius. "If that were the case, the three of us would be dead by now. It looks like we have help. Our assassin has turned sides."

The city was in turmoil. Everywhere he looked, Krow saw people struggling for survival, on the steppes, along the bridges, in the streets far below. It had been a battle at first, but the citizens of Tyrnael were unaccustomed to the horrors of warfare, as war had not intruded upon their land in over a thousand years. Even their best soldiers lacked the martial skill for combat, for much of what they knew had been passed down through the ages, becoming more ceremonial than efficient, and now the ring of mountains once protecting them from invasion would be their undoing.

At the wheel of the *Cloud Breaker*, he could but watch events unfold and despair, as eloai and highborn scattered into the alleys to be ambushed, and families barricaded themselves in their houses to have rooftops collapse atop them. Survivors scrambled for refuge beneath the wreckage, only to have war horgs tear them from their holes moments later. Like worms, bogrens crawled up from the earth, twisted instruments fast about their limbs. From under the causeways, they swarmed like spiders, newly hatched and hungry. But here and there were victories, men learning the ways of battle while in the midst of it, channeling their warrior ancestors from within their essences. Likewise, the women fought as ferociously and died as readily. But to the avian's keen eyes, none were so bold or so cunning as one of his own.

A head rolled onto the deck, drawing a line of blood, startling him no less than the first time. With the grace of a kite dancer, she descended, perfectly balancing herself atop the bowsprit, one foot behind the other.

"Must you do that?" he admonished her.

"It was heavy."

"Why not leave it in the streets?"

"They're my trophies." She drifted onto the deck, dragging the horg skull by the hair, and into the net with the rest.

"How many is that?"

"I've lost count," she said, shaking the wet crimson hue from her feathered blade.

"You realize, if one were to catch you—"

"They won't. Horg are like pigs. They can't look up."

"I did not bring you all this way to go hunting, Avia. I need you to be my scout, to see who needs lifting."

"I am saving them my own way, Krow. One less horg means a dozen less dead."

"Perhaps you are right."

A volley of arrows, trailing fire, reached for the underside of the hull, but he managed to steer clear of them. What damage they had sustained—holes with burnt edges in the sails—was a result of their efforts to evacuate the people.

"There!" She followed his gaze to a stepped structure, a squared-hilltop rimmed with snow. The bogren army had pushed their way to the outskirts, and the humans were gathering from all directions, clamoring onto the edifice.

"Quickly, Avia, lower the burners."

She moved to decrease the flame, when the whole of the ship shuddered. Part of the gunwale was missing, split beams hanging in the wind. An enormous rock was in its place, bound in iron spikes, and a chain was hanging down from it.

Avia drew her sword and extended her arms, gliding alongside the *Cloud Breaker*. She spotted the horg who had hit them, and folding her wings against her ribcage, sword firm against thigh and heel, she went into a spiral, as a flurry of arrows shot up from below. Shafts broke against her steel, falling away from her face, but in the process of deflecting them, she lost control. Careening down and down, a lamppost knocked the weapon from her grasp, and she found herself tumbling, tossing up rocks and snow.

"Avia!"

Without a crew, the *Cloud Breaker* was slow to maneuver. Krow could not hope to both steer and man the burners, but neither could he stand idle, leaving one of his own to die. Cursing the day his wings were taken from him, he leapt from the wheel, stopping short as two young boys emerged from below the floorboards.

"Don't worry! We've got it!" Colin was turning the fire. Toby was standing beside him, watching with curiosity.

"What in Aza are you two doing here?"

"We wanted to help," said Toby.

"So you stowed away?" He was furious, screeching like a caw. "This is war! If anything happens to you, Thulken will have my head!"

"What about Avia? Shouldn't we be rescuing her?" Colin cried.

Krow looked to where she had crashed. People were gathering around her, defending her, but bogrens were amassing by the hundreds. Many young men had already fallen to keep the diminutive creatures from their avian savior.

"Down!" he ordered. "Take us down!"

The burners turned to wisps of blue and the *Cloud Breaker* began to dip. Avia, all the while, was being lifted from tier to tier, from the arms of one into the arms of another. They were halfway to the top of the steppe, but the bogrens were gaining, as were their giant, lumbering cousins.

Krow steered into the city, watching the streets expanding around them, the terraces rising on either side. In no time at all, they were being assailed from the parapets. Arrows peppered the hull, and a sudden roar drew his gaze away, to where the mainsail had erupted into an orange and black cloud of fire and smoke.

"The ladders!" he squawked, putting his weight into the wheel. "Drop the ladders! The rigging! What have you!"

The galley dropped, the keel skimming the ground, breaking through cobblestones thick with snow, knocking over lampposts and shattering windows. Bogrens locked their greedy eyes upon the vessel, but it ascended again, a wagon caught up by its anchor like a minnow on a hook.

With Colin and Toby at the burners, the fire at full blast, Krow wheeled into the stepped hill. Eloai and tradesmen and highborn caught onto the ladders, climbing over and into the ship. They came arm in arm, the wounded and the dying and the strong, strangers helping strangers, lone figures with blackened faces, families with tearful children, and young men playing at hero.

Avia was last to arrive. Upon seeing her, Krow took to the air, as the boys led the survivors to the rigging. They cut the ropes and freed the ladders, and the people below watched bogrens drop from the underside of the ship, gray bodies smashing through shingles, impaling on weathervanes, breaking against the stony ramparts.

"Captain Krow, sir," Colin said timidly, "I think we're losing kerosene, sir."

"We lost a tank in the explosion," he answered. "Go check Avia. See if she's all right."

One of the men approached him, a soldier by the battered look of his armor. "Take us over to that tree. I can watch over your mate. She's badly hurt, but she'll make it."

"She is not my mate," Krow said. "I love a human."

"Is that why you're here? Why you're helping us?"

"No . . . I am here because, well . . . because of Radia."

"I understand. The name is Hugo."

Krow steered the ship away from the center, and from the white and gold spire about which everything turned south. Like all bird men, he possessed an intuitive sense of direction, knowing the way to the Great River and the One Sea, and it was along this line that he could see the majestic camphor, crowning the skyline at the edge of the city, taller than any structure save the Compass Tower itself. Despite the deathly chill from beyond the encircling mountains, the tree looked unaffected, its boughs remaining free of frost, its leaves maintaining a deep, sun-drenched green.

"Why the tree?"

"She is there," Hugo answered. "Sleeping on the bier. Zaibos thought to demoralize us, giving us the body, to be paraded through the streets. That was his greatest mistake. We mourned her passing. And then we rallied."

"A giant plant, however big, is indefensible," Krow admitted.

"We will fight to the last man."

"There'll be no chance for fighting, only slaughter. You cannot see things clearly. Humans never do. From up high, I can see them gathering like termites. Thousands more breaking from the East."

"We could use the tower. It could be a place of refuge, if we could get to it."

"I cannot ferry you. Fuel is nearly spent, and I can only take thirty or forty at once. But do not lose hope. We have men on the inside."

"What good will that do? If thousands are coming, as you say, there may be no one left to save. What we need is time. Time is the master of all."

Krow turned again to the Compass Tower, his eyes tracing the remnants of every street and walkway reaching toward it. He did not know whether Demacharon and Ecthros had managed a way inside, or if they were betrayed by their bogren guide. If they failed, the people of Tyrnael were doomed. Krow could abandon them, taking Avia and the boys to Yefira, but he did not agree with Thulken. Zaibos was a disease bound to spread throughout Aenya. In such a world, his wife and child could never be safe.

"There is a bridge leading to the dark hemisphere—" he said to Hugo.

"The Great Eastern Gate, I know it well. Was shut for ages, until Zaibos opened it, releasing those monsters into our homes."

"Well then," Krow went on, "if what you need is time—time is what you will get."

Madame Latima's job was simple. With the aid of her eloai daughter, Vasila, she tended to the camp, sweeping the leaves and shoveling the snow. It was hard work, and in stark contrast to the seclusion with which she was accustomed. But at Esse's insistence, Latima agreed to lend her hand to the cause. Doubtless, the young seamstress turned revolutionary was smitten by Hugo's charms, for she had never bothered with politics, or anything else beyond the point of her needle. Eloai were not born to think, after all. Who could have put such fancy notions into her head but him? And yet, even Latima had to admit that something had to be done about the usurper.

It happened the night after Radia's body passed through their street. She had been stitching a shroud for a child—a child cooked alive by the king—as Esse and Vasila labored with a passion she had never seen in them, reams of white fabric piled at their feet, their fingers working the gold thread for a hundred unicorns. It was at that moment that she realized she could not stand to sew another funerary shroud. She put down the needle, stood abruptly, and turned to the girls, saying, "Where do we go?" And by the look in Esse's eyes, it was clear to her that the girl had understood right away.

When Latima was brought before the still and cold body of the princess, who was dressed in gold-laced white linen, she fell to her knees and wept. It was as if all the sorrows for the dead were embodied upon that solitary grave, and every awful thing she had pretended was not happening came pouring out of her eyes.

When asked what duty she would have liked to be given, Latima could think of only one. And thus, she became Radia's caretaker, cleaning the bloodied tunic until it gleamed again, and mending every loose thread. At dawn and at midday and again at sundown, she washed the princess's hands and feet and brow, and was always brushing her golden hair until it rested perfectly about her shoulders. Since the body did not seem to suffer the ravages of time, no one thought to burn or to bury it.

Now Tyrnael was engulfed in flames and dust and echoed with the screams of the desperate. But for Latima, it all seemed far away. She pushed everything from her mind as she did when tasked with a job, and with the sun at its zenith, the time had come to cleanse her lord. With a zeal that never waned, she pumped the water from the well into a special ceramic pot,

boiled it under an open flame, and carried it with clean towels
to the place where the body rested.

The great tree had grown suddenly in the night, embracing
the princess in a sepulcher of wood and leaves. An ascent of
fallen boughs had been carefully positioned over its roots, and
a makeshift walkway leading to the alcove in the camphor's
folds, so that the people could more easily visit and tend to her.
It was here that Latima stopped, frozen with dread, the pot
tumbling from her hands. A cry erupted from her small frame
as she collapsed, the dress about her knees growing damp in
the wet snow.

Vasila, hearing the wailing of her mistress, was
immediately upon her. "Madame! Oh, Madame! What ever
could it be, that you should cry out so?"

"Good Vasila, help me to my feet, will you?"

The young eloai did as she was told and, hand-in-hand,
they approached the spot where the body had been. Vasila
became hysterical. "Oh, what has happened? Radia isn't here!
What are we to do?"

"Think, dear girl! They've obviously stolen it!"

"Who? Who would do such a thing?" she cried, fighting
back her tears.

"Who else but the usurper!"

"Oh... Oh..." She was hopping now and pulling at her hair.
"I cannot fathom what they must be doing to it! To our dear
beloved! Those monsters!"

"Don't think such evil thoughts!" Latima admonished her.
"You're not bred for it. Neither of us is."

"If only Esse were here. She'd know what to do."

"Esse? What does she know? She's no different than we
are. She can't even—"

Madame Latima was then interrupted not by something
Vasila had said, but by what she was doing. Given their
predicament and her reaction to the missing body of Radia, the
young eloai was unexpectedly calm, and even her tears were
beginning to dry against the back of her hand. She spoke not a
word, but walked slowly away, stooping now and again.

"Get back here, Vasila! The perpetrators may still be afoot!"

"No, Madame, I think not. Just look!"

Latima did as Vasila bid, and she saw it also. The ground was flat, blazing like white crystals with freshly fallen snow, but in sections it was pitted, with what they slowly recognized to be footprints. Vasila even removed her shoe to make certain. More remarkable still were the clovers, and the baby's breath budding from each impression. Hope had become such a rarity in Tyrnael, that the young eloai girl was afraid even to consider it. "Could it be?" she asked, turning to face Latima. "Do you truly think?"

"Indeed I do. Radia is risen!"

They were both weeping, holding one another like giddy children.

"Radia is risen!" Vasila agreed. "But what shall we do now?"

"I shall go one way, and you another. Find everyone you can and spread the good word. Tell them that Radia is risen!"

Ecthros had not expected the interior of the tower to open into the vast, vertical tunnel that stood before him. Zaibos was vain, Demacharon assured him, and was sure to be watching the battle from the top of the stairwell.

The Hedonian refused to rest, bounding upward without pause, as Ugh came up after, climbing more than walking the stairwell. Ecthros followed in their shadow, wondering how the toddler-sized creature and the old man could do it. Higher and higher they ascended, his legs aching with every increment, this coupled with a growing sense of vertigo and vulnerability. They were out in the open, exposed to attack from all sides. Fighting armored soldiers in a place where he could run and hide had been terrifying enough, but here there was nowhere to go, except down, and very quickly. The steps were tall and far apart, each rising to meet his shins, and after the first hundred or so he stopped counting them. It was not long before he found himself leaning against the curved inner wall, his feet too heavy to lift.

"Demacharon, sir, perhaps we could stop for a breath?"

"No time for that, boy. Every moment we waste is a moment we lose. If Zaibos learns we're here, he'll set up countermeasures, perhaps organize an offensive. Here more than anywhere, he has every advantage."

"I shouldn't have come along," Ecthros admitted. His hand was at the wall, his lungs drawing hard, Demacharon high above him. "I am not much of a soldier. Or an archer for that matter. I'm not really much of anything."

"I did not ask you to join me."

"I know," he said softly. "You go on. I'll stay with Ugh."

The commander gazed long at the boy standing under him, measuring him like a new recruit. "I didn't ask you to be here, but I am grateful that you are."

"Why? My arrows can't even penetrate their armor. I should be out there, with Krow."

"I've led many young men into battle," he answered, stepping down to sit with them, "and if this should be my last hurrah, I am proud knowing that an honorable man fought beside me. Besides, even the best of soldiers cannot plan for every eventuality. Sometimes, the smallest factor can turn the tide of battle."

"Me? Turn the tide of battle?" He chuckled. "I can't imagine it will come to that."

Ugh sat in the boy's lap, listening intently with his eyes, but said nothing. Ecthros sensed only that the bogren was sympathizing, without fully understanding.

Demacharon set a hand on the boy's shoulder. It was strong. Reassuring. And yet there was a finality to it that frightened him. "Ready?"

"Honestly . . .?" He gazed wistfully at his bow. It was a family heirloom, all that he had of his father. But now it felt small in his hands, and of little consequence. "I'm not like you. I am scared to die."

"You wouldn't be living, son, if you weren't at all afraid," he said, and after some silence, added, "It is not how long we live that matters, but how we live."

"All I wanted was to see her again, just her face, if only once more."

"I know. We all did."

"But does it even matter," the boy remarked, "all this fighting?"

"How can you ask? Tyrnael is—"

"That isn't what I meant. I suppose, what I meant to say was . . . is it naïve, to think as she did, to believe in the goodness of people?"

"I'm no philosopher, but there was a time I was convinced, that there is no righteousness but what might permits. I was mistaken. Even if we fail today, Zaibos cannot last, because the people will not stand for it. There is a light within us all, to guide us. You and I have seen that light. We've met her."

Ecthros pulled himself up, gripping his bow in one hand and an arrow in the other. "I think I'm rested up, commander." He smiled, but his heart was not in it. "Lead the way."

They made it a quarter circle from the spot where they had been sitting, when a metallic echo sounded from above. Zaibos's praetorian guard was descending upon them, jangling in their obsidian-black armor and red aarok-plumed helmets.

"I don't like the look of these guys," Ecthros remarked, nervously fitting an arrow to his bow.

"Stay behind me!" Demacharon shouted, rushing headlong into the oncoming host, his gladius and two-sword drawn. Ugh, short and gaunt as he was, went into hiding, tucking himself behind a step.

Two-by-two they marched, heavy in their mail, the poleyn covering their knees bending awkwardly. His swords could find no purchase, no seam between the steel plates, yet he compensated with brute force. Their double-hilted blades swept to and fro, threatening to open him at the gut, but he deflected their blows with his own, slipping under their defenses to get at their greaves and the tassets girding their loins. With a cacophony of iron against iron, reverberating across that vast chamber, the Hedonian pressed them back. Ecthros watched the first assailant plummet from the stairwell, making no sound as he fell to the lower level, landing like a stack of kitchenware. Demacharon was still wrestling with another guard when a second detachment came rushing over the steps to join the fray.

Eyeing his target, Ecthros bent his bow, but found no opportunity. A better archer could have risked it, but he was more likely to kill Demacharon than the man he was fighting. The boy then realized what he had to do. Rounding down the tower, he came to a new vantage point, directly across from and below the guards. His shafts ricocheted from the masonry, the steps, wherever they were not. But it was enough of a distraction to turn their attentions away, giving Demacharon the chance to hurl his rival through a window.

The moment was short lived. Seeing that his arrows could only draw their attention away, the remaining praetorians joined their weapons into a phalanx of three, to advance upon the Hedonian. Demacharon had no choice but to withdraw, his gladius blunting against their steel, his nigh-invisible sword useless at his side, as it could but shatter against their mail. Ecthros watched as he continued to descend from whence he had come, over the spot where Ugh lay in hiding. Going unnoticed, the bogren sprang up as they passed over him, smacking his ax into the back of a knee, knocking a guard to his death. Not knowing what had hit them, the other two fell into confusion, and Demacharon charged. But before he could reach them, the man to his left appeared to slip, or jump from the stairs. The lone defender shrank, tossing his weapon to claw at the back of his cuirass. He proceeded to twist and to flail every which way, like a marionette possessed by a madman. Despite his silence, and the visor concealing his eyes, his agony was unmistakable. As if dealt a powerful blow, he collapsed backward, writhing upon the steps. Demacharon rushed over him, forcing the helmet from his head. The face was young, innocent, but deathly pale and slick with sweat. His veins were breaking through his cheeks and brow, and his throat was pulsating with a purplish welt the size of a child's fist.

Seeing no other sentries, Ecthros raced up. "Is he dead?"

Demacharon turned and smacked him hard across the face.

"Hey—that hurt!"

"Look."

The black and fire-orange colors of a tiny spider showed distinctly against the curved wall. It had been crawling on him, but the commander managed to dislodge it. His cheek was sore, yet he welcomed the sensation when thinking on the alternative. "What is that?"

"A pain spider. Its body is covered in poisonous hairs. The pain has been known to drive men to suicide. You're lucky it just shed, or you'd be looking a lot like him."

Ugh examined the arachnid with fascination. It did not appear particularly dangerous, so he pinched it between his fingers and popped it into his mouth.

"Eh . . . is he going to be alright?"

"Don't know much about bogrens," Demacharon answered. "He may be immune. But I know we've got little to worry about, at least when it comes to spiders."

"Our assassin strikes again?"

"Yes, and if he's as clever as he seems, I'd wager he's waiting to make his final move. He wants Zaibos as badly as we do, and is getting into position as we speak, coordinating with us, whether we know it or not."

Fires spread, and monsters sprang up from the earth, and blood ran in tributaries between the cobblestones. But she took no notice of it. At any moment, a stray arrow could find her body, or a horg's mace crush the life from her, but it did not matter, for no worse fate could befall a mother than what had already transpired. And so, she remained, rooted to the spot where her child had fallen, cradling the small, limp shape, washing and washing and again washing her daughter's bloodied brow.

"Good woman, why do you mourn so?"

She did not face away, to see who was accosting her, answering simply, "Why else? I have lost my only child."

"Do not be dismayed, Marta, for you are gravely mistaken. Your daughter is not lost. She is there. In your arms."

The woman could feel the warmth, and the light, intensifying about her. It was as if the sun, long absent and forgotten, had emerged from a dismal sky to color the world. She turned, at last, to see with whom she was speaking, and was blinded.

"Who . . . who are you, that knows my name?" She could see only the silhouette of a girl, masked by a brilliant golden halo.

"I know you, Marta, and your daughter. I know all people. But you have forgotten me. Where is your faith?"

"How can a mother have hope, when her child is dead? Look. See with your own eyes!"

The little girl's complexion was like milk that has gone sour, her blonde locks streaked with crimson, tangled by the stone deep in her forehead. She could not have been more than four or five. And as if witnessing this for the first time, the mother began to sob.

"Do not weep," the luminous silhouette implored, "for your daughter is only sleeping. Please. Look again."

She stopped, wiping her eyes to do as the strange girl insisted. And when she dared to look again, it was hope that found her.

"We must away, Amalthea, for we are needed elsewhere."

Marta's face was awash, but now with fresh tears, different tears from those she had, only moments ago, been shedding. "Please! Let me thank you! Let me sing your praises. I will do anything you ask of me—"

The girl climbed into the mist and onto the white mare which formed from it. "Love one another," she said, departing, "for it is the heart of my power."

The unicorn bore the young woman on its back, and as one form they raced through the war-torn streets, a star blazing from her forehead, butterflies and fireflutters waking in their wake, swirling to the sky to herald the goddess. And all who saw them found hope renewed, and broken hearts were once more allayed. But those who had come to maim and to kill were blinded by the light. Unable to see, bogren and horg fell into a panic, shrinking into the holes from whence they had spewed.

On she rode, like a white flash across land and water, over the river where the bridge had collapsed, over the base of the mountain with its white crashing waterfalls, and into the gates of the Compass Tower.

The stone slipped from her forehead, and the girl caught it as if playing a game. Rubbing the sleep from her eyes, Naone tugged at her mother's fingertips, remarking, "Look, Mama! Radia woke up!"

Zaibos watched his city fall to ruin and smiled. Bloodsnot's army had performed admirably. Even from the height of the Compass Tower, he could make out the scarlet tinting the streets. It was a beautiful sight, the veins of those denying him having been opened, the weakness of Tyrnael gushing dry. But there were still people in hiding, and the main force from the dark hemisphere was cut off. From nowhere, a flying galleon had crashed into the Great Eastern Gate, destroying it and everyone upon it. It was a noble sacrifice, sparing a good number of the citizenry, and yet, in keeping with his larger scheme. Zaibos needed the people, for when the day was won, there would be work to do. To reclaim Aenya, he would need delegates, and treaties composed by greater minds than that of bogrens. When the last of the world's empires would fall to him, he would need governors, and men of letters to arrange for taxation. More importantly, he wished to have these events recorded. For after such a day, who would dare oppose him? Tales of his victory, and the ongoing massacre, were sure to echo through history until the end of time.

A clash from below drew his focus away. Something was happening on the tower steps. Perhaps they were sending a small force to destroy him. The fools. Did they not know he could not be beaten?

Nine praetorians stood in a semi-circle about the throne. They were as he had made them—utterly obedient, living for no other purpose but to serve. Like stone sentries, they never moved, never spoke. Even as the sounds of battle intensified, echoing up from the tower shaft, they did not stir. Lesser men were stationed on the steps to deal with intruders. And yet, the most elite of his guards were beginning to show signs of agitation. He could see it in their aggressive posture, in the way they gripped their weapons and turned toward the din of battle. Were they hungering for a fight? To do as they were trained? No, he could not allow any display of agency, of free will. He raised a fist, gesturing that they return to their positions. But they did not obey.

Zaibos grew ever furious as he watched them orbit the room, dancing and twitching and twisting.

"You dare!" he cried. "Back to your stations at once! Or I'll have you cooked alive for this insult!"

Still, they did not heed him. Their shields were the first to drop, followed by their sarissas. He knew something was amiss when one of the men collapsed and started to convulse. Another was clawing at his back, to get at something inside his armor, until running and throwing himself from the ledge. A third drew his sword, only to cut his own throat.

It was a horrifying sight, watching the nine of them fall, one after another, but Zaibos did not cower from it. Instead, he waited, until he was certain they were dead, before moving to examine the body of the one closest to him. But before he could pull away, a swarm of spiders crawled from every crease and joint in the praetorian's armor.

"Assassin!" Zaibos surveyed the room, turning in one sweeping motion, his mace—Bonecrusher—firm in hand. "Show yourself!"

Pacing the compass face, the lines etched into it indicating the same southerly direction, he could find no sign of intrusion. And in his fury, he dragged the bodies, one by one, tossing them from the tower. But not all were dead. One of the men was still suffering, and soon to expire, Zaibos surmised, but alive enough to give answers.

Wrenching the helmet away, Zaibos was taken aback. If the face had ever been human, he did not recognize it. A throbbing, discolored mass of purple met his gaze. What could be seen of the eyes and nose was greatly deformed, and as for the mouth and chin, it was missing entirely, but for the iron rivets driven into the skull with a steel plate—the blade came at him before he could see it, the dirk breaking against his mailed collar.

"Eros!"

He tightened his gauntlet about the assassin's wrist, wrestling the dirk away, and after a brief contest of wills, the weapon slipped to the floor.

"How could you have been so naïve?" His head of spikes reverberated with a metallic timbre. "To believe that you—an abomination—could have had any relation to the heir of Solon? To think you and Radia shared the same mother?" Zaibos proceeded to haul him to the edge of the compass floor to meet the sky, the assassin thrashing with what little strength remained in him, forming inhuman groans from the place where a mouth should have been. "You were deceived! Bewitched! You saw only what she wanted you to see, and for that, you have been made to know misery. For that, you will die." But before he could be thrown from the top of the tower, a bubble in Eros's cheek burst, spraying them both with infant spiders. They skittered along the assassin's neck and onto Zaibos's outstretched arm, finding their way inside.

Eros fell onto his ribs, half-alive, snaking toward his dirk. Zaibos was still reeling, the splinters shed from the spiders' hairy bodies stabbing at him like needles dipped in fire, and yet he succeeded in kicking the blade further from the assassin's grasp.

Somehow, despite the pain permeating every thread of his body, he managed command of his faculties, lifting Eros's gelatinous head from the floor. "You think to make me suffer? Me!" he cried, his morningstar poised to strike. "I am the Lord of Agonies! Not you!" With that, the delicate webbing keeping

Eros's skull intact came unglued, spraying Bonecrusher with puss and brain.

They paused at the summit of the stairwell, breathing hard. Demacharon was first to speak. "When I get in there, find someplace to hide."

"But—"

Offering no reply, he stealthily crossed the vestibule leading to the rooftop throne. Ecthros, his arrows readied, followed like a shadow. Ugh came last, like a loyal dog.

They watched the carnage as it transpired, the nine praetorians being killed off, and the ensuing brawl between Zaibos with Eros. The assassin lay with only half a head, the top part of it dissolved, the lower masked by an iron plate. Vengeance was denied him, and yet, he had bought Demacharon considerable advantage. It was three against one now. Eros's sacrifice allowed them to go unseen and unheard, the boy and the bogren taking positions behind the raised dais.

Zaibos brooded over the corpse, leaning against his giant morningstar. He looked to be gasping for air, but it was difficult to know for certain. Demacharon studied his armor, but there was not a crease to be seen, not a hint of naked flesh he might hope to injure. If the king had a weakness, the assassin had failed to find it, so what hope did he have? *Severetrix.* Defying all that he knew of weapons, if the Zo had indeed made Zaibos's armor, as Nessus told them, he prayed that a blade forged by the Zo could penetrate it.

Scooping a shield from the body of a guard nearest him, Demacharon crept ever closer, his two-sword eager for death. At that moment, as he raised the unseen edge to strike, a single thought occurred to him. His promise to Radia, a lifetime ago, that he would never kill. Never take a life in her name. Despite having cut short the lives of so many that very day, he had yet to murder anyone in cold blood.

"Hedonian!"

Zaibos swung around, Bonecrusher nearly tearing the shield from his grasp. "You've got one more execution to carry out," Demacharon answered, goading the king to attack, "one more subject loyal to Radia, the true heir of Tyrnael." The ball of iron came at him from below, the impact lifting him from his feet, throwing him off balance.

"Radia is dead!" Zaibos cried. "I saw to it myself!"

He looked for an opening, to move from behind his enemy's defenses, but every blow he received rattled his bones, sent him staggering back. The king's strength was uncanny, his resolve unshakable.

"I reached into her chest," he went on, "and pulled out her heart."

"That may be, but you cannot erase the memory of her, what she stood for!"

Down and down, the blood-red morningstar continued to punish him, rendering him to his knees, punching through his shield, a spike coming within a hair of his eye. Hooking the shield away, a mailed fist sent him sprawling. He retreated, wiping at his lip, but it continued to flow. Zaibos advanced like something monstrous, invincible. He could feel the rush of air as Bonecrusher came circling. Without a shield, he doubted he could withstand even a single a blow. His only advantage was speed. He could outmaneuver the king, tire him out, wait for a mistake and strike.

"You believe yourself morally superior, but I know where you come from, Hedonian. One does not command legions by compassion. Your heart is as black as mine, and if you had not lost your homeland, you would be as I am now, bestriding her throne!"

Lesser men could be thwarted by taunting. It was a common enough tactic. Demacharon was not a lesser man, but a rage stirred within him, and he could not help moving ahead despite being aware of the danger. As Bonecrusher flew over his head, the gladius in his left punched between the spikes. Pain shot through his wrist and the short sword rang to the floor. He followed with Severetrix in his right, stripping the blood-paint from the king's helm, leaving only a mark.

"You are deluded! Deluded by the great lie all men tell themselves. *There is no good! There is no evil!* There is only power and the will to use it."

He reached for his gladius, but the morningstar moved with unexpected swiftness, glancing against his hip and forearm, the spikes ripping through his flesh. Wracked with pain, he hit the floor, slinking away with the little strength that remained in him.

Zaibos loomed over him like the Taker himself, Bonecrusher dripping with his blood. "I will achieve what your people never could. Tyrnael will be the seat of a united Aenya."

"You cannot build an empire on hate. It is what destroyed us. And it will destroy you as well."

The mask gave no reply. But as fist and morningstar went up, Demacharon lurched forward, Severetrix in hand, the imperceptible edge directed at the king's mailed groin. Despite its workmanship, the blade was fragile. It was like fighting with glass. And now, in his most desperate need, it could either wound his attacker or shatter.

There was a sharp sound, like the snapping of a harp string, and Demacharon knew that all was lost. Only the broken haft of the two-sword remained in his palm. The upper part was missing, a mirrored sliver in the sun. But there had also been, sounding in unison, the distinct chime of an arrowhead.

"Get away from him!"

Ecthros was standing a short leap from the king, his bow drawn against his cheek, his first arrow having ricocheted and fallen at Zaibos's feet. And he was quivering, quivering in his courage.

"I remember you," Zaibos replied, "the boy from Yefira. Have you come all this way for revenge? No, I think not. I think you came because of *her*."

"Shut up! Just shut up!" The young archer could hardly hold still enough to aim, and his tears were blinding him.

"Are you afraid? That I will do to you what I did to her?"

A second arrow flew, directly under the king's eye socket. But the king did not flinch. "I'll do it!" Ecthros threatened. "I'll shoot you through the eye."

"That's impossible."

"It's not impossible! My father could do it! He was a great archer! The greatest who ever was!"

The morningstar went clanging to the floor and Zaibos leaned forward, raising his arms in an act of surrender. "Show me."

Demacharon sat up, seeing what the boy could not. He was being lured. "No, Ecthros, don't do it."

Even when he was not shaking with fright, Ecthros failed to hit his targets. And now he was desperate to calm himself, to aim for an opening scarcely the width of the arrowhead itself, but before he could loose the fletching from between his fingertips, there came an echo, softly clopping hooves from the stair below. They looked to the source of it, and their eyes brightened, the warmth returning to their worn bodies. It was like the morning sun, washing into the room after a long gloomy night.

"Brother."

Zaibos looked visibly shaken. It was in his voice and his mannerisms. "How . . . How can you be alive?"

Radia dismounted from Amalthea and stepped forward. She was radiant in her white funeral gown, with hair like fiery gold and eyes like the moons, her face ageless and eternal. "Life and death are entwined. The one begets the other. It is the natural course of things."

"But I pulled out your heart . . . the source of your power! You cannot come back!"

"My power was never something you could take away," she answered, "but you could not have known that, for you see only with your eyes. My true heart, dear brother, resides in the love shared between the people of Aenya. That is something you failed to destroy."

Zaibos did not answer. He simply lifted his morningstar, advancing upon her.

"No!" His cord snapped, the arrow ricocheting from Zaibos's iron facade. A moment later, the king proved Bonecrusher true to its namesake, and the boy's forearms were shattered along with the bow he was holding, the pieces of his family's heirloom caught up in the spikes. Ecthros limped away, but Zaibos would not allow him to escape.

"Even if I cannot kill you," he said to Radia, his gauntlet closing about the boy's neck, "I can kill everyone and everything you love."

Ecthros was frantic, thrashing with his shredded, broken limbs to pry the king loose. It was a fleeting moment. Demacharon moved quickly, but the boy paid no attention to his would-be savior. Resolved to his fate, he found that for which he most longed. His eyes now fixed upon hers, he slowly grew still, and a look of tranquility froze upon him.

She did not act, nor speak, and her glow was greatly diminished. Already, the room was growing cold.

"So, it appears you have a weakness, after all. Think, now, how much greater is hate. Without love, you would not be suffering as you are now. You could watch him die and feel nothing."

"Zaibos . . ." she murmured, paralyzed as he approached, his morningstar raised to destroy her.

"There is only one way to stop me," he cried. "You must kill me yourself, but you cannot—can you? You may be the goddess of life, but I am the bringer of death!"

Demacharon knew what to do. He had always known, but had been afraid, afraid of that which awaited him. The wife and child he was doomed never to see.

Forgive me.

Zaibos was vulnerable in two places. Two very narrow places. With the two halves of Severetrix cutting into his hands, he found them both.

34

Radia

As the ice was beginning to thaw around them, the people of Tyrnael wept. From shingled rooftops and chipped windowsills to vine-wrapped terraces, their tears ran down into the streets, pooling between broken homes and the feet of ruined families. Sounds of mourning joined with the gentle patter of sudden rain as the evidence of bloodshed was washed away, though the memory of what was lost could never be.

Quietly, they left their hiding places, gathering in the squares, carrying loved ones in wagons and on makeshift biers. Their eyes were heavy, and their hearts full of fury, but they were silent, for no words could suffice to tell what each had witnessed. But now was not the time for story, only contemplation, to drink deep the enormity of all that was come and gone.

The clouds were scattering, turning to gold and fiery reds. A shaft of sun broke from the gray haze like an arm reaching down to ignite the Compass Tower, and in seeing it they knew. The world would be right again. Zaibos was dead.

Radia had never felt more alive. The essence of what it meant to exist was coursing through her veins a thousandfold. Her senses were attuned to the whole of Aenya, to the longing call of every songbird and the laboring of every insect, to the growth of every blade of grass to the wanting wail of every infant. It was her greatest source of strength, and her weakness also. This was the tide she had been holding back by drinking the centaur's poison. The world was a sea of miseries, and yet she could feel the ebb and flow of love keeping the darkness in check. Part of her had long recognized the truth of herself, but she had been afraid of it, in the same way, she knew, the caterpillar sometimes fears becoming the butterfly. And yet, she was still the daughter of Solon, and a friend of Demacharon and Davos and Ecthros. Only by focusing on them, on the memories of her mortal life, could she keep from losing herself entirely, her awareness of having been Radia.

A lone Hedonian soldier stood beside her among the dead. Too much had happened in too short a time for him to give voice to it. She could feel him more intimately than a lover, as if they shared a single body, a solitary mind. Seven praetorians were decaying in their armor, their sarissas and shields intersecting the compass lines etched into the floor. But at the feet of the two survivors, three were fallen—the king bleeding out from his eyes, from where the broken halves of the two-sword were planted, the headless assassin, disguised in the beetle-plate of the Silent, and the boy with his bow.

At last, she closed her eyes, shutting out every other emotion, and the room dimmed as if a cloud was passing before the sun. The immediate sorrow brought her to her knees, as she reached, torn between Ecthros and Eros. Demacharon did not ask what he was thinking, but she knew. Her feelings for the boy were apparent, but what could the assassin have meant to her?

"He was my brother." Her small frame shuddered, the loss too great to contain. In that instance, she was Noora, with all the frailties of a mortal being.

"Your brother? How? Are you not the daughter of Solon?"

"The king found me in the garden nursery. I was delivered by a phoenix. Eros's mother carried me in her womb. I was his twin."

"He was a killer. That you could have any relation to that monster—it's unthinkable."

"I am Life, Demacharon—sister to all brothers, mother to all sons, daughter to all fathers. You named me after your long-lost sister. That was no mere coincidence. Have you not kept Noora in your heart all these years? Only Zaibos was blind to my true nature, for he has never loved anyone, not even himself. As for Eros, when he first looked upon me, he saw the actual face of his mother, from when she was very young, and he was innocent. I feel him in death, see him standing along the shore beyond."

"You want to bring him back, don't you?" He was straining to speak, for the severity of his injuries was beginning to rush into his brain. But like a true soldier, he shrugged the pain away, maintaining a pretense of strength, as if she could not sense him.

"I cannot," she answered. "He has moved on, crossed over the waters of Lethe. Somewhere in Aenya, this very moment, a mother awaits his spirit. But this one," she said, turning to the limp, sleeping form of the boy, "he stands by the river, yet does not drink from it. He longs to remember, to return to me."

"If you can revive him, why do you weep so?"

She brushed at her cheek, surprised by the sudden dampness. Whatever divinity she possessed, in that instance, she did not feel it. As he had not yet tasted from the waters of the river, she knew he could return, but her mortal aspect could not help but lament his passing. "I was Noora once . . . we were young and we were foolish, and in another life, we could have been lovers." She pulled the boy close, resting his head upon her bosom, to mourn and call his name, touching her lips to his so that he might find his way.

"I will make this right. Bring the rest to me. Bring everybody."

Demacharon could not be certain where dream and reality diverged, or even whether there was any true distinction. He did not have the words to describe what she was doing, knowing only that she seemed to be plucking at the harp strings of existence, and that the melody was harmonious. Like anyone confronted by what is beyond their comprehension, he was left with imprecise labels like *religion* and *magic*.

Ecthros was alive and beaming, still rubbing the crust from his eyes as if he had been sleeping. Whether he could even remember his final breath, Demacharon could not tell. Only Radia seemed to matter to him, and yet the boy looked long and wistfully upon her.

The remaining eloai in the tower, who had been made to swear allegiance to Zaibos, now spent the morning washing the compass mosaic of bloodshed, and removing the bodies of the Silent and the king, which were sent to the catacombs below. Demacharon aided where he could, but his every action stabbed at his insides, and after a time he was forced to rest his gaze upon the Goddess, where she sat upon her throne, overseeing the people assembling with their wounded and their dead. And as the day waned, he witnessed many impossible things—the crippled walking, the blind seeing, the deceased waking as if from a nightmare. Mournful faces all turning to the light.

Into the eclipsing night, Radia worked tirelessly, though there were many even she could not save, bodies buried that could not be retrieved, and souls too far removed, having passed onto the next life. At some point, he asked her why some traversed the river, while others did not. "To cross is to take the most natural course," she explained, "just as it is natural to sleep and to wake, just as an infant must escape the womb. But some hesitate, compelled by some unfinished duty to remain." And a thought occurred to him then that he could not escape. *Astor. If she had been with me that day by the shore, would my son have returned to me?*

The last to be brought to her were the most badly broken, Krow among them. Had Avia not delivered his charred remains from the ruins of the *Cloud Breaker*, Demacharon would not have recognized him. Radia labored furiously over the dead avian. It was not unlike a woman birthing a child, and he came to realize that, in some way, all mothers are goddesses.

His wounds were severe, but he did not bother seeking her aid. There were others to be saved. More deserving than himself. So he did what he could to dress his punctured flesh and carry on, hoping to hide his anguish behind those who suffered more greatly.

Tyrnael basked in the turquoise glow of the greater moon, and the Goddess was spent, excusing herself to her bower as she faded back into the shadows. And yet a celebratory feel was in the air. The Compass Tower filled with people sharing stories, reciting songs of old and breaking bread, and children casting joyful spells with their games and their laughter. Unicorn banners were made into kites and flown from the parapets, signaling to any who could not attend that the usurper's reign was over. And, for a brief time, the memory of their losses was lifted.

High above the masses, songbirds perched over the queen's dais, and the curving wall behind the throne, and a blue finch settled upon the unicorn's horn. They were singing the morning into being, and Demacharon wondered at them, for he had not noticed when the birds were absent.

Hugo stood hand in hand with Esse, and Avia and Krow were beside them, and Ecthros and Tobias and Colin also. Even the bogren had not shied away, despite his aversion to humans, having somehow managed to befriend the unicorn.

Radia arrived in a garment of air and starlight, the ethereal fabric tumbling from the steps and down into the streets and across the horizon beyond. The world seemed to bend and shimmer about her naked form, as if the whole of the city were insubstantial, and she the only true thing in it. But from her face, none could look away, for her countenance was luminous to behold, her moon-hued eyes ageless, the zeal and wonder of youth made manifest in her smile.

Esse turned to Hugo, handing him a woven crown of laurels and flowers of dazzling color. He climbed slowly, falling before her bare feet, proclaiming, "Hail, Radia! Daughter of Solon, She Who Is True North, Goddess Who Walks amongst Mortals, Queen of Aenya!"

She smiled, unexpectedly bashful. Noora was still there, peering from behind a veil of divinity. "That will do nicely, Captain."

There was a moment of doubt, as to the proper etiquette required before the new sovereign. Hugo backed away, prostrate before the queen, and all but Demacharon and Amalthea followed his example. Far too proud for bowing, the unicorn pranced in circles about the throne.

"Please," Radia implored, "stand up! Do you show humility before the oak? The aurochs? Your dearest friends? You do not, and yet I am all these things, and more."

"We will do as you ask," Hugo answered her.

"Then listen, for I have much to say to you, and much to ask. First, let us speak of my adopted brother. Zaibos was cruel beyond measure, but he is to be pitied, for the life he could not know, and the connections he could not make." She paused, knowing that to say such things, even for her, must seem to the people like a blasphemy.

Esse was next to address the queen, her voice sounding scarcely above a whisper. "Where were you?"

"What do you mean?"

Hugo touched her shoulder, to halt her speaking, but she brushed him off. "We've lost so much, and suffered greatly. If you are, indeed, Zoë returned to us, why did you not come sooner, to stop these things from happening?"

"I feel your sorrow, Esse, more deeply than you can imagine. But there are things beyond even what the gods can do. Death, suffering, Zaibos himself—they are all part of the natural order, and have been since time immemorial."

"Then, are we doomed to forever repeat these events? Can you do nothing to prevent them?"

"Where gods fail," Radia answered, "humanity may triumph. There is a way to transcend suffering. It is the path that leads to compassion."

"But these are mere words," the eloai pressed her. "Words that hold little weight to those who choose cruelty."

"Compassion is understanding. What one does to another, he does unto himself. To this, Zaibos was utterly blind. You do not yet fully see it yourself, but you feel the truth of it. That is the reason I am here. Bring the people to me and I will show them. Not only those in Tyrnael, but everyone, everywhere. Despite what the usurper stood for, and all he proposed, we agreed on one account, that our people must come out of seclusion. We can no longer hide behind our myths. Mythradanaiil must be known for the real place that it is, and therefore, we must rebuild the great bridges in the hope that Aenya may again be united."

Hugo stepped forward suddenly, forgetting himself, and with whom he was conversing. "That is a mighty task. How do you suggest we go about this?"

"It cannot happen by force, as my brother believed, but through diplomacy, commerce, and the trading of ideas."

"O My Queen—" he started, remembering his impropriety.

"Please, Hugo, just call me by name."

"Yes, indeed, *Radia* . . . Respectfully, I must point out that journeying to this land remains perilous. There are rivers of ice to navigate. Sheer cliffs. Unless you can move mountains, trade with the outside world will be nigh impossible."

"The mountains move themselves," she answered, "only too slowly for mortal eyes to perceive. In a thousand years or so, the passage will open. It is not so long a time to wait for a deity."

"What can we possibly do then, in the interim, with the scant years we are given?"

"Go out and tell the world that the Goddess walks amongst you and that she has come to bring an end to the Dark Age of Aenya."

"The outer nations have their own faiths, their own gods," Hugo contested. "Many will reject you. They may even raise arms to oppose you."

"I will speak to them in dreams," she said, turning to her Hedonian protector, "so that they seek me out themselves, wherever they are."

"And if still they do not believe? What then?"

She smiled, her mismatched eyes seeming to peer ahead, to the future awaiting beyond the ring of mountains. "Belief does not matter. Only love. And let me add this, so that it is clear to all of you—*whoever harms another, does harm to me, and whoever shows love to another, shows love to me.*"

"I will have it written," said Hugo. "So it is never forgotten."

Avia stepped forth now, addressing the throne with a bow. "My people are known messengers. We can travel the whole of the planet in less than a cycle. I will deliver your message to those in high places, to the Ascendency in Nimbos, to King Frizzbeard of Northendell, and to the Caliph of Shemselinihar."

"Nature knows little of governance, or treaties, or lines drawn on maps. Your knowledge of the outside would be of great use to this court, Avia of Nimbos, and so, if you are willing, I would like to appoint you my official herald."

"It would be an honor," Avia said.

"There is one more thing," Demacharon added, with some hesitancy. "A man has come into the world. He is no king, and he commands no allegiances, but like you, he is laden with destiny. They say he is the Batal of Legend, a descendant of the very first king of Aenya. I know not if he still lives, but if he does, Avia's people may know if it. His name is Xandr. Shall I reach out to him? Or let him alone?"

Radia considered this for a moment. "Somehow, I feel that I know this man already." Turning then to the bird woman, she said, "If I were to write him a letter, to summon him here, would you deliver it?"

"Such is my duty, Most High One, but of this man you speak, and his consort, they are Ilmar, outcasts from the civilized world, wanderers, and will no doubt be difficult to locate.

Should I chance to find them, they may not receive one of my race, as our past dealings with them have been less than fortuitous."

"We have shed blood together," Demacharon revealed. "And they will trust in my summons."

"But how will they know the message is from you?" the avian inquired.

He was slow to reply, for his mind was dulling, but with some effort, he managed to recall the words he had last spoken to the Ilmarin. "Tell them . . . tell them that Radia seeks an audience with the *Skyclad Warriors*."

The bird woman bowed, her feather-crested head shimmering. "I will await the queen's hand."

Demacharon was feeling faint. A numbness was coming over him. He could not feel his feet or his fingers, and the bandages about his torso were growing damp. Perhaps it was that he had not slept the whole of the night. Either way, the proclamations of the court were growing indecipherable, and he became acutely aware that he was missing much of the proceedings. Regaining some measure of lucidity, he listened as Krow despaired over his inability to serve the queen.

"Would that I could go and spread the good word, but without a ship to navigate the skies, I am of little use."

"You gave your own life freely," she answered him, "for a people not of your kind. I can think of no more deserving of reward. If you so wish, it is not beyond my power to mend your wings."

Overwhelmed by the possibility, the bird man stood dumbfounded. And then, upon further contemplation, the delight upon his feathered features waned, as he adopted his usual sullen appearance. "For the love of a human, my flight was taken from me. Now you say that what I did, I did not do for my own kind, but you are mistaken. Humans are my kind. My wife is human, and my son is more human than avian. I wish to be no different."

Before Radia could reply, Toby chimed in, offering the whirlydinghy he and Colin had built. "It's quite small, but you can still use it," he added, "to deliver news of the queen. She's called *The Radia*, after all."

"A noble gesture, Tobias. You will grow into a fine man, and you will live a long life, one of consequence, *that* I can promise."

She stood to descend from her throne, her starry raiment flowing like mist over water. And, as if she were no more royalty than the lowest of laborers, she moved from person to person, addressing each of them by name.

"For your kindness and your loyalty, I wish to grant you all a gift."

Hugo wanted nothing but to stay on as captain of the guard. "I would have no one else," the queen replied.

The eloai wished to become a handmaiden to the queen, but Radia refused the offer, declaring, "Esse, you have proven that there is more to a life than what is written in their essence. Henceforth, there shall be no distinction between classes. No more eloai. Clothing that marks one's station is to be abolished, for each shall present themselves as they are, without shame or judgment, whether you choose the accoutrements of the praetorian, or to live freely, as I have made you.

"But most vital of all my decrees is this, the Committee is to be abolished posthaste. For it is an affront to me, and has become a cause for great sorrow among my subjects, Eros chief among them." Her dazzling glare fell hard upon Demacharon, forcing him to look away, lest he lose himself in her eyes. "I know what you felt for my brother, your contempt for him lingers still. But temper your memory by the knowledge that his heart was broken by his own sense of empathy, by the suffering his mother—our mother—was made to endure, by a system that was set in place ages ago. He was what the Committee made him, and in his madness, he did what he thought just. This must end. Never again will a child of Tyrnael have such a cause for matricide. For no one who is born to this land will know what it means to be called an *abomination*. The genesis of new life shall be decided by love, as Zobaba intended, since the first mating."

Hugo turned to the young girl beside him, standing in her short white peplos and bare feet, just as Noora had been, and Larissa. A longing was in his face, and she returned his gaze in kind.

"As for you, dear Esse, if you wish to continue your craft in my service, you may, so long as you let me sew beside you, as your pupil."

"Or . . . as a friend?"

Radia answered with a smile, turning then to Amalthea. "You've borne me on your back, and have shown me the truth of myself. What can I offer, to one who is herself divine?"

The unicorn was clopping gently along the rim of the dais from hoof to hoof, whiter than crashing foam, her horn a glittering star. "Unicorns do not know gratitude, nor resentment. These are human qualities. So there is nothing for you to amend or reward. I only ask your pardon, for I do not belong to this or any world, and so must slip away, into another story. But as you have need of me, I shall ever be near." And with that, the white mare jumped into Radia's shadow, through the dim silhouette of the Goddess stretched across the wall, and disappeared.

"What of you, Ecthros? What do you wish of me?"

"I would take a kiss," he said sheepishly, "but since you've already given me one, I won't ask for another."

"I know you miss Noora," the Goddess replied, "but she will always be here, whenever you wish to speak to her."

The boy's heart was heavy with unrequited love. Demacharon could feel it, the way he once longed for Niobe, on his long campaigns from home. But Ecthros was not such a fool, to imagine himself courting a goddess.

"I have a long journey ahead of me," he said at some length. "My uncle has a brother in Graton. It's a small town, far to the south, with a delightful view of the Sea. I've never seen the Sea, and I feel it is my duty to deliver news to him of his family."

"In that case, I will send you off with a strong wind."

Ugh was hanging in and around Ecthros's thighs like a toddler, ashamed of his hideousness. But to the surprise of everyone, she lowered herself to his height, gently nudging his fingers from his face.

"Little bogren, you've proven most remarkable of all. You have demonstrated that there are no evil races and that perhaps, someday, others like yourself may come forth, to make amends between human and bogren kind. You are indeed *good*. What would you have of me?"

"I only ever wanted a friend," he admitted, "but she's go away."

"Who's gone away?"

"Radia."

"But I am right here. I am your friend."

"No," he murmured, "you're not her. You're too big. But Ugh finds new friends."

"That's right," Ecthros remarked, taking him by the hand. "Me and the little fellow have been through a lot. So we're hitting the road. Together."

It was a fine low-moon morning, or as Radia called it in the ancient tongue, *Springtime*. The moons of Aenya shone like faint apparitions in the vast blue canopy above them, as the sun continued to climb, blanketing the city in its warmth. And yet, Demacharon could feel none of it. His heart was light, but a coldness permeated his being. One by one, his wounds were opening, where Zaibos's spikes had driven through his body.

"Praetorian," she said softly, gently, "you have fulfilled your promise to me, and then some. From this day onward, all acts of valor shall be measured against yours. Your story will be played out by children for generations. What reward can satisfy such loyalty? What could I possibly offer you, my dearest friend?"

"My Queen," he answered, "I have done my duty. That is all. My reward, if I was to have one, was to see you safely returned to the throne. Other than that, I wish for nothing, nothing but your release."

"Have I been such a bother to you, that you wish to take your leave, above all else?"

"Quite the contrary. My heart aches to think I shall never see you again, but I have an appointment, you see . . . one that a man may only delay, but never put aside, and you've kept me from it. You've kept me from it for far too long."

Radia came near him. Her light was dimming. "And who will protect me when you are gone?"

"Hugo is fine and honorable," he replied, with whatever strength was left in him, "and I believe he will serve you well."

"You are my knight, Dimmy. I will have no one else."

His time was nearly gone. He was fully aware of it, for the darkness was closing about him. But could she feel it also? How could she not? "You are awakened," he murmured. "You've no need of a guardian."

"I'll always need you."

The floor was spinning, but she caught him, lowering him gently to the floor. Everyone was surrounding him now. He could hear Ecthros, calling his name, but it sounded from afar. The illusion of reality was falling from his eyes.

"You are not so badly wounded," Noora said to him, and in her quivering voice, he could hear the mortal part of her, a human girl of fifteen, pleading with him to remain. "Let me save you. Please."

A cluster of loving hands was groping at his body, tugging off his leather cuirass, tearing at his clothes. There were shouts about what to do. Desperation etched on every brow. But the bandages beneath were saturated, and the tiles about their feet were turning crimson.

"Stay with me," she was saying, but he could scarcely hold her in his vision. He blinked, and felt himself departing, the details of the room becoming less and less substantial.

There is only one constant. For she exists in both realms simultaneously, and she has always been there, always been with me. I had only to turn into the light to find her.

She is gloriously green, like a meadow when living things begin to sprout, and her hair the gold of sunset, nebulous and infinite as the cosmos, and upon it she wears a crown of concentric bands, manifesting every living thing, mammoths and saurians and wakefins and fireflutters, avians and merquid, bogrens and humans. And I realize that she is only as I perceive her—a young woman—for every creature shown upon her divine headdress is but an aspect of the Goddess in all her myriad forms.

A hand reaches down for me, but it is not as I have dreaded, no person I have wronged. He seizes me, and I am lifted powerfully into his embrace.

"Welcome, brother," Davos says to me.

We are in the throne room still, but the walls are of pure light, as are the crystalline minarets in the distance. I see souls of the lost finding their way into the city, like drifting lanterns upon a stream, and without trepidation, I peer over the void. We are leagues above the clouds, the whole of Aenya swirling below us like a golden pearl. I have arrived where I thought never to belong. The City of Light.

I ache to speak with Davos, but the girl urges me to follow, and I am captivated, her will becoming my own. There is a higher plateau above the dais, which I had not known was there, a place I could not have hoped to find without her to guide me, and without questioning, I begin to climb the stair.

"They are waiting for you."

"Who?"

"You'll see." Even in this, her most divine state, she is being coy. Playful. Like a child with a long-kept secret.

At the top of the stair, an open archway beckons, and I see two shapes standing under it, a woman and a young boy. The Goddess releases me, and I continue to ascend.

I see them clearly now, across a long luminous passage, and they can see me. I am running to them because they are waiting. They have waited a long time. And they know my name.

Made in the USA
Columbia, SC
22 June 2024

bf253e47-8e12-4649-9a3e-2c2eeda94253R01